DARK ROUX

Toby LeBlanc

DARK ROUX

Published by Unsolicited Press.

Printed in the United States of America.

First Edition.

Lyrics for "200 Lines: I Music Not Speak French," written by Hadley J. Castille and published by Flat Town Music Co., reprinted with permission by Swallow Publications, Inc.

Attention schools and businesses: for discounted copies on large orders, please contact the publisher directly.

For information contact:

Unsolicited Press

Portland, Oregon

www.unsolicitedpress.com

orders@unsolicitedpress.com

619-354-8005

Cover Design: Kathryn Gerhardt

Editor: Kay Grey

ISBN: 978-1-956692-26-6

For Lena and Louis

Lâche pas la patate.

Roux

/roo̅/

noun

noun: **roux**; plural noun: **roux**

a mixture of fat and flour used in making sauces.

Recipe:

Go pee.

Get a beer.

Heat 1 cup of oil, butter or rendered fat (vegetable oil has low smoke point) in a thick-bottomed pot or skillet until a pinch of flour fries in it.

Add 1 cup of all-purpose flour.

Stir deliberately and consistently, BEING CAREFUL TO ALWAYS KEEP THE MIXTURE MOVING SO IT DOES NOT BURN. (This step takes the longest. It is hard work. You will need to be patient. You will be glad you went to pee. Let your beer keep you company.)

Add oil if it becomes pasty, flour if it becomes too wet. Mix the wet and dry as evenly as possible. The texture should look like melted chocolate. Lighter roux is the color of caramel. Dark roux, like milk chocolate. (When I was learning to make a roux, I would ask my wife to find an old penny the color of the roux she liked).

Add the trinity (green bell peppers, celery, and onions) to start nearly any Cajun dish.

William

Chapter 1

He says the hook is barely beneath my skin. But it must be deeper.

"Hold still, *coullion*," he growls. This burns. His bulbous fingers rotate and twist the treble hook until it releases. It's a miracle I don't fall into this dirty ass water. The bloody hole in my right hand, my computer hand, is God teaching me a lesson. At least that's what my mom would say if she knew it'd kept me up last night, betraying everything I've been taught to be. God I can't wait to leave this place. I'm shook from any pleasantness a daydream can provide with the serious look on Paw Paw's face. He grabs my remaining good hand and studies it. Holding it gently in his leathery paw, he proceeds to crush it with a vice-like grip.

"Nah I bet you not tinking about you udder hand no mo." He smiles to say "you're welcome." His bent, agile legs scramble across the shifting aluminum boat back to his pole, bait still in the water. Years of punishing sun turned his skin a deep ochre, making it hard to imagine it was once something tinted white. "Nah, you go sit down and suck on dat. You done scared mah fish and I got to go find dem. *Fils d'putain*!" I wish I didn't feel ten years old every time he gets irritated with me. It's easy to see he thinks a hook hole in a sixteen-year old's hand, even if it is currently getting infected, is not a legitimate reason to cut a fishing trip short. Far be it from me to mess up the rhythm of his life. He's moved back to humming his same old Cajun tune. Between verses he pitches a three-inch bait, covered in sharp barbs, between two small cypress knees, one foot apart and twenty yards away. "If you not gonna catch no fish den you can *donne-moi une bière*."

He might say I'm not holding my mouth right when I work a crank bait. Today he seems content to quietly mock my lack of ability in this sunken hell. He doesn't seem to care that I don't care if I get a fish in this boat. Not making eye contact, I grab one of his lukewarm Schlitz out of the live well. Looking at it makes me want to vomit, and not because of the bacteria seeping into my open wound. The memory of the night he got me drunk on this stuff during a game of *bourré* looms in my throat, threatening a seizure-filled vomit. Even though I was nearly unconscious, it still took me over two hours to lose all of my money. He said he was proud.

We left the interstate bridge over an hour ago. Only he knows how deep in the Basin we are. If we leave soon, we probably won't get back to the landing until after noon. Paw Paw will want to stop at Tante's house. That will take another couple of hours. This day won't end.

"I din't know what bored meant 'til I learned English. You need to stop bein' all *nervine.* Dese fish can tell when you get antsy. You gonna make us have to pull up and go to another spot. *Lâche pas la patate*!" I don't know how he thinks I can finish strong.

"How long before you decide there aren't any fish?"

"Long enough. I know dey somewhere in here. Probly just need to change baits. Troll me over to da nex drain."

On a day when using the trolling motor sounds like a reprieve, it doesn't work. Pedal pushed… check. Twist the handle to forward… check. This will be my fault somehow.

"Um…Paw Paw? I think your trolling motor is broken."

"What'd you do to it?" his voice even more threatening with fishing line in his teeth.

"Nothing."

"Notin…*mon cul.*" Ambling over he scolds, "*Mais* you din't even connec it to da battry!"

"How was I supposed to know I had to do that?"

"You should know because you old enough to have common sense. You read dem books and play on you computer all day but you doan got da smarts dat matter. You too old to have me figurin' all dat out for you all da time. *Mon Dieu*!"

Another word and I get a slap. If Child Welfare Services had a navy in this swamp, I bet they'd put all of the Cajun nonks, dads, and Paw Paws in jail. I see a picture of empty boats with social workers' cards taped to trolling motors floating in my head. How many times have his hands ended up across my face? To look at those hands now, they are so different than they were a few years ago, now gnarled like the cypress knees surrounding us. He struggles with the wires and battery. His grunting falls in sync with the droning of the cicadas. I used to study him when he'd work on things like this. Instead, I watch a couple of hyacinths, left over from the warmer months, bob in the ripples made from his struggle in this boat. "Ah. *Mais la*!" he exclaims. The old man manages to get the connector close to the post and bump it in with the heel of his hand. "*Ça c'est une belle gratte*!" he shouts. "That's how I been keeping *ça* battry since I first started taking you fishing when you was tree."

"Now bring me over in dat little cove," he commands, wagging his grossly oversized chin and nose in the direction I should take. Trolling is like using a joystick. But I need to switch to the other hand. The hook hole still burns, and I want to use this hand later, even if it is for the wrong reasons. But there's no room for shame in this boat alongside the stink, and the sweat, and the pain.

Getting into the truck at the landing is like Communion in church: the end of the suffering is near. A look of silent judgement finds me over the lid of the livewell, little more than a large, dingy ice chest. There would have been three fish in there if I hadn't hit a wasp nest while casting, the bugs rushing the perceived culprit, Auguste Chenevert, making him drop the fish and almost lose his pole. I stay in the boat waiting for him to back the trailer up. When I peer over at the other kid at the landing, a kid at least three years younger than me, he is pulling what looks like his own grandfather, boat and all, out of the mucky coffee-colored water. Paw Paw doesn't trust me with a truck and a trailer, and I don't blame him. He backs up, the old Ford's brakes straining as it sits precariously on an overused ramp, wet from the other fisherman. He hops out and is back aboard this floating aluminum coffin in seconds.

"Go hook up," he yells over his revving engine. I stand at the front of the trailer as he lines the boat up and gets a running start for the trailer. He's up quickly and nearly smashes my hand waiting with the safety clip. I get back in the truck before I mess up anything else. We are almost out of the parking lot before I realized I didn't winch the slack out of the strap. I tell him I forgot something in the boat, quickly crank the wench, and am back in the truck explaining I forgot I already had what I needed before he has a chance to figure out what happened. He grumbles at this, but much less than he would have should his boat have come loose on I-10 or the Breaux Bridge Main Highway.

Kerosene smell pours from the old man inside his cramped cab. The layers of oil caking his hands finally seeped into his blue veins. The plastic canteen of Canadian Club he sips certainly does not help the smell. Playing at his house when I was a kid, I would smell him coming from working outside before I would see him. Once I even smelled my dad to see if that's what all grown men smell like. Paw Paw's odor does not circulate through the open windows of this truck because of damp air coming from the impending rainstorm. The weather is as drunk as everyone else in this place. The smell of mud, and the life rotting within it, is strong enough to singe my nose hairs. No matter where I am here it stinks. At least there is some semblance of coolness as I hang my head out of the window, especially since it's my only air conditioning. Stringy dust-colored hair sticks to my forehead despite the wind blowing through it. I close my eyes. A digital image of flesh from the night before flashes through my mind. A quick turn of my stomach and I push the thought away. Last night it was a sin; in this truck it's vomit-inducing.

"When we get to you *tante's* house you can help me fry dese *sac-a-lait*. I know she misses you. You've haven't been there in a while."

"Paw Paw, I don't like fish."

"You used to."

"No, I've never liked fish. We go over this every time I come fishing."

"*Mais,* den you never had dem—"

"—cooked right? You say that every time."

"Watch you mouth, *lapin.*" A corporal punishment tone gathers like the thunderheads around us despite the smirk on his face. He likes when I stand up for myself, even if he won't say it. His eyes break from the road for a glance at me. "Why you always so *bouder* witchou *babine* hanging down like dat? You look mad all the time." There's no world where I'd be able to explain all the reasons I hate being here, doing these ridiculous things, in a way he'd understand. I look out the window into the sulking clouds instead. "You know, I'm proud of you, Willy." This is a trap. "You came fishing today when I know you doan like doin' it no mo. *Tu es un bon garçon.* A good boy. My prayers have been paying off. If you'd only learn French." If my parents thought it was important for me to learn French, they would have talked to me more in that language. Why can't they just let it die? Maybe people would like it then, like Latin. Despite his inability to ever let a compliment lay undisturbed, a warm feeling, something akin to fulfillment, rises from my gut. I absolutely hate it. If I trust this, I'll never leave. With a deep breath in, I go to tell him I can't stand the sound of the mispronounced French in this place, but I'm cut off.

"Dey buy them spensive shoes but can't keep a car fixed. *Fils d'putain*!" It's awkward before his old Ford stops. The old man grumbles as he sifts through the wrenches, screwdrivers, and other dangerous metal-looking objects on his floorboard. Glinting in the February sun are shiny bladed rims on a rusting old Pontiac Bonneville. Above the hooptie, lat muscles of a six-foot-tall Black teen crop up over a well-formed chest. An older woman I guess to be his mother stands slightly in front of him. Their unblinking eyes lock on Paw Paw.

"And he's probly crankin' that old lady outta her food stamps."

I can't see how he can judge anyone else about how they spend money. He lives in a rotting shack off Main Highway near Breaux Bridge, fixing junk into makeshift tools, sustaining himself on rice and whatever he can get out of the water or from the woods. The man should have caught something incurable. Instead, the man is incurable. This place is so bottled up and shelved like Mom's wine. And just like my mom, everyone here is content with what is cheap and easy. I need so bad to taste something different. But I'm bottled, too. At least for a little longer. He totters toward the Black family, his clunky frame small and arthritic, but solid as this old Ford.

When this hits the news tonight I'll be the little white asshole, stringy hair stuck to perpetual sweat on my forehead, limp pasty arms with no muscle tone, folded over a belly made of too many Doritos, explaining why I sat in the car and watched my racist grandfather get his ass beat. I can even picture the camera zooming in to my brown eyes and peach fuzz mustache, centering on the zit I can't get rid of at the end of my overly sharp nose, as I tell them I thought he deserved it.

My view is broken when they disappear behind the open hood. I gasp as the young man reappears without him, only to hop behind the wheel and turn the engine over. The old woman comes around smiling, but Paw Paw is just as smug as when he left the truck. The young guy, who couldn't be much older than me, reaches out a huge hand. Paw Paw stares at it. He knows what to do with an engine, but has no idea what to do with a Black man's appreciation. Finally, he shakes it and starts back for the truck. It's good to know I'm not the only kid who can't seem to ever please him when it comes to engines.

The concoction of motor oil and sweat wafts as he leans in the car; the physical exertion made it stronger. It fills my nose as he leans close to whisper.

"Reach in dat glove compartment and pull out da pistol."

I must be hearing things. But the expectant look on his face tells me that's exactly what he said. The cab spins as I hand him the snub-nosed .38 special.

"No, not dat, *coullion.* Gimme da money behind it. You gonna make dem tink we tryin' to rob dem."

A smear of blood from my hand is left on a roll of cash that I guess is a thousand. He flips back my bloody bill and pulls two twenties off.

"Take dat gun out of sight."

Looking at my hand I see the barrel pointed toward my grandfather. It was almost higher than the dash, in eyesight of the pair. I stuff it back into the glove compartment. I look up to see the woman backed into the opening of her car door with her son in front of her. As he hands him the cash, the muscled kid ventures a smile at the old man. It quickly turns to a frown as my grandfather opens his mouth. This is all too familiar. Paw Paw walks back and starts up the Ford, peeling onto the road faster than I have ever seen him drive.

"I din't give dem enough money to get into trouble but I bet dey will anyway."

"What did you tell them?"

"I told dem to go get good spark plugs dat work and stop spending money on shoes. And nah we not gonna have time to stop by you *tante's* house for you to fix her computer. If we do, it's gonna be dark when I'm driving home." Thanks to my grandfather's racism, and that poor petrified family, I'll live normally again sooner rather than later. "It's good to help people, Willy. Even da ones who won't help demselves." I've lost track of how many times I've told him I don't like that name. He can't stand to let me like my life.

Chapter 2

Free from the stench of men and motors, I go inside. Mom left a perfume oil warmer on and whatever misnamed floral scent is circulating the house. Retreating from the smell, I go to my room. One day I'll be able to chisel out a place to belong in greater than one hundred square feet. There are several college apps hidden in my closet I know I need to work on, but I don't have it in me to think about what to put in the essays. The best time killer is waiting in the corner of my room. My sore and bloody hand hesitates before my wounded finger clicks on the icon for Netscape. It's too close to when Mom comes home to start some porn. But curiosity is a powerful thing. I've had pictures from that new site I visited last night swimming through my head all day. I click on the last site I visited and go to lock the door. When I return, many of the thumbnails are loaded. Men touch themselves while they watch me watching them. It feels different than watching girls do this. This is probably just an intellectual, even academic, curiosity. But I don't look away. I'll just be added to the column of "weird, depraved" people who populate the world outside of Acadiana. Paralyzed, my tortured finger remains poised, trembling, deciding whether or not to click on one of the thumbnails.

My mother's air horn voice rings through the air. It's repetitive and desperate. She wraps my name in her shrill, desperate tone. Psychological brakes are slammed so hard my brain wants to pop through my forehead. The finger in traction leaps into painful action and covers my tracks by exiting the screen impulsively. It musters up enough energy to unlock my door half a second before she rounds the corner. I'm back at my computer looking entrenched before she darkens my doorway.

"There you are—right where I left you last night. Did you have fun with Paw Paw?" Her butt fills the doorway. The loud red dye in her hair dulls the other colors in the room. Even her face, full of painted expression, sucks in life's energy.

"Yep."

"Did y'all catch?"

"He did."

"Did you even fish?"

"I did."

"Did Paw Paw say anything?"

"Like what?"

"I don't know. I just wanted to see what happened." Playing my role, the quiet one, might just let me make it out of this without her knowing what I was looking at. Maybe there is a God.

"Did you eat?"

"Yeah," I lie.

"Ok. Well let me know if you get hungry again. I could pick you something up at Dean-o's or something. Oh, and I think there's something wrong with the internet on your computer. I tried using it this morning and it did something… weird."

"Huh," is all the panic teaming through my veins allows to come through. The one time I don't cover my tracks completely is when she decides to brave tech alone. What if she went to the site? Should I ask her about it? No. That's stupid. It will only confirm I did something, and I didn't really do anything. I looked at a picture I accidentally ran across. Yes. That's the story. It is a virus that popped up when I was working a school project. I can wait to see if she says something about it. That shouldn't take too long. Not so much because of what this is about, but because she doesn't know how to keep her mouth shut.

As she retreats, the smell of coffee mixes with a waft of alcohol. Something is up. She usually drinks at home, not at work. Although that isn't considered weird in a place where people drive hay bailers while sipping daiquiris. Why do I care? All that matters is she doesn't get curious about what's on my computer. Time to start a new habit of wiping my history each time I log off.

Playing video games is much safer. Absorbed in Starcraft, I lose track of time until I hear the crash in the kitchen. Next to a counter at the corner of our square kitchen, in a pile of pots and roasting trays, sits my mother. She is trying to stand up but seems confused as to whether to use her arms, legs, or both.

"Mom, what are you doing?"

"I was making some fucking dinner! I get hungry!"

"Ok, Mom. I was just curious."

This is an act. She wants me to dig it out of her. She wants me to beg for the guilt she thinks I deserve. I could bend my own rules and indulge her this time. This is different. I need to pull out every stop to make sure she doesn't think her perfect little Cajun boy is gay. If I become the family's sick secret, it's all I'll ever be. An overturned bottle of wine drips from the counter onto the floor as she tries to pick up a roasting pan and she loses her footing in the puddle on the floor. Still paralyzed in forming a plan of to how keep my mother, or worse, my grandfather, from believing I'm an evil little pervert, I can only stare at her awkward attempts at balance.

"You gonna help me?" she rasps in accusation.

"I… sure." Not sure if I'm helping her up, or picking up the pots, I go for the pots. They seem the most rational.

"You're more concerned about the pots?" As I switch to helping her up, I get, "Never mind. Why don't you just go hide in your room like you always do? It seems like none of the men in this family actually want to act like they're in it."

Things are looking up. This might not be about me after all. It might be run of the mill injured mom stuff. "What are you talking about?" I ask sweetly.

"Don't act like you're not avoiding me the moment you walk in this house." I can't be sure, now. I'm in a trap. If I push back, and she knows, it'll be thrown in my face and into the open where my worst nightmare, one worse than having to remain in this place through adulthood, will start unfolding. If I play into whatever imaginary slight she's talking about, she'll pull me in tighter, and I'll be the little sweet boy she always knew me to be. That I can handle… for now.

"I don't try to avoid you. I just don't always know what to say to you."

"You sassing me?"

"No ma'am. Don't know what you need, is all."

Here they come. Tears are on tap for her. "We aren't much of a family anymore, are we? We don't even know each other."

Her plight uttered, the cry turns to a full sob. Funny how her wine-soaked brain makes her see more clearly. She spends all day avoiding the fact her daughter and her husband don't come home and her son hides from her.

"Yes we are, mom. We're the same family we were before. Everyone is just… growing up."

"You mean growing away."

"I know it looks that way."

"Because it is that way! We didn't act like this in my family. We spent time together. Paw Paw would come home to us after working in the shop all day and drink his beer and ask us about what happened. Momma would cook something and we'd talk. When I was little, I used to talk to my mom and dad until I would fall asleep mid-conversation. But you are the only one who spends time at home anymore and I barely see you. I'm so alone!" I wonder if moms in the North act like this. "Promise me you won't leave like your sister or stay away like your father."

"No, mom." Well, at least it's not a lie. Unlike my sister, Addison, I intend to leave this town. And she doesn't have to worry about me working with roughnecks in the oil field like Dad.

"See, you're a good boy. *Un bon garçon.* You're my favorite."

Silently putting away pots to avoid looking at her, I hear glass clinking in the background, signaling more wine being poured. As the last pot goes into the cupboard, she announces she is tired and heading to bed. Drunk must be stronger than hunger.

"Do you want to come lay in bed and watch TV with me?"

The request hangs in the air, sucking all sanity into it. Would pretending I didn't hear her work here? Her silence tells me she is waiting.

"I'm kind of tired, too," I declare neutrally.

"You can fall asleep in my bed."

"I… uh… I like my bed. I think I'll sleep better in mine."

"Fine. I'll go be alone. Again."

When morning arrives in all of its awkward glory, I am greeted with her contrite silence. At least it's silence. Staring out of the window on the way to Addie's game to make sure she doesn't think I want to talk, I count the restaurants. After a few blocks I come to the mathematical estimation of five fast-food restaurants per square mile. None highlight plant matter on their menu. No wonder this tiny city has one of the top heart hospitals in the country. May 21, 2000 cannot come fast enough. The hangover keeps Mom in silent shame the whole way there. My life is attending one long softball game where I pretend to like something because it's "the right thing to do." In a perfect world I'd get twenty bucks and the afternoon at my arcade in the mall. Or at least somewhere air conditioned.

"Where can I find you after the game?" she inquires. Meticulous fingers sharpen the spikes of her perm to poke through the top of her visor. Could that be an apology for last night? There are much fewer of these than restaurants in this town.

"Um, I guess here. At the car."

"Ok. I think I'm only going to hang around for fifteen or so minutes after the game. Addison is too busy with her softball friends to spend time with us, like usual." Artists could take notes on the way she paints the truth.

There is something about the smell of boiled peanuts that's fishy. I mean literally fishy. That smell is everywhere in this place. Fresh air doesn't exist. There's no breeze. It's either too cold or too hot with this humidity. The bottoms of my feet sweat. I shouldn't complain. In a few months I won't be able to get dry with the oversaturated ground steaming beneath me.

As I search for any semblance of moving air, I see someone looking familiar-ish. The kind of familiar that leaves us both confused. His face has a half smile. What will eventually be a thick blond beard hugs just his chin. His hair is a tone lighter and has a fullness that only good breeding can produce. He walks as if the stadium is a runway. People this attractive and self-assured always make me uncomfortable to the point of wondering if I'm doing anything in life correctly. He looks directly in my eyes, making it all the worse. With sudden self-consciousness, I run my fingers through my sweaty brown hair and suck my gut. The "Stussy" written across his shirt makes my Target brand shirt fit even worse than usual.

"Do you go to Comeaux?" I ask. Way to be a stereotypical teenager, William.

"No. ESA. I party with some of the Comeaux people," the specimen acknowledges. He has an easy smile.

"Um…"

"Well, anyway, I'm Jared. Who are you here to see?"

"My older sister catches."

"Really? My older sister is pitching. Crazy. My sis is always talking about how she looks up to your sister." Jared looks inside the park. "You're not watching the game?"

"Just stuffy in there."

"It's not bad under the awning."

"We're not under the awning. We're up on the backstop."

"Well that's dumb. It's humid as balls in this place." He says it so matter-of-factly I can't be offended.

"I agree." The judgment of my own parent's choices must amuse Jared because he smiles.

"Then you should sit in our section. I have extra tickets. My parents never come."

"Sure," I venture tentatively. Busy inventorying my deficiencies, I look around to see who else notices his error in stepping down a few rungs on the social ladder.

Jared's seats are perfect – far enough below the awning to not have to deal with sun and overinvolved parents, and far enough from the top to not have to deal with kids who treat it like a playground. Having been to years of softball, I can tell instantly Jared's sister is decent on the mound, but would probably see a bench more. Either Jared doesn't know or doesn't care. He yells encouragements the entire time she is on the field. He screams again as his sister's fast ball slaps into my sister's glove. His face is much lighter in complexion than the sun-beaten farm boys around here. It turns bright red as he screams, almost the same color as his sister's jersey. One more curveball for a strike and she retires the side. She does a little curtsy as she comes toward the dugout.

"That girl loves to be seen."

"Can't be worse than my mom. She makes us sit close to the backstop so maybe one of the cameras will get her in a frame."

"Which one is she?"

It's not that hard to point out the round woman with red, spiked hair in the third row. How do you tell another teenager how unhinged your mother is without scaring them off? But it seems like I don't have to. Unfiltered laughter bursts from him. My first reaction is to be offended because, well, I think I'm supposed to. Except his laugh gives sound to the ridiculousness that is my mother. I laugh, too.

"Think of the exact opposite of that, and that's my mom. No style, no personality... just a pretty face and a lot of money. She's always in high heels, even when she comes to these games. Even at home." That was meant to put me in my place. His dad probably got his money as a heart doctor in Cali and travelled to Lafayette because healthy lifestyles don't lend themselves to a market based on coronaries. Looking around the stadium, seeing what he sees, I get how opposite from civilized life this is. "Hey, I mean that in a good way. My mom is a Stepford wife. You've got to be cool if you came from that." And like that, I'm cool again. Never thought my mother's hideous hair could do that for me.

The Lady Cajuns lose what should be a fluff pre-season game. The reason is none other than Jared's sister, who forced three runs. Jared gets quieter. Then he completely stops talking. His eyes never leave his sister in the dugout. When she is out of sight, he heads for the gates. It was nice to spend time in his world. I'm glad I'm leaving before he figures out who'd he'd been hanging out with. As I turn toward my mom's car, Jared proves he remembers my name by calling it out.

"Come hang out with us tonight. I'm having some people over. Nothing fancy. Drinking and chilling. Might be able to scrounge up some weed. You down?"

"Um, sure."

"Hurry up and put your number in my cell and I'll pick you up. I have to hurry. My sister will be in serious sulk mode. I got about two hours to get her ready to go out, get drunk and forget about it."

Chapter 3

The wine is not helping whatever endeavor Mom is undertaking in her room. In her doorway I see her trying to muffle the swearing as she tries on this year's gown. She shimmies to get the dress up over her fleshy ass. Over the years the ruffles and sequins have repopulated the areas that used to show skin. She thinks no one in Krewe de Bijou notices she's aged and gotten bigger. Jared will arrive early to pick me up. Because nothing good ever actually happens by chance in my life, a good mood will need to be planted for her. Complimenting her dress for her ball seems like a safe bet. But I take too much interest and stumble into talk over what I will do while she's at the ball. I try to back pedal out of it by saying I'd like to go out to a party for the first time in my life. I'm stupid for thinking any amount of smoothing her fragile ego would help.

The interrogation begins. Watching her judge everyone with reckless abandon makes me never want to tell her anything real about me. If she'd seen the porn, she's had all day to bring it up or act weird. It's good her attention is elsewhere. Jared probably won't show, and this will still be worth it. But that's not my life. My life is Jared showing up early, wheels screeching into my driveway, and blowing the horn. The look on my mother's face, the recognition that I'd already made plans without consulting her, is almost as bad as her finding dude porn. In a split second I weigh an attempt to stop my drunk, sequin-clad mother from pressing a near stranger on his family history and upbringing against confirming there is something to hide in my life. The latter is heavier by a mile.

Her big body hisses through the front door faster than I've ever seen it move. She rushes up to Jared in a green flash.

"What's your name?"

"Jared Simmons, ma'am." There is a pause between his name and "ma'am." He's not used to saying it. He looks at me as he does, eyes wide as if to ask if I am seeing this too.

"Don't look at him! Look at me! Jared where are you going with my son?"

"To my house, ma'am." There is no pause this time.

"And where do you live?"

"Greenbriar, ma'am."

"Hmph." My mother attempts to sound haughty but I can tell she is impressed. He's the class of people she'd always wanted to be associated with, erasing the worst parts of being Cajun. "And what will you be doing there?"

"Watching movies, ma'am. I like to keep it low-key."

"Uh-huh. And who will be at your house?" Her tone is softening. The playful yet polite way he answers her questions shows her she has no power over him. Here is one more thing about him I covet. In seconds he removes her from the warpath and is talking to her as if they're old friends. He already feels like a buoy in my life. She throws a time for me to be home over her half drunken shoulder. In his car I tried to find out how he pulled off that magic trick.

"Once you meet the folks at my house you'll see. I do a lot of drunken reasoning. Sometimes with people's parents. Here's a beer. Go ahead and get started." He upshifts as we get out of my neighborhood. In the cup holder is a cold bottle of Abita Amber. I'd seen my dad scoff at these in the grocery store. Something strange happens when I sip it. I like it. It doesn't taste like fermented sweat or horse piss.

He hits Johnston Street and flies. Fifty, sixty, then seventy miles an hour. My eyes scan the horizon for cars that might threaten the trajectory of this Supra. The hum of the modified engine, the lights flying by, brings me to a place where thinking doesn't work well. In fact, it's dangerous. In moments we are in Greenbriar, an outside world inside Lafayette. I've only driven through it with family at Christmas to look at the elaborate light displays. We'd all longingly look at the mansions. Even Dad would "ooo" and "ahhh." Tonight, Jared and I pull up to a remodeled plantation style home. Gaslight lamps hang from the antique brick wall, signaling through the dark how rich this person is. I panic at the sight of several cars in the horseshoe driveway. Every single one of them must go for around thirty thousand. Through the French doors I'm transported to a mythical place. The furniture is all antique. Warm light glows from lamps made when Paw Paw was an infant and probably imported from New Orleans. Populating the corners and sofas of this museum are scholars from Lafayette and Comeaux High, the rich kids of Saint Thomas More, and the elites of Episcopal School of Acadiana. I am in the company of unicorns. Cutting through the drawl, I hear what might be a Chicago or New York accent. My empty bottle is replaced by a full one without my noticing. Anxiety usually moves me to the edge of any social setting, making me appear aloof. But the eyes here dart or stay downcast, like mine. Finding no stories about fishing or football or fools, I talk about things I care about:

"The reason the Clintons are effective is because they don't bother appealing to the dying Christian morals."

"They should have stopped at Final Fantasy VII."

"I think David Foster Wallace is our Oscar Wilde."

Jared bounces between little covens of intellectuals, never using an unwelcoming tone, never letting his shoulders droop, always holding his head high as he laughs at jokes ("What does the South and mustaches have in common?"), making each person feel like he's the only human alive he wants to talk to. It makes more sense now why this angel of men approached a geeky Cajun kid in a ball park. I'm his pity invite, a social service. I'd be mad but his personality is so affable, so humanistic, it makes him even more angelic. I grow more uncomfortable learning how perfect he is, the gulf between growing by the second.

Pizza arrives and I am encouraged to eat despite nobody knowing who paid for it. A skunky smell appears. When the pipe comes my way, I fumble it. After a knowing look from Jared, he slips next to me, whispering instructions, what sounds like the instructions of life, close to my ear.

"Hold your thumb over the hole while you inhale, then let go."

After a first drag tasting of lighter heat, I figure out the concept. Another new thing happens. I stop worrying. Whatever concern I have about coming across to these amazing creatures, or when I'll get home, or if this can happen again, disappears into smoke. I'm here – the here I've always wanted. Time, something that drags me through life, with pain, flits into night until only a few party stragglers remain.

"Dude, your swamp accent keeps getting thicker and thicker the more fucked up you get. I can hardly understand you. Jared? Where'd you find this guy?" one of the Saint Thomas More stragglers slurs at me. The fuzzy, warm world I'd stumbled into this evening flips onto its head. I'm outed. "Where are you from? Like, really?"

"Alright. That's enough, guys," Jared tells them. While his manner remains gracious, his voice shows some irritation. "I'm tired. I think it's time for you to go anyway." The two giggle and get up, debating on where to finish their party. Jared sits next to me on this imported couch as the door shuts.

"I don't really know those two. They started showing up at my little get-togethers about a month ago. I'm pretty sure they're here for the weed. But, hey. Did you have fun?" He waits for a response. People in my life look for responses only to confirm what they think. Working really hard to enunciate without the nasal sounds or the ridiculous sing-song intonation, a way of talking I'd spent the last several years trying to rid myself of, I respond.

"Yeah, man. This was great. I haven't had this much fun… like… ever."

"Probably because you don't get out much."

"I mean, I do. Just not with folks like this."

"What? People your age? Intelligent people?"

Does he not see the giant gulf between his side of the couch and mine? He's got the life I've wanted. He's supposed to feel sorry for me. It leaves me wondering why he asked the STM guys to leave, like he wants to belittle me on his own. Since I don't know the rules here, I walk through the trap.

"Um…yeah. Pretty much."

"Yeah. I could tell. You fit in here. But I wouldn't recommend it. They're all so fake. You're different. You're the real thing." I wish I wasn't so high and drunk. Here is that strange directness and honesty from before. He might actually be paying as much attention to me as I am to him.

"I really like hanging out with you." My words hang heavy and gross like the air outside. The truth is completely overshadowed by my gawkiness. This will be the last time I'll hang out with him. This is why I should never be honest.

"I really like hanging out with you, too." Reeling from the drugs, the booze, and the constant jarring of the conversation, I don't know what to do with affirmation from the prince of my fairy tale land. Finally turning to him to find possible explanation from his expression, I encounter his face inches from mine. He looks directly in my eyes like he did this morning. Then he looks at my mouth. He kisses me. Or, I kiss him. I almost wish someone had stayed so I could know how it's really happening. But we are definitely kissing. It's a long kiss. Despite having nothing to compare it to, I know it's a good kiss. The stubble on his chin, the little hairs I wish I could grow, scrape against my skin. I'm all twisted, screaming inside and simultaneously silent. What stirs my eyes open is the sensation of him getting up. I'm paralyzed brain down.

"Want to light another bowl? Or do you want another beer? Both?" In the course of one afternoon I went from a cloistered momma's boy to going out, drinking, smoking, and now kissing… a dude. How is this my life?

"I don't think I should."

"Ok. Do you want to watch a movie or something?"

"I… uh. I think it's time for me to go."

"Uh… ok. Are you alright? You seem freaked?"

"I'm cool. Just getting late. And I'm… my M… I…"

"You're freaked."

"No. No. I… no."

He smiles. It could be patronizing. Or it could be something else. But there is definitely some sort of recognition, some knowing.

"Don't worry about it, man. I'll bring you home. I'm getting tired, too." The Supra retraces the road to my house much more slowly, making silence between us deeper and longer. When a person feels something their whole life, it's normal. And what this is, all of it, is not normal. But it's nice. It confirms what my family and my friends and everyone here knows: I'm not normal. Liking this is not normal. Tonight, not normal was not a problem. I was not the problem. In fact, the only time there was a problem is when normal showed itself. That, or I'm trying to explain away my weirdness with weird people in weird situations.

"I didn't mean to make anything weird, I swear."

"You… it wasn't. It's just… can you get me home?" I manage to stammer.

When I venture a first look since the kiss, the solid guy I'd met earlier in the day looks like a scared kid. An ancient part of me, something I wish wasn't there, says he is a monster. He nods contritely and pulls up to my house. My head tells me to run inside. My legs keep me in the open car door. My insides tremble, same as they did in front of my computer a few days ago. I look again at him. And an echo from deep in my head tells me he is what my family protected me from. Why do things that make me happy also hurt? I close the door and he rolls down the window.

"Thinking about being at the parade tomorrow. Meet me in front of Graham Central Station if you want to join."

I walk faster until I'm inside.

Chapter 4

The searing pain and loud cracking is coming from my toes. Paw Paw stands above me, gripping another toe to crack.

"*Allons*! You momma said you was gonna be ready when I got here. Now we might miss da sunrise." Several seconds pass while I squint at him blankly. "What's wrong witchu, *cher*? I'm speaking English! *Tu préfères je parle en français?*" This is Mom getting me back. Something tells me I will be going fishing early the morning after any night I go out from now on. "*Ne me'ga pas comme ça! Tu es haïssable.* Get you ass out of bed and put some clothes on. We should be at da landing by nah."

"Paw Paw, I'm supposed to go help out at the church to get ready for Ash Wednesday," I lie.

In the glare of the flashlight, his small graying eyes bore into me. The rusted old gears in his head turn. "God gonna understand. Getchu clothes on."

The stakes are set. Months of scorn will follow if I make him waste gas and lose fish. On my way out I pass my smiling mother in her silk robe, hair looking newly spiked. She hands me the small ice chest filled with sandwich, chips, and Gatorade. "Have fun *et bon chance*!" she encourages with too much relish.

His old Ford clunks down I-10, hitting every bump. The boat in tow makes the truck sway in the road. Seasick, I worry I am about to spew remnants of pizza and alcohol across the dash. He cusses at one of the other three drivers with whom he shares an empty highway. As we pass a carcass on the road, I'm forced to listen to a story about a possum that chased him. Now he moves on to advice on how to talk to people, as if people talk the same as they did in 1955. So when he comments on the smell of alcohol coming off of me I keep my eyes closed, willing myself to be unconscious.

"William I'm talking to you."

Evoking my full name gets my attention. "No, sir. No drinking."

He starts to slow the truck and pulls over onto the side of the interstate. He throws it into park and fishes out his flashlight, shining it into my face.

"You lyin', boy" The flashlight stays unmoving in my eyes. "Why you lyin?" Should I say it was a few beers and I'm sorry and it won't happen again? I know he doesn't want the real story.

"I had some drinks with friends last night."

"Why you was lyin'?"

"I… I didn't want you to be disappointed in me." He is not as surprised to hear me say it as I am.

"I'm disappointed 'cause you lie." The light turns off and I hear the truck start.

Biology class skipped the chapter explaining how alcohol can seep through your pores. The smells of this primordial place are even more dank than usual. In the Basin, every boat passing by sends a curse of wake my way. It takes everything to stay upright in this piece of aluminum. The vomit burns at the back of my throat. And, as if the God I pretend to pray to wasn't angry enough, I am constantly made the center of attention by the endless amount of fish jumping on my line. The old man dashes back and forth across the boat, putting fish in the livewell while trying to catch something himself. After the seventh or eighth fish the old man is downright giddy. I smile.

"Dere you go Willy! You finally holding dat mout on you face just right! Dat's da purdiest smile I seen all day!" He starts to two-step, right here in the boat. I lose my balance and almost fall in. In the middle of righting myself I get another bite on my line and set the hook perfectly. "Dat's some livin' right dere, *cher*! You can't buy dat at da sto!"

A laugh escapes my lips. I don't understand how he gets happy on so little. This simple thing, making my Paw Paw happy, makes me happy. The fog of the hangover loses its grip a little. Or I'm leaning into it. My feet do some awkward jig as my next fish hits the deck. The *sac-a-lait* on my line pops and jumps at the bottom of the boat. "I found me a dancing partner!" I exclaim.

The Old Man keeps a beat, stomping and clapping. "You not gonna find a better dance partner 'til you weddin' day! Be cahful. You gonna have to go find dat fish daddy and ask him for her hand, or her fin."

My feet slow and I busy myself with getting the hook out. How happy he is with me stands in stark contrast with what I did last night. Pictures of last night, and how that kiss felt, gurgle in my stomach. If he knew how unCatholic and amoral I've become, his love would turn to a burning hate reserved only for the atheist Yankees of the world. But shouldn't I be able to feel something without filtering it through endless unforgiving morals? Like the screws I'd strip working on engines with Paw Paw, I'm getting in too deep while losing my chance to back out. The second I start feeling what they want me to feel I'll end up like this fish: caught and powerless to whoever's hook is set in me. Waiting to see if my grandfather will have pity on my clumsiness to free this fellow is fruitless. Paw Paw's feet stomp and his hands clap. He sings "Colinda" now. The big fishy black eyes look up at me, gulping air that can't save him. He'll die on this hook, go in the livewell, or go back to where he came from. Doubling down on my efforts, I hear Paw Paw sing, "*C'est pas tout le monde qui peut danser tous les vieilles valses des vieux temps,*" as the hook mercifully releases. With one last sympathetic look, I drop him in the livewell. Paw Paw always said I need to think like a fish to catch one. Never thought I'd have to feel like a fish on life's hook for it to happen. It's too literal.

A content silence finds us on the way home. For a moment I stepped inside his world. It feels like understanding. Glancing at him as he drives his death trap Ford, he appears closer, the distance on this cracked single bench seat shortened. I breathe in the damp, cool, earthy, feeling, its touch deep in my lungs.

"You found a piece of you on da Basin today, T-boy. I knew you would."

"Hmph," is all I can muster. The silence was so nice.

"When you leave here, you'll miss fishing." He knows I'm leaving for college. How? He never stays in my house long enough to dig in my closet to see the application packets. I was sure when he broke the silence I'd have to feel guilty, or pray, or both, for my lack of acceptable Cajunness. If he can see my shock, feel my wide eyes on him, he gives no acknowledgement for it. "It's hard to make you momma happy. She always hurt about sometin'. She ain't happy 'til she's miserable. Maybe dat's why she married you daddy. Be nice, dough. She tryin'. She cain't help she's stubborn like me." The admission gives him a chuckle and he looks at me, pride twinkling behind his gray eyes. "And I'll keep how you got drunk between you and me. I won't even tell her you kissed somebody last night."

My eyes widen more and I flatten against my seat like he front-ended a brick wall.

"How did you know?"

"I din't. You just tole me. I'm good at fishin' in an out a boat, me!" he exclaims, slapping my knee. His eyes stay on the road as he starts to hum. "Just be cahful wit dem Black girls. They can turn you a different color," he works into the melody. His tone is of someone with experience. Something I'll leave sitting in the humid air. I've had enough of what Paw Paw might know. I'm safer with him being a white supremacist than a homophobe.

Waking from my afternoon, post-fishing nap, I have to orient myself. It's the same day. The stench of fish fry is still in my nose. Thankfully, I got away with only having to choke down a little bit before getting to nap off the rest of my hangover. Feeling refreshed is cut short by a deep voice. Instead of Paw Paw's sing-song tone, gruff punctuations echo down the hallway to our room.

"Hey boy. Come calm your mother down," my father instructs from the doorway he just burst into. We stare at each other for several moments as he waits for me to jump up like one of his shop hands. "Well?" he beckons.

"I'm not sure what you want me to do."

"Never mind. I don't need you acting like a prick, too." He leaves my door open to spite me. I hear Addie squeal when she walks in and sees her dad is home. In mere moments, the power struggle between my sister and mother will begin. Getting my pants on, I find them in the kitchen, my sister stirring my mom to a simmer, something I'll have to deal with later. I leave the kitchen, not wanting to participate a moment longer than I must. Addie follows me, walking in her partial squat, like she is about to sit behind a plate or pounce.

"Saw Dad's truck. Figured we'd get to this, but I was hoping to at least make it to parade time before it started." It's like she's apologizing.

"Yeah."

"You alright?" She looks me in the eye, like she can read me.

"I'm fine. What?"

"Nothing. You look, I don't know. You look happier."

My stare beckons her to say something of value.

"Things still bad here?"

"They're manageable," I say as flatly as I can. I know where this is going. She's as predictable as Mom.

"They'd probably leave you alone more if you learned to meet them halfway. Like if you tried talking some French with them or something. You at least could start learning what they're saying about you right in front of your face. That's why I learned." Here is round one: the advice. It's a mystery to me why everyone wants me to learn a language unrecognizable to the country that spawned it. Without an answer from me she gets quiet, still trying to catch my eyes. Next round is where she apologizes for not being a better mom than Mom. One was more than enough.

"I'm sorry I left you here to deal with them all by yourself."

"It's cool. I'm out of here in like a year. Just like you." Her face gets sad. She flutters her oversized brown eyes at me in pity. This is the final round, where I save her from herself just like I save Mom. Today I'll do it again, just to get on with my life such as it is. "What Addie? You left to go to college. Normal people do that. I'm not mad at you for it. Our parents are what they are. This was always going to happen."

"Yeah but I worry about what it's doing to you."

"You make it sound like I can't take care of myself."

"Well you shouldn't have to—"

"Look," I interrupt, "I'm leaving the crazy in this place in a little over a year. I already have some applications printed out. My GPA is solid. I've got some good practice test scores on the ACT. It's going to happen." She gives her fake smile and I decide it's time for a shower.

"What do you want to drink tonight? I'll call in an order to my friend. My treat." As much as she can't admit it, she's just like Mom. I can't ever end a conversation on the first try with either of them.

"I'll catch a ride but I have some friends I'm going to meet instead."

"What? Who?"

"Not telling."

"Oh come on, asshole. You didn't even have sleepovers when we were kids and now you have friends you're going to go out with on the Sunday before Mardi Gras? Spill."

"Seriously, not telling. I'm not going to have friends for the first time then have my sister stalk me and freak them out."

"I wouldn't do that."

"My ass," I say pulling down my boxers. Giving my left butt cheek a jiggle, I show her where to put her lips. Dad has the living room occupied, drinking beer and watching TV, which makes mom stay in the kitchen. Addie will leave me alone for a minute so she can get her Daddy fix without interruption.

The fight begins earlier than I thought it would. Our escape plan needs to be bumped up, which neither me nor Addie mind. In the car she mothers me as if she can't hear Beatrice Mouton screaming at her husband, her voice reaching us through two sets of glass. As she hassles me about not having enough clothes on for the weather, I put one of her softball sweatshirts from a crumpled pile of clothes on the floorboard, relishing her embarrassment as she thinks of her brother going out in public with a woman's sweatshirt. If she only knew. It's enough, and she leaves me alone about who I'm going out with tonight.

Arriving at the softball field I run my next gauntlet to freedom. My sister's friends crowd me, reminding me how long they've been watching me grow. My gruff exit to meet Jared is met with a longing look from Addie, another thing reminiscent of our mother. When I arrive at the gaudy multi-bar Jared said he'd meet me in front of, I am alone for a while. Mardi Gras revelers file past on their way to Johnston Street. The nauseatingly loud purple, gold, and green pervade every stitch of clothing. Crass humor, the greasy smells, and bad fashion also drape the drunken, puking masses. It's easy to spot Jared's tall lean figure and blond hair against the dark haired, dark skinned natives. He lets me know his friends are near Fatima Church, so we cut back toward Cajundome Boulevard to avoid the hectic Albertson's Curve. It's a respite from the dueling Booty and Zydeco music, the last bit of quiet for a while.

"Thanks for letting me come out with you," I say.

"My pleasure."

"So is it going to be like last night?"

"Listen. About that—"

"Are there going to be guys there who find a Cajun accent offensive?"

"Oh, those guys. Yeah. They'll be there. But if they start that shit again we can leave."

"*We* can?"

"Yeah."

He wants to say something else, but we are overtaken by a drunk showing us his hairy tits. The stranger and I scream "*Ayyyyyyyy* Mardi Gras!" in unison. It satisfies the stranger and he keeps walking, drinking, and screaming to no one.

"Did you know him?" a surprised Jared asks.

"No. Don't need to. It's Mardi Gras."

"I don't know if I'll ever get used to that."

"You should." We are approaching the throng surrounding the parade route and I have a moment to wonder if I was just using my Cajun culture to impress the guy, or because I actually like Mardi Gras. Unlike his friends, he seems to appreciate it. But with Jared I have to see it through new eyes. It's a lot nicer when he's looking at it.

We find an opening in the barricades and make our way across. We almost trip several times; beads, kids, and drunk people surround our feet. This is an introvert's nightmare. We find his Saint Thomas More friends, my judge and jury from last night. Their little spot is sad. The music is coming out of a car with its doors open. There is no food table. There is only one ice chest, and not even a big one. They're out of place here and they know it. They try to critique the drunken, dancing fools around them the way they did politics, except here they sound ridiculous.

"So how many years have you been coming to Mardi Gras?"

I don't know which to be more confused by, the question or the person asking. Memories from last night are a bit fuzzy but I think this is the guy who said my accent is funny. And what does he mean by "coming" to Mardi Gras? Mardi Gras is.

"I don't remember my ever not doing Mardi Gras if that tells you anything."

"That's awesome. I mean I didn't come last year because we had just moved here. So this is my first one."

"Well," I say reaching down into his ice chest to pull out some beer. "Let's get you initiated right." We crack them and clink them. He chugs like a frat boy in training. They are all impressed when I produce the Crown Royal my sister came through with.

We hear the sirens and the police motorcycles blast past. The outsiders stare wide-eyed. The pulse of the first high school band makes the ground throb. The STM kids wave like idiots. I want to explain bands don't throw beads, but they don't seem to care. The out-of-towners do some sort of white boy shuffle when St. Martinville High plays DMX. Everyone else is dancing, too. Grandmothers shake their big butts alongside twerking middle schoolers. Nudging Jared, I urge him to join his friends. He smiles and turns his head back to the float without moving. The outsiders scream for beads, but we're kind of in the middle of the route. The first float dumped a lot of its beads at the beginning and will now be in conservation mode to make it to the end of the route. Their only chance of getting any is if they know someone on the float, which I seriously doubt. One of them even screams "Show me your tits!" to one of the women on the float. Everyone, including the woman whose breasts are in question, gives him a confused look. It doesn't deter him from flashing his own bird chest as a suggestion. She chunks a nice handful of beads to someone way further down the line. Discouraged, he bends down, picking up beads off the ground and putting them around his neck before strolling over to us.

"Bitch wouldn't throw or show," he says as if he is speaking a local lingo.

"You know, you're not supposed to wear those," I respond.

"Wear what?"

"Pity beads. Never pick up beads off the ground."

"What's wrong with them?"

"You didn't come by them with an honest grab," I respond. "They're tainted, like bad luck around your neck now," I add. He looks at them and shrugs.

"Plus you never know what liquid is on the ground. Could be beer. Could be something much worse," Jared finishes. We laugh quietly as the outsider walks away, trying to discreetly pull the beads off his neck to throw them in some bushes. We sit through a couple more floats. Looking at Jared, he seems content but not interested.

"Listen," I say while looking around, "this spot is kind of dead. Let's go further up Johnston.

We continue swimming through a sea of drunkenness, sidestepping the occasional fight. We pass Ground Pati, moving further past what I will always call the University of Southwestern Louisiana, and continue all the way past University Avenue. The walk doesn't feel long because the Crown is halfway gone. There are much more people our age here. At the crossroads at Jefferson Street, I consider taking him to the Strip. From what my sister says, anyone can get into The Keg. But Downtown looks more alive these days. Jared deserves something better than the tired bar my sister and parents went to. We detour to the higher-class Jefferson Street. As it happens, most of the bars have their doors wide open letting people in and out at will. Bouncers function only to ensure there are no fights. We walk right into Amanda Scott's and into the pulse of bass. Sweaty bodies pepper the dance floor.

"Should we get a drink?" I ask.

"You're not drunk?"

"Of course I am. But it's Mardi Gras!" I slur.

The bartender suggests their special of the evening, Long Island Iced Teas. We join the fray and clumsily bump to the beat, laughing at how ridiculous the course of our night has been. My small, boring life exists only in the past. How fast I've gotten used to this only confirms how this is the life I should be living. Without the old rules, I thrive. I don't need to escape into a game or porn. The drunker we get the more we dance, and the better we think we are at it. Looking up at Jared I see him looking at me. It's similar to the smile he had after we… after we did that thing. This feels new, too. It's not how the guys look at girls in porn, or how all of Addie's one-night stands look at her. It's not like the other guys at school, or even the girls, look at me.

Our bodies brush up against each other. My heartbeat seems to be coming from somewhere near my teeth. It doesn't stop as I feel something moving much more cleverly than a hip near my crotch. Old rules echo in my head, a remnant of my old life. During Mardi Gras taboo rules. It could be the alcohol, but I don't want to move his hand.

Chapter 5

"Smells good," I lie as I walk in the kitchen. She stays silent. Bad sign. "What are you cooking?"

"Chicken Fricassee and fried livers, green beans, cornbread."

What is it with the food in this place? Gravies, sauces, fried and boiled: it does the same thing as the people in this place. The flavor built by slow simmering sucks you in while it works to kill you from the inside. Today's menu was written by my grandfather. "Who else is coming?"

"Paw Paw, Tante, your sister, maybe your dad." She's straight and to the point but not unpleasant. I have no idea of what to do with that.

"K."

I leave the kitchen in time to see my aunt walk in. She greets me warmly with a pinch of suspicion. The cryptic demeanor is the same with my sister when she arrives. Something is definitely going on, and it looks like it's about me. The voices of the three women calmly seep from the kitchen until Addie decides to rejoin me in the living room.

"What's going on with mom?" she asks in too loud of a whisper. This just might not be about me.

"I don't know. I think she's pissed at me, but I don't know for what."

"Well you have been a douche lately."

"Thanks queenie."

"You think she knows about you messing around with that boy?" For a moment I thought I'd pass out from all the blood shifting directions. Sifting through the fuzziness from Mardi Gras night, I look for memories of people having seen us. I was so drunk there is no way of knowing. Fuzzy recollections of an awkward hand job in Jared's car dislodges, getting uncomfortably clear. Having someone understand more about the mechanics of my body than I do, despite all the time I've spent "discovering" it, is much more uncomfortable while sober. The lie I'd told myself, of being too drunk to know what was happening in that sordid moment, will have to be my cover.

"If I noticed don't you think Mom noticed? Maybe she doesn't know what's happening. She's probably in denial anyway. But she can pick up on stuff. And if Paw Paw caught wind of this…" The more I try to make hate in my eyes sear her soul, the more she seems to take pleasure in it. I want to run. I want to hit her. She's just like Mom. All she needs is a bad color job and for that ass of hers to grow bigger to match her spitefulness and manipulation. "Calm down. I don't know anything. Well, at least I didn't." She smiles lovingly. That was Paw Paw's trick. With the same smile she asks "Are you being gay because you think it's cool? I hear people do that."

"I'm not gay," I declare a little too harshly, willing the color to return to my face.

"It's ok Will. It makes sense. You've been quiet all these years, flying under the radar."

"I'm not gay."

"Will, it's me. I'm not going to tell Mom. Or Paw Paw. I gain nothing from that."

"You're right you won't tell them. There's nothing to tell."

She stares at me, waiting to see if it will make me magically tell a truth she'd like to hear. I stare back expressionless, the natural look of my introvert face. Paw Paw's patented shave-and-a-haircut-POUND-POUND breaks the deadlock. God, or whatever, bless him. Another moment locked in that stare would have either broken my calm, or I would have broken her collar bone. Addison opens the door for Paw Paw and gushes, switching seamlessly from my most recent interrogation. She lets him go in the kitchen to sort the chickens out, before she follows in like a hungry fox. She'll never have enough drama.

"Will! Come eat!" my aunt calls. It's over now. Addie is going to tell them. She's been waiting for this hour since I showed up in this family sixteen years ago. In a few moments she will go from being the town drunken slut, to the favorite. Stepping toward that room feels like an execution march. A plate is already on the table with way more food than I could eat, a last meal filled with food looking like cat vomit. I'm waiting for her to proclaim my death sentence: the little faggot freak of the family. I've never heard a Cajun French word for that, but I'm sure they'll make one up.

"Dad, did I tell you Will has a little friend now?" It's my mother's voice starting the crucifixion. How many people know?

"No. He tole me. Dat's good."

"When did he tell you?"

"When we went fishin'."

"What's he like?" my aunt asks with too much interest.

"He's nice enough. But Will doesn't even invite him in for us to get to know him," my mother answers for me. I feel my face get hot. It only confirms guilt. Dad always says never blow when you're caught. I shouldn't have thought the word "blow." Damn it. There's another memory from Mardi Gras night. The color in my face drains back out. This is why teenagers are despondent and hate the world. And I hate that I'm like other teenagers. It's over. My escape, my chance at a happy life, is over. My mom says something, but I can't hear it over the end of my future roaring in my ears. Paw Paw's voice cuts through it with an even loader roar.

"*Mon Dieu*, Bee. It's not like dat's his boyfriend."

Addie's eyes are on me. I don't need to look up to see them. I shove a forkful of food in my mouth.

"Daddy this is not like when we were growing up. We either knew everyone in town or we were related to them. Nowadays—"

"He's gonna be able to go to war in two years, Bee. You got all dese opinions about tings you doan know nuttin' about and you tink we want to hear about it."

My executioner turns out to be my savior. All this masculine bullshit they've tried to indoctrinate me with turns out to be useful. His love of privacy, his need to turn me into a man, prevents me from being the family's dirty secret. To my knowledge there has never been a gay Cajun kid, ever. I don't want to be the first. Their damning focus returns to him for the rest of the evening. I know what this means. My grandfather taking my side against his girls makes me public enemy number one. At least it's better than the truth. I excuse myself from the table feeling satisfied.

The effect of Auguste Chenevert is strong on my mother. She doesn't bring up my "friend" again for the rest of the week. Despite the expanse of livable moments this has allowed me, my leg bounces while I play Red Alert. Why am I so *nervine*? Shit, now I'm even using French words to talk about myself. I've been spending too much time with the old man. It's not going to help me if I just get nervous when I'm around Jared and his friends. I have to stop thinking that he, and everything he makes me feel, is some sort of exotic imported thing. Easy to see why I feel that way. Everything good in this place came from the outside. I pull the computer cord from the wall.

At least there will be weed and beer at Jared's regular weekend house party. That should help. What won't help is trying to make small talk, still knowing I'm the outsider. I'm a party favor or something. It's only Jared I'm going for, even if I can't figure it out. It's not fair. I want to figure out what's happening, want to talk about this relationship thing. But there is no one in my family who is any good at relationships. Even if they were, they wouldn't get this. I don't even get this. The only person who could help me figure this out is the person who is causing all my confusion.

The pistons growl as Jared's Supra enters the driveway, his car clearing its throat to catch my attention. When I exit my room, the house is silent. Only a single lamp is on in the living room. No explanation for my mother's absence. Too good to be true, I still leave through the laundry room window. Entering Jared's car silently, we depart for his house. I'm so freaked out I don't realize we haven't said a word to each other until we're in the driveway of his mansion. He grabs my shoulder before we walk inside.

"Are we cool?" he asks.

We? Are we a we? What kind of we are we? At least half of this we is me, and I am not cool. His perfect eyes study me, looking for something in my expressionless face. But I don't know what I could show him that wouldn't freak both of us out. The boy looks like he might kiss me. I hear my heart in my ears. I squeak out, "Yeah. It's hot though. Let's go inside," even though it's just a cool March day.

The moochers already tapped the keg, so I help myself. Quietly joining a conversation, not saying a word, I wait for the beer to start working. Air is filled with smoke and talk, and they're both wearing thin. Are these conversations the ones I was sure spoke to my core the last time I was here? Hearing them trickle out of their mouths sounds different, or rather, not so different. Juxtaposing the regular gene pool rejects at my school, those that pride themselves on impulsiveness and lack of judgement, these tout affluence and a better vocabulary. The magic of the first night falls away like cheap veil. All these interactions are for the same purpose. Every word these rich kids utter is meant to convince those around them of the same stupid thing: they belong. Wrap it up in a Northern accent, with more money, and it's still the same bullshit I've lived with all my life. I know I'm white, but I'm not this kind of white. This is flavorless. Regardless of Jared admitting his hate for how fake it is, he sure looks comfortable. What looks fake now is how he acts with me, when no one else is around. Why I was nervous earlier starts to make sense. I took it for my lack of social graces, for breaking rules I was set to obey long enough to escape for good. Looking around this room, I see it was an instinct trying to tell me about these people, this place. This was only a temporary escape, and a false one. I consider my Paw Paw's offer to come get me. But I shouldn't make him drive at night. My dad is the only person I can think of who wouldn't ask a ton of questions. Letting myself into some rich sitting room, I pick up a gilded receiver.

"What are you doing calling me?"

"Figure I'd make your dreams come true. I'm at a lame party and don't have a ride home."

"A party huh?" Dad asks pleasantly. "T-boy I'm a little busy right now." It's an invitation to convince him.

"Too busy for a free beer? I'll buy if you order."

He says he'll be here soon. It's common knowledge I shouldn't ask where he's been. It's not like I want to know anyway. Biding my time, I feign interest in a political conversation. When Jared questions where I've been I return a warm, reassuring smile. His calm lasts until my dad honks. He leaves his conversation to meet me as I'm about to open the door.

"Why are you leaving? Who's picking you up?"

"My dad. This party really sucks."

"You hate your dad."

"I hate this party more."

"You don't have church in the morning. Stay." He could be joking or judging me for being an ignorant, hocus pocus Catholic.

"It's cool." His light-colored eyes watch me close the door. He'll be back to talking with the people he belongs with the minute it clicks, I tell myself. It was a nice dream. But that's all it was. I'm not like him. And his presence in my life is making my escape that much harder. It's better this way.

The inside of Dad's truck smells like it did when I last rode in it two years ago: Drakkar cologne, dip, musky sweat, and stale beer. I move some work gloves and safety glasses to the back seat.

"Put those goggles where I can see them. I've been looking for them. So where we going T-boy?"

"I'll let you choose."

"Let's go to Parrain's. There will be some people I could introduce you to."

We rocket down back roads and he spits into his most recent empty beer can. He's quiet at first, listening to Alan Jackson and humming along. For a moment I thought he would make picking his son up from a party at midnight as normal as driving home from work. But that's not that normal since he doesn't come home.

"So what were you doing there? I thought you only liked playing video games."

"I met some new friends."

He looks at me seriously. "Girls or guys?"

"Guys mostly. But some girls."

"Just wear a condom. I'm not paying for grandbabies this early. You need some condoms?"

"No, Dad. Thanks though. So what's this bar?" I ask, changing the subject quickly.

"Place I go after work. They have 'Bikini Fridays.' Too bad it's Saturday. Most of the same old boys will be there." Like anywhere you go in this city, we go from pitch black back roads through cow pastures, to well-lit suburban streets. Broken neon light comes through a giant glass bathroom block window, leaving no question to the lack of class inside the establishment. The parking lot is littered with trucks and motorcycles making parking spots more like parking suggestions. Inside, the place is dingy with the sticky dust indigenous only to Louisiana. Quickly I'm introduced to old Cajun men. Introduced as his son, I'm met with equal measures of pride and apprehension. A Bud Light is thrust into my fist. Men violently shake my father's hands and grapple him about his shoulders. Older women treat him like a son or a brother. The younger ones treat him like a father or a sex symbol. A king presiding over his court, he lets out belly laughs. It's no wonder Mom can't get him to come home. Here is where he reigns.

One woman gets closer than the others, wrapping her arms around him from behind, lips touching his ear when she talks. The red scar on Dad's neck flares purple. Her Wranglers are tight and her halter barely contains her freckled boobs. He says something and she looks over at me before lurching forward without trying to mask how drunk she is.

"You're Will?"

"Yes ma'am."

She smiles and looks back at Dad before turning to me again. "So polite, *cher 'tit bébé*! And you're handsome like your daddy, too! My name is Linda."

"Nice to meet you." She turns back to my dad and gives him a thumbs up before walking past him.

"How does Paw Paw say that? *Quoi tu peux faire avec une femme comme ça* ? What you gonna do with a woman like that?" After chugging what's left of his beer, Dad looks at me seriously. "I don't think your mom should know. She'll probably think the wrong thing. That lady has had a thing for me for a while, but I know better than to stick my dick in that alligator's mouth."

He's baptizing me into manhood. The amount of pleasure he appears to derive from parading me around is gross. I always knew this is the type of man he expected me to be, but it's even worse seeing it than imagining it. Thoughts of time with Paw Paw and his version of manhood cross my mind, confirming how bad this must be to daydream about fishing trips and fried water critters. I only wanted to get out of a crappy teenage party. It would not have been difficult to continue feigning interest in debate over the merits of Ivy League schools I'll never go to. "How about a shot with your old Pops! Trudy! Get us a couple of red snappers! And maybe shots, too!"

Getting drunk seems like the only way out of this night.

Chapter 6

"Did you get drunk with your father last night?"

"Good morning to you too, Mom."

"Did you?"

I don't say anything. This is better than her wondering about why I left in the first place. She turns red and gets silent. In my fuzzy hungover state I play the game wrong. She goes into the cupboard and violently pulls down pots and pans. My head splits open with each pot. It will happen any second. Dad will hear this and be in here. Barely finishing the thought, he shouts from the back.

"What the *FUCK* Beatrice?!"

He comes to the front in his boxers and undershirt, tucking his dick back in the button hole, purple blotch of scar on his neck looking like it might pop off of his skin.

"Why in the hell you got to make so much goddamn *noise?*"

"I thought that's what you do when people are sleeping. At least I'm not drunk while I'm doing it. And at least I'm not getting our underage son drunk while I do it. The worst that can happen when I'm making noise is that he learns how to cook."

"Holy shit Beatrice! You're going off about bringing *our* son home safe?"

I make my exit from the room. The fight may be over me, but it's not about me. Let sleeping dogs fight, or whatever. I go back to my room and fire up my PC. The whir of my tower starts to drown out the shouting. I've barely logged into the internet when I hear my father burst through his bedroom door across the hall, cursing under his breath. Moments later my door opens.

"You coming, my boy?"

It is not a command, and it is not a question. It's a plea. She beat him this time. The purple in the scar on his neck carries a deeper hue. That was not a normal fight. Whatever he wants from me, I'm sure I don't have it.

"Paw Paw is coming. It's Sunday."

His hurt look turns to rage. He looks away for a moment before turning around and walking out with a barely audible "piece of shit" on his lips. And he wonders why we don't hang out.

The load screen for Starcraft finally appears when I hear, "Will, could you come help me in the kitchen?" It's not safe to weasel out of it today. Arriving where my mother stands at her cutting board, I can't tell if I should duck or get ready for a hug. She violently chops onions with a smile only Da Vinci could paint.

"Can you wash the bell peppers and celery, *mon 'tit garçon*?"

"Sure." I can tell the knife in her hands is dull compared to the words she has in her head right now.

"I'm sorry about me and your dad. I think that had been building up for a while. I just got mad at the thought he was taking you out drinking." She pauses to grab another onion. "Have you been doing that a lot lately?" she asks with sweet innocence.

"Not really," I answer as uninterestedly as possible. I finish with the celery and begin to quickly wash the bell peppers.

"This is not like the Will I know. I mean I'm so happy you've been hanging out with your new little friends. I don't want you staying out all night and not coming home like your daddy. Besides I've been lonely lately and missing you. How about you stay home next weekend and we can do something together?"

Paw Paw's knock comes to the rescue again. Hopefully leaving the conversation on how she is happy I have friends will give me some room to spend more time alone. Paw Paw gives me a gruff hug and asks where my mother is. He hands me bags reeking of something fishy. I drop it on the counter and try to leave the room as he tells my mother he saw my father peeling away. I'm almost to my room when I hear, "*'Tit garçon,* come wit me to my truck. I need you help. Get me a flathead." All I'm asking for is some computer time and silence. He's standing at the open hood of his truck when I get outside. After a few moments of fiddling, he looks over at me. "You hungover?"

"Yeah." No use in lying. He goes to the driver's side and pulls out a jar.

"You done pissed you momma off and she turned around and pissed you daddy off. She used to do dat shit to her momma when she was mad at me. Shooo, dem two fought like barn cats."

"Well then do you know what I'm supposed to do so she doesn't act like that?"

"I'm her daddy. I don't have to worry about dat. Drink dis. Blackberry moonshine. I call dat *Lune Noir.* My neighbors been buying it from me like dey don't sell beer in da sto."

His hand shakes as he holds the jar out to me. The color of the liquid is somewhere between purple, blue, and red. The floating bits of berry make it look like stagnant swamp water. He's waiting. Unscrewing the cap, I close my eyes, and gulp. It burns like hell but doesn't taste like it. Towards the end of my coughing it borders on pleasant.

"So you didn't need help on your car?"

"Gus? Naawww. I've had Gus since da 1975 election in Breaux Bridge. The man who became mayor gave me dat so I wouldn't run. Has never given me trouble as long as I keep his oil fresh." He grabs another jar from under his seat and a black Magic Marker from the floorboard and writes the date on top. It's more of a struggle than usual and his handwriting doesn't look like it normally does. He sighs as he finishes and meets my eyes. "I'm gonna bring dat up da road to one of you neighbors. We got to talkin' last week and he tole me how much he misses his grandpa's pot lickah."

Chapter 7

I cast between two patches of hyacinth a foot apart. I've gotten better. I don't know if Paw Paw notices. He doesn't say anything about it.

"I tink dis all fished ott, *cher.*"

I hook my bait on a post behind the eye and sit down ready to motor to the next spot. Paw Paw cleans up his gear, giving me a grave look. It's like I did something wrong but I can't think of what it is. "You in ma seat," he says. I wait for an explanation but there is none. He wants me to drive, I guess. I scoot behind the wheel and wait for instruction. None comes. He fiddles with his coveralls. I try to start the engine, getting only coughs and sputters. I try again with no result. There is still no instruction. I try to think practically and go through the steps I've seen. Knowing the old man, there is some sort of subtle art of backwards engineering needing to be performed. Without a clear origin of the impulse, I pull the key out slightly and turn it slowly, to hear the engine hum in consideration. With one hard turn of the key it gives a loud familiar growl, coming to life. It might be a smile I see on Paw Paw's face out of the corner of my eye. "Take it slow back down dis bayou," he tells me. Easing the throttle forward, the front of the boat raises slightly. Not knowing how I know, I trim up the motor and the bow drops. Something must have sunk in from watching him all these years.

Putting along, he looks lovingly at the leafless cypress trees and the brown water under a completely grey sky. He sticks a finger in the water and tastes it. The flavor meets his approval. I never can tell if he does things like this for effect, or it actually means something.

"You not hungover today, *mon petit.*"

"Nope."

"You not spendin' time witchou friends no mo?"

"Not as much."

"Someting wrong with dem?"

"I don't know. Maybe. I don't know if I fit in with them."

"I tink you got it backwards."

"Huh?"

"Dey gotta fit witchou."

"I don't think I fit anywhere."

"Yeah you do. You just ain't found it yet."

It feels like he wants to see me. Or at least he's trying to understand where I fit in his world. Maybe it's time to show him I don't. "Paw Paw. No. I'm a Cajun kid who likes video games and doesn't like spicy or fried food. Accordions make my ears bleed. I hate humidity. I don't like living here, but I don't know how to live anywhere else. I think you're giving me more credit than you should."

"I swear you din't know you were unhappy until you saw it on TV." He sighs and looks back over his bayou. "You daddy don't wanna work wit his hands no mo. You momma made dat sto. The old ways stop workin'. I did dat when I didn't want to work in da field and wanted to be a mechanic. You gotta take what's dere and make it work for you. *Mais* you might have to leave Lafayette or even Louisiana." I look at him to make sure it's my grandfather talking, the man who thinks Louisiana is what the sun revolves around. "Dere's only oil and doctors here. If you don't wanna be one of dose, you gonna have to leave. *Écoute mon fils.* I fought in Korea. I ate me some Korean food. Dat's good, yeah. Only reason I don't eat it nah is dey ain't got no Korean restaurants here. Dere was a piece of me over dere I din't know about. Nah, when I talked about dat food witchou Maw Maw, she tought I was crazy. But dat don't change da fac I like it. I'm still a Cajun dat likes Korean food. Sometime you gotta leave home to find home. You gotta go where you can find da most pieces of you. *Tu comprends*?"

His eyes go back to his bayou. He sees something I don't. Something I miss when I look at the brown water and grey cypress. I wish I could see it, too.

"How come you never told me that?"

"You neva ask." Trying to pick another question I could ask, I'm interrupted. "But you always gonna end up paying someone too much money to fix you car if you doan start learnin' engines."

At our dinner table I take a few bites of fried fish. Paw Paw watches me the whole time from his usual spot without saying anything. Every nerve in my face is suppressed to mask my reflex to gag, but I don't. Something tells me he knows, though he barely strays a look at me while he bickers with my mom. After he leaves, I try to go to my room, but I'm headed off by a cry from the kitchen.

"Are you going out?" it screeches desperately. I didn't want to before, but now I do.

"No."

"Oh." My mom sticks her head out with too much excitement. "Want to watch a movie with me then?"

"K. But I'm warning in advance I might fall asleep."

With my eyes closing at the end of the opening credits, my mother starts to rustle purposefully.

"I'm so thankful I get tonight with you. I had said a prayer earlier in the day that I'd get to spend more time with you and look what happened. It's the little miracles. *Tu connais*?"

I grunt in response with my eyes still closed.

"Will, tell me about the boy you've been going out with lately?"

"He's nobody. Thought he was someone I could hang out with."

"Yeah but why won't you talk about him with me?"

"Mom, it doesn't matter. We're not going to hang out anymore."

"Y'all had a falling out?" Falling out? I wish she'd come right out and say if she knows something. No. That's crazy. I haven't talked to him since that party.

"Something like that. Can we talk about this later?"

"Sure, *mon petit.* I'm glad I'm getting some time with you. I was afraid I was losing you." This I can handle. It may be miserable, but it's familiar. But it's broken by a sound, a quiet sobbing trying not to be quiet. I keep my eyes closed and hope beyond hopes she thinks I can fall asleep that fast.

"Will… I'm so alone."

I open my eyes and look at her. This is easy. All I need to say is how she has me. Then I'm supposed to lie and tell her I'll be here forever.

"Why do you say that?" flies out of my mouth.

"Your sister is gone off to college and she hates me. Or she's dating someone. Either way, she's gone. Your dad… let's just say we're not a happy couple." Sugarcoating this must make her feel a bit more like an appropriate mother in the middle of telling her son her personal business. "And you, you're getting friends. You're going out. You don't even talk to me about it."

"We just did. And I haven't left. Paw Paw is still here too." There we go. That's more like it.

"Paw Paw has his own life. He doesn't need me. No one needs me anymore."

"Oh, Mom—"

"It's true! I'm going to turn into a lonely old woman like this. Please don't you leave me, son. Go to school but promise me you'll live here."

"Maybe if you got some friends, Mom, you—"

"It's not the same. I've been going out more, not that you've noticed. I need you to stay here. Stay home."

"I'm leaving, Mom. I'm going away to college after next year." My ears are terrified but my tongue is relieved. All the hiding, pretending to be something I'm not, has been in service of this. It's easy to see now I'm free to be unhappy, and free to find all my pieces.

"Where are you going?"

"Does it matter? I'm going away, Mom. I can't be this little Cajun boy anymore. This place isn't me. This food isn't me. These people aren't me." The door inside me, the one I shut on Jared as I walked out of the party, flies back open.

"How long were you going to wait to tell me?"

"I don't know."

She stands and stomps over to a window. "I thought you were different. I thought you cared about me." She is begging for me to go back to our lie.

"This isn't about you."

"It isn't? I'm your mother! I'm who brought you into this uncaring world! The one who wiped your ass and fed you. I was your friend when you had none! And now the minute you make a new friend it's ok for you to leave? Tell me which part isn't about me."

"This isn't normal, Mom."

"What? What isn't normal?"

"It's not normal to spend your whole life down the road from your parents. It isn't normal to look at the rest of the world as strange and amoral and cultureless. It isn't normal to judge how good a person is by the color of their roux and who their cousins are."

"You are too young to understand. You're trying to decide who you are by who you don't want to be. You will see how much family matters when you go out in the world and no one loves you like we do."

"That's just it. Our family is not the whole world. We've never joined the rest of the world. We are so stuck in the past. We live our lives looking through a keyhole at the rest of the world never wondering if we're the ones locked away."

"You act like you seen things! When our ancestors got here we had nothing. It was only because we stuck together we—"

"Paw Paw told me I should leave."

Her mouth drops open and she pales. Even her red hair seems to dull some, the spikes losing their point. Her shoulders slump and a look of defeat pulls her cheeks down into jowls. She looks older. Sadder. About to cry.

"You're right. You need to find your path. But you don't have to use my father to try and hurt me."

She grabs her jacket and her keys and walks out the door. There are no dramatic pauses. The car starts. The silence left in the house is broken only by the tinny sound of someone laughing hysterically on TV.

Chapter 8

The only evidence of her still living here are the groceries she drops off while I'm at school. As a bonus, she's made my favorites: mac and cheese and her homemade baked chicken. She is nowhere to be seen when I walk out of my room. Should I apologize for not wanting to be like the other men in this family? I'd be apologizing for telling the truth. What am I supposed to do when she sticks me between two of the morals she beat into me? The mac and cheese tastes bland, which means sanity is on its head. And to make this more confusing, my sister shows up begging to talk to Mom.

"Why does everyone think I know her mind?" I snap back at her from my computer chair.

"Because you live here. Why haven't you been answering the phone?"

"Addison, go away. I said I'm not her keeper. I'm also not your son. One mother is enough."

"Why are you being such a prick?"

"I've been feeling honest lately. Can you go now?"

Sounds like those from a small animal murmur behind me. As if I need a PMSing sister ruining the only thing I have left to enjoy about living here. If she can't appreciate my time or space, I won't tiptoe around her feelings. I stand up and spin around, ready to shove her out of my room. I'm stopped by wet streaks of mascara dripping down her olive, round cheeks.

"What is it?" I ask.

She starts to cry harder.

"Addie, it's ok. Tell me. I'll stop being a prick."

"Tell Mom I need to talk to her." But she doesn't leave.

"Addie, I don't have the ability today to play the game where you expect me to pry it out of you to show I care or until you decide it's ok to tell me."

The pleading, scared eyes she finally brings up to meet mine are the same ones I saw the day she heard our Maw Maw died. Something is seriously wrong. I almost feel bad about considering the potential of the family shit pile shifting off of me. I exhale loudly, for both of us. She looks up, thinking it was a breath of condemnation. But I smile and open my arms. Making good on not being a prick, she collapses into my chest and cries harder. I've never hugged her because I wanted to before.

Chapter 9

It's disturbing. Mom isn't showing up at Addie's game. Addie is playing at her worst. I still don't know what to make of her crying the whole way here. She always spills. Addison Mouton is known for the size of her mouth, in more ways than one. Part of my pinky finger wants to feel worried or even sorry for her. She's not trying to say anything about me and another boy now. She could do me a favor and break Mom's heart even more than I did, and I can go back to being the good one.

As I finish thinking about my status in the family, I look over at my grandfather squatting on the bleacher beside me. He wears his usual sweat and oil-stained coveralls, but with a new bright red baseball cap.

"*T'as faim*?" he asks.

"No I ate before I came here."

"How's you sister doin'?"

"Ok. This isn't her best game."

"Where's you momma?"

"I don't know. She wasn't there when I woke up this morning."

He gets quiet and stares at my sister in the dugout.

"You a good boy coming with you sister to her game."

"Thanks."

He continues to watch, quietly, until she gets up to the plate. Two balls and two strikes in, she nails one to the fences. The outfield miscommunicates and she slides in for the triple. Paw Paw hops up and down, screaming.

"*Cher 'tite fille.* She still good, yeah! I remember when she couldn't even hit. Look dat girl now."

His joy is contagious, and his pride is addictive. Warm contentment, for her, for me, spreads in my chest. I will it away, still not wanting too much sentiment to weigh me down, preventing a clean getaway.

"I'm going to go away to college, Paw Paw," I say to prevent my resolve from getting eroded.

"I figured you would. You gotta do what you gotta do."

"You don't sound happy about it. This was your idea."

"My idea was for you to find where you gone be happy. Not for you to give everyone else *misère* in da process. From what you momma tole me, you act like she beats you. You not tryin' to work it out wit her. Dat's not how we raised you."

"All that stuff has been building up for a long time."

"Part of growing up is respectin' *sa famille.*"

"They need to act respectable for me to respect them."

A white flash overtakes my vision. I didn't even see the old man move. The sting arrives on my face before I realize I've been slapped. "*Tu a besoin un calotte,*" he tells me. It's unclear whether the sparsely filled stands are used to public corporal punishment, or merely condone it. No one budges or looks. He returns to watching my sister silently. The slap makes my face hot. It stings more than a slap should. Searching for a solid reason for why he'd think I need that, I find nothing. There is only one thing to do now: nothing.

After the Lady Cajuns are off the field, and Paw Paw is done cheering, he tells me we are going for a ride.

"Where you friend live?"

"Who?"

"You friend you used to drink with and carry on."

"We're not—"

His steel grey eyes lock on me from underneath the new cap brim. If the look wasn't enough, the nostrils of his oversized nose flare and his mouth flattens to a thin line. He's never looked at me like this before.

This is the look he gave the enemy when he fought in Korea. I give him Jared's address in Greenbriar.

Breathing normally for the first time since telling him Jared's address, I'm happy to see only Jared's car in the driveway. Having this angry fossil with me when I'd meet his high-class parents for the first time would give me a stroke.

"Go be witchou *Americains*," Paw Paw tells me.

"What?"

"Go ahead since you don't want us. I'll work out getting you clothes and tings from you momma. That's you home now."

"Paw Paw come on. I get it. I messed up. I'll smooth things over with Mom."

"You not listenin'. I'm telling you to go. You don't need to live with her, with us, no mo. I'm giving you what you want. No hard feelings."

A look over at him in the driver's seat and I can tell he means it. His eyes aren't set on me like a Communist, like they were when we drove here. He understands and might even wish me well. It's clear he's known I've wanted to live in a place like this, with people like Jared, all along. Today he is bending to me, finally giving me what I want, and asking nothing in return. I look back at Jared's house, at the gas lamps, the antique red brick, the glass French doors. He'd take me in without having to ask. This could finally be my world. There'd never be too much spice or constant frying in the kitchen. It would be quiet. There wouldn't be a nag to come home to or spend an afternoon fishing on murky, reptile-infested water. And that's exactly what's wrong with it.

"Take me home, Paw Paw. Please."

Chapter 10

I hear a pot bang. It's a little soothing. Always I've craved the quiet in between the noises. It turns out the noises are what make the silences real. When the phone rings, I feel a sort of smug anticipation of her yelling at the receiver, as if the phone company could not be trusted to carry her voice on its own. Coziness is cut short by a bloodcurdling exclamation of "Noooo!" Mice jump into my mind. Mom freaks at anything small and furry. But she said "no." She doesn't tell mice "no." Erring toward impulse, I get up from Dungeons and Dragons.

When I get to the kitchen, she is on the floor hyperventilating, phone lying next to her. No one is left on the line. Staring forward, her eyes scare me. They're a million miles away.

"What Mom? Mom! Talk to me! What happened?" But I know. And the far-away, morose look in her eyes confirms it. "What happened to Paw Paw?"

Her face contorts in pain and anger and fear.

"Daddy got in a wreck. They think he had a stroke. They're going to take him to General."

As her eyes go to focus on a point I can't see, a sound emits from somewhere deep in her throat. It could be a whine. It could be a stifled cry. It's childlike. Slipping into the role of the adult in the room is easy because it's so familiar. Today it doesn't leave me bitter because I know it's what my family needs.

"We need to go," I declare.

"Yes," she says.

Not a single car ride in my life was accompanied by silence. Today I want meaningless chatter, off-key singing, or even endless questions—anything to break the stab of the silence. The hum of the engine isn't enough to break this maddening pitch of quiet. It's too full of awful possibilities. Only days ago I'd walked away from a change because it was too good. Can I trade that change for what this change might be? It might be nothing. It might be an exciting Saturday night me and Paw Paw talk about over fishing tomorrow, next week at the latest.

I smell him before I see him. The musk of sweat lays heavy over the emissions of plastic and disinfectant. The bandages over the deep cuts on his arms, the faded gown, and his skin are all sterilized toward white. The dried blood and mud in his hairline stands out. The gown slipped down a bit to expose the deep V of his coverall tan, which has much less contrast than it usually does. Only his face looks like it might belong to him, except it's tired and slack. The wrinkles around his lips, which always crease when speaking French, look like they've been ironed out. It's the first time he's ever looked fragile, looked old. He won't be fishing tomorrow.

A Yankee doctor enters the room. He might be from California. He might even be Jared's dad. His demeanor is cool, full of rehearsed concern, as he explains Auguste Chenevert was found still in his truck after it had crashed through the concrete barrier of I-10 and fell roughly 20 feet to the water below. The culprit of the crash appears to be a stroke. None of them know how he is still alive. None of us know what he would have been doing on I-10 heading east at that time of night. My eyes land on a bag poking from the cubby in the wall. I open it as the doctor leaves. His coveralls are there, covered in mud or swamp water. They're same coveralls he came to the game in. The same ones he wore when he drove me to Jared's and told me to choose. Alongside them is the new red cap he'd worn. It looks completely untouched.

"My Daddy," Mom gasps out. These tears are controlled and made for public consumption. She walks over to him and runs her hands over his head and through his thick gray hair. She sniffles and kisses his forehead.

"*Je suis ici. Je suis ici,*" she chants over and over. Her hands rub his head the way they would mine when I couldn't sleep. I get angry. A hug and a kiss is plenty. If he were awake he'd yell "*Je n'suis pas ton chat*! *Mais,* I'm nobody's cat!" She doesn't have to respect him today. She has him where she wants him. He needs help, and he can't swat away her hovering over him. For several minutes I watch and wait, hoping she will stop this obscene little ritual. If anything, her movements become more manic and her voice more pleasant. It only serves to drive the point home. Even being treated the way he hates doesn't wake him. Tunnel vision takes over as I stare at his nearly lifeless body, a picture of what normal from today forward could be. I feel sick. My mother doesn't even notice when I slip out of the door.

The click of the door is followed by the sound of my name. I wonder if the shadows of nutria on the island in Girard Park are calling to me. The utterance of my name helps me realize I'm sitting in duck shit.

"Will, are you ok?"

"Yeah. Walked away to get air, I guess."

"Mom said that was five hours ago."

"You saw him?"

"Yeah." Her eyes well up. "It's bad."

"Mom can't handle it."

"I know. But you don't look like you're handling it well either," she says while pointing to my ass in the mud.

"Don't really know how I got here. Just know it feels more friendly than what's waiting for us over there."

My sister doesn't mind getting dirty, but there needs to be a reason. Hunting, softball, mudding in truck are usual reasons. I cannot for the life of me figure out what her reason is to sit next to me in this filth.

"You're right," she breathes out. This would be so much easier to deal with if the other people in my family would act normal. Never in my memory has she said I'm right. She explains we need to get back to the hospital because Paw Paw's prognosis is not good. Her voice breaks as she tells me, and she gets lost in a sob. Without having to think about it, my arm goes around her, and I pull her close. It doesn't matter that it's not normal.

"Come on," she says, sitting upright, exhausted by her own tears. "Let's get back in there. Lord knows what Mom is doing. She's not going to be able to move this forward on her own."

Re-entering the room, covered in mud, our mother is leaning over our grandfather, cooing as she did when we left. When she straightens at the sound of us, I can see his pallor deepened. She faces us and I know Addie can see the same distant, nearly absent look in her eyes. She smiles warmly, freakishly calm despite all the disconnected life in the room.

"Paw Paw is gone," she says.

Chapter 11

From my viewpoint on this over-upholstered couch I have a bird's eye view of the man closest to what I thought an adult should be like. But he doesn't look like that man. He could be his brother or distant cousin. They've slacked his skin to make him look peaceful. They've powdered his face so his sallowness looks like coffee milk rather than a used coffee filter. People file in and hug my mom, my sister, and me. My mom smiles while she sobs, telling them he is with God now, proud she is on show. My sister competes with my mom for the gracious martyr award. My father broods and holds back tears, saying nearly nothing to anyone.

The priest shows up and proclaims he'll be saying the rosary in French in honor of Auguste. We bow obediently. The performances go to intermission and the eyes are no longer on me. I raise my head to look at Paw Paw. They didn't put his favorite rosary in his hand. It always seems weird when they'd do that, but his rosary would be the only authentic thing in this circus. They've waited until there is nothing left of him to protest before taking it. I lose it. I know my mother has that rosary. There is no other place it could be. Her head is bent in reverence, tears still cutting trails in her heavy powder. But she is smiling. On the day that should be the worst of her life she smiles. Like that rosary, this whole room is in her pocket.

Getting up to leave with tears in my eyes, I hear the hushed utterances of "*pauvre bête.*" Let them think this is all about his death. While it would be downright fun to tell them all it's about who he left me with, I won't make this all about me, not like my mother has. Outside it's wet and cold. A front came through. The blackbirds argue in the big palm bush next to the door. I smell something cooking, something greasy. It's hard to tell if the nausea is for the greasy smell or the disgusting shit show inside. My stomach commences growling the longer my deep breaths take in the smell of the food.

"You should come back inside." My sister gives me another thing to hate in this moment. So, I don't respond.

"Will, you need to get inside."

"I don't care what they think, Addie, no matter how much you want me to."

She grabs my shoulder and spins me toward her. "Listen you fucking brat. That's our grandfather in there. You need to be a fucking man and pay your respects. You can't leave his funeral because you're *bouder* and need to come outside to pout!"

"Bouder. *Mais*, I need to go respect him, me? God damn this place. Damn everyone in it."

Fuck her. While readying my next barrage of bitter reality, she starts crying. It's not her injured manipulative cry. It's like the one she had next to the duck pond.

"We've been acting like this could never happen. That he'd always be here making sense of it for us. What are we going to do now?" she blubbers.

Her hug is warm and genuine; the exact opposite of the one I'm giving back. She doesn't seem to mind. When she's satisfied, she pushes me to arm's length and looks in my eyes lovingly. I'm put off by how nice this feels, how real. The contrast from the scene inside is disorienting. She leaves me with the greasy smell, birds, and humidity. The door to the funeral home closes silently behind her. I hear tinny Cajun music and the smell of crawfish. I know it's not coming from Meche's Donuts across the street. I follow it to the back of the funeral home where a door is open. Inside I catch a glimpse of age-spotted hands, buzzing a blur around a mass of crawfish spread on paper. I look around to see if I've ventured over to another portion of the building –

a restaurant or someone's living room. Before I can determine where I am, I hear an accent as thick as my grandfather's call toward me.

"*Vien voit ici, cher.* Dere's plenty!" The bespectacled eyes peeking through the crack in the door make no doubt of who she's talking to. Closer, I see a back room to a back room of the funeral home. The two old ladies beckoning me look familiar. I place them as the Daughters of the Diocese who greeted all the mourners.

"I think I'm lost," I try to say innocently.

"No you not, *cher*. You followed you nose to *da* right place." The one with bigger glasses stuffs a paper towel over my father's ill-fitting tie. As I look down at the pile of crustaceans, I feel a familiar disgust rising. This is the food I hate most. The wet cracking of the carapaces as you open them, the garlicky spice that never seems to get out of your mouth, and the earthy taste of mud on every tail, all of it awaits me even if I can get past the smell. But being in here is so much better than being in there.

Sharing some smiles, and a meal from the earth, is where Paw Paw would me want to be. It's a welcome in French. The only due that needs to be paid is that I eat. Unpracticed at peeling though they are, my hands vigorously tear at a medium sized mudbug until I get disfigured tail meat out. I'm sure I will throw up as it goes into my mouth, but I need something to show me he's still here and didn't take it all with him when he left. When my gag reflex doesn't engage, I open my eyes while chewing quickly to see two very pleased… no proud… Daughters of the Diocese. Having witnessed my struggle to get to the little tail meat, they continue to push a pile of peeled tails to my spot at the table.

Being the indoor geek of the family means I'm not missed often. Thankfully I was out of sight, out of mind once the rosary was over. I weave my way back into the crowd and people assume I was there the whole time. We pay our last respects and I don't look at him. There is a role to play, to look strong, so as a pallbearer I can carry the one who was really strong. He wasn't tall. His muscles were thin, a man always waging war to hold weight against a humid Louisiana sun that steals appetite. Only his width can explain the weight of the casket. Or it's the opulence of his coffin that makes it heavy – yet another thing he would hate.

The heft makes me sweat against the humidity in this suit. Puffs of air smelling like crawfish boil steam travel up my neck from underneath my shirt. While I'm having the hardest time physically, my dad is having a harder time emotionally. He almost drops Paw Paw's head when he reaches for his handkerchief. We get him on the little stainless-steel accordion cart and wheel him to the front of the church. The priest admonishes us for not being as Catholic as Paw Paw. He then proceeds to tell stories about how Auguste would always outfish, outhunt, outcook, and outrepair him. He gets teary-eyed when talking about how Auguste seemed to naturally understand the things he spent years in the seminary figuring out. Heads nod all around me. Knowing him together, knowing how he helped us define our lives, makes me connected to these people, maybe for the first time.

Graveside, I look inside the hole where my grandfather will remain for eternity next to Maw Maw. The place on my face where he slapped me begins to ache, reminding me of our last interaction. When his casket finishes lowering, it makes a sound similar to when his hand met my face. Even the spinning I felt afterwards returns. What goes in the hole with him? If something small like his rosary can't go in, why does all the laughter, all the times he tried to make me a man, all the kisses he still gave me as a teenager, have to go in with him? The spinning gets worse as I stare at the hole and taps is played. The picture of Jared's house floats in the hole. Because that's all it was. A hole to bury pieces of myself in, pieces of Paw Paw, pieces of this place and these people I don't know what to do with but are more a part of me than I can admit. Without those pieces I will be as cold and dead as the man who was less ashamed of me than I am. The centrifuge in my head breaks loose and I vomit on the headstone of a Boudreaux. Looking down I see how much crawfish I ate. Dad's hands are now on my shoulders. I vomit more. When I look up at my father's red eyes, I'm met with tenderness I'd only seen in one other man's eyes. I vomit again.

No one will question me going to my room. The last thing I need today is my aunt or my mom making a big deal about what I'm eating. Sitting in my computer chair I stare at the blank screen, quietly refilling my stomach with mac and cheese and boudin. The boudin is gone first. A knock to my door interrupts the understanding silence. Trying to decide if I could feign sleep, my hand on the door ends the debate in my head.

"You ok?" Addie inquires with less genuineness than earlier in the day.

"Yeah."

"Yeah me, too." She enters the room and sits on my bed. I return to my plate. Silence. Could we sit in each other's company, avoiding the bedlam in the living room, without having to talk? I remember I am not that lucky when Addie says, "Mom pissed me off."

My answer is a blank stare.

She smiles and then doesn't. "She tried to tell me that Paw Paw would be upset with me for the way I'm treating her today. I mean, seriously! She's going to invoke my own dead grandfather's name to try and control me."

"Hmph."

"I mean, she's always projecting what she thinks onto him. You know? I mean, that's crazy, right?" With my inability to play this game, she finally asks. "Do you think he would have been mad?" Her face watches mine, beseeching support. This isn't about her. This isn't about my mom or my dad or my aunt. It's not even about me. It's supposed to be about him.

"I'm not sure, Addie. And you know why I'm not sure. Because he's dead. We can't ask him. You got a problem with Mom? Deal with it. Tell her off. Stop talking to her. Do whatever. Because what Paw Paw thinks doesn't matter anymore. Because Paw Paw isn't thinking. We have to figure it all out now."

"You shut your fucking mouth! You think he can't hear us in heaven?"

"Maybe. If there even is such a thing. And if he does, he—"

She stands up, disgusted. "All the faggots and drugs you've been fucking with have messed you up."

I've spent weeks dreading someone saying less than that. And I couldn't care less. I feel like I'm watching it all through backwards binoculars. I've tried to change for them and I can't. It's hard to tell if changing even matters anymore. "I've been learning to think for myself. Paw Paw taught me to do that." I say it as much for me as I do for her. "Get out. The chances of either of us feeling better around here are pretty slim."

Chapter 12

Our house was always a fertile ground for lies. The silence he left drowns out any chance of loud opinions or inconvenient truths. In this game of chicken, the loser is the first one to open their mouth and acknowledge life is harder now. The silence is protective without Auguste Chenevert around to make sure we can't say what we think about each other. We are only allowed to talk about the big question: Why was he on I-10 in the middle of the night heading eastbound? Mom wonders if he missed the exit to home since he was about to have a stroke. Addie seems to think he knew the end was coming and just wanted to go fishing one more time. Dad, whom I'd barely seen since we got drunk together, even takes me out to lunch to hear his theory: he had a woman he didn't want to tell us about.

The room we give each other allows me plenty of opportunities to work on college applications. Even if I end up at my closest choice, Tulane, they won't visit me there. They think New Orleans is Mars. The right essay topic finally came to me. Growing up in a Cajun household has a lot more to it than I ever appreciated. Afterwards, I even hesitated before checking "white" in the identity column. The word just makes me think of Jared and his Northern friends. I see now I'm more "off-white." Thinking about Jared causes my stomach to flip, something I should be used to by now. When I sit with it, I realize it's flipping at the thought of walking out on him and the world he opened me up to without so much of a backward glance. That wasn't my world, but neither is this, especially since Paw Paw is gone. Tears sting my eyes as a deep, real, grief finds me. The longing for his confidence, his concern, makes me pull out his red baseball cap, the one he wore the day he died. I'd taken it from my mother's room earlier in the week. Since she took his rosary, I can't feel bad for stealing the hat. She can't have everything of his. His coveralls had mildewed and smelled terrible. But his hat is fine. I hold it up looking on the inside for a hair, a fleck of skin, anything that would be left of him. There is nothing. The hat is immaculate. His faint smell is gone from it now, overpowered by the cloth and plastic odors of a new hat. Turning it back over I look at the logo. I'd only noticed it was red and assumed it was a USL cap in support of my sister and her "baseball." Instead I read a logo in black that says "Kim's Korean BBQ" with a little pig underneath. I log into Netscape and find where this restaurant is located: Baton Rouge. Auguste Chenevert died on the way to get his spicy Korean BBQ. I put on the hat.

Wiping tears, I fluctuate between being glad no one is home and wishing one of them was here. After several minutes I accept none of them would get this. They'd always think it was odd that Paw Paw died getting food they've never eaten. They'll think he's weird for liking it. He just wanted to have all the pieces of himself. That's what he wanted for me, too. That's why that door was hard to close on Jared: I closed off pieces of me. All I've done in my life is try to choose some pieces over others. I don't want to do that anymore. Placing Paw Paw's hat on my head I find Jared's phone number.

"Don't call me," Jared proclaims. But he doesn't hang up.

"I need to talk to you."

"You're too late."

"I fucked up with you."

"Yeah you did." But he still doesn't hang up.

"I want to tell you what you deserve to hear."

In a little over ten minutes, the speed freak picks me up at my house. He gives me a quizzical look about not needing cover from my family, but I don't acknowledge it.

"Head toward Broussard," I tell him. "I've never seen your school, ESA. Let's go there to talk."

He turns off of Highway 90 down a dark road and he stops in front of a cluster of interconnected buildings. All sit about two feet off the ground, similar to my grandfather's old house. A big difference is how new and well-kept they look. The oaks, illuminated by the headlights of his over-engineered Supra, look like they've been cared for. We find our way to the middle of the buildings, me following Jared's tall slender frame, with the orange security light making his blond hair look like it's on fire. We sit on steps outside of what must be a third or fourth grade class. Pictures of the kids smile at me in the security lights. Several of the kids don't look like they're from around here.

"Y'all have a bunch of Indian kids at this school. Like Indians from India."

"Yeah. Don't you?"

"Like, three."

"That's weird."

He produces a joint and I see no reason to turn him down. Maybe it can even help me figure out what I want to say to him. Our smoke intertwines with a nearby oak, twisting and writhing with the Spanish moss.

"My grandfather died."

"Recently?"

"Yeah."

"Shit. I'm sorry. I didn't know. What happened?"

"Stroke. Wreck."

"Holy crap. That sucks. So, I guess that's why you started acting so weird," he says with some relief.

"No," I reply, watching the smoke continue to dance with trees. Watching it turns out to be more relaxing than the weed.

"So then why?"

I pull the brim of Paw Paw's hat back some. "Let's go somewhere else. I thought this was the right place to talk about this. But it doesn't have enough of the right pieces. "

"Joint isn't done."

"Smoke in the car. We're in the country. People don't worry about stuff here."

I guide him to Tante Marie's. Specifically, I want to get to Cousin Vilain's catfish pond. For a moment I think it's a bad idea. Not because there is barely any light and we are both high. More because Jared's Supra is straining through the mud even though he's in a low gear. He groans as it seems like we're going to stall. It feels colder and wetter out here. Fifty degrees, cold by a Cajun's standard, feels more like it's in the thirties. Jared puts the roach in his ashtray and closes the windows. We pull up to a slightly drier patch of dirt. Through the cluster of trees on our right I can see the security light outside Vilain's momma's house.

"You know you're washing my car, right? Where the hell are we?"

"Catfish pond."

"Who lives there?"

"Family."

"They have guns?"

"Of course they have guns." More white appears around his eyes. "Don't worry. My cousin is in jail and his momma is sound asleep. Stay here and I'll show you why we came here."

My feet squish through the mud rimming the pond to a cypress shed splitting the distance between us and the house. It's been seven or eight years since I was last here. But like the roads, I don't need light to find what I'm looking for. Paw Paw always said he wanted to take me catfishing at night. The fishing poles are in the corner of the shed. They're the same ones I used when I'd walk out to this pond, bored of my mom's conversations with her cousin. I take a while before I catch myself expecting to see Paw Paw's silhouette walking from the house to join me for a few casts. Without needing to search for it, I find a bag of large chunked dry dog food in the left corner of the shed where it always is; even though their old yellow hunting lab died last year. There is something to be said about Cajuns never changing. I grab a handful of the dog food on the way out of the shed. Having made my way back, I hold out one of the poles to Jared. He remains immobile, staring at me in disbelief.

"What?"

"Take it."

He continues to stare as I fix a couple of humidity-softened chunks of dog food to the end of my hook. I do the same for his. I pitch our baits far out into the pond. With only moonlight as a guide, the past and intuition will tell me when the fish hits. An owl hoots. Paw Paw would say he's letting me know I'm about to get a bite. Instead of getting annoyed at the superstition, I get excited about the fish the owl told me about. A bit of swamp gas, *feu follet* Paw Paw would call it, ethereal as our smoke in the school yard, dances over the water. My eyes venture to Jared who wears a completely confounded look.

"You're not holding your mouth right," I say with amusement. For years I thought this was superstition, too. Tonight, I realize Paw Paw was telling me to smile.

"What?"

A big tug gets my hands busy before I can explain. In a few moments I have a large catfish on the bank. I dance with my fish, like I did that day in Paw Paw's boat. My steps are a little better since I'm high and not hungover. At least I think they're better. Careful not to get stung by the fins, I work the hook out in one quick movement. The catfish looks beautiful in the moonlight.

"Satisfied? Can we go now before someone puts holes in us?" Letting the fish go, I watch it happily glide off to what it knows, caring little for its ordeal out of water. Hopefully it will be smarter next time, not biting onto just anything dangling in front of it. "We'll finish this conversation at my house. I hope I have some towels in my car for our muddy-ass shoes."

"I'm not done fishing. *Lâche pas la patate.*"

A quizzical, or annoyed, look spreads across his face. They're indistinguishable in moonlight. "Why the hell are we here, asshole?" he rasps.

"I told you I'd tell you what you deserve to hear." I put my pole down and wipe my hands on my pants. He looks at them in disgust. "You'll never understand how much that kiss, the way you looked at me, the way you touched me, meant to me. There were pieces of me I didn't even know were there and you found them."

He smiles and takes a step toward me, running his hand between my legs, "After you shower I can find those pieces again."

"Stop," I say pushing his hand away and taking a step back. "There's other pieces you can't see, that you didn't touch. Pieces I'm still figuring out. That's why I can't be gay with you. Not right now."

"Will…" His tone softens. "Will, listen. I freaked out, too, when I was coming out. It's normal to not want this." His eyes glisten. The glint of moonlight outlines authenticity in his eyes. He genuinely wants to be with me. The door he opened inside of me swings wide again, but I know now I don't have to walk through it, at least not yet. There are other doors to look for. "Can we go smoke and talk about it?" he asks.

"I thought I had it all figured out. All I had figured out is what I don't want. I'm not a bunch of 'eithers' and 'ors'. I'm a big 'and.'" The honesty of it feels clean, giving a final rinse to this moon-bathed mecca.

"You're not making any sense."

"I am. You can't get it. You were raised… like you were. But—"

The moon light converts to searing white light and pain, followed by cold wetness. My eyes struggle open against mud and duck shit. When I get to a sitting position, he is standing over me. I wipe muck and blood away from above my left eye.

"You're worse than everyone else here. They may be dumb, but you're stupid. You're self-absorbed. You've been so busy trying to be somebody, you never saw me as a somebody. You don't get to be better than me! You are not better than me! Asshole! You were supposed to be different from all the posers who keep coming to my house wherever I go. Listen to you. Full of self-righteous Southern-fried bullshit. I shouldn't have picked up the phone. Don't call again. And I'm not your weed hook up. I only do that for friends."

Still sitting in the mud, I watch the Supra's lights flash across the trees. The pain in my head makes it hard to determine if the crickets are on the inside or outside of my head. The smart thing to do would be to go to my cousin's house and call someone to pick me up. But I don't want that right now. It's not because I have to explain. I just don't want to freak out Tante Marie. She's worried enough for Vilain to not have to worry about another cousin going down a wrong path. If I want to reach civilization before daybreak, though, I need to get moving. Walking back down parish roads, down unlit highways, and past dimly lit gas stations, my head starts to clear. The pain over my eye purges the high I'd been feeling. It also serves to sober my understanding of what I'm facing when I go home. My world is different now. Tolerating the difficulty isn't going to work anymore. We won't be able to love each other without becoming something new. It's going to be hard and painful. It makes me miss my Paw Paw. But at least I caught a pretty catfish tonight.

After walking several miles, I'm on the outskirts of Broussard proper. Jared is probably already home or at a party, trying to forget my confusing ass. I don't blame him. I'm an "and." The only person who knew how to do this, to crave kimchi and be Cajun, is gone. Speaking of Korean food, I remember the hat and the mud Jared knocked me down into. I pull it off once I find some good light. There is not a speck on it. The tightness in my stomach, the one always warning me of danger, melts. It allows me to fully feel the cold. I'm shivering. I don't need help to get out fish hooks any more, but I need to learn how to ask for a ride. Finding a pay phone outside a convenience store, I fumble in my pocket and find a quarter. After a promise to explain more, my sister agrees to pick me up. Covering her seat with a sweaty old gym towel she pulls from the floorboard of her truck, I carefully slide in.

“Oh my God you stink! What are you doing here? And why are you wearing Paw Paw’s hat?"

"Wanted to go fishing."

"Is that blood?" she asks, touching my eye.

I flinch. “Jared hit me. We went to get high and fish. I told him we weren't as alike as he wanted us to be. That's when he hit me."

"What the fuck is wrong with you?"

"A lot. But I'm working on that."

At home Mom’s car is in the driveway and Dad’s is gone. Addie puts her ten-year-old Silverado in park.

“You can go. I'll handle this," I say. Her look of sisterly concern softens. She smiles as she slugs me in my arm.

“I'll be at *Tante's* Sunday," she needlessly reassures.

The house is quiet. There’s no loud TV or screaming. Mom isn’t on the phone. I slip off to the shower. I’m hungry. My clothes in the wash, I go to see if there are any leftovers from the reception. I find Mom at the kitchen table staring down at its surface. Her hands are flat against it as if she was about to get up but changed her mind. With her back to me, I get to look at her for more than a moment. Her thick thighs don’t spill as much over the sides of the chair. The red in her hair faded. Walking around to the front of her, I see a distant smile draped across a tired face.

“Mom?”

She looks up but her hands stay flat against the tabletop. “Hey *mon p’tit.*”

“You ok?”

“Oh yeah. Just thinking. About… well... everybody. Sometimes I have to stop and look at my life. I hardly recognize it anymore. One day you'll see. You wake up and wonder how you got here." If only she knew that day is today. But I don't need her to get me anymore. Turning to see me for the first time since I entered the room, her eyes focus on the cut on my eye. "My God, Will! What happened?"

"Can I talk to you?"

"You can always talk to me. What happened to your eye?"

"I know what I must look like to you with the way I've been acting lately. Going out all the time. Drinking. Getting weird friends. I'm not much like the Will you're used to."

"Hmm." That could be agreement. She keeps looking at my eye.

"I'm tired of being angry all the time. When the time is right, let's talk about what happens next."

Looking at me with warmth she says, "*Mon 'tit garçon*. You look like *mon 'tit garçon*," she smiles warmly and stretches her hands away from the table toward me, signaling an embrace. Bracing myself for the awkwardness of my mom hugging her "little boy," I lean in. It's not tight and clutching. It's not worried and shaming either. It's just a good mom hug.

Chapter 13

We pack up the chocolate eruption and fish fry Tante Kathy can't find in Breaux Bridge. On the drive there we catch a crackly signal from an AM station in Ville Platte. We sing "200 Lines," my Mom shouting the chorus "I must not speak French on the schoolground anymore." When we get to the end of the song, she whispers the line one last time. Only she says it in French, staging her own little Cajun rebellion. We both laugh. Somewhere out over the Bayou Teche, Paw Paw is smiling.

I lean my head out the window. I can smell the Henderson swamp even though we're still several miles away. I want to go fishing, but it'll wait for another day. Unlike the rusting overhang of the Pont Breaux bridge, the green oaks never look any smaller no matter how big I get. Even though I know how much people hate having to pressure wash it, the bright green mold growing on sides of houses, signaling the approach of spring, is kind of pretty. Never bothering with our comings or goings, nature follows its own time. Never intimidated by what we try to build, and only managing to destroy, it grows around and through everything. No matter how big we think our lives are, we'll always need its permission to follow our plans. It's comforting somehow.

Before my aunt can initiate, I'm in her arms. She hugs like my mom does now, or maybe the other way around. Better yet, her clothes smell faintly of Paw Paw. She offers my cousin's room and the use of his computer, but I decline. The accents and the smell of the food are what I'm craving today. I try not to think too deeply on what it might mean. The meaning will come from the doing.

My mom is fussing at her sister for not having the fish fileted. They cluck back and forth in French. I understand more words. "Time." "Go." "Decision." Quietly, I make my way to the sink and start to filet. A well recorded series of memories inform me better than any Saturday afternoon cooking show how to cut this catfish. I only mess up once before my brain and hands are working together. It's involved work. When I look up, they're staring at me.

"*Il sourit,*" my aunt whispers behind me, remarking on the upturned corners of my mouth. They beam proudly at me. Behind her my sister walks in. She's wearing the face she uses when she's fighting back tears.

"I brought Schlitz," she announces. We all give a little cheer.

Addison

Chapter 14

The next pitch will show if she really is doing the opposite of what I tell her. I call a curve and she gives me a changeup. Not only is she *contraillon,* but she's cocky, too. The ball ends up in the dust and the runner at first takes off for second. She's lucky I have an arm. Even after I throw the runner out, she isn't any less cocky or more appreciative. Coach doesn't even scold her when we get in the dugout. She says something about bad calls. I roll my eyes, hoping she's looking. I've known some of these girls since slow pitch. This team and this game have given me all the love I need, and I've given it all back plus *lagniappe,* for the last twelve years. Making sure the whole team hears, she tells me I need to be in her office before I leave. Now I have two prima donnas to set straight.

In the twenty minutes it takes her to get to her office I'm able to get all the mud caked to my cleats rubbed into her new carpet. Then I take them off and let my feet air out on her desk. Her nose doesn't even wrinkle when she finally walks in.

"You were giving bad calls today, Mouton. It looked like you were doing it deliberately."

She's got an uppity Freshman pitcher who thinks she knows better than her senior catcher. But Coach either doesn't see it or doesn't care. Either way, I traded the winningest coach in this school's history for a woman with bad judgement aching to make a name for herself.

"If it came off dat way I'm sorry," I say with extra accent to remind her California ass where she is.

"You don't like me, do you Addie?" My last coach would have never made it personal. Liking her even less now, I smile bigger. "I mean I figured you wouldn't. You're the one all the girls look up to. For good reason. You're a great catcher. And I'm the new coach coming in and changing things. Do you think we can figure out a way you can finish out your senior year with the glory you deserve? We could have done this a much nicer way. I have a team to put together. If you don't want to get on board, you don't need to be on this team. You'll sit the bench next week. That should give you time to think about what role you want to play. I think we're done here," she finishes flatly.

There's nothing to say as I get back to my locker. Everyone is out of the showers and dressing. Their eyes haven't left me since I was in coach's little glass office. They don't need to be lip readers to have seen the looks on both of our faces. I drop my cleats and socks into my locker. They'll want me to crack a joke, put them, and myself, at ease. While I try to shove the corners of my mouth up, I think about how I just had some gay Yankee try and rip my team, and my life's work, away from me. Too pissed to joke, I grab my bag, still dressed in my sweaty uniform, my humid hair approaching an afro, and walk out the door.

Chucking my bag in the back of my truck, I try to open the door. I know it sticks. I know I have to be gentle. But I'm so pissed, gentle is not in my repertoire. Not being able to open the door only makes me more pissed. I just need to get away from here and get a drink. Right now. Hand still on the door, a scream reaches out upward toward the sky coming from somewhere deep in my chest. That little soap opera wasn't enough to make me this angsty. It's the fact my life is like this damn door right now. I try to open it up, try to get inside and move, but I'm just stuck.

"You ok?"

A deep voice echoes from my ears to my chest, landing somewhere near where the scream came from. It makes me startle and turn to see a large, dark-skinned Black man in a white tank and sweats. He's muscular, easily strong enough to hold someone down to have his way with them. Trying my door again, it's still stuck.

"You look like you could use some help." He doesn't sound like Black folk I've heard before. He sounds educated, high-class even. So much so I'm conscious of how strong my accent is. He's less country than me.

"No. Don't need help. Just want to be left alone."

"Don't think alone will work for too long if you can't get in your truck and you don't have any shoes."

My anger sent me out the locker room barefoot. Only my ankle braces stand between me and the cold, damp pavement.

"I'm fine. If you can walk around in an undershirt, I can walk around without shoes."

"You Cajun girls are something else. I meant your feet would get torn up. But you're worried about it being cold. This ain't cold."

"Who said I was Cajun?"

He points at my jersey with the large "LADY CAJUNS" printed across the front, indicating his comment was about my team affiliation. He keeps the same sympathetic look he's had since he walked up. My face gets hot. He smiles. It's a nice smile. Pulling on my door desperately, I will it to open. It doesn't budge. This is the most jammed it's ever been. My truck has betrayed me. He walks toward me.

"What the hell do you think you're doing?"

"Wanted to see if I could open it for you."

"Back the fuck up! I don't know you."

He puts his hands up like I have a gun on him. "I'm Dave. David Johnson. I play on the football team. I was walking by…"

"Don't lie to me! There's nothing back here for you to be walking by."

"Coach had us at the stadium and…"

"It's not even a stadium, it's called CAJUN Field." The emphasis in the name should remind him who belongs here, no matter what his class is.

"Ok. Field. Whatever. I was heading back to my apartment."

"Stop lying! There aren't any apartments near here."

"Beau Chenes apartments aren't too far."

It didn't occur to me that he could be living near here, on the white side of town. This guy really must not be from around here. Still, Beau Chenes is a long walk barely wearing a shirt in sixty-degree weather. We're in this standoff, his hands up, mine on the door handle refusing to budge. We both look at each other and realize we're studying one another. His eyes size up my big Cajun curls, my thick eyebrows that need to be plucked, my button French nose above my Paw Paw's thick chin, and the muscles in my arms. His eyes don't go down to my round bottom like all the other Black men's eyes do. As he watches me, I take stock of his close-cropped hair, his dark, stained cypress skin, his long nose, and his square shoulders. Despite his powerful frame his movements are easy and gentle. The pieces of my life getting squeezed in the locker room crash up against all this weirdness between me and this oddly pleasant Black man. Insecurity pressing up against this freaky curiosity creates a bunch of pressure. It comes out through my hand and I break the black handle off the truck. The door swings open. I swing my not quite big enough butt inside and slam the door shut. It stays ajar. I'll have to hold it all the way home, alternating driving with the stick. It'll be hard, but not as hard as all this. I start the truck.

"Care to get out of my way?" Dropping my Chevy down in first, I pull away. It's like I hurt his feelings. It bothers me enough to watch him grow small in my rearview. A drink at The Bulldog will fix that.

Chapter 15

Quick Screw always leaves me happy drunk. I do my best to enjoy it because all the sugar from the Crown and the butterscotch schnapps will feel awful coming back up my throat tomorrow morning. The sugar high buzz makes flirting with the new pitcher's boyfriend even better. From across the big back room of Graham Central Station, quivering with the beat of booty music, I feel his eyes on me. This place is so clean, so corporate, the eyes on my butt feel dirty. At least it's nice to have a new place to drink. This sophomore has no idea what to do with me. If that young pitcher is his type, then I'll break his mold. I haven't decided what I should do to the rest of him once I'm done with his mold. I flip my dark curls a couple of times and lean a little further over the top of the table so my ass has that nice curve. When I catch him and smile, he looks away. He's in my garage and I can drive him whenever and wherever I want.

"What are you doing, girl? He's not close to your type." Jennifer says from behind me. She has another round of Quick Screw.

"I don't have a type," I correct.

"Yes you do. Tall, athletic or rich, and duuummmmbbbbb."

"Well at least he's dumb." I laugh.

I need to broaden my net, quit fishing in the same holes. There are guys my mom knows, but I can't trust her judgement. My cousin knows lots of guys from all around, but I don't want to catch whatever she's giving them. What else? A face, strong and dark, outside of my truck window, hovers in my mind, replacing the ones I'd been considering. No, absolutely not. I know what happens to girls who do that. Besides, it'd be all weird: music so the whole neighborhood can hear, laughing too loud and too much, and talking so I can't understand them. And then there is all of the complaining. They get everything for free and it's never enough. That's not my life.

Looking back at the pitcher's guy, he smiles boyishly. His dimples remind me of the ones on the boy in the sixth grade, the one who liked me. Being the overweight kid meant I didn't have many friends, much less an admirer. I liked that he liked me. And it wasn't until I told my Dad about it that I had to care he was a Black kid. Daddy said he wanted only one thing, and he probably picked me because Black guys always like fat girls. It was hard to believe at that age I could cry that hard and that long into my well-worn Strawberry Shortcake pillow that night. But after I told the kid he couldn't like me (Terrence was his name) I cried for the rest of the day. He immediately started hitting on my closest friend, which only served to make the tears flow faster, harder. It took two weeks for me to stop wincing when I saw Terrence.

"Jen you like Black guys, right?"

"I like guys, yes."

"Don't be a smartass. What's it like being with a Black guy?"

"Um, so, I'm not going to give you dimensions or anything."

"No, like, what's it like to date them, ya freak?"

"Damn. Settle down, girl. What's it like to date them? I mean I've only dated one Black guy so I'm not an expert—"

"Forget I asked" I retort. Eventually I'll learn to follow a first instinct.

"No, I'll tell you. It's like dating anybody. Troy worried about what I thought too much. But at least he worried. I will say he always smelled different than white guys. He—"

"I don't think I could get over the smell. I'm just being honest."

"I didn't say smelled bad."

The pitcher's guy heads for one of the smaller rooms. Seizing the opportunity, I tell Jennifer I will see her tomorrow.

Chapter 16

Soon I'll be eating the food that gave me this ass and it always gets rid of hangovers. I'll hug my momma and act like we get along great. She'll fuss, moving her big butt across the kitchen like some shrimp boat caught in a storm. Paw Paw might even come. I miss him, but I really don't want him to see me looking so rough. Good news for me is my dad is here. I haven't seen him in so long. The bad news for Mom is my dad is here. Which means that it's also bad news for me.

Pulling up to my parents' house, I'm transported back to an eighteen-year-old version of myself. I'm part excited, part nervous to be with everyone. As I open the door, Dad comes barreling out of the hallway. It's such a treat to see him, I wrap my arms around his big belly squealing, "Daddddyyyyyy!" While breathing deep the smell of cologne, tobacco, and beer, I plant my feet firmly on the ground, hoping he won't leave me again today.

"Damn it, Addie!" he yelps. He smiles while he does it, letting both of us know he doesn't mean it. But the smile fades quick. Mom has already pissed him off. He gives me a quick squeeze and plops into his recliner. It only adds to the mixed effect of returning home. No one could count how many times he's done exactly this after a fight with mom. He'll lord over the TV for hours.

"Can we talk later?" I ask in my sweetest voice.

"Go talk to your mother first before she gets pissed off at you, too." There's no coincidence he stopped coming home after I left for college. There was one less person for Mom to make miserable, and he didn't want her to take it all out on him. It would have been nice for him to stick around at least until Will was out of high school. Sometimes I think Dad pays for my apartment out of guilt since he never has to come home to face this. But I have no room to talk. "You might want to get a drink before you have to fight with her on top of that hangover," he says with a knowing smile. It's good to know I still make him happy. I sing my greeting as I walk into the kitchen, trying to diffuse whatever tension waits for me.

"Hi Addie. Come help me clean up. Addie! I know I taught you better than that! You barely spend time with your family and now you show up late without bringing something?" At least it's all familiar.

"Oh. Sorry, Mom. Wasn't thinking this morning."

"You got that from your father. You be careful or you'll be like him."

Other people have the ability to hold their tongue. Will can do it. That gene skipped me and landed right on him. "I'm here like you asked, mom. You don't need to project your frustration at Dad on me."

"Don't you start that psychobabble bullshit with me. You go and take some college classes and now you think you talk around me?"

Eyeing the door, I think I should leave. If I can't hold my tongue, I know what I'll hear: she'll never understand why I go to school to play ball with a bunch of girls. She got Dad in her third semester and dropped out. I can't seem to bring home a degree *or* a man, so why the hell am I in college. But that won't stop her from showing up to every game to convince everyone she's mom of the year. Will's awkward ass finally joins us, and I am saved.

"Whatever. Hi Will."

"Hey."

"What have you been up to?"

"Noth—"

"Now you're going to ignore me?" She's mad, madder than I could make her by myself. Someone got under her skin.

"Will isn't trying to fight me so I'm going to talk to him."

"So that's how it is. You're just going to disrespect me."

"No one is disrespecting you, Mom. I'd prefer to have this visit be pleasant and have a good Lundi Gras." I use one of her best tricks against her. If you make the other person out to be the problem, you win.

It feels good to check on him like a good big sister would. Guilt gnaws at me when I come home and see who I left him with. But he's the same grumpy nerd. Maybe the grumpy will help him stand up to mom. But he'll end up at Circuit City selling electronics like the other nerds. He keeps swearing he'll leave, trying to ride that dream all the way through high school. As we move our conversation to the living room, I wonder why he can't see this is what growing up is like. The house is as it was when it was built fifteen, twenty years ago. We can change pictures, buy a new couch every once in a while, or even enclose our back patio… but we don't leave. Life would be so much easier for him if he just learned to be happy where he's at. All of the video games make his world a fantasy. He's in for a harsh reality check when he gets out of high school and realizes it's even harder to make friends, find relationships that don't hurt, and have people praise you for exerting the least effort. He gets *bouder* telling me about it as we talk just outside the kitchen. If I can make him pout, life will eat him. If I remind him about the good parts of living here maybe he'll start to get it.

"What do you want to drink tonight? I'll call in an order to my friend. My treat."

"I'll catch a ride but I have some friends I'm going to meet instead."

"What? Who?"

"Not telling."

"Oh come on, asshole. You didn't even have sleepovers when we were kids and now you have friends you're going to go out with on the Monday before Mardi Gras? Spill." Maybe the little punk has a few secrets after all.

"Seriously. Not telling. I'm not going to have friends for the first time then have my sister stalk me and freak them out." As if. He's the one who will chase them off.

"I wouldn't do that."

"My ass," he says while giving me a full moon of his white ass. There's not even a tan line above it. I really like that kid, but he'd be closer to normal if he spent more time outside. As Will pulls up his pants and walks away, I spy Daddy in his old spot on the La-Z-Boy.

"Hi, Daddy."

"Hm?" he looks up at me with his grumpy, defensive face. He realizes I'm not Mom and softens. "Hey."

"What are you watching?"

"Some goofy alien movie with Tommy Lee Jones."

"Ah. Can I join you?"

"You gonna fight with me?"

He must be hungover. Dark circles frame his eyes. The little veins in his nose are red. All I need to do is offer him another beer and he will be happy with me. I sit down quietly next to him, drinking a beer of my own, and wait.

"How's the season starting?" he asks. Even though he no longer participates in the single greatest thing he ever taught me, I can let it go if he can smile at me and remember I'm his little girl.

"Not bad."

"Good," he concludes.

"You got any good stories for me?" I coax.

"Shiiiitttt, you know I do. Have I told you the latest one about Yank?" He straightens in the recliner. His narrow eyes widen. I wonder if he does this when his friends ask about me.

"Oh lawd. What did that freak do now?"

"I went gator trapping with him and a friend of his and we come up on this big ole gator. Yank grabs the .22 but it's an old thing and the bolt is rusted. He can't get the damn thing to move. So his dumb ass grabs the Marine Ka-Bar he keeps in his boot, because Yank keeps big ass knives on him you know, takes off his shirt, and dives in after that gator on the line."

"Holy shit! Did you go in after him?"

"Hell naw! You crazy?"

"Well then what'd you do?"

We're able to continue on like this for longer than usual since Mom is busy sulking or hovering over her precious little boy. Mom should thank me for the mood I'm leaving her husband in. But she can't let it last. They're back at it in minutes. It provides the perfect diversion for me and Will to slip out.

"Whoof. I'm glad we're getting out of that." Their shouts leak through the windows as he gets into my car. "Will, are you going to have enough clothes with that light jacket?" His look tells me to back off. "Will, I'm not leaving until you get something more on your arms." Without looking at me, he reaches in the back seat and pulls out one of my generic ULL sweatshirts. I don't know if he will wear a girl's sweatshirt to embarrass me, or if he is really that socially inept. "Nevermind." I throw the truck in reverse, still switching hands between the door and the steering wheel so I can shift.

At Cajun field my teammates fawn over him. I forget many of them have seen him grow up from an awkward kid to a more awkward teenager. All of us watch in shock as he walks away, his arms swinging, instead of hanging limp and gawky next to his Dorito gut, like they usually do.

"Who'd he say he was going with?"

"I don't know. He won't tell me," I tell Jennifer while watching Will walk away. "It's good he's making friends, and even better he left the sweatshirt in the car. He might get beat up on a night like tonight."

Our group for Mardi Gras this year is mostly athletics folks. There are a couple of frat guys, but they will be preoccupied with getting an underage sorority girl drunk tonight. There are a few Ag guys, but damn, they are so dumb, even for me. And I can't ever get attracted to the nerds. The pickings are slimmer than they used to be. Everyone is graduating or getting married. A shiver goes across my body while picturing a baby on my hip. In a perfect world I could live like some girls do where you can party, and have your career, or have a family, and no one cares one way or another. There's no point in worrying about it though. Everyone here figures it out at some point. I'll get out of school and Dad will know someone with a job or a girlfriend will know a guy. It will come together. I have time. Maybe I should go hang out with my Paw Paw instead. I need my door fixed.

"I figured out why you were asking about Black guys."

Spinning away from the sight of Will's silhouette I meet Jennifer's very pleased eyes. "What do you think you figured out?"

"I was at Corey's apartment last night…"

"You a ho!"

"Don't try to change the subject. Corey told me the tight end was asking around about you."

"And what else did Corey tell you?"

"He told me this guy, Dave, is a really nice guy. He's from Missouri somewhere."

"Missouri?"

Jennifer smiles bigger. "You look interested."

"In what? A Black guy I met once in the parking lot creeping around my truck."

"Why you gotta be like that?"

"Because he's only interested in the one thing all Black guys are interested in."

"So how come you don't let him get his hands on your one thing like every other white dude in athletics?"

The Bud Light going in my mouth comes right back out. Jennifer only laughs harder.

"Don't worry *cher 'tite bebe*. Your dark secret is safe with me."

Jennifer's promises are always solid. It doesn't stop me from getting really drunk. It must be one of those good, hard, Mardi Gras drunks, because I do not recognize the ceiling when I wake up. I crawl off a mattress on the floor in a dorm and get dressed. "It's 5:30 in the morning," says the nerd I was just in bed with. He seemed a lot cuter last night.

"Gotta get to my spot," I respond with dissatisfaction leftover from the night before. "They said they'd have beignets. I'm hungry and it's free."

"Stay a little longer," he pines sweetly.

"Oh, honey. No. I gotta get going. Stop by later on Johnston at the church near that fast-food restaurant."

"Wait, which fast food—"

"Gotta go. Happy Mardi Gras!"

At the spot across from ULL, I smell no vegetable oil. I see no bag of powdered sugar. I am pissed. Jennifer steps out of her dad's RV.

"I got Screwdrivers or Bud Light."

"I'm hongry. I thought you said there'd be beignets."

"My daddy is the one who promised to make them and he's inside asleep."

"He's hungover, too?"

"I think he's still drunk. But! Look what Cain dropped off on the way to his spot." The glorious smell hits me before she has a chance to flash the white of the butcher paper.

"Boudin!" we call out in unison. The greasy, pungent innards squirt out of the casing. This, with a Bud Light, is the perfect Mardi Gras breakfast. We silently squeeze and chew our way through two links before Brach, the catcher on the men's team, comes stumbling down the middle of Johnston, between the barriers, with a greasy brown bag in his hand. Even more coonass than me, I have a feeling what's in the bag.

"Now I know you not gonna pass by without saying hi and giving me some of those *gratons*!"

A smile breaks out on his face as he walks over to us. "Shooo, I'm still pie-eyed. I din't even recognize you. How you do, *cher*?"

"Hungover, but those *gratons* will help. Quit holding out!" Brach is so drunk I don't even have to flip my curls. If there is one thing that will finish off this hangover, it's fried pork skin and fat. As he opens up the bag, I hear a car approaching. It switches lanes at the last minute, missing Brach only by a couple of feet. He wobbles, watching the car drive away. "You know they don't have the streets sealed off yet. I mean, the barriers are up but obviously cars are still coming through," I scold.

"I doan care, me. They can go around like dat asshole did. *Laissez les bon temps roulez, cher*! Happy Mardi Gras!"

"Happy Mardi Gras!" we cheer back. When he is out of ear shot, we have another moment of synchronized thinking, saying "He's gonna die." We giggle into our cracklins and beer and find our way to some lawn chairs. Everyone else will trickle in eventually. This will be the last bit of quiet for today. In a few hours this ghost town, littered with the beads, doubloons, cups, and paper bead clasps from previous parades will convert into the best party of the year. The perfume in the air is a mix of fried goodness, port-a-potties, and stale beer. There are so many reasons why I couldn't leave Louisiana, hard winters aside. Just when I think I might have found the makings of hot coffee, my cousin arrives looking worse for the wear. Her hair is in clumps and mascara has run halfway down her cheeks. When I hug her, she is sticky.

"Well look who got beat up by Mardi Gras," Jennifer welcomes.

"Girl, don't ever go to Mardi Gras parties at frat houses. The Sigma Nu assholes poured dish soap all over the floors, opened the front and back doors, and then went slip and sliding naked. Some dude busted two teeth out when the basketball pole in the back stopped him."

"Don't tell me you did it too."

"Someone had to go further than that momma's boy. He just didn't know how to aim hisself."

Jennifer and I nearly fall out of our chairs laughing. Helping herself to beer and boudin, Tiffany sits without another word. As long as she gets her dose of attention, she's ok. She was like this even when we were toddlers. But things changed between me and her during high school. She's not used to me being the pretty cousin. She may have the boobs, but I have the ass and the face. At least that was the consensus of the football team's internal ranking system. Since then I've made sure to put up more of a fight when she's around. Twenty years is long enough to think she's hot shit in this family. When Jennifer's dad comes stumbling out of the RV and heads to the ice chest, we make sure not to break his painful silence. He joins us after cracking his Bud Light and taking a long, draining swig. We wait for our Mardi Gras buzz to set in.

As Jennifer's dad's headache abates, he lights the propane burner and starts the Jambalaya. He was smart enough to chop the trinity the night before. The smell wafts and a random old guy shouts "If pussy smelled like that I wouldn't come up for air!" The keg arrives around nine as we finish the initial twelve pack. The throngs of people are getting thicker and louder. That means we can finally turn up the music. We start with some Cajun but quickly move to Booty.

A member of the LPD, who wishes he was a state trooper, stops by and tries to write us a ticket for our four-foot-tall professional grade speakers positioned on each side of the RV. No external speakers, he says. Only car stereos are allowed this year. The old grandmas across the street rock in their SAS shoes while booing him. We turn the speakers into a car stereo by loading them into the bed of a truck. We seem to make everybody happy, including the cop who didn't like the hostility he was feeling.

The sirens start and I take off my sweatshirt. Aside from it getting warm, I need more dexterity to jump over some baseball players who are standing in front of me. Almost missing her behind the mask, I glimpse bright red hair and realize it's my mom. I call Mom's first name to get her attention and she pitches me some good beads and a moon pie. When the next float arrives, Jennifer gets an old man's sweaty cowboy hat after she flashes her tits. Tiffany thinks she can do the same but I'm sure everyone in this zip code has seen her tits. She gets a slightly larger throw than regular trash beads. She walks back, drunkenly dejected. The boys look to me for the next show. I smile coyly, saying I need a fresh beer. I walk back to where Tiffany sits to give her some moral support. Instantly I regret it when I see her crying.

"There's no crying on Mardi Gras!" I offer as cheerily as possible.

"Oh fuck you, *Moutchon.*"

"Only Paw Paw can call me that."

"You and your faggot brother! That's right. I was talking to some high school kid from Comeaux who snuck into the frat house last night and he told me your brother was at some ESA party this weekend with a known fag."

"Tiffany, what—"

"Whatever, bitch."

She walks back into the throng of parade revelers. I'm really wishing I wasn't so drunk right now. Will would never, ever go to a party. My last recollection is him telling me he was going to meet friends. Shit. Maybe he did go to a party. It doesn't take much for people to start talking in this town. People talk even when you don't do anything. Maybe he should stay home with Mom where it's safe. He doesn't know how to handle all of this.

Enough of this worrying. It's the wrong day for that. It's probably Tiffany's jealous bullshit anyway. I refill my beer, chug, and take a running start for the beads I see sailing toward our uppity pitcher who just arrived.

Chapter 17

It's like they're not even trying to make a cross. A big black smudge on my forehead, along with the fresh French bread I'm bringing, will stop an argument with my mother before it has a chance to start. I need all the time I can to talk to Will. In the lion's den, where Mom and Tante are, I kiss cheeks. Making sure to put the bread in the way of her cutting board where she will see it, I get a half assed "Hi" from my mom. Aunt Kathy looks squirrely. Something ain't right.

The not-subtle-at-all sideways glances tell me they want to talk, and children like me are not welcome. I'll figure this out later. But they have given me an idea how to get what I want from the little troublemaker.

"What's going on with Mom?"

"I don't know. I think she's pissed at me, but I don't know for what."

"Well you have been a douche lately," I seriously joke.

"Thanks queenie."

He's acting like nothing happened night before last. I exhale, not realizing I was holding my breath. Listening to Tiffany is always a bad idea. But the skinny little bitch had just enough righteousness in her tone to make me think twice. What the hell. I can ask him. As a big sister it's my job to keep him from going down a bad path.

"You think she knows about you messing around with that boy?" His face gets pale. My stomach flips like it does when I think about whether our coach is seducing that nasty pitcher. Will is about to ruin my life. I don't need people thinking I have a fag for a brother. It's not a big leap to start thinking his softball playing sister is a lezzie. God damn it why does he do everything the hard way? Wait. What am I talking about? He's not messing around with a boy. More likely he thought some guy was his friend because he talked to him. Maybe the guy is gay, the poor little marsh hen, and Will wouldn't know or even care since most of his human contact is limited to our mother. In that case I need to scare him straight.

"If I noticed don't you think Mom noticed? Maybe she doesn't know what's happening. She's probably in denial anyway. But she can pick up on stuff. And if Paw Paw caught wind of this…" His eyes fire up with rage. Now I've got him. He doesn't get enough tough love. He'll thank me once he grows up. "Calm down. I don't know anything. Well, at least I didn't." He still gets so upset, like when I'd prank him as a kid. There's so much happening in the world right now for a naïve soul like him to get caught up in. "Are you being gay because you think it's cool? I hear people do that."

"I'm not gay."

"Will, it's me. I'm not really going to tell Mom. Or Paw Paw. I gain nothing from that."

"You're right you won't tell them. There's nothing to tell."

Searching his hurt young eyes, we're interrupted by a familiar knock. I rush to the door and throw my arms around my sweet Paw Paw.

"Alright, *Moutchon. Tu es une sottiseuse.*" He's been calling me "stump" for as long as I can remember. He's the only person who could get away with that, and with telling me I'm "goofy."

"I'm not goofy, Paw Paw! You know I love you."

"*Ou est ta mère et ta tante*?" Before I can answer he's looking me over. I know what's coming next. "*Mais* you getting tick, *cher*. It's good dey feed you like dat at college." When I was little, I was *pitié* and needed to eat. In the fifth grade, when Dad started going offshore more, I ate… a lot. Been thick ever since. Being a petite little Cajun girl is never happening again, no matter how hard I try. There's no way I'll starve myself like the sorority girls. I'd rather love fries and have thighs. I'll swallow his little harsh remarks along with the food today.

Heading to the kitchen, the real adult interrupts the kid talk of my aunt and mom. While I can't hear what Paw Paw is saying, I hear his growl. Mom and Aunt Kathy are both getting put in their place. I give them a few minutes before I follow him in.

Over fricassee, and the bread I brought, Mom and Tante gossip and Cousin Vilain. I'm still glad I missed his goodbye party. I may be thick, but they are ugly. And I don't need someone spotting me around them. Thinking about the last time I went there, when me and the cousins got drunk and skinny dipped in the catfish pond, I almost miss when they switch their attention to Will.

"Dad did I tell you Will has a little friend now?" I feel sorry for the kid. But he needs to learn how this works. His faces changes colors twice while they talk about this new kid's influence. It feels good not being the family fuck-up. If he wasn't Bee's precious little boy, there would be room for me to get bad grades as long as I graduate. If they think he's gay, it won't be so bad if I don't have a boyfriend yet. While they're worried about his soul, the job I work to make ends meet will make it seem like I'm the responsible one.

"*Mon Dieu*, Bee. It's not like dat's his boyfriend."

The pallor of Will's face wanes as blood returns. This is impossible. Mom finally moves in for the kill on someone other than me, and Paw Paw saves him. I'm fat, but Will shouldn't be bothered about his gay rumors. Will can't even look up. He knows how good he has it, how unfair this family is. I rip off a big piece of French bread and stuff it in my mouth. The two vultures that circled Will for half a second fixate on Paw Paw and his last doctor visit. Normally I'd tell them to leave my Paw Paw alone. If Will doesn't have to squirm today, maybe he should have to. To no one's shock, at least not mine, Paw Paw doesn't think his medical history is their business.

I was so sure before dinner last night that Will could never leave here. But that conversation showed we're on the same playing field. It's me who's stuck. Cajun girls become godless ingrates when we don't sacrifice everything for our family's happiness. All the love I felt for this place just a few days ago on Mardi Gras day becomes a cage. It's heavier than the meal accompanying the conversation last night. Now, at the plate, coach hounds me to finish my swing. The basics of softball are ingrained in my muscles, so her getting all *fâché* isn't going to help. This isn't about mechanics. My bat knows what's approaching. That's why it's so heavy. It knows large shirts and stretchy waste bands are all that will fit me once I stop swinging. The weight waiting for my body, the weight of my family and this place, is on just my bat for now. Getting ready to leave this sport, the only thing that wasn't a game to me, stings. Adulthood says that softball isn't serious; at least not serious enough to make league play out of it. This is proof adulthood is stupid and unfair. How is avoiding pregnancy and getting fat on plate lunches behind a reception desk more mature? Slinging my bat on my shoulder, I walk off the field. The eyes of the girls are on me like they were in the locker room. They are wondering the same thing as me: what the hell am I going to do next? God has to sort this out for me. In and out of the shower, I head toward the truck, wondering if there is anyone at the Bulldog worth drinking with.

Just a little ways down Cajundome Boulevard I see the same Black man that wanted to help me get into my truck; the tight end who's been asking about me. From this angle it seems he was positioned well. He's walking in the direction of Beau Chene apartments. Now I'm really convinced he was telling the truth. It's even chillier than the last time I saw him, but he's still just got a tank top and flip flops on. I slow my truck and reach across the bench seat to roll down the passenger window.

"Don't you own any clothes?"

He smiles easily, showing off bright white teeth. There's not an ounce of gold in them.

"Yeah. I like cooling off after practice."

"You want a ride?" The words come from practiced hospitality. That was ingrained early in life, but all rules have exceptions. I immediately regret asking him. I start to panic at the thought that he'll accept and consider if I could speed away.

"No, thank you." He says coolly and without any condescension. "It's a short walk."

The way he looks at me has no judgement. His black eyes, eyes the color of Paw Paw's cast iron jambalaya pot, don't seem real. Everyone's eyes judge me, even Jennifer's. It's always just been a matter of how much judgement I could tolerate. Looking in the direction of his apartment, I estimate it is less than a mile. I shouldn't be spotted by anyone in that short a distance.

"Get in."

We take off quickly, but he doesn't say anything. He ventures a look at my door where I've run a bungee cord through a gap in my window, around the frame of the cab, back through a gap in the sliding glass back window to hook back on itself, securing the door shut. He doesn't say anything, but I can see him smile out of the corner of my eye.

"I told you my name," his booming voice reverberates around my truck cab. "Can you tell me yours." Many a Black man has asked for my name. I've never told a single one of them.

"Addison."

"Thank you for the ride, Addison. I thought I had freaked you out the other day."

"You did," I say a little too honestly. "But that wasn't your fault. You were trying to help. You deserve to have it repaid."

"Well it's kind of you. I don't see Black folk in cars with white folk much around here, unless they're riding in the back of the truck. I appreciate you letting me ride in the front." My heart, which was beating near my throat the closer we got to busy Johnston Street, falls past my pelvis.

"Well then those people weren't raised Cajun," I say with much less condescension than I did the last time we met. His gentle demeanor makes me want him to feel like he belongs. He seems nice enough.

"So you're Creole Cajun?"

"We're Cajun. Creole means Black."

"I'm sure that line isn't blurry at all. I thought French people didn't worry about stuff like that. I thought y'all were the cooler Europeans." The gentleness in his tone takes a playful turn.

"We're Americans," I retort. I didn't like the sound in his voice when he said "cooler". Because I sure as hell ain't no pussy Frenchie. He looks at me for a long while, daring me. "How would you know?"

"Seems to me Creole and Cajun are just about the same. Cajun seems to be something white people made up to differentiate themselves from Black folk. Then your accents could be 'quaint' instead of 'foreign.' Your food would be 'interesting' instead of 'ethnic.'"

"Shows what you know. Cajun is white. Check your history. That's big talk from someone who comes from a place with no culture."

"Whoooaa. You don't know about Missouri."

"And I don't need to."

"Why?"

"Because I would never move to Missouri. Cajun girls don't leave Louisiana."

"Do you even speak French?"

My cheeks flush out of habit. "*Un peu.*" Yankees usually follow it up with "How big of a boat do you paddle to school?" Even people from around here who aren't Cajun scoff since their pure English tongue instantly makes them better than me.

"That's fire," he responds. He smiles that smile. We reach his parking lot. These apartments are as nice as they looked from the street. I want to go. He seems to sense it. He opens the door, but his big body stops halfway.

"How do you cool off after practice?"

"Look… I'm not going to fuck you," flies out of my mouth.

"Whoa. Slow down. It ain't like that. All I have are guy friends. Sisters in these parts are… different. Truth is you've been real nice. Was just trying to make a friend." Something stirs the calm black pools of his irises. He doesn't flinch when our eyes meet. He doesn't look at my body. He doesn't look away. It's enough to make me wonder what he sees. I end up smiling. He smiles back. It's a really nice smile.

Flipping through TV channels in my apartment after that encounter does nothing to occupy my mind. Why am I so *nervine?* He invited me out for just a drink or two. Turning through the door of my bedroom I see too much of myself in only panties and tee in the big standing mirror. My ass grows in its reflection while my boobs shrink. The cellulite, something I usually don't notice as much, appears in all its glory, smeared from waist to my knees. The pimples along my jawline show bright pink. In each of my pieces I can advance the clock, catching a glimpse of a body just like my mother's. It's enough to make me want to play sports forever. I put on baggy, comfy jeans I usually wear to the grocery store. My hair is frizzed from not having dried it right out of the shower. No one should recognize me. This outfit screams "We're just friends." It's a free drink. I'll come home right after. Another look in the mirror and I picture those eyes on me. I picture that smile. I put on a nicer tee shirt and walk out of the door.

In the well-lit parking lot of the softball field, I pull directly under a light and turn down the Mystikal I've been listening to. A Kia sedan pulls into the parking lot. It's strange for a random person to be here.

Out of the very clean, unassuming Kia steps the man I am waiting for. No extra gold trim, no rims, no trunk rattling from bass – just a nice car. His Ecko pants are baggy but not off his ass. His Polo looks like it's been pressed. He's almost too pretty. He's serious but doesn't act full of himself. It must be because he's a Yankee. He walks up to my truck door and I roll down my window from where it was drawn down to let the bungee through.

"You gonna get this fixed?" his voice booms.

"My Paw Paw will fix it," I squeak back.

"Of course you have a Paw Paw who fixes things." Despite looking me right in the eye he pays no attention to my "what is that supposed to mean?" face. "I know a place we can go," he says.

"Ok. Get in," I say.

"No. I'll drive. I don't trust your hoopty."

"This truck is indestructible."

"The truck may be, and you may be, but me in this truck… I got tint on my windows. We're safer in mine."

"Where are you taking me?" I ask, feeling an old fear rising in me.

"Someplace we can be safe and enjoy each other's company." That doesn't instill a ton of confidence. The suggestion is not as strange as how genuine he is. Nothing in how he talks makes it sound like he's giving a line. It's still hard to handle the way he looks at me. He hasn't said a thing about how I'm dressed or my lack of makeup.

We're almost at the downtown library, near all of the new bars. But he keeps going, all the way to the Evangeline Thruway. We turn north and now my stomach finds a new way to knot. We are heading to the other side of town, near Simcoe. He turns again, going several streets away before parking in front of the Carmelite Monastery. He parks along the road and exits.

I want to bolt. This is one of the worst neighborhoods in town. While I sit cautiously in the car surveying my surroundings, he looks back at me from in front of the car, his easy smile spreading across his face. He leans into what I'm worried about, gently pulling me away from it, and it leaves me feeling like I'm falling. It's wrong and fun at the same time.

"I'm not dressed right to go into any club," I say, as I slowly exit the car, still looking around.

"I know those aren't your best jeans, but I'm sure you'll be ok."

"Why are we going here?" I ask, trying not point out that I'll likely be one of the few white girls in these clubs. And I'm not like those other white girls that will be in there.

"Because you front a lot. You have this big tough exterior. But that nice, pretty woman who gave me a ride home today wasn't frontin'. People front because they're protecting something. Something important. If we're gonna be friends I want to get to know the real you. We won't do that in a bar you've been to a million times. Besides, I don't need to stop every few minutes and talk about football with some yokel. There's more to me than football."

He said I was pretty. And he didn't say it to get in my pants. It makes me want to find out more about him other than he's a Yankee football player. But as soon as I close the door on his immaculate car, I feel how Eve must have felt after she took a bite of that damn apple. He hums as we walk, as if that could put me more at ease. It makes me wonder if it's the last thing I'll hear before I'm raped and choked to death. I'm about ready to turn and run. But a pair of eyes, almost as black as David's, stare at me from a porch. They are young eyes underneath a cascade of plastic barrettes clipped to hasty twists of hair. I'd put the little Black girl's eyes at eleven or twelve. Those eyes are afraid. We watch each other as I walk past. Dave continues to hum, seeming to know she needs that. He was afraid of being in my truck, now this little girl is afraid of me in her neighborhood. These people keep acting like they're the ones in danger. It's not right for them to feel afraid of me. I try to make my gaze a little kinder, to signal it's ok to this little girl. She continues to stare, the whites of her eyes still visible until the night consumes them.

As we near Simcoe, the people walking the streets, shouting to one another in the dark, puts me on edge again. We approach a brightly painted club, it's roof low slung. He pays for us to get in and the thick bouncer smiles non-threateningly at me. Briefly, I consider how a white bouncer at one of the clubs I go to would have looked at Dave. Inside, I survey the surroundings in case I need to leave fast. Dave's hand touches a spot on my back never touched before as we head for a high-top table in a dark, wood toned room. There's been the gruff hand between the shoulder blades. I've had the horny hand on my lower back. This hand is smack dab between those two spots. Only one other table has patrons. It's a Black couple. This feels comforting to me for a reason I can't figure out. Dave goes to the bar immediately and comes back with a Bud Light for me and a *frou frou* drink in front of him.

"What is that?" I don't even bother to hide the accusation in my tone.

"Sex on the Beach. Ever had it?"

"Not the drink," I guffaw. Blood drains from my face as I imagine what I made him think.

"You should try it. This is grown folk candy," he responds without innuendo.

My eyes range over the empty bar. "So this place is hoppin'."

"They'll be here later. You dance Zydeco?"

Hip Hop, Rap, and Booty are all I've ever danced to in clubs. All my experience with Zydeco and two-step was at festivals or in Paw Paw's kitchen. It's been a few years, and I'm not sure I'm ready to relearn in public.

"Not really."

"Damn. I was hoping you'd show me."

"You mean one of Corey's hoes couldn't teach you to Zydeco?" I tease.

"So you've been asking about me." The low light in this place is much appreciated. My face is so hot I want to hold my beer against it. Instead I take a big chug and think of how to counter.

"Yeah. Wanted to know who the guy was at my truck."

"A guy who's interested in getting to know you. I told you already. There's no reason for me to lie. I know there's more to you past the hard-ass front."

His dark eyes glitter in the neon lights. Also reflecting in them is my silhouette. What must I look like in those eyes? He smiles his smile. This time when I smile back it's not just a reflex.

People trickle through the door. From the looks of it I'll be the only white person in here tonight. But they don't seem to mind. I don't think I do either. It must be the alcohol.

Chapter 18

Over the past three days I've been like a combat vet on the fourth of July. Every conversation with someone is a possible indictment. When someone asks what I've been up to I mention softball, family, or the Bulldog. I change the subject when they ask if I've been seeing anyone. Maybe for once, in this little town, no one saw what I did. Or no one cared. I can't decide which is more likely. Do I care this much about what people think? I can't be like my mom. I shouldn't do that to myself. Jennifer running late for our little meetup helps life to feel regular again. The shit-eating grin she's wearing tells me I am about to dive into the sweet comfort of gossip.

"So you went on a date with him, huh?"

"Oh, come on! How'd you hear about it?" My yell is loud enough to get a few people's attention over the loud music of the bar we're in. It's not like it matters. My life is over.

"Calm down. One of my girlfriends was there that night and saw y'all dancing. But she's not in the business of spreading your business." I exhale and finish off my beer, before asking for a shot of Crown. "How could she have seen me? There weren't any other white people there."

"She's not white," she says with a tinge of accusation. "She said you were smiling the whole time." The memory of teaching him how to Zydeco in two songs, having him swing me out, having him ask me real questions, comes running back. "You're smiling right now."

"Shut up."

"Did you fuck him?"

My eyes narrow. She knows I will kill her. "No, Jennifer. And I'm not going to."

"Why not?"

"I don't need to have this conversation with you."

"Then you are going to fuck him."

"No, I'm not."

"Why not?"

"Well for starters I'm not a ho."

She blinks and smiles. And then looks a little more serious. "Addie, for real? Girl, this whole bar thinks you a ho."

For too long I wait for her to start her donkey laugh. It never comes. Her over-mascaraed eyes watch me to see if I'll laugh in acknowledgment of what she thinks is obvious. If the girl known for sleeping with Black guys is the one to tell me I'm a ho, then my reputation is even worse than I thought. Smiles, long hugs, flirts: I got all those guys wrong. Those little gestures weren't innocent. They were down payments on what they were sure they could collect on. Tiffany's chest from Mardi Gras, the lack of looks they drew, and the looks I got instead, have new meaning. They weren't *hoping* to see me flash. Why the hell am I finding this out now, after I went out with *him*? There's no coming back to my life, to good little party girl Addie, with Dave in the mix. Would they find my truck if I drove it off the Atchafalaya bridge on I-10? It doesn't matter. If this is how they see me I can't fall any further. I order another drink and shot. Jennifer looks sorry for telling me.

"Don't need to say anything else, Jen."

"I don't think you're a ho."

"It's cool, Jen."

"I mean, that's my point. I don't care what people say. I love you. You my girl."

Turning around I catch a rich-looking frat boy's eyes moving off my ass. The shot I take is fire all the way down, promising to burn away my worry. Drink in hand, I decide to go introduce myself to Mr. Rich Boy.

It blurred somewhere after I said "Hi." Judging from the feelings in my head, stomach, liver, and lady parts, it was a very rough night. I'm glad I can't remember any of last night. The extra guilt, aside from the normal blackout, is bad. Not knowing how many sins you've committed is a sin within itself. Hearing I'm a ho came before the booze, unfortunately, making the memory crystal clear. I grew up a good little girl. My biggest problem used to be just being a little bit tomboy and chubby. Life shouldn't be this hard. I want to go back.

Something greasy from Mel's Diner would help this hangover. When I get to my truck, though, someone has easily detached the bungee and made off with all of my tapes. At least the tape deck is still in the dash. I'm glad I didn't take my dad up on the CD player. Staring at the contents of my softball bag strewn about my cab I realize it's not food I'm craving. This hangover is more about waking up in a life I don't recognize. A piece of honesty and a slice of love is what's needed. Things like those would ease my unsettled stomach and pounding head. My broken door is my perfect excuse to go get them.

Palmettos dot the jungle of young oaks and grey trees in overgrown pastures. Driving past the humble homes off Main Highway in Breaux Bridge makes time move backwards, all the way to when life crawled out of Bayou Teche. I slow down and let cars pass. My Chevy's tires crunch on the gravelly potholes of Paw Paw's driveway. Time and my heartbeat slow down as I watch an egret take flight from the water nearby. The brick of his house is duller than when I was a kid. The wood of the porch is weather worn. But nothing has moved (except for maybe an extra engine or two on sawhorses under the overhang of his garage). The front door opens and his silhouette etches behind the glass of his screen door. The sour sweetness of something rotting comes running up my nose. Motor oil mixed with mud wafts from his shed. It's the smell of childhood. It's the smell of not worrying about who I need to be or what I need to do. Don't get hurt while I play outside. Watch out for snakes. Be a good girl.

"Qui est la?" he yells from inside.

"*'Tite Moutchon*!" I announce. I don't mind being his stump today.

"Mais 'ga la! I din't know you was comin'!"

"I know. I missed you. And I broke my truck."

"Aw ma '*tite fille*," he hums while opening the door to kiss and hug me. I bury my face in his musty shoulder. "What you did to you truck? You always breaking tings. You break my boats. Jam my shotguns. Birdnest my fishing rods. You need to break more hearts, you."

"You look good, Paw Paw." I smile, watching his grey eyes dance as he looks at me.

"I doan know how to look any udda way. You want some coffee? You look like *un lapin qui a couru de le cocodril.*"

"More like a rabbit that ran from the *rougarou* rather than an alligator."

"*Shoo*! I make dat coffee tick, den. I'ma find sometin in da icebox for you, too. *Assis-toi*!" He bustles off to busy himself with his percolator. He sings a tune to himself and I catch the words "...*a la traine*." I've known him to insult people under his breath, but I'd rather think "messy" is part of a song, not about me. Several of our school pictures, curling from the humidity, are still tacked to his walls. My sixth-grade picture holds a prominent place on the wall. That was the year someone liked me. That was the year I learned to hate my body. My cheeks fill out the top of the 8x10 while my torso, awash in the sea of a neon pink surfer T-shirt, threatens to blind anyone looking. Even my hair was big, twelve-year-old curls frizzed by the hot rain that washed through that day. The only little thing on me was my button nose. I wish I were that small again.

The wood paneling and cabinets have thick layers of dust. You can tell when Maw Maw died because of where the framed pictures stop. Many objects have gone unmoved, maybe since before I was born. Now they have electrical switches with frayed wires dispersed among the knick-knacks to keep them company. He brings out some crackers and hogshead cheese. As we each heap the congealed pig's head on top of the crackers, smiles break out on both of our faces.

"If you Maw Maw would have tasted like dat I might not have ever left to go fishin' or huntin'."

"Paw Paw!"

He giggles and gets up to get the coffee. As he sets down his bent tray, with the same mismatched mugs he used when I was a child, there is a knock at the door. Paw Paw grumbles. With him there is such a thing as too much company. He opens the door violently in preparation to scare someone from his porch.

"Clement! Whatchou doin' on my porch?" he shouts.

"I'm bringing back you lawnmower. My son-in-law came by with a new one for me. *Bien merci*, Auguste!"

"*Mais* you welcome, *monsieur*. Leave it dere. I'll come get dat later." The whole conversation finishes without the screen door even opening. Closing the heavy wooden door, he walks back to the hogshead cheese and me. "You didn't invite him in?"

"Clement? He wouldn't have come in."

"Why not?"

"Because he's Black."

"Well I could see that. He was friends enough to borrow your mower. He's not friends enough to come in the house?"

He looks up at me confused while attempting to use his twisted index finger to sandwich a piece of head cheese against his cracker. His poor hands don't work like they used to. It's bad enough they're all twisted from the arthritis, but now they seem to have a mind of their own from time to time. "We not friends. We neighbors. I known Clement since he was ten and I was twenty-five. Tings were different back den. Dey taught da Blacks to stay away from whites."

"Is it because our ancestors owned slaves?"

"We worked the land and da bayous, same as da Blacks. We din't own no plantations. We made good neighbors. *Il est comme nous autres.* You might even have some cousins on you Maw Maw's side dat's Black." "Nuh uh!" My tone manages to be playful in time to cover up my shock at the tone he used to say Clement is like one of us, and then tell me I have Black cousins, with the same emotion he'd use to tell me to pass him his crescent wrench. As if he heard my thoughts, he eyes me seriously and lets out a "hmph" to challenge me to say different. If there's a question of Black blood in me I prefer to keep it that way than make it a clear statement.

"You ever been in his house?"

"Never."

"Why not?"

"Just din't go in. It's not like now. Sometimes I tink it's better now. People don't worry so much about what udder people tink and dey friends wit who makes dem happy. Me and Clement, we cut from da old cloth. Don't know how to do any udda way. When you get old like us you doan wanna change no mo."

"Why—"

"Beb, I'm not gonna answer no mo questions 'til you tell me why you keep askin' why." Because I want so much for him to say that one part of my life, though strange, could be moving in a right direction. But I pushed him too hard. He's pissed.

"I just like knowing how you think about people and life and stuff."

"*Mais la,* you spoiled! You had everything given to you, more than I ever had. Now you want me to give you how to tink. I doan have a way to handle people or life, just to take it as it comes."

He's not lying. He's a real self-made man. He's never had to question what the next step would be. Me, I don't know what's right anymore. The only thing that has ever been right, the only thing that didn't make me feel I was fat, or a ho, or too tomboy, is softball. And now I have to give it up. Auguste Chenevert never has to worry about what anyone says, that he went crazy when his wife died, or that seventy-five is too old to go fishing in the swamp by himself, or too young to say he can't drive at night. He doesn't even seem to care that anyone would know he married a woman who was part Black. I wish I could do it like him.

"But what if—"

"C'est pas de tes affaires! It's not you business how me and ma neighbors get along. You tryin' to make simple tings not simple. You so worried about how udda people play dey hand you never play you own. Just like when you lose *bourre*, you gonna end up with no tricks, nuttin' in you hands."

Simple. That's what I came here for. Somehow, I screwed that up. There must have been something important I missed between talking about this Black neighbor, whose house he wouldn't set foot in, and then acting protective of their friendship. I can't look when he scolds me. While I wipe my eyes, he leaves the room. Crying upsets him. I should have saved it until I got home. I've overstayed my welcome, but the jar he returns with says otherwise.

"Dis ma *Lune Noir.*" The bluish/purplish/reddish liquid inside jostles, blackberry bits dancing throughout. I've never said no to Paw Paw and I'm not starting now, even if it means I need to sneak out back to puke in the overgrowth. Turns out it's good, like everything Paw Paw gives me. As I sip, he turns on his old Victrola. Amedé Ardoin cries to us in the time of a waltz. The needle, fuzzy with dust, skips and skids across his priceless 78 RPM record. Paw Paw takes my hand. Despite the twists of his fingers, and the slight shake in his palm, his hand is sure of everything. He pulls my wet eyes toward him, twirling me. Feet shuffle 1-2-3, 1-2-3 through the kitchen, around the table, across the yellowing linoleum. The house shimmies on its foot-tall pillars. His grip is firm. When I was a little girl he'd sometimes leave a bruise. Today his painful lead is the most wonderful feeling. The stamping of our feet let loose a hundred memories. Our rhythm connects with a sense I can't find anywhere else. I'm his *'tite Moutchon* again. And all this stuff isn't more important than a dance and some good food. It never has to be more complicated. I smile.

"Nah, tell Paw Paw what you did to you truck."

Back in my apartment, with a buzz from the moonshine, a fixed door handle on my truck, and a feeling life is back to how it's supposed to be, I want to go to bed and sleep, hoping memories of Paw Paw's sweet *Moutchon* will play in my dreams. Instead I'm greeted by a ringing phone. The only person who calls on a Sunday afternoon is my mother. Weighing options, I decide I'll have less to deal with later if I can just get told I'm a bad daughter for a few minutes. I'm sure I deserve it anyway.

"Hello."

"Hey," says a subtle boom.

My heart leaps between my ears.

"Hey."

"You want to see a movie with me?"

My father, my locker room, my whole life tells me the answer is no. It's social suicide. After listening to Paw Paw break it down, I'd say it's downright confusing. Paw Paw thinks friends should be the people who treat you right. End of story. It's simple. It's a measure I've never used in my life and look where it's gotten me. Paw Paw said he wishes he had a chance to be friends with whoever he wanted. Dave is everything I've looked for from people. Just so happens he's the wrong color. That should be everyone else's problem, not mine. Still, I need to start slow. I think Paw Paw believes things have changed more than they have.

"How 'bout you come here. Go to Blockbuster and pick something out. Whatever you want is good."

"You want me to grab you something to eat?"

"I'm not going to sleep with you." It tumbles out. I feel my face become sullen.

"Good. Because I hadn't planned on it tonight, either."

Chapter 19

I'm rethinking this daddy-daughter date. They used to be a weekly affair, starting as trips to Showbiz Pizza and then road trips to New Orleans, shopping sprees, and hunting trips. They slowed to a trickle as he worked more at the shop, and then stopped altogether. Even though this is what a good daughter does, this time could be better spent. It's not like he's put in much effort toward family lately. From what Will says, he isn't around much. Will could use a male presence in all the mommy madness, and he doesn't get to see how much fun Dad can be when he's not grumpy. I can't tell if he's grumpy right now. I munch my Old Tyme shrimp po-boy with only the screech of the Girard Park swing and the distant traffic to listen to. Our feet grind across the gravel as we swivel next to each other. He buries himself in his po-boy, swinging next to me.

"You remember when I used to bring you here when you were a kid?" he finally asks.

"I thought that's why you wanted to come here."

"Yeah, maybe so."

The way he invited me here and isn't saying much makes me think he wants to talk about something serious. There can only be two things that serious: he is sick, or he is leaving mom. Man, I hope it's the second. We'll be able to work with heart stuff. I can stay up his butt about exercising and eating better. Cancer I can't deal with. He's being quiet for too long.

"You alright, Addie?"

"Me? Yeah. Doing fine. You?"

"Oh I'm good, babe."

Quiet again. Damn it, he's killing me. It doesn't help that his scar on his neck is all purple, like he's got something hard to say and it's stuck in his throat. “I’ve been worried, no, thinking about you more lately. We don’t get to do this enough anymore.”

He’s being too careful with his words. “We have busy lives now, Daddy.”

“I know. Just… wish we could talk more. You know?”

“We can talk now." I got the door wide open for him to tell me he’s sick. Please God, make him leave Mom.

“You remember that time we went fishing with Paw Paw and he shot some nutria. I think it was the first time you saw nutria. Those ugly little bastards grossed you out. You even screamed when you first saw them!”

“They still gross me out. I don’t even like staying in this park at sunset.”

“Yeah. I remember you said you were glad Paw Paw shot them.”

“Yeah. I think they should all be shot.”

“Hmmm.”

He takes a big bite out of his Po-Boy, smearing Jack Miller’s barbecue sauce across his face. His choice in Po-Boy is almost as weird as this conversation. He chews for a while. Maybe I'm doing what Mom does and making this deeper than it is.

“You want to go fishing soon?” I offer.

“Yeah. Maybe.”

“Paw Paw says the basin has been high. Maybe we can do Patterson or something like that.”

“Mmm-hmm.”

“How’s work, daddy?”

“Work? Work’s good, I guess. Always like a derrick. Up and down. As long as it doesn't tank like it did in the eighties, we should be good.”

“You still like what you’re doing?”

"Yeah. Gets the bills paid."

Conversation starters have officially run dry. He's not giving me anything. Comfortable silences stopped more than five years ago. Craving comfort, I think of Dave.

"What?" he asks with a full mouth.

"What?" I repeat with an equally full mouth.

"You're smiling."

"Oh. Just thinking about something one of my friends did recently."

"Like what. I could use a good story."

"Oh, it's stupid. "

"Those are my favorite."

"Tiffany showed up at Mardi Gras all bruised and bloody. Told us about how she schooled some frat boys on how to slip and slide on concrete."

"Ha! Did I ever tell you the one about Yank and the alligator?"

As I listen to the story again, I see my happy daddy return. If I want to find out what this lunch date is about, I'd have to go hunting. Except I don't feeling like hunting at all. Paw Paw always said snakes don't bite when they're full. Dad thinks my smile is because I'm filling up on stale stories. My smile is bigger, more satisfied, as a result of a few moments with one of the other men in my life. I'm so full it's like I've never eaten before.

It's enough to even make me want to be nice to the newbie pitcher. Coach notices at practice. "You two seem to be communicating better," she says after the newbie smacks a decent fast ball into my mitt.

"Anything for you, Coach," I reply with marked sarcasm. This is for my girls. Her shitty coaching deserves no respect.

"You don't need to remind me you don't like me, Mouton. I was just letting you know I see you making a positive change."

Putting my gear back in my locker, I don't notice Jennifer approaching until she is right in my ear. "Did you fuck him yet?" Jennifer asks in a not-so-whisper tone.

"No," I say happily.

"I'd expect you be this happy after you fuck him."

"We're… we…"

"For chrissakes… don't turn into a Lifetime movie. Go shower and we'll get a drink and talk."

"I can't," I mumble as I shove my stuff in my bag, smiling bigger. She returns the bigger smile. My cleats chatter across the floor, my feet skipping to my truck. In the parking lot a few football players loiter after evening drills. They joke amongst themselves until I get nearer. "Haven't seen you around, Addison," one of them shouts and laughs.

In slamming my door I hope I've left the impression I'm pissed. My truck rumbles to life. It doesn't matter. They don't care if they piss off a ho. I force myself to think of being with Dave in a few minutes, far away from this place. But I can't leave this place. The refuge of my apartment, watching a movie next to him on a couch, is only a vacation from what waits outside my door. Vacations suck. Like when I went to Colorado, they talked about my accent. In Texas they talked about what (and how much) I ate. In Florida, for Spring Break, they still had something to say about the guys I would hang out with. Opinions are faster than a sunset on the Basin. Worst of all, opinions held by enough people eventually become the truth. No matter how lovely Dave's eyes are when they look at me, clean and shiny, they can't make other eyes unsee me as the fat-assed bar whore.

Once inside my apartment, my legs lose their resolution and I wilt to the floor. I'm never getting out from under their eyes. Maybe that's why I'm with a Black guy. Maybe some part of me, deep down, knows there's nothing else left for me.

When the knock at the door comes, I freeze. Since my collapse, I've pulled myself into a sitting position against the door. I can't see him. He'll be supportive. He'll be honest. He'll take all the shit and shine it into gold. The shine will leave when he does. And it'll be worse because I will have given the opinions one more right to truth. Then he'll come back and smile that smile. It's a sick cycle.

"We can't hang out, Dave," I yell through the door.

"Where are you? Are you on the floor?"

"Please go."

"Are you ok?"

"Yes. Just go."

"Are you hurt?" If he only knew.

"No. You need to go."

"You sound upset." Tears roll down both cheeks. His deep voice is so nice. I'll miss it. "I knew this would happen." The tears come harder and faster.

"You knew I'd be a whore?"

"Yeah. I did."

Self-pity didn't plan for that response. His ability to see me, see the me I wish I was, makes this even harder. Desperately in need for someone to walk into my life and tell me what I'm supposed to do here, who I'm supposed to be, I sit. He must think I have some choice in this.

"We shouldn't hang out," I say again through the tears. His car starts and the sound of the engine fades. Bringing my knees to my chest, I curl up on my floor and welcome the end of a life I was supposed to be starting. The phone screams at me and I have no will to move. It stops ringing for a moment before ringing again. The incessant noise is making it hard to wallow. A third time it rings, and I get up to check the ID. It's been an unknown number for the past three calls. It stops again, only for a second and rings a fourth time. I don't even get time to say hello.

"You gonna make me call four times before you pick up?"

"Where are you?"

"Gas station around the corner."

"Dave, we—"

"—can't hang out. I know. But we're not hanging out. I'm a guy on a pay phone around the corner. You're a girl in her nice little apartment. No one knows we're talking to one another. So, some people found out about us?"

“Yea. Well… I don’t know. Some of your teammates said something.”

“What’d they say?”

“Nothing. But they just wanted me to know they know something.”

“What'd they say?”

“Said they hadn't seen me in a while.” A big, booming laugh comes from the other end. “This isn't funny. People don't think you're an alcoholic coonass ho. Some kind of Lafayette Monica Lewinsky.”

“No, because they usually think worse. Besides. White people are too concerned with other white people’s private lives.”

“Don’t do this race thing right now.”

“What race thing?”

“This isn’t the same. When you’re a man, you be with who you want to. You don’t have to worry about how you’ll take care of yourself or if you need to find someone to do it for you. If I can’t walk the narrow line of being a pure Southern woman, without also being a prude, I’ll end up being some stereotype. That’s all I’ll ever be anywhere I go.”

“Well, some of that’s true,” he says calmly, choosing his words as carefully as my dad did earlier. “I get what it’s like to be close enough to acceptable but just different enough to have to try and thread the needle of people's expectations."

"You can't get it. They don't expect something of you… something you can't give."

"Addie. Baby. Everyone expects something. Everyone expects me to be on the street slinging drugs. People expect you to be uneducated, barely speak English, and eat roadkill. The only reason we're on the phone in the first place is because we expect something different from our lives."

"Easy on the roadkill," I half chuckle. There's simplicity in his thinking I crave. But graduation is waiting for me in a couple of months and I don't have a job. I'm farther from being married and having a family than when I started college. Hell, I'm even sucking it up at softball, the one thing everyone can agree I'm good at. Listening to him is wishing on stars. They're so pretty, but they're all small and far away. This could never work. It's not just the people at practice. It's Dad killing him, then me. It's mom being overly nice so she doesn't let on she was raised to think about Black folk the same way I was." I know if I keep him in my life, I'm just going to end up spending more time with him. Eventually, I'll be ruined. "I don't know if I can do this, Dave."

"Sure, you can. You, more than anybody in this place, can go after what you want. You're bigger than what they tell you to be."

"How do you know?"

"Because you're like me."

"How do you figure?" I ask, the incredulity at his challenge pushing my tears back.

"I knew I was taking my life in my hands hanging out with a Cajun girl in this place. You knew you'd be risking, too. Yet here we are."

"Talking on the phone."

He must be smiling because I can almost hear it through the receiver. “Want me to come over?”

“Yeah.”

“One thing… what’s a coonass?”

“It’s not racial. So don’t go there.”

“I won’t. What is it?”

“Honestly, I don’t know. People just always call us that when they want to talk down to us.”

“Baby, you need to learn what people are saying when they make an ethnic epithet towards you.”

“Whatever, Yankee.”

“You know Missouri is in the South, right?”

“Just get over here.”

Several nights over the next week are spent innocently watching movies on the couch. When not in front of my TV, we spend hours on the phone like a couple of eighth graders. It’s easier to manage people’s opinions this way, avoiding them all together. I’ve never spent this much time just focusing on being close to someone, getting to know them. Not even my own family. Each day I get home a little earlier from practice or a game to call him. I even call when we’re on the road. We talk about things usually kept to ourselves: movies, books, and families. We neglect other parts of our lives. He neglects books. I neglect friends.

Tonight, we won't talk on the phone. It’s weird to have a guy say he “needs a break” and trust it’s only an interruption. With a whole night to cut loose, I struggle to think of people I even want to hang out with. It feels weird, somehow not Cajun, to sit at home and avoid trouble. It’s easier to breathe without trying to stay afloat amongst everyone’s opinions. But there is a person with whom I’m safe from opinions. It’s only because she deserves those rumors more than I do. Besides, I can always say I’m hanging out with family.

"What are you doing calling me so late, cuz?" Tiffany drunkenly garbles through the phone.

"I need to get into some good clean trouble."

"Well, shit. Come meet us at the USL horse farm. We're about to go muddin'."

Before I can ask who "we" are, the line is dead. Guaranteed whoever my cousin is with will bring out her more charming qualities. The horse farm looks empty when I get there. Tiffany has sent me on drunken goose chases before. But a flashlight flickers from inside the old barn. Following it I'm engulfed in the sweet, earthy smell of horses. They're unhappy, stomping and puffing in their stalls. Glimpses of wet black eyes shine back at me from the moving light. When I get to Tiffany, she is making out with some drugstore cowboy, flashlight dangling from the hand on her ass. He may work this retirement home for thoroughbreds, but by the look of his pristine white cowboy hat, this barn next to a strip mall is the deepest in the country he's gotten.

"This isn't trespassing?"

She stops mid-kiss to check my identity but doesn't bother removing her arms from around his neck.

"Nope." After a final long kiss, and what looked like maybe a grope of his crotch, she asks "Where's your friend? Let's have some fun!"

His friend turns out to be an actual cowboy, sweat and mud stains covering his worn baseball cap. He also turns out to be kind of cute. We pile into the cab of a newer model truck.

"You don't think someone's gonna see headlights going in circles back there and call some cops?" I interrogate. Tiffany shoots a look of drunken conviction in response to my question.

"Don't need headlights. There's plenty of moonlight," Drugstore Cowboy responds.

"You have to stay in the big, back pasture. Way away from the coulee," Real Cowboy says.

"Shut up Derek. You can leave my truck if you're gonna be a bitch."

The Drugstore Cowboy leaves his daring eyes in the rearview mirror, glaring at the cute country boy sharing the back seat with me, before putting the truck in gear. He slams the gas and Tiffany lets out a squeal for effect. She never did that when we went mudding with my dad. Drugstore flies across the bridge spanning the coulee and hits his first spin after about a hundred yards. The mud is not as slick as what is generally good for mudding and his tires catch, jerking the truck and tipping it. Grabbing his seat, I brace for a roll. Instead he guns it forward, riding on his two wheels for a minute before the truck rights itself. That shit would never have happened in my Chevy. Drugstore is all balls as he tries another donut. I yell in protest, but he cuts the wheel harder. Something gray flashes past us as we spin and I feel the bed hit something, trying to tip again. Thankfully, Drugstore has the presence of mind to stop. The smile on Tiffany's face is in full contrast to her eyes. Our Real Cowboy is looking out the back window.

"I can't tell for sure, Kent, but I think your back end is on the edge of the coulee. You for sure took out the fence."

"Fuck! He's gonna make me pay for it," he looks at Tiffany. "Y'all are gonna help me pay for it, right? I mean, we went riding together." Tiffany's desperation always manages to find the absolute worst excuses for men. They were always bad, but with Dave for comparison, I can see exactly how bad. She looks as if she'll agree to his ridiculous request, so I cut her off.

"Fuck no! You're the asshole who decided it would be a good idea to come muddin' in the middle of the city, with your lights off, by a giant cement coulee! You, and whatever money got you this shitty truck, are going to pay for it." Turning to the cowboy next to me I tell him, "And don't you lift a finger to help him fix this fence." In the green light from the dash I think I might see him blushing.

Drugstore gets out, mumbling about the bitch in his truck, to assess the damage. Real Cowboy and I step out to join him and my feet feel the slope toward the coulee. We're close. Walking only a foot and a half, I realize his tires are hanging off the back. Drugstore stands on a piece of broken hurricane fence hanging over the coulee. Whimpering just audibly enough to hear, his hands caress the back of his truck.

"I think this tire is bust over here. Fence is wrapped around the corner of your bumper too," Derek the Real Cowboy calls from the other end of the truck. "I'll go get the tractor."

"No! Don't! The old man will be doubly pissed we used his tractor."

"Kent, I really don't think there's a way this gets better tonight."

The only reason I want to stay is to watch Drugstore cry. Even over the sound of the revving tractor engine, I can hear the bumper squeal as the fence pulls against it. The bumper stays attached and takes some fence with it. Maybe Fords do have some redeeming qualities. Unfortunately, he doesn't cry. Disappointed the night ended so early, I walk to my truck. Tiffany stands under the security light, visibly hurt by the way Drugstore touches his truck instead of her ass. I almost feel bad for her. While the nice thing to do would be to offer her a ride, it's not my job. Just like my brother, she needs to learn the hard way. Derek stops me right before I open my door.

"I could use a ride."

"Alright. Where to?"

We agree we are too sober. He doesn't say much on the drive to the Bulldog. It's his first time here. The awkwardness of his smile is enhanced by the horny glow of neon beer signs. A bunch of the regulars, including athletics people, watch as we walk in. I should have thought this out more. The eyes all around me make walls close in. It's too late to leave. They've seen us. Nothing good will come of this. Or could it? If I could give them what they want, one sorry coonass girl getting drunk with a white country boy, I'd be free to spend time with a man who treats me right. My whole life has been spent trying to not to be who they think I am. Freedom might finally come from just being what they expect. One night here could give me all the cover I need. For their benefit, I laugh louder at Real Cowboy's attempts at humor. It emboldens him. Derek buys my beer. He's cute and a gentleman – good combination. A month ago I would have been all over him.

"Your cousin is—"

"You don't have to finish that sentence. I know what Tiffany's like. Your friend is—"

"Don't finish that sentence. He's a co-worker. That's all."

"Hmmm," I say, surveying the eyes looking at me.

"So it's Addison..."

"...Mouton. Derek..."

"...Patin."

"*'ga ca.* Who's you daddy and what color is his roux?"

"*Mais* you know it's dark. And my daddy, he's Henry, him."

"I thought I knew all the coonasses at USL."

"I'm not in school. Just work at the horse farm when my Dad isn't planting down in Kaplan."

"And you farm?"

"Yeah."

It stalls. Like I put on an old broken-in shoe, one I've outgrown, I get uncomfortable. I smile and finish my Bud Light. Their eyes are all on me, ready to spread a different rumor. It'd be so easy to take advantage of the cover, to show them the good Cajun tomboy who was just going through a phase. I don't have it in me. Not anymore. Dave messed it up. Because I only care what he thinks. The only thing that matters right now is this guy is not Dave.

Setting down my empty bottle I say, "Thank you for the beer. It's time for me to go."

"Wait! Hold on. Let me buy you another one."

"Thanks, but I really have to go."

"I still don't have a ride," is the last I hear from Real Cowboy Derek when I walk out of the Bulldog.

Chapter 20

My heart is beating out of my chest the way it did during my first kiss at thirteen. Of all the things I could be doing right now, sitting under the covers with him watching Sportscenter is the most thrilling. His arm moves around me, and I snuggle into him. I nearly pass out from blood swirling throughout my body. He smells unbelievably good. As I breathe it in more, his arm flexes and tightens against me.

"I'm glad you came over."

"Me too," he replies.

No man has ever just wanted to sit next to me, to hold me. No man has ever spent hours trying to know me. I'd always have sex with them without that. Even if I didn't really feel like it. And they'd never stay. Here's Dave, doing all those things, and it's time to admit it to myself. I want to have sex with him. Those old fears, old worries, I don't want to care about them anymore. I pull closer to kiss him. Pulling off his shirt, I glimpse his perfect torso. On his left pectoral is a tattoo of a scribbled name, something more to get to know about him. I run my hand over it while touching as much of his body as I can. As I start for his shorts, he stops me.

"Are you sure?" he booms at me.

"Don't question it. I don't need any more of that."

"But do you—"

"Shhh!"

To convince him further I shed my own tee and bra. Removing his shorts, I reach down, satisfying a burning curiosity. He's big, but not freakishly so. He brings my face up to his, kissing me, and then my neck. My shorts come off. His touch doesn't take, doesn't want something from me I don't readily give. We go back to my bed, kissing as we spread out on the sheets. He wants to touch, to caress more. I'm done with that. He notices. He notices lots of things, like the right speed and when to pause. He follows my breaths and my moans. He knows when it's time to switch it up. As if I needed any more perfection, any more of what I've waited and wanted for, I feel everything tighten in me before a big, leg-quaking release. Every thought, every worry, every last piece of what I should be, ebbs away like a tide going out, riding the receding aftershocks. I hardly notice him finish.

When he lies down next to me, he pulls me onto his chest. His heart beats with a boom similar to his voice. The skin beneath my face is moist and smells of sweat. I breathe deeply, letting it out as a sigh.

"Yeah?" he asks.

"Yeah." I respond.

"Me too," he closes.

This is all it has to be: simple. We lie for a while. His skin smells so much better than the other skins I've pressed my body against. It smells familiar, like home. If only I could bottle it. My hair spread across his chest is hopefully absorbing this, saving it for later in my day. His breathing starts to even. Pretty sure he's fallen asleep, I look up. His eyes, barely open and glassy, center on me. He smiles his smile. The warmth from it spreads from my eyes into places of my soul I didn't know existed, or didn't exist until now. Something deep down in me knew this love was out there, the kind white boys don't seem to have anymore. But here it is, waiting for me in the last place I would look.

My life finally feels like it's moving somewhere. It's still out of focus, but that's getting better. After Dave leaves, I know exactly what could make things even better.

"Paw Paw do you want to go fishing tomorrow? Dad said he'd go with me, but he never called me to set it up."

"I'm going witchou brudda tomorrow. I got room in my boat, doe."

“Oh.” I never get to see him and now I have to share him? But this is good for Will. Maybe he’ll finally man up with more time on the water. I’ll make more time to go see Paw Paw later. Besides, I know how to spend that time. "I wouldn't want to intrude on your man time. What about next weekend?”

“How 'bout I come to you game, *Moutchon.*”

“*J’aime ça, moi*! Come to my apartment after and I’ll cook something.”

“Aw, *cher. C’est pas un grand-chose.*”

“Paw Paw I want to. It’s a big deal to me. You haven’t come in a long time.”

“*C’est* OK. *J’te verrai.*”

Without needing to get up early to drive to Breaux Bridge I can stay out late, and with Dave at a football party, I have the night to myself. I think I’m done with mudding and Bulldog petty bullshit. Staying home sounds good. It doesn't stop Jennifer from calling me from the Bulldog.

"Addie. What the hell, girl? Why haven't you been coming to hang out?"

"I can barely hear you over the bar noise."

"Get your ass over here." Her s's are a little long. She's already drunk.

"I'm staying in tonight."

"You have your special friend there?" The tone in her voice is meant to tease. I'm not biting.

"Not tonight. I want to stay in and watch a movie."

"Wait. So you have been spending time with him. Did y'all —"

"I'm not kissing and telling."

She gasps. “Stop it right now, Addison Mouton. How was it?"

“Dave? He’s kind of a Cajun in a Black man’s body. I mean… you know.”

She laughs hysterically. After a few moments she comes back coughing. "Come to the bar. My treat tonight. We'll celebrate."

It's so nice to have someone I don't hide from, who gets excited for me when I'm excited. "Not tonight, girl. I need a night to chill. Drink one for me."

"I'll drink more than that for you. Good night, love bug."

Popping my movie in, I snuggle under my blanket. It still smells like him. Smiling, I end up thinking about his smile, and smile bigger. The way Jennifer reacts makes me think I’ve been focusing too much on what the wrong people think. What she thinks of me, what Dave thinks, even what Will and my mom think, are more important. Breathing into the blanket deeply, I think about a future that’s wide open. It leaves me feeling hopeful instead of paralyzed. Halfway through the movie I nod off, but I’m startled awake by pounding on my door. It's like a police knock. Worried some of my drunken sins have come home to roost, I open slowly. It’s Dave.

"Hey! I thought you were out tonight,” I say cheerily opening the door wider.

"I was. Can we talk?"

He doesn't sit, so I don't either. Anger has never crossed his face that I’ve seen. It doesn't suit him and I'm waiting for him to start laughing at the prank he just pulled on me.

"Who was the bubba you went to a bar with last week?"

The blood runs out of everything. "He was a guy who needed a ride home."

"Uh huh. Where did he need a ride home from? And why did that entail drinking with him?"

"Dave, I just met him that night—"

"I hope that wasn't meant to make me feel better."

"Hear me out. He was with my cousin who was trying to sleep with this guy. The guy at the bar was his friend. When my cousin's guy wrecked his truck—"

"You know what – just stop. I don't care. I tried being sympathetic to you worrying what people think... thinking you a ho. I see I'm just another Black man to you. I see you trying so hard not to be with a brother you turnin' yourself into a slave."

"If you'd listen to the whole story, you'd know I left him in that bar with no ride home. Put your timelines together and you'd see I called you to come over right after. I knew it was wrong."

"You took Bubba to a place where you knew people would watch and talk. You wanted them to see you. You wanted them to stop thinking you could be slumming it with a Black dude. See, what that tells me is you'd rather be a ho to a bunch of white dudes than have a real relationship with a Black man."

This is how it works. I make the hard choice, I choose the person I… love… and it bites me in the ass. "That's... that's not how it really is."

"How it really is. What are you about say? You feel something? You want to tell me when there are no eyes other than mine to see it, that you have some real love for your side piece? I'd convinced myself the Addison I saw when it was just the two of us was the real you. God damn. My momma was right when she said I was being naïve. I prefer the racism in Missouri. At least there you know right away when they hate you, instead of being baited with some Cajun hospitality bullshit first."

"It's your turn to stop. You're making it into this whole Black and white thing. I do care about you. I do want this. That's the real me. But it's not as simple as you're acting like it is."

"Oh, it's simple. I was your Black stud. I hope I scratched that itch raw for you."

Until now, what was happening slipped my attention. After we danced and laughed in a place I thought was dangerous, while we quietly watched a movie, in the innocent phone calls every night, and the not so innocent time in my bed, the space Dave took in my life was growing, little by little. Before he showed up tonight I was saying how his opinion is now as important as Jennifer's, my mom's and my brother, even my Paw Paw. If I have to be honest though, it's more important than any of theirs now. I can only see now that I may have lost him. The horror associated with figuring this out too late is only made worse with glimpses of futures disappearing before I can enjoy them. The hurt from twelve-year-old Addie, rejected for rejecting someone else, races back. The little girl who rejected someone who cared about her, because her daddy told her to, did it again. My daddy didn't have to say a word. I finally found love and acceptance and cast him aside. The favor is returned as he pushes me away because of a misunderstanding. In his dark eyes I search for the gentle softness that used to hold my image. I looked so beautiful in those eyes. But there's nothing coming back now. No one really wants to know. No one has the patience to know how confusing, how contradictory, how fucked up I really am. No one, not even him, can accept me. I can't accept me. A new truth, the one I've been avoiding all these years, finally surfaces. I'm alone. Now I always will be.

"And now I see I was just your white trophy. You can go back now. Brag to your hood friends about the white ass you pulled."

It was always going to be like this. I keep telling myself this while I drive to my family's house. My hands take me there without knowing why or what I am looking for. Part of me is mad that I even felt anything, that I'm crying now. My mother's car isn't there and I feel strangely sad. I find Will in his normal spot in front of the computer. Knowing he's not what I came here for, I ask for Mom.

"Why are you being such a prick?" I accuse Will following a surly welcome. For my troubles, I get a sarcastic teenage brother reveling in my pain. If I expected a loving mother with open arms or a father who'd threaten to dismember the one who'd hurt me, it was as much a dream as getting a man to love me. My head gets the memo. Why can't my heart accept it? My heart must be connected to my feet because they stay stuck to the floor.

"What is it?" Will asks. How can I answer that? I want my mommy and my daddy? Could you give me a hug because I threw away the only person who treated me like I matter? It's all coming undone now. "Addie, it's ok. Tell me. I'll stop being a prick."

"Just tell Mom I need to talk to her." My shoulders turn, trying again to leave, but my feet stay planted. Regret spills from my eyes with no promise of stopping. You can't get out a lifetime's worth of tears in one night. Making another unsuccessful attempt to leave, Will lets out a big, exasperated breath. I brace myself for more sarcasm. He opens his arms. Folding into his embrace, his wordless acceptance, I remember this is what I came here for. It's just not who I expected it from.

Everything left for me in life feels trivial right about now. In the locker room before the game I speak to no one. I don't look at their eyes. Not because I can't handle what they might be thinking about me. Today I don't care. As we wrap up the first inning, I drop the ball, and almost miss another completely, solely because I gave the opposite call of what I meant. Since when did the pitcher start throwing what I call? I'm so used to people being against me. The coach looks genuinely concerned. Now I second guess if her concern was always this genuine. I tell her I'll shake it off. My mind gets buried in the game. If nothing else, at least I know this part of my life. At bat I swing at the most ridiculous pitch. Given how far inside this bitch is pitching, I consider stepping into the next pitch, ending a lot of my troubles for today. Stepping back from the plate to collect myself I look up at Will and see Paw Paw joined him. He's even wearing a new red hat. I feel some energy return. The next pitch is the slowest fast ball in history crossing right over mid-plate. I get enough of it to get it to the fence. The other team sucks so bad I turn what would be a single into a triple. In true Paw Paw fashion, he leaves the game early with Will. I don't have it in me to join the locker room and their party. I'll just start crying again. I'm off, straight to my truck and back to my apartment, so Paw Paw doesn't wait. Except he ends up getting there a lot later. Weird it would take so long for him to drop off Will. He sits in the living room while I shower, flipping through cable networks he never sees on his own TV. Curls still wet, I head straight to the kitchen, grab him a beer, and start on my seven steak.

"You din't have to go tru all dis *tracas, cher.* I'd be happy wit a sammich, me." "I wanted some rice and gravy."

"*C'est comme tu veux, Moutchon.*" It officially doesn't bother me anymore. It's the name of love now. "*Ça va?*"

"*Ça va.* I'm ok."

"You doan look ok."

"I got a lot on my mind."

"*Tu me raconte.* Huh? You let you Paw Paw know all about it."

"It's a bunch of stuff. You don't need to worry about it. I've made some mistakes and I need to deal with the consequences."

He fiddles with his wedding ring and then takes a long sip of his beer followed by a muffled burp. He rubs his big, curved French nose and lets out a big sigh.

"When you Maw Maw passed *je faisais drôle.* I din't ak right. *Tu comprends?* Now I know it looked like I was strong and wasn't bothered, but I wasn't myself. I did some tings I'm not gonna talk witchou about. But when I finally came out of dat, I went to church and ask God's forgiveness. Tings got better afta dat." "Thanks, Paw Paw. But I don't know if everything gets forgiven," comes from my mouth before my teeth set into my tongue. I hope beyond hopes he doesn't ask what I did because I absolutely cannot lie to my Paw Paw.

"Den ask again. And if *Jésus* doan listen I'ma go pass him a slap. You tell Him!"

I chuckle, feeling my pulse slow a little. Air feels easier to breathe. I stir my gravy. "Don't you blaspheme, Paw Paw," I say while letting the steam wrap around my face.

"Me and *Jésus* came to an understanding many years ago. He knows better dan to abandon my grandbaby."

"Paw Paw, *je t'aime*. I hope you're right."

"*Mais* you kick dem with dem tick legs. Dat doan work, use you hard head. *Tête dur* like yours could crack a diamond."

"*T'es fou, toi*! I've missed you Paw Paw. Let's spend every weekend together."

"No *'tite Moutchon*. You grown now. You 'bout to go get you a big job and a husband. You need to be spending time wit dat." I clear my throat to ward off whatever horrible thing wants to come out. Heading to the ice box he asks, "You talked to you momma 'bout what's botherin' you?"

"I tried, but she wasn't there. Maybe God was trying to tell me something. She and I have a hard time communicating."

"*C'est vrai*," he agrees before cracking his next beer. "You two alike in all da bad ways and not in da good ways. Still it's good to try again."

Back at my pot the gravy is starting to seep out of the meat. Steam rises from the rice cooker. Outside, a car passes with way too much bass, enough to rattle my windows. We both look up.

"All these Blacks!" pops out of my mouth with more force than I expect. It's enough force to make Paw Paw look at me cautiously.

"Dey been doin' dat a lot?"

"They all do that. They're all pieces of shit."

"Nah, *Moutchon*. It's not right to make it…*plus simple*…too simple like dat."

“You’re the one always telling me to make things simple!” Tears burn like the rice steam from the backs of my eyes.

“’Cept for tings dat aren’t right.”

My lips purse to make sure the fire in my stomach doesn't shoot out of my mouth. It must be so easy for him. He makes all of the rules. He gets to say what truth is. Everyone listens to him. He doesn’t get that we’re two different people on different sides of life. His path made sure he was in the driver’s seat, with hands always tight on the wheel. I steer nothing. Here, too, I’ve lost the resolve to hold to a picture of me. His strong, sweet *Moutchon* turns into an angry, wet mess. Paw Paw’s arms wrap around me while my legs crumble like well-cooked meat. He half carries, half drags me to my couch, smoothing my wet hair.

"*Ma 'tite Moutchon.* You always quick to *fâche* like you daddy. I remember you got angry at small tings when you was little. Maybe you get angry at big tings nah dat you big. No matter whachou or anybody else tinks, wedder big, small, angry, happy… you have to just pick you path forward. You can’t ever know where it’s gonna end up. When you old like me you see it doan matta. You who you are. Tings are how dey are. Between you, da tings, and God, everyting gets figured out. Just pick a place and start moving it forward. Don’t matter where you been."

Wiping my eyes, I peer into his cloudy gray ones. His eyes can’t see what I want them to. For the first time in my life, I'm wishing it were someone else's eyes looking at me like that right now. Now I know I need to talk to Dave. I check on my seven steak.

Chapter 21

A week passes before I run out of excuses. Test, game, tired… I've found something every night. Tonight, there is no excuse. The music is off. There's no TV in the background. Staring at the phone I say a prayer for Dave to call me instead and make this easier. I nearly leap out of my skin when the phone rings. My heart overtaking my tonsils, I check the ID. It's Mom. My heart plummets.

"Hello?" I say dejectedly

"Addie? It's Momma. Paw Paw's been in a wreck. He and his truck took a dive off the I-10 bridge in Henderson. I think he'll wake up soon. I need you to come find Will. He left out of the room and he's been gone for five hours. I tried getting a hold of your dad but he's out... wherever."

My mind and my heart reverse course with the surfacing picture of my injured Paw Paw. My only consoling thought is this could be another exaggeration by my mom, a sick attempt for sympathy at his expense. The possibility disappears when I walk in on the doctor explaining his prognosis.

"He's going to be ok, Addie. *Tu comprends?*" There's a gruffness to Mom's voice. She doesn't want me to cry. Today I shouldn't have to be strong. "Addie, he'll be fine." She almost sounds angry. Nothing about this is fine. My life isn't fine. It's worse than I thought. That man in the hospital bed in front of me, he's very not fine.

"I love you Paw Paw. *Moutchon* loves you."

"Oh, he knows honey." Her tone sweetens at the prospect of consoling me. I continue to ignore her.

"Come back to us, OK? I'm worried my door might break again. You know how to fix things. I'll cook for you. Come back and I'll make you some more seven steak."

"He hears you, Addie. Keep talking! Look at his heart rate! *Bon Dieu*!" My eyes glance over to the paper slowly coming out of one of the machines, but there isn't a change.

"Mom, what was he doing on I-10 heading east after dark?" I ask, still looking at the paper.

"Addie, go find Will. He was so dazed. I'm worried he's into some trouble. Like, God forbid, drugs." Like every other hard thing in her life, she wants to run from it. There's always this push keeping me at arm's length. She doesn't want me to join her in worrying over him. It's sickening to watch her talk to him, sucking in whatever goodness he has left. I wish she'd let us love him together. If only she could let me close enough. Then maybe we could love each other. The thought makes me see even more clearly how simple it would have been to let Dave in more. Now both Dave and my Paw Paw are gone. I feel like throwing up.

"I'll look for him," I say, excusing myself from my mother's vacuum.

Outside I rub my bare arms and wonder where a computer nerd without a sense of direction goes. There are a few restaurants in the Oil Center, but he doesn't have any money. The planetarium is most likely closed. The memory of a younger little brother looking at a starry ceiling, seeming happy for once, reminded me of another childhood place. Girard Park is easy walking distance. I start at the swings and work my way around the walking trail. I eventually see a silhouetted figure slumped near the pond. As I get closer, I call his name, but he doesn't turn. Crouching in duck shit and mud, I put my arm around him.

"Will, are you ok?"

He seems so fragile, so lost. It's hard to be the strong one here. As I listen to him talk about our mother, there is a resolve I've never noticed in him before. His jaw sets before he speaks and his eyes are on mine. It's mature. Watching that look, like he could see a way forward that I can't, is enough to make all that we're losing snap into focus. I may not be able to see where to go from here, but I'm keenly aware of where I've been.

"Nothing is going to be the same. I overheard the doctor say that, even if he wakes up, he won't be able to walk. There won't be fishing trips with him anymore and dance parties in his kitchen. He won't be able to speak. His stories about how it was, his French, the songs… they're all gone. Doc said his memory is likely shot, remembering only the oldest things. All that's left is what we'll remember from him. He won't recognize us because we're too new." The last thread holding my heart together breaks. His hug helps to mend it.

His hug gives me a new thread, one we've tried to form our whole lives. It binds us all the way back to the hospital room where our mother bends over Auguste Chenevert as if she were praying at his alter. She looks up at us, peace and horror filling the corners of her mouth and eyes. "Paw Paw is gone," she says.

In the days while we prepare to say our final goodbye, we keep away from each other. Without Paw Paw we don't trust each other to hold a conversation without burning it all down. Mom plans the funeral. Dad disappears into work. Will disappears into his room. Without Dave, I disappear back into softball. We reappear to each other at the funeral home in Breaux Bridge. A sea of faces stretches out. Cajun. Black. Creole. There's a couple of Vietnamese guys standing in the back. They're packed in like my cousin's catfish pond. I immediately start crying again. I don't know why looking at people I don't recognize would make me freak out like this. Maybe it's because I've always thought my Paw Paw belongs only to me. He belongs to so many people. And they belong to him. He would love all these people in one room where he could see them. He would hate it at the same time because it's such a crowd.

My family looks beaten. Even Tiffany looks defeated, my cousin's ever-present smugness absent from her face. Only my mom is cheery.

She directs me over to some flowers in a corner. The irritation of being ushered away from Aunt Kathy, Tiffany's mom and my favorite aunt, is gone once I see the girls on my team sent flowers, Easter lilies full of sweet fragrance, along with a small bouquet of roses to Will. I've been feeling so lonely. But here is proof of their love. Tears come harder. Cheeks kissed, I can finally head to his casket. The group of distant cousins finishing their "Our Father" move away, realizing I'm his granddaughter.

Slipping my hand underneath his, pushing a recently bought rosary aside, I want to feel his weight. Looking at his face I can stop holding back. He looks younger. He looks like he did in the pictures from my birth. A shudder moves through me. The last thing he said to me was to pick a place to start. It doesn't matter where I've been. I doubt he thought his casket would be where I'd have to start from. And how could I not think of where I've been? Where I've been defines me. It defines everyone in this room.

The Vietnamese will leave here and go back to work because that's what they've always done. We Cajuns will get drunk, if some of us aren't drunk already, and then *fais do do*. And the Black folk… I can't finish that. Not in front of Paw Paw. He sees me now, knows what I'm about to think is not right. I'm not right for thinking it. The only people who could help make me right are gone. My knees wobble. I'm dizzy. I hurry and sit down on the maroon velvet couch in front of the casket to start the rosary.

Putting my head between my legs, I can hear the whisperings from behind me. When the ground starts to feel solid again, I sit up and look back. My head feels like it's trying to float. These people think I'm overacting. They think I'm playing a part for them like Mom does. When a loud "*Au nom de le Père,*" begins the rosary, I appreciate a moment to not have eyes to perform for. Through the Mercy of Jesus, Will gets up to run outside. They'll see me go after him and know I'm a good big sister. Outside, Will stands looking out over the parking lot.

The only one who was trying to show him how to be a man is gone now. It's so sad that I, a woman, must take over the job.

Chapter 22

The softball field is on my right, again. This is the second time I've passed it. You'd think I'd prefer the girl sweat and chatter of the locker room instead of the smell of two-day old tears and the quiet inside my truck cab, the sound of my life without direction, purpose, or definition. Without him. Which him? Does it matter? Do you have anything else God? As if You're even there. My stomach feels like a shrimp boat in a hurricane. I pull over to dry heave. Have I turned into that girl? That stupid irrational girl who gets sick every time she feels something? Even when I've been hungover from Quick Screw, I didn't feel like this. Maybe it's just because I'm about to start my period. What day is today? I should have started my period four days ago. This is weird. The women in my mom's family can set our watches by our periods. All this stress could be doing it. Or could it be something worse. It's been a couple of weeks since Dave and I...

At the K&B on Congress I pull all three pregnancy tests they offer. Going all the way back to my apartment feels too far. In minutes that seem like hours I'm back at the field and force myself to go into the locker room. Everyone is already on the field practicing. After peeing on all three indicators, I read it may take two weeks after sex for the hormones to show. All that means is I can't be sure of what they'll say. My eyes never leave the indicators. Eternity passes at least two times. Finally, the allotted time runs low. No line on the first. I close my eyes and exhale, shaking the hand not holding the tests, trying to force blood back to my extremities. It'll be ok. God won't give me more than I can handle. When I look back at the tests to see the other two turn positive, and then the first turn positive after mocking me with a blank screen, I understand how crazy both me and God are.

"Are you there?" I ask God, or maybe even Paw Paw. My voice echoes off the tile.

"Yeah?" comes back through my stall door. "Addison?"

My heart skips. It sounds like Mom's voice. All these years I've wanted her to let me have this place, this sport, all to myself because it loved me more than she does. Three little lines slice through those years and tie me back to Momma. I can't pull my drawers up fast enough to open the stall door. It doesn't matter if I greet her with my shorts only halfway up.

"Addison? What's wrong?"

"Oh… Coach. I'm ok." My stomach plunges in disappointment, clenching my chest in the process. I'm too emotional to have hidden the tests. My coach's eyes zone in on them.

"You sure?"

My mouth tries to say yes. But my body finishes betraying me, reaching out for Coach like a toddler lost in Target reaches for a cashier. Sobs vibrate through me. She holds me so perfectly. The way I'd want my mom to hold me.

"Can I help?" wafts through the opening to the bathroom. I look up to see my sassy pitcher standing there. There's no point in hiding the tests from her either. "Let me take you home," she says. "Or is there some other place better for you to be? Your parents?"

"No," comes out of me before I officially decide how to answer. It doesn't feel right, given I was just grasping for my mommy, any mommy really. But it sounds right. The sound of no comes from some place much more real than the alternate universe of this bathroom. It's the ten-thousand-foot view I got while watching my Paw Paw slip away. It's a "no" to "will I ever be enough?" It's a "no" to can I be a good daughter, a good sister, or a good woman. Everything I've done so far has made all the answers "no." It's a "no" to preventing myself from becoming some bad Cajun stereotype. What am I talking about? I just proved I'm a stereotypically fertile Cajun. But there's a new factor to consider in those questions. Someone I haven't met yet. Someone I don't know how I'll be able to meet. But I do know I can't start those questions with "no." And "no" is all that's waiting for me at my parent's house. I need to go where there is a better chance for some "yes's."

"I need you to take me to Dave's apartment."

My tentative knock is followed by earsplitting silence before Dave opens. From the serious look on his face, I wait for him to tell me he wants nothing to do with me. And that will be that. But, worse, he doesn't say anything, at least for a while.

"How'd you find out where I live?" he finally asks.

"One of the guys on your team."

Another long, painful stare.

"Can I come in?" I ask.

He moves his six-foot frame out of the doorway. I exhale, realizing I'd been holding my breath. His apartment is as spotless as his car and much more tasteful than mine.

"This is nice."

"Yeah. Despite my roommate." He motions for the couch and we sit. Holding this is hard. It needs to happen now.

"I think I'm pregnant." Another long painful stare.

"Think?"

"Yeah. I missed my period and took a test. I took three tests. They're all positive.

"Addie, you didn't think this might be an outcome of getting busy without a condom?"

"I was caught up in the moment. Like I thought you were. Weren't you worried about it?"

"I tried to ask but you shut me up. I figured you were on the pill or something."

"I'm Catholic. We don't do that. Thought you knew that."

There is a long, incredibly painful pause. "I can't be a father right now."

"Excuse me?" I can honestly say with all the messy things rolling around in my head, this was not one of them. His face doesn't change and he might be serious. "I don't think you have a choice."

"No but you do," this is getting worse by the second.

"You know what we call having an abortion? *Detruire la famille.* Destroy the family. It's an abomination. I just told you I'm Catholic. It's not an option."

"Now you're gonna be righteous. You ain't been to church in all the Sundays I've spent with you. You white folk always get religion when it's convenient."

"Don't start that shit again! That race bullshit! Don't talk like you know me!" comes out with too much force. He calmly smiles back.

"I think you're coming to my point. We don't know each other. You want to make plans. Plans for two, maybe three people, who don't know each other."

This is wrong. I thought I was taking charge of my life. Where things are supposed to be getting better, I have a man who sees me, and this kid in me, as strangers. He's telling me to do the unthinkable. I was so stupid, thinking this would be different, that he would be different. More than likely this is him not wanting to pay child support. With a president backing him, making sure none of them take responsibility for anything, why should he? I can't do this. I'm not built to be alone. Alone I will screw this kid up. My mind races to all the ways I will turn this child into a drunk, mindless, insecure brat. Panic assumes control.

"I have an idea. What if we move somewhere away from here and all this mess? Maybe back to Missouri? You can—"

"Stop. Heellllllllll no. I lost count of the crazy things coming out of your mouth. You think it'd only be hard for this kid here? What do you think it's like for a mixed kid? That's even assuming I trust you. Which I don't. You're still two-faced. So no, moving with you back to Missouri is not a good idea."

A small smile curves my lips while I stare at the floor. Tears hit me like summer thunderstorms lately: hard, hot, and messy. But I don't feel refreshed and clean like I do during the summer. These tears flood me, set everything afloat, make the ground beneath me sink with every step I try to take. It was dumb coming here expecting to get what I want by trying to please everyone, screwing myself more than I screw dudes in the process. When I complicate something, I do it all the way. *Lâche pas la patate.* The simplest thing is still the truth.

"I fell for you."

He gives me a big booming chuckle. His face looks almost pleased when he looks at me. I'm aching for his arm around my shoulders, the sound of his heart in my ear, and reassurance this will all be ok.

He wordlessly gets up to open the door for me. "We'll figure out the paperwork later," he says as I walk out. Barely through the opening, he closes the door behind me. The newbie pitcher starts to smile when I approach the car. She sees my face and looks away. She doesn't seem happy that she was right and I should have gone to my parents. Paw Paw said to try. Me and Mom have been good at disliking each other since Dad started leaving the house. Now we are tied in our loneliness. My choices made us alike in a new way. My nausea from earlier returns. My pitcher stops with me at the new CC's by Albertson's. I grab a large coffee for her and Mom, and a decaf for me. I don't know what I will say to Mom. Panic starts coming back. I need help. I need to do the right thing. When we pull up to the house and she's not there my heart sinks. Mom would say it's a sign from God. Paw Paw would say try again. At this moment I don't even know if Paw Paw's listening anymore. I wouldn't want Paw Paw to see this. I wonder what a child of mine would want. It makes me panic more. Panic is a luxury. Panic is what I let myself fall into when life gets hard. Looking at the empty driveway of my childhood home, the place where things were always simpler than I let them be, there are mental pictures of the people who'd bail me out when I made things too complicated.

Paw Paw, Dave, Dad, Mom, and lately, even Will. They were always there, saving me from myself. This empty driveway is just what's left of the bridges I've burned. I didn't even bother driving off them, like Paw Paw did.

Where was he going, anyway? Why'd he miss his exit? Mom wants to think it's because he was sick. It doesn't take a college degree to know his stroke caused him to go into the Basin but it didn't make him miss the exit. He was leaving, going God knows where. He didn't want us to see it. It was his little secret; one he took with him to the grave. What would he hide from us? Could it be the man who I was sure was impervious to the world worried about what his family thought? One thing is for sure, Auguste Chenevert didn't see the point in explaining his life to anyone. Whatever he was doing that night, he was doing it on his own terms. Could that be it? Paw Paw knew his family wouldn't accept wherever he was going, so he didn't bother. His truck went off the bridge on the edge of Cajun country; he almost made it out. If only I had that in me. With every decision I end up retracing my steps, trying to make sure it's right. It only ever slows me down, eventually stopping me completely. When that seven steak was cooking, he told me the only way through this is to pick a place and start moving. He would have started with his family. I ask my pitcher to drive me to my momma's work.

"Addie! What are you doing? Don't you have class or something?" Mom sings as I come through the door. She makes her way through the maze of displays. Drinking paraphernalia, Southern charm, and uniquely Cajun local gifts are all on sale here. She nearly knocks over a mannequin in a very form fitting, jeweled, and somewhat revealing, Mardi Gras bodice (on post Mardi Gras clearance) as she rushes to the front to meet me.

"Yeah. I skipped. I wanted to come visit."

Her shoulders relax. "*Mon Dieu*, you make your momma's heart happy. And you brought coffee. I taught you well." She smiles and sips, before smiling even bigger. It feels good to make her happy.

"Have you been doing ok, Mom?"

"Me?" She's surprised to hear me ask it.

"Yeah."

"Oh, I'm fine."

A customer enters. The bustling that fills our home with anxious energy works great in this industry. She looks after them, anticipating needs. As I watch, the browser turns into a buyer with quite a hefty sum at the register. Mom comes back to hear me letting out a big sigh.

"That was great, Mom."

"What? That? I'm just peddling my trinkets."

"I know but... ok I have another question. What made you decide to do this? Like what was life like before this job, when we were, I don't know, closer, what was it like for you? Like when we were babies. I know dad was gone a lot then, too. Back when he was on the rigs. It was just us and you."

“Why do you ask?”

“I figure I don’t know some things about you. I could learn something.”

She’s as shocked to hear it as I am to say it. But she doesn’t question it.

"It was nice. You and your brother were a couple of *of tête durs*: hard, hard heads. But after I’d threaten the wooden spoon when y’all wouldn’t listen. When y'all got to be too much, Maw Maw or Aunt Kathy would come over."

"I remember them visiting. I didn't know it was because we were a handful."

"It wasn't always helpful, if you want me to be honest."

"Huh?"

"Your Maw Maw could be mean. Always telling me I was doing something wrong."

"That sounds like her. She was always telling us we were being *canaille* even when we weren't."

"Your aunt, too. She still loves to boss me around."

"Not Aunt Kathy!"

"*Oui,* Kathy"

"I don't believe it."

"Ok fine. Wait until you start having kids. Will or your Dad or Tiffany… somebody will always have something to say about what you're doing."

An old impulse wants to say she's wrong. This is just her anger, her jealousy, her insecurity, blaming people for her difficulties. But I know she's telling the truth. Dad would never accept a mixed baby. Will would be no help. Tiffany would rub this in my face across the family, across the city, until we die. It'll be just like Kathy and my mom. I'm starting to understand why mom is so bitter. What about mom? Would she just reject me and this baby? She wouldn't because she knows it's not right. But her love would only be coating for her disappointment, for her own shame. My family won't accept me, or this baby. No matter what I choose moving forward, they will always look at my life as a set of mistakes I'm trying to make up for. Two Addies will exist: the correct version before the baby, and the incorrect version after the baby. Neither of them is really me.

The door opens again. In walks a woman whose eyes light up when she sees Mom. They embrace more tightly than she and I ever have.

Both turning to me she says, "Addison this is Julie Denburg, my partner here."

Looking at my mom quizzically, the woman flashes a smile. After all her years of oversharing, never leaving room for interpretation on what she's feeling or thinking, Mom made another life for herself she doesn't share with anyone. She's not ashamed or even apologetic.

"Addie was just—"

"—going. I came by for a visit. But I should really go. I can't miss all of my classes today." If she doesn't need to apologize, doesn't have to feel *honte*, for making her own life outside of this family then neither do I.

My life feels like an onion in a crawfish boil: layers peeling away without anything holding it together and making it look like it once did. Even my nerdy, home bound brother is different. When I picked up Will in the middle of nowhere, in the middle of the night, after his first fight with a guy, a guy I can't even be sure he wasn't gay for, it makes it all real. The most unnerving part of it all was how despite being covered in mud and blood that night, Will seems to have his life more together than me. When I asked what was wrong with him, he could accept there is a lot, but he's working on it. He's not afraid to work out where he's from. He never apologized for being messed up. Guys get away with never apologizing. You know what… screw that. I'm a tomboy and that's close enough.

Another unrecognizable piece of life is the new role I take on the team. Coach puts me at third base coach for the rest of the season. She's worried I'll take a ball to the stomach. Since I'm being honest lately, I'd say this feels good. Feeling even better is overhearing the newbie pitcher telling the second-string catcher how she'll never be as good as me. I'd say that's love. This game might not have to be over for me after all. There are a lot of softball teams needing coaches around the country.

The idea stays with me as I take the same route I always take, back to my lonely apartment. It was only a week ago that my life felt open and easy like Johnston Street does on this Sunday evening while everyone is at dinner or trying to make the last mass. Now my life is the same street, but with the noise and confusion of Mardi Gras day. The picture makes me laugh out loud. The laugh breaks down in my throat, crumbles in my chest, and collapses somewhere near my heart. My heart is breaking because it knows I can't stay here. I don't know how any momma ever raised a mixed Creole baby here. Could they have been less racist back then? I don't believe that. Which means they must have been stronger than me. I don't believe that either. If they could have left, they would have.

Already I'm too worried about what other people will think about it than what I think. Turning toward the place I'm supposed to, the Church, will mean I'll get people who say they want to help, while they tell me how evil and misguided I've been. Why does that love have to hurt? I won't use religion as parenting. The Church will be worse than the Bulldog. I don't want my baby growing up with people telling them they're not Cajun enough, or too Black, at the same time. No. I need to leave this place. Shreveport could be a good place to land since it's still in Louisiana. But being in the state without being around Cajun people will only make me more homesick. I need to go further; Houston or somewhere. It could be my shot to teach a little "me" not to worry about what other people think. Looking at my red eyes in the rearview, on my face I didn't bother to put make up on, I see what a forty-year-old version of me could look like. I won't have red spiked hair. I'll have a big ass. What else will change outside of this place? What will stay the same? In my next kitchen, will I still dance around the table? A smile breaks across my face thinking of dancing with a little, darker version of me. There won't be Cajun music on the radio, though. It's likely they won't sell boudin at the gas station. They might not even sell alcohol on Sundays. There won't be Paw Paw, even my momma, to coo at my baby in French. Big alligator tears spill onto my softball sweatshirt. Looking around at the businesses, the foliage, the black weather wear of the concrete, I miss it all already.

My breath starts to even as I think about turning the truck toward I-10. They have not repaired the concrete rail on the Basin where my Paw Paw went over. I could easily go through the orange plastic fence there. Even if my soul doesn't make it to where he is, I won't be stuck between all these worlds anymore. At least Hell would give me an address. Thinking of my taillights sinking into the swamp, I wonder again where he was going that night. Being Cajun didn't decide what he was allowed to do. He didn't want us to know. He didn't ask for our understanding or care if we'd be ok with it. Seems that if you can't make your home happy, our choices are to conform completely or rebel. I've tried to find some sort of middle way. Paw Paw knew there isn't one. I have my two choices, leave or die. Like he said, I need to pick a path and move forward. From here, in this moment, the path is obvious.

Turning around, I find my side street near USL. Houston seems like a big place, but maybe that will mean more chances to have my own life. I'll need a better job for better housing… and day care. I don't even know what to look for in a day care. My grandfather's grey, firm eyes drift into my mind and my breath catches. After I force my lungs to slow, I remind myself he'd expect me to find my answers. Even though I never thought I was doing it right, he never seemed disappointed. I inch down my street, holding his grey eyes in my mind. My mother's judgment, my brother's condescension, my dad's indifference; I found none of those things there. It must be why I sought him when I was lost. Reflected in those eyes are who I want see when I look at myself. The acceptance also saw all my flaws, letting me know I don't have to be those things anymore. I don't have to be judgmental, condescending, or indifferent to what I find inside of me. It's especially important now since there is someone else inside sharing my life with me. I'm… excited. This little person will be a piece of me I put in the world. That's not a bad thing. Panic, fear, denial, excitement, hope – that's the real me. It's a good thing, because sitting crossed-legged on my welcome mat is a large, hunched figure with his head down. As I exit my truck, he brings his dark eyes to meet mine.

"Hey," his boom vibrates toward me.

Chapter 23

Rockin' Doopsie blasts through my open windows. Cars pass me as I slowly drive down Main Highway in Breaux Bridge on the way to Aunt Kathy's. I'm savoring all the sights. Missouri won't have swamps and bayous like this. It'll probably be cornfields or something. Where will I get seafood there? I need to make a good étouffée. That's how I can start thanking his momma for convincing her boy to bring her grandbaby, and the baby's momma, home. They better know this baby and me are leaving every spring. I can't miss Mardi Gras.

Dave's mom told us to come right now. We told her we needed to finish finals. Now I'm not sure if I can. She said we need to rip it fast like a Band-Aid. She knew how I'd start missing things, second-guessing. Maybe she'll know more of me than my mother. Untethered, the baby and I, we'll float along a sea of unfamiliar. It'll be good for the baby, could even be good for me, but it won't be home. This seemed so simple when David told me we could do this. It's just about family. That's something Paw Paw would understand. But now I have to choose who my family is. It's no wonder I've spent all my life avoiding choices. Choices are always goodbye to something.

As I pass Paw Paw's house the air gets sucked out of the cab. I might not ever again see my grandfather's tattered house bordered by Bayou Teche. In one day he taught me to cast, how a bump from a bass feels, and to drive a boat on that bayou. I drove right over a submerged log even though I saw it. I figured the motor would shred it. When I heard the engine grind, I turned around to see splinters in my wake. Paw Paw could tell by the sound I'd bent the prop. When I'd bring my truck to him after taking on a muddy field, having shred the transmission, he'd give me only a few curse words in French before spending three weeks rebuilding it. He can't fix what I break anymore. Who will yell at me when I'm stupid for taking on more than I can handle? It'll have to be me, I guess. Whether or not I can do this, not only for myself, but for a child, makes me wonder again if driving off of the I-10 bridge would have been the smarter choice. But I'm my Paw Paw's kin. Cajun mommas don't give up, especially when family is at stake. Momma. That's a big word. Big, but at least it's just one thing. Keep it simple.

Going to Aunt Kathy's on a Sunday afternoon, instead of Paw Paw's house, doesn't feel the same. Everything is already changing without him here. Now that I'm thinking about it, it could make this the best time to leave. This place won't make as much sense without him in it. I can find a new fishing hole in Missouri. I can find a new bar for when I'm due for a break from the baby. I will have new people. Maybe people who leave here are not as crazy as everyone says they are; as I said they are. Looking through Aunt Kathy's screen door, I see the two matrons of my family with their backs to me, watching Will… clean fish? I'll miss so much more than I thought. I'll miss my brother finish turning into a man. He was supposed to be the one to leave, not me. The only thing I could clearly see in my future, sitting in the stands watching the girls play my sport, won't happen. What will Yankees think of some girl from the swamp who chokes back tears because she can't have boudin for breakfast?

Clearing a sob from my throat, I burst through my aunt's screen door. "I brought Schlitz," I declare. They all give a little yelp. I celebrate by cracking one for myself, swallowing fast.

Beatrice

Chapter 24

Nobody else will like these. I feel bad for getting them only because I like them. But they're so cute, little charms on the bottom of wine glasses. Maybe they'll be a thing. That's silly. I'm glad I didn't buy too many. Now I'm regretting them more because I don't know how to delete in this damn computer program. I hate this thing. I wish we could go back to ledgers. You don't have to worry about Y2k bugs, or whatever they're called, with a pen and paper. Julie insisted though. And she doesn't seem worried about the Y2K.

"Julie! How do I fix this?"

"Fix what?" she shouts from the back of our boutique.

"Fix… this?"

Julie comes out of our tiny little stockroom swinging those thirty eight year old hips. I don't know why she does that. It's not like I'm going to date her.

"Bee! You break my computer?"

"I don't know, *cher*! I can't tell when I'm doing right or I'm doing wrong."

"Let me do it."

I can't say I'm not relieved. My wine is a little low and needs recharging. In the stock room I uncork the Merlot and notice Julie's wine glass is empty next to her new-fangled cell phone. "Who were you talking to back here?" I prod innocently.

"My casino crew."

"You have a whole crew for that?"

"Well, yeah. You want to be on my crew?"

"Oh honey I got a Krewe, except it's with a 'k'."

“Well in my crew we end up with money instead of throwing it away to other people.”

“That’s half the fun! Have you ever been on a float holding all those beads! You feel like a queen!”

“You’re still throwing beads you paid for to perfect strangers. You should try coming with us one weekend! Do something for you.”

“I do stuff for me,” I shout to the front after finishing the glass and pouring another. She thinks my life is like hers. Young, single, beautiful – things I haven’t been in a long time. And it’s not like we’re alike in other ways either. There must be something wrong with her if she’s not married by this age. She never seems bothered about not having kids. She goes out all the time. It’s not much of a life. Makes her a good business partner, though. She’s got a knack for getting people through the door of Louisiana Treasures Boutique and keeping the books. I’ll say another prayer for her tonight. I’ll thank Jesus she walked in the same day I started thinking about closing this place. I can pray she finds a nice man, too.

“There. Fixed," she says as I walk back to the counter, handing her a refilled glass of wine. "I can enter in whatever you were trying to. What is it you were trying to type in?”

“Oh I can do it, *beb*. You don’t need extra work.”

“Is it… these? What are these?”

She picks up one of the little charm wine glass things. Watching her face, I wait for her to tell me what I’ve already figured out. She turns them in her hand and looks at me.

“Wine charms? They’re silly little accessories for your wine glass,” I say.

“I like them. They’re super cute. What’s our price point on these?”

“Three dollars,” I return.

“How much did we pay for them?”

“Two dollars.”

"Aw Bee, these are seven bucks, easy."

"That's too much."

"Nope. That's business. Good business. I keep hoping you'll catch on."

"I'm not going to catch on to overcharging people out of their hard-earned money."

"Tell that to the guy who makes all the beads you pay too much for," she sasses.

Looking over my glass, I see it's two o'clock. Daddy and Will might be home soon. "Julie let's knock off. There's no one in here. No one's coming in. Not this close to Mardi Gras."

"Bee you got two boxes of inventory you haven't entered yet."

"It'll give me something to do Monday." She stares at me for too long. "What? Do I have wine teeth?"

"No. You're… you're coming with me."

"To do what?"

"To have a life."

"I do have a life."

"Yeah. And it's time you start using it."

She takes me to a hippie house. I can smell the oils they put on their skin when we get out of the car. We're on the wrong side of the Evangeline Thruway. For a second I think she took me to some Black person's house, but then the hippie who owns the smell comes walking out. She hugs Julie. It's a long hug. They both have their eyes closed, which makes my skin crawl with a new possibility. Is this why she swings her hips when it's the two of us? She better not be thinking what I think she's thinking.

"Bee, I want to introduce you to my best friend and roommate, Jackie." Jackie's smile is unnervingly warm. I feel the look on my face. She holds out her hand.

"I've heard a lot about you, Bee."

"I'm sure I'm not as bad as Julie says."

"She hasn't been able to mention anything bad. Only that you can be too sweet. Come inside. I can make tea. Or do you drink coffee? I have both."

This is moving in the wrong direction, fast. Do I look like an old lesbian? I knew I shouldn't have let the beautician give me spikey hair. Still, it's wrong to refuse an invitation. They may be lesbians, but I got my own sins to worry about. Entering a room full of light and plants, I stand immobile in the entryway. The furniture is covered and probably mismatched. Bright paintings cloud the walls in no specific pattern. Agreeing to sit only on the edge of what might be an armchair, I sip my coffee. Jackie drinks Community. I misjudged her. Nobody bad drinks Community. And she puts the right amount of cream and sugar. She didn't even need to ask. The girls exchange their pleasantries with an air of youth I haven't seen since my daughter was in high school. I'm trying so hard to figure it out I almost don't notice when they've both turned to look at me.

"Are you afraid that chair will eat you?" Jackie asks. Not the chair, no. Comparing my edge-sitting to their lounging, their legs almost crossing each other on the couch, I see what they mean. I scoot a little farther back. But not too far. I could catch something.

"There you go. Act like you'll stay a while."

"Oh, I'm sorry, but I can't stay for too long."

"That's right." Jackie looks back at Julie. "You need to get back to Will." There's no point in hiding my discomfort in her knowing my son's name. I look over at Julie, too.

"Bee, Jackie has been my best friend for years. I tell her everything."

"Yes, I need to get to Will." My legs ready underneath me to get up.

"Oh. Julie. Did you decide if you want to go to New Orleans tomorrow?" Jackie asked.

"I think I'll stay here and help Bee get ready for Mardi Gras."

"Oh, honey. You go have fun in all that craziness. I can handle it here." I encourage. The idea of having a little space between me and her sounds good right about now.

"I know you can. But I don't want you to handle it. Besides, it'll give me time to wear you down to come with me to New Orleans or the casino another day. We'll worry about that after your Mardi Gras Ball and the parades and the big sale."

Here I was trying to give them the benefit of the doubt when they really do want to wear me down. It's time to go. "We'll have to see. But Julie, I'm so sorry. I really can't stay gone too long. They'll be waiting for me back home."

"Of course," Jackie cheerfully chimes. "A mother's work is never done. It was a treat to have met you. Oh, I have something I want to give you." She floats into the next room while I stand, taking my cup to the sink. Jackie flows back in cutting me off and grabbing the cup out of my hand. She replaces it with a small crucifix, like one from a rosary.

"I know you heard about that church that burned in Basile."

"Those poor people. And that poor little priest."

"Well I drove down there to help with the cleanup when I heard. The priest and I got along and ended up laughing through most of it. Such a nice man. In the end he gave me that and said it's what was left of his rosary. Julie tells me how devout you are. I think it belongs with you."

"Aw, Jackie. That's so sweet. But I couldn't—"

"It belongs with you, Bee."

Truth is I don't want this. While it probably is very holy, having been prayed on by a priest and lived through a fire, it doesn't belong to me. That priest didn't give it to me. And even with the correct intention attached, I'm sure whatever connection this had to God is gone now that it's been in her possession. "Jackie, really, I—"

"It belongs with you."

This is the second time I've been tested for my graciousness. I nod and thank her and slip it into my purse. The two of them embrace longer this time. When the engine starts, I feel some relief. That was the first and last time I'll go with Julie Denburg anywhere.

"What did you think of Jackie?" she asks.

"She seems nice."

I rush home and immediately wonder why. My son is at his computer where he will be all night, ignoring me. It's no use trying to have a conversation with him because all I get are one-word answers. There's only one thing left to bring me any feeling of comfort or love. In the pantry I lift my box of Franzia, and see I still have half left. That's plenty company. I wipe the wet around my eyes. My daughter chooses a ballpark over me. My son chooses a screen. I guess those are better than what my husband chooses.

That's the thought. That's the one I don't like thinking. The one where younger, thinner fingers are moving through his hair. The one where our vows mean more to me than to him. I'm a silly and ridiculous wife. And with the glass finally filled from my little spigot, I gulp it all down, the sweetness as cheap as the feeling that goes with it. As it sinks, it carries the burn from my eyes to my throat and chest. All those thoughts get washed down as I refill. Silly doesn't mean much for a woman my age. What's left to try and have all that pride for? Another skill, one I know I'm already good at, is dodging mirrors. My body is best handled in pieces. This white piece of flesh here, this rumpled cellulite there, none really fits together anymore into something I could call my own. Being an absentee landlord of this once nice vessel, I keep a neat house and a glamourous boutique to offset it. The days when I looked like Addie, curly hair to flip and a tighter butt to swing, are long gone. Remembering the way I could turn a head reminds me of the new dress I left on the coat rack behind the front door. I'm so busy trying to do for Will, I forget little things like that. I smile as the sequins glint, rubbing the polyester between my fingers. Mardi Gras is always my Christmas. Life goes loose and what's left is laughs, and color, and passion. People are nice and have fun. On top my float I can give all those beads away. They call my name, all of my friends, all of my family, and I get reminded of who loves me. Going through my favorite memories from the past few years apparently makes me thirsty because my wine is gone again. And now I'm hungry.

"Mom, what are you doing?" he asks from behind me as I try to get a hot meal. Does taking care of myself look that foreign to him?

"I was making some fucking dinner! I get hungry!" That little brat wants to come out here when I drop something and disturb his games.

"Ok, Mom. I was just curious."

To make it all worse, I see I knocked over the new bottle of wine I uncorked a minute before. It's all over the floor before I can save any of it. Might as well pick up these goddamned pots. These old knees are making it tough to stand. And he's standing there and watching me struggle. "You gonna help me?"

"I… sure." After lumbering toward me, never seeming to be able to get his arms to swing in time with his legs, he bends down and starts grabbing pots. Pots are more important than me in this house now. Pots. Seems like every man in my life gets distracted by something disappointingly small when it's time to love me. He tries to start helping me up but makes my balance worse. It's not really help if I have to tell him, anyway.

"Nevermind. Why don't you just go hide in your room like you always do? It seems like none of the men in this family actually want to act like they're in it."

"What are you talking about?"

“Don’t act like you’re not avoiding me the moment you walk in this house.” I should have pointed it out a long time ago. He’s been doing this for months, or even years. He’s been so ungrateful. All I’ve done is try to be a good mom to him. But he’s gone off in some other direction, exactly like his father.

“I don’t try to avoid you. I just don’t always know what to say to you.”

“You sassing me?”

“No ma’am. Don’t know what you need, is all.”

My little boy lays it out in black and white. I’m always thinking about what they need. I’m looking at my eyes and chin on his face. We’re the same people. But he still can’t see what I need. He doesn’t even like me, or maybe love me enough, to figure out what I need. Everyone here acts like they’re done trying to like each other except me. They keep treating love like a chore. It’s our blessing. Even if it doesn’t feel that way they have to keep trying. *Lâche pas la patate.* The wine must be wearing off because the tears are back. Like a frozen turkey dropped in a fryer, tears explode from within. All the truth that had been under pressure comes up in a horrible geyser.

“We aren’t much of a family anymore, are we?”

Chapter 25

Things started getting fuzzy about the time I remember getting hungry and deciding to cook. What was it I wanted? Oh, rice and gravy. What the hell was I thinking? I could burn the house down cooking while I'm that drunk. And there's something about Will, too. I feel like I should be mad at him this morning, but I can't remember what for. Christ. What did I do? What did he say? I'm too embarrassed to ask.

Doing what I'm supposed to do, I ask forgiveness. The Church says I should ask Jesus, God, and the Holy Spirit for forgiveness. After nights like last night I never can face them. Since I was a girl, getting in trouble meant I'd have to face Daddy's disappointment face, his set jaw, his furrowed forehead. I picture those on the Trinity. While they may give me absolution, I've always gotten the understanding and consoling I need from a woman: the Virgin Mary. She's the mother I wished I had and the woman I wish I could be. In the dark of the room, in my empty bed, I say my rosary. The words are repetitious. I haven't really heard them in decades. It's the trance, the beseeching, the rhythm, and even the click of the beads I seek. Each bead passing between my fingers takes me further from my mistakes and closer to being loved again.

With less hangover I can get ready for Addie's game. I wish, so much, that she still liked to see me there. When she stopped coming to see me after the game, and leaving straight away with her friends, I knew she was telling me something. She was telling me how she feels about family. But one day Addie will understand a mother's love and appreciate how I was always there. I'm not so sure Will can understand. He's so lost. Any time I try and nudge him toward the right things, he fights. He's young to be so bitter. Given what I can't know about last night, I'll leave him alone today. If I spoke some truth he didn't want to hear… I'd rather let it marinate. If he told me something horrible, or

I did something… silly… I don't think bringing it back up right now would help. So I ask Will where I can find him after the game.

"Um, I guess here. At the car."

It doesn't matter. Addison doesn't care about her family when her friends are around. Every year that goes by she cares more about what they think. Making my way to my seat, I see my usual stadium neighbors. Dr. Robillard and his son, Betsy Fontenot and her husband, and the Johnsons are already there. I'm glad the Fontenots came. I can talk Mardi Gras shop with Betsy. Squeezing my hips into my seat, I can smell her sweat mixed with good perfume.

"Poo yie it's hot for February!" I exclaim.

"I don't even put my short pants away anymore," Glen Johnson says.

"Dr. Robillard where's your wife?"

"Sick," he responds flatly. He doesn't talk much. I've never understood that.

"Well I'm glad she has you," I offer back. All I get for my trouble is a forced smile. I'm glad Betsy's husband sits by him. Maybe his nice nature will rub off.

"Betsy, I have something at Louisiana Treasures you have to see."

"Oh yeah? *Qu'est que c'est*?"

"You'll have to pass a visit and see!"

"Beatrice, don't set me up to come buy some crap, now!"

My laugh is met with a smile from her. I can't tell what kind it is. Does she think the things I ordered with her in mind were crap? I mentally run through the Mardi Gras masks I've shown her over the last year. Re-imagining the faces and words she used when she would see them, I remember how unkind and gruff her reactions were all these years. Thankfully, the game is starting and I can focus on my Addie.

She is looking good, despite this crappy pitcher. I always love when the girls in her dugout cheer. I love to cheer along. When she calls those good pitches, and that ball sails home, I let out an "Addie-girl!" like I have since she started playing back in middle school. I always feel so bad for her poor hands and knees. There's so much of my Daddy's toughness in her, though, she never complains. So many of the rosaries I pray in hope that Addie will make our relationship like Daddy and me.

"Will didn't want to come today?" Betsy notices after the end of the second inning. She's trying to make nice after that sass earlier.

"No, he's here. Somewhere."

"Oh, I see him."

"Where?" I ask, surprised he's not still in the car.

"Look up near the top. Under the overhang. He's sitting next to some other boy."

The boy's handsome. I'm pretty sure I've seen him before. His mom is the blonde lady who wears heels to these games. They come from money. How in the world did Will make friends with *him*? Watching him for a minute I see his shoulders hunch. He runs his hands through his hair, the way he does when he's nervous. He talks without making eye contact. But the other kid is laughing. It's like finding out a secret. No, it's more like finding out I was gypped. Conversation doesn't come hard for him with a stranger, but it sure does in our house. My heart sinks. He thinks he's a better breed than me.

The picture of those two hangs in my head for the rest of the day. Mardi Gras balls are God's grace. They provide some happiness in the middle of all this *misère*, something to lighten and simplify life. My dress fits, thank God. The woman I see in the mirror looks different enough from the forty-three-year-old always in jeans or shorts. Leaving behind my worries from the softball field, I notice the sequins reflecting something I'm always looking for. If only I could wear things like this every day. It's enough that I want to share this good feeling with Will when he walks in my room.

"Whew. *Bon Dieu*! You know I think you're right. It doesn't look half bad. Your ole momma's still got something."

"What is the theme this year?" he asks sweetly. Maybe my boy is back.

"Amazon."

"Wasn't that the theme last year?"

Even this one, the one who lives with me, doesn't pay attention to my most important thing, a thing just for me. "No that was Caribbean."

"Ah."

"I had one of those big Carnival headdresses last year, remember?"

"Oh, yeah. So you said the ball is tomorrow night?"

"Yeah. I feel bad we aren't going to Cousin Vilain's going away party because of the ball. You should go, though. Your cousin could bring you." *Pauvre* Vilain. He never figured it out. His momma and his daddy cut him loose when he was Will's age. Now look at him. Will never appreciates why I try to show him the right way. It's by God's grace he stays so shy and never wants to leave the house.

"Mom, I've only met Vilain two or three times. I don't believe I'm the one they were thinking about when they invited you for his send off to prison."

Here it is. My children think they're better than their blood. They can't appreciate what happened to us when they broke up our families and the Cajuns were tossed to the sea. He's so spoiled. He's never relied only on family to get him through this world. "The whole family is invited. And don't act like you're better than him. Y'all have the same great-great-grandfather."

"Yes ma'am." When I look away from the mirror, I see my sweet little boy's face. The one I used to see a year ago. My God, I hope this lasts. Taking a sip of my wine, I savor the moment.

"You mind if I go to my own party tonight?" *Comme ça*, the little boy is gone.

"Do I know this person or their family?"

"No, but his sister is on the team with Addie. She was pitching today."

"That no talent?" He hasn't wondered about how I would feel about this. And he's picked the worst set of people to be social with. A good mother feels what her son feels. He's excited, I see it now. But he doesn't know what he's getting into. Those people are not like us. From the looks of them, they come from some liberal city in California. Not talking about it, the way he and I co-existed for so long, will not work this time. And it won't have to. I hear the little degenerate's car in my driveway.

The handsome young man in his rice rocket is smart enough to exit his car to meet me. I'm shocked to hear him use manners. He says all the right things, that they'll just watch a movie, and they live in a nice neighborhood. If I tell Will he can't go now, he'll end up telling Paw Paw and I'd have no good defense against him. Hell with it. I have my wine and a Mardi Gras ball and parade to get ready for.

Back in my room, as I sob at this ungrateful world I'm living in, I try to get out of my dress. The zipper isn't reachable. In the mirror I see a green monster flailing around like a caught fish. New tears in my eyes blind me as my limited mobility makes me fall. Bawling forces me into taking deep breaths. The breaths are not as difficult as they were, leading me to believe I ripped my dress. My hand reaches behind and feels my bra. Did it rip the zipper? Getting out of it and spreading it on the bed, I exhale seeing it still completely intact. Miraculously, it unzipped by itself. Worrying about my dress made me stop all this damn crying in time for me to answer my sister's phone call.

"Hey, Kathy."

"Bee what the hell is wrong with you? Why are you going to that Mardi Gras ball instead of Vilain's going away party?"

"Daddy told you?"

"Who else? Lord knows you weren't going to have a spine to show up or even tell me."

"Oh, come now Kathy. It's not like that."

"It is like that, because it's always been like that with you. You're selfish Beatrice. Think about what that's going to be like for him, all locked away from his family."

"I do think about him Kathy. I pray for him every day and even dedicate masses to him. I also pray for those poor people he stole all that money from."

"Listen to you. So high and mighty. How is what he did different than what you do? You can't make your husband happy enough to want to stay home. But you sure don't have a problem helping yourself to his money, buying those fancy dresses just so you can feel special." This has happened our whole lives. I try to be kind, to be thoughtful, but Kathy finds a way to tear me down, to use my own good intentions against me.

"Kathy, that's—"

"You're not special. Momma and Daddy treated you that way because you're so fragile. It's time you grow up and realize the truth about you."

"Why you so mean, Kathy?"

"Truth hurts, Bee. It's sad you think honesty is me being mean, when it's the nicest thing I could do for you. But go. Go dance with other people's husbands and drink your wine. You know how to keep your little fantasy going."

It's enough. I hang up on her. This time it's not to prove a point. Having the child who came from your body, and your own sister, tell you how little they think of you in less than an hour, is enough. Why I picked up that phone I'll never know, because this is what she does when there's no one around. Standing in my empty house, pouring another glass of wine, I wait. Numbness arrives to carry me through a little more of my life, bringing a little courage with it. Since I've been shunned twice tonight, might as well go for three. Maybe I won't feel this one as much. Even though I don't expect John to pick up his car phone, he does.

"Hey, John"

"What's up Bee? Everything ok?"

"Oh yes, sweetheart. Fine. I'm just calling about tomorrow night."

"What about tomorrow night?"

"The ball, John? I'm going to pick up your tux tomorrow afternoon. We need to leave the house by five-thirty to be at the Hilton."

"Aw, Bee. Crap. I'm sorry. I can't make it. I'm on my way to Houston for a sales call."

I get quiet, trying to hold on to the numbness. But I'm losing. Home is another hotel for him. And the only hotel where he's not with one of his *putains*, his little playthings. Somewhere in my quiet I hear my sister's voice, scorning me for my selfishness. She'd want me to consider what this life must be like for him and what it got me. Her voice does not leave me *honte* today. It ruins my numbness and makes me angry.

"It's ok. I'll… It's ok. Will you be home for lunch tomorrow? I'll be cooking something."

"What are you cooking?"

"What do you want?" I know what he doesn't want: gumbo. That should have told me something was wrong with him from the beginning. It's even my best dish. Everyone says so. Man who doesn't eat good gumbo is not right.

"I don't know. Just wondering." He pauses. He might realize how he sounds. "I'll be there sometime in the morning."

"Ok, my love. See you tomorrow. Hope the trip isn't too much *tracas*."

Still there are no tears as I pour the next glass. Sin or not, anger feels good. Like I could burn it all down. It's a feeling I'm not supposed to feel about my family, so I wait for it to change to disappointment. That doesn't hurt as much, probably because I'm used to it. All the pain is worth something if we stay a good family.

I could use a real voice of comfort and direction right now. The wind can always listen to me, carrying my troubles to God. Except the wind, like God, never speaks directly. Guesses and hopes are what's left after I toss my prayers into the wind. I down the rest of the glass, refill it, and make one last phone call before my words slur. Before the night is over, I'd like to hear the voice of someone who I know loves me.

"Daddy, *quoi t'es après faire?*"

"*Quoi y a?*"

"No, nothing's the matter."

"Den why you callin' me so late."

"Will just let me know he'd like to go fishing with you tomorrow."

"Willy *a dit ça?* Maybe dat boy finally gonna come 'round."

Chapter 26

"*Nous avions de bonne chance aujourd'hui* ! Willy caught him five *sac-a-lait*," my Daddy's voice sings out as he comes in. The mood could not be more unlike the one I sent them off in this morning.

"That's good! When was the last time you were that lucky, Will?" I ask, trying to seem happy for him, but still so suspicious of what made the change. My thoughts go to the possibility that Will started talking about me. But then why is Daddy so happy?

"Dat doan matter. We gonna pass us a good time. I'm gone clean fish."

"Ok, I'll work here in the kitchen. Will, go help your Paw Paw."

A look passes between them. "Nah, Bee. I'll clean dem. We'll call you when dinner is ready, Willy."

"Dad, your rule is you clean what you catch. Will needs to clean his own fish." The rule is never bent, much less broken.

"Not today. I clean dem faster anyway."

"He needs to learn."

"He knows how."

"Dad—"

"Bee, *tu passer*!"

Will said something. There's no other reason my father would take up for him when he's never done anything for his grandfather. The number of people loving me back seems to be shrinking by the hour. I head into the kitchen, like Daddy told me, while Will retreats to his little cave. This picture is all wrong.

I am in the middle of mixing the potato salad when Daddy walks back in with his cleaned fish. He sets them down on the counter and I get to work breading them and dropping them in the grease.

"Why you make potato salad? We not havin' gumbo."

"I thought it would go well with the fish," I offer.

"You not gonna fry some potatoes?"

"I will if you want some, Daddy."

"*Mais* doan do dat just for me, *cher*."

"Well I don't know what you want, then."

"Bee, doan you talk to you Daddy like dat! You like a nasty ole barn cat."

Will said something about the other night, the one I don't remember. It's like Kathy used to do. She'd tell Momma and Daddy something when I wasn't around and they come back spoiling for a fight with me. Momma never bought her bullshit though. Daddy always did. Like I'm sure he's buying Will's now. But Will can't appreciate how I've managed this all these years, how I've fought back without anyone seeing. I know how to get my daddy to prove that he loves me.

"Why you standing like dat? Witchu hip all to da side like dat," he asks.

"Oh my back is messed up again, I think. I'm glad you mentioned it. Because since you're my *traiteur* and you're here…"

"Nah I tole you, I don't know how many times, Bee. I taught you how to treat dat. You know all da prayers and you know what to do. You can fix dat."

"I never got the call for it, Daddy."

"Calls don't work da same for everyone. *Maman* got it in her dreams. I got it while I was at work, me. You gotta be listen' right to get you call. God don't talk to us all da same way. I can't do dis forever, no. You gonna have to be da *traiteur* in da family. And you a good one. I seen you work on Willy and Addie."

"Yeah but for little things, like warts."

"It's all da same, Bee. Like I said. I'm gonna be gone one day."

"Daddy stop talking like that." The fish I'm pulling out of the oil slips and drops back in, splattering hot oil onto my hand. I scream and curse. Before I notice, Daddy pulls all of the fish out of the oil with one hand. The other hand grabs one of the unbattered sac-a-lait and holds the cold tail against my skin, tightly in his old, leathery grip. He mouths a prayer and tells me to hold the tail there. He wipes his hands on his pants before putting one paw on my shoulder and the other on my right side. He pushes in and up on my right hip. He tells me how to breathe, and our breaths fall in time together. We've synced again.

"*Ma 'tite* Bee. What I'm gonna do witchu? You hip wasn't bad." The hum of his words take me back to a time when things were simpler, when I knew people loved me. "You just worried 'bout sometin. Worry gonna kill you faster dan da ting you worried 'bout. Dat's why I'm gonna be around for a while. But you still gotta learn how to do all this for when I'm gone." There's no reason to start thinking about this, even if he insists on bringing it up all the time lately. He's still healthy and spry. His face is one I know better than my own. The seams of his face are deeper from all the laughing and talking French. There's so much light behind his eyes even if his eyebrows are a lot scragglier and whiter. "Nah. Finish dem fish. *J'ai faim*. And I'm sure Willy is hungry, too." A quick pour of Community and he's at his normal spot at the table, gulping away. That gulp is how I know he has plenty of life left in him. That's how he takes life in, in gulps. Back to my fish, I know I can feel better about my family with him here.

That is, until I hear the back door open. The pleasantness of things the way they should be is interrupted by the way things are. John's big belly arrives in the kitchen before he does. A smile, perched on his face to make him look innocent, follows behind.

"Mr. Chenevert! I didn't know you'd be here today. It's good to see you!"

"John. *Ça va?*"

"Oh I'm doin' alright."

Not bothering to even put down his bags, he leans over and pecks me roughly on the cheek.

"Hi, John."

"Hey, Bee. Let me go put all this up and I'll be right back." Amazing how much peace he can ruin in under twenty seconds.

"How long was he gone dis time?" Daddy attempts to whisper.

"Who?" I whisper back.

"John."

"Oh I don't know. I stopped keeping track. You know how this job is."

The last of the fish comes out of the fry and I see Daddy staring down the hall, none too pleased. He likes John less and less as the years go by. Which makes me love Daddy more and more. I should have listened to him so long ago.

"I'll go get Will," I say as I put his plate in front of him and refill his coffee. In the hall John and I meet up. He still has his bag in his hand.

"You're not even going to stay and eat with your father-in-law?"

"Yes I am. I was putting this in the truck so I don't forget it."

"As if you'd forget you were leaving."

"Bee, I just walked through the door. Don't start."

There's nothing to start since there won't be a finish. Will's got his headphones on while he plays his video game, so I shake him to tell him lunch is ready. I'm ready for a fight but he gets up and walks into the kitchen where the other two men sit silently eating. As Will takes his place, and I put a plate in front of him, I realize what kind of meal this will be. My plans to sniff out what transpired between Daddy and Will crumble in the presence of total silence between three men who don't know how to talk to each other.

"Daddy you been huntin' lately?" I err toward getting John and him talking.

"Jus rabbits. Nuttin' in season. I been catchin' some frogs. Y'all want some?"

"We still haven't cooked all the ducks John brought home this past season. I don't have room in my deep freeze."

"Hmm," is all Daddy says. John doesn't even look up at the mention of his name.

"John, has work been busy?" I ask with as much interest I can muster. He doesn't even hear me. He continues to shove fish and potato salad into his face. "John?"

"Hmm?"

"How's work been?"

"Good. Busy. Old Leonard got me runnin' all over the place selling these tools. I can't wait to get this damn liberal out of the White House so business is good and they come to us." Except he'll find another excuse to not be at home, like he's too busy at the shop.

"You ever get out to da rigs?" Daddy asks. Now we can have a normal family dinner.

"Me? God, no. That's mechanic work."

"You too good for mechanic work, John? Dat's how I fed you wife and her sister in da sixties. Dem rich Texas boys din't want to be out on dem rigs so dey got us to do it for dem."

"Aw come now Mr. Chenevert. I meant no disrespect. They got guys especially for that is all I'm saying."

"I bet dat's what dem big bellied Texas men tought, too." Get him, Daddy. "Beside, you can do some good fishin' at da rigs. We used to pull up all kinds of stuff. *Les tambours, les plies, les sheepheads*; and we'd cook dat right on da rig. And we din't have all dem safety rules, no. Dem company men would've shot us if dey'd known we was using open flames near all dat oil."

John laughs. He only laughs like this when Daddy's around. It's a little boy's laugh. "Only thing missing was some beer!" he adds.

"Oh we'd get our beer. We'd catch so much fish we'd trade some to da fisherman who would come to our rig. We'd lower down a bucket and dey'd send some Schlitz up. Nah, da company man definitely din't want to know about his coonasses drunk on da job."

They both roar with laughter. I smile and look over at Will. He's slumped, poking at his fish. He needs to be talking with his father and his grandfather, learning how to be a man. But today it's best not to mess with him. Not without knowing what he told his grandfather. So I send him back to his video games. John and Daddy continue talking in the next room. It leaves me hoping John will get in a better mood and he'll come to the ball with me. Before my hope grows, Daddy is back in the kitchen kissing and hugging goodbye, saying he can't be out too late. So I clean, even things I know don't need cleaning. John watches his stupid shoot-em-up movies and I wait. What I'm waiting for, I can't tell. A sign from God on how to handle this loveless marriage would be good. The strength to say what I feel would be good too. A good wife doesn't act suspicious of her husband. But a good wife also takes care of her house and her marriage.

"It was good to see you and Daddy laugh."

"Yeah," is all I get back from Johnt.

"Y'all used to visit like that a lot."

"Yeah." Easing into this is not working.

"John where are you going to be tonight?"

"Told you, Bee. Gotta work."

"On Lundi Gras?"

"Don't start."

"John, I don't ask you for much—"

"Damn it, Bee! Don't you act like some sort of victim here. You knew what this life was like when you married me. Your daddy did this work for a while. You like your house? You like this ball you're going to? Because you're not going to have these things selling junk to housewives. Until you're responsible for the roofs over thirty other people's heads I don't want to hear it. Have fun at your ball. Because I'll be working."

"John," I attempt.

"Shut the hell up, Bee!"

He turns the volume up to drown me out. This is pointless. And I knew it. Retreating to the kitchen, I grab my flask and fill it with Jack Daniels. It's not my usual, but it's Mardi Gras. A little goes into my red Solo cup. Who will care if I show up to a ball already drunk? Pouring a little more into the Solo cup, I hear the door open again. Now Addie's already here and the circle of ungratefulness is complete. Let's hope we can get through dinner easily enough so I can make it to the ball.

"Hi Addie. Come help me clean up. Addie! I know I taught you better than that! You barely spend time with your family and now you show up late without even bringing something?" God bless the poor soul who decides to marry her.

"Oh. Sorry, Mom. Wasn't thinking this morning."

"You got that from your father. You be careful or you'll be like him."

"I'm here like you asked, mom. You don't need to project your frustration at Dad on me."

"Don't you start that psychobabble bullshit with me. You go and take some college classes and now you think you talk around me?"

"Whatever. Hi Will."

"Hey."

"What have you been up to?"

"Noth— " Now they think they can act like I'm not even in the room. So hateful.

"Now you're going to ignore me?"

"What options have you left me? You want to fight. I don't. Will isn't trying to fight me so I'm going to talk to him."

"So that's how it is. You're just going to disrespect me," I'm so mad I'm almost stuttering.

"No one is disrespecting you, Mom. I'd prefer to have this visit be pleasant and have a good Lundi Gras."

So hateful. I could have never talked to my mother this way. Her hand would be across my face for the tone alone. My mother, my sister, and my cousins talked down to me like this my whole life. Now the only other woman in my family is doing it. I should slap her. I need to slap her. But I'd end up being the villain they seem to think I am. When I try to tell them how they've turned into monsters, whom I know I didn't raise this way, a lump forms in my throat.

"Well you have a good Mardi Gras," is all I can get out before escaping to the back porch.

The wind blows through the pines above. Deep in the folds of my heart, in the parts I don't share with anyone, that sound comes home to roost. Its whisper was always there when I'd run outside, just like this, waiting to tell me I could do it. I could be quiet because a day would come when I could speak. I could tell my momma or my daddy whatever they wanted to hear because making sure I stay close to them was always more important. The wind holds my secrets. Most of all, the wind doesn't judge. Its attitude never changes no matter what I said into it. And as I tell it my secrets today, huddled in my little gazebo in the corner of the yard, I hear the familiar whisper. I shudder at the cold before asking: When is the day I'll harvest the love I've sown throughout my life? I thought it would be my wedding day. Then when I had babies. Then when my momma died so I didn't have a woman to be beholden to. But the day still isn't here and, if anything, it seems farther away. I don't know what days I have left that are worth waiting for. How many prayers, rosaries, even novenas I said, asking God to open my family to my love. And when that didn't happen, I prayed to have this anger, this resentment, taken from me. But here I am, driven from my house by people who I'm supposed to love and who are supposed to love me.

This can't be God's mercy, because God is fair. He doesn't want me to suffer any more than they do—despite my best efforts to save them from their hateful selves. I know he cannot want me to live as an exile from my own home when my sister gets to have her family come to her whenever she wants. I'm at least as deserving as all these Protestant women in these neighborhoods and their perfect looking little families. Thinking about how Mary stuck with her son, even with a husband that never seemed to be around, reminds me I can find the grace she did. Having never given birth to the Son of God, I need a little more than grace to steel my nerves. In the kitchen I pour another bit of whiskey. I think about starting with Will and working my way to the living room, but in walks John. My nerves and belly are on fire, but my face is as cool as the other side of the pillow. I guess I'll go with what's in front of me.

"Is there any *sac-a-lait* left? Or potato salad?" he asks.

"John, I don't want you to go back to work tonight."

"Tough," he says picking through the breading and crumbs on the greasy paper towel.

"Fine. Then I'll tell it like it is. I don't want you going to another woman's house tonight."

He looks up at me with his nostrils flared, his bloodshot eyes opened as wide as they go. "What?"

"You heard me, John." He walks toward me. He's never hurt me. But there's a reason I never said this. It could be a mistake to stop respecting that feeling.

"I'm going to believe you're drunk right now. Drunk and not crazy. And I don't know where this drunk bullshit is coming from, but it's going to stop right now. I'm heading to work tonight. That's all there is to it."

Twenty-three years of marriage and I'm condescended to, just like my own daughter did earlier. There's nothing left of the man who was so happy, so giddy, the day we said I do; just a shell that looks like him. A shell who doesn't look at me like the mother of his children.

"What about this home? What about me? You always have a priority that doesn't involve us. You always —"

"I'm going to give you one last chance to stop this bullshit." A vein in the middle of his shiny forehead bulges toward me. On the edge of his face his jaw is setting. Shoulders square back like they would at bars when he was in his twenties and spoiling for a fight. Despite all the whiskey, my heart beats out of my chest. With the exception of a few quick punches exchanged with my cousins under the pines of my grandmother's house, I've never been part of anything physical. Surprisingly, I'm not afraid. I want the next thing to happen. If he does it, I can finally stop waiting for it.

"If you beat me, what do you think my Daddy will do?"

His jaw relaxes. His shoulders hunch. "Huh," he says with a slight smile. He wants to say something clever. The smile fades, along with his presence in the kitchen. Truck tires peel out in the driveway and John is gone to return who knows when. Well, since the kids left somewhere in the middle of all that, I guess I did technically take the house back, even if I'm alone again.

The green dress sparkles from where it hangs in my bedroom. Left on its hanger, I transfer my wallet and other odds and ends from my purse to my clutch. Digging around for my dark red lipstick I feel something funny. From the bottom of my purse comes the little crucifix what's-her-face gave me. How long has it been since someone gave me something? And she didn't even know me. My world is upside down when strangers think about me more than my own family. I put it in the clutch and apply my lipstick.

Chapter 27

By some voodoo I manage to get my flask out of my bra without flashing George Hidalgo. Now I can't get it back in. George smiles a little too much. They don't even put a break in between that two-step and the waltz we're now slowing down for. So, I politely say I'm tired and head for the sidelines. Plopping down on my seat next to Betsy Fontenot I let out a big breath. She insists on always being between me and her husband. She smiles like a cottonmouth. I don't know what she's worried about. Between the fur in her husband's ears, and his skinny legs, he looks like a damn mule. John really should be here. He is no fun on the dance floor but at least he'd make all of these sideways glances stop.

Pauvre bete, Mr. Hildago. He looks pitiful across the dance floor. It must be two years since his wife died. I bet it's hard coming to these balls without her. We're both pitiful. I don't even know where my kids are right now. I hope they are having fun. I hope God is protecting them.

"Bee why you frownin' so much on Lundi Gras?" Since Alice Hoffpauir started heading Krewe de Bijou, she thinks she's in charge of how much fun we have, the bossy old goat.

"I was frowning thinking about my kids. Hmm. That didn't come out right." She's even got me watching what I say now.

"Why don't you go get another dance with Hidalgo instead? He's had his eye on you all night."

"He has not."

"What's he doing right now?"

Sure enough, there's old Hidalgo, looking away when my eyes reach him. He fumbles his Miller Lite all the way to his lips. His head turned, I can see how he still has all of his hair. John hasn't had hair like that since his early thirties. Ok Beatrice. That's a sin. You're married. And he probably misses his wife. Now he's looking at me. He's caught me laboring through all this in my drunken head. Wait, is that a wink? It must be, because now he's walking toward me. What am I supposed to do? What do other married women do without their husbands around? Panic tells me to go to the restroom.

The toilet seat is pleasantly cold on my ass. Everything needs to go down a degree or two, to slow down. Whiskey is like a hot lover: gets you worked up fast but leaves you feeling dirty and used after. My breath runs back in my nostrils as I fan myself. Holy shit, I'm drunk. My thoughts come in fits and spurts, interrupted by the slamming of stall doors and conversations of other drunk women. Trying to hold the thoughts in my head, hold my dress above my waist, and hold my purse under my arm, proves to be too much of a juggling act in my current state. The purse falls to the tiles, spilling out. I dive for the rolling lipstick and fall headfirst into the wall of the stall. Not wanting to kneel on the dirty, sweating floor to get my balance, but not having a sure footing in these damn heels, I let my head continue to balance me against the stall wall as my left hand chases after the lipstick. My bare ass is now wobbling in the wind. Wind is what it is because all this *misère* after that jambalaya has farts busting out of my ass faster than I can catch them. Having caught the lipstick, I use my head to push off the stall wall and plop back down on the toilet. It's only now I can see I knocked open the stall door in the commotion.

Standing outside watching me are Betsy Fontenot and Alice Hoffpauir. Betsy's smile is that of a snake with its fill. Alice looks like she just found her next party. Behind them I can see in the mirror my hair is flattened on the side I used as a counterbalance. My makeup runs with sweat. My dress falls underneath my bare ass, into the toilet.

"You got it, Bee?" Alice asks.

A stare is all I can offer back.

“You need some help?” Betsy hums as if she’s singing along to my embarrassment.

“No,” I finally respond, “I think I got it now.”

I sit up, pulling the door shut, feeling water drip down from dress onto my calves. My teeth sink into the heel of my hand until I hear them leave the bathroom. Then the sobbing starts. How much more do you have for me, God? What did I do to deserve all this? I don’t know how I’m getting home. I should have thought this through better. Feeling so *honte*, so ashamed, I don’t think it matters what happens now. I need a fire exit. I pull my soggy underwear back up where it belongs and wonder if there are alarms on the back doors. Picking up and then dropping the contents of my purse convinces me preserving my dignity doesn’t matter now. The last thing I pick up is the crucifix Julie’s friend gave me. Its wear and tear looking out of place in a pristine Hilton bathroom, the Savior attached still seems serene. It’s timeless and simple like the ones I’d see on rosaries at the Five and Dime when I was a kid. This is the only friendly thing I think I have in my life right now. It's like when Julie walked into my shop for the first time. Her first impulse was to help. Like sun after a good afternoon summer thunderstorm, a small smile appears long enough to stop the tears.

Almost no words pass between Julie and me when she picks me up. She barely let me finish my tearful phone call to tell me she was on her way. We go about a mile before I realize we are not heading toward my house. A sober thought finally arrives. Julie might have been otherwise occupied when I called her at midnight on Lundi Gras. Wherever she is taking me, I'm not ready to handle any more *tracas*. I need home and a bed, my own empty bed.

“Julie, I’m sorry. But home is back that way.”

“I know. I’m not taking you home. You look like you could use some taking-care-of.” The words are a chorus. They’re the words I wanted when I walked in from the wind earlier today. But who is saying them is suspect. I’m getting pictures of some séance or a feminist pep rally. "We'll tone down our weird, wild women stuff. We want to make sure you're ok." In this damn whiskey drunk I can't tell if I'd been talking out of my head, or she knows me better than I know myself at this moment.

The hippie smell still hangs in the air, making me sleepy and making my headache lessen. Jackie is standing in her cluttered hallway with a cup of coffee in one hand and a bottle of wine in the other. "Do you want to crawl out or dive in deeper?" A deep belly laugh begins before I know what is happening. Having asked myself that question many a night, I collapse to the floor, still laughing. I'd be asking that question of myself, alone in my house, had I gone home. Continuing the hysterical laugh, I point to the coffee. She tosses a sweat suit my way and motions to the bathroom, handing me the coffee on the way. The bathroom is spotless. She doesn't have kids, so I don't need to feel bad about how dirty our bathrooms are at home. Again, I struggle with the zipper on my dress. Without knowing how long I've been doing this, Jackie walks in, unzips my dress, and refills my cup. It all happens before I have a chance to protest. With how fast she came in and out, it's hard to think she was trying to see me naked. The lacy bra I bought last week, for no one to see, comes off too. Naked except for my panties, I look in the large mirror. I see something that looks like it crawled out of a crawfish pond. My legs wither. Words try to come out of me, trying to explain what happened to me to make me like this. But the whiskey still rules my tongue and only nonsense makes it out of my mouth. So focused on my lamenting I never notice the hands cleaning my face and pulling the bobby pins from my hair. They pull the sweatpants over my legs and the top over my head without ever touching my body. There is no choice but to accept their help. Strangely unconcerned by the fact these two women, whom I was convinced were some *sorcières*, are brushing out the hairspray and refilling my cup. This time a tablespoon of white paste is stirred furiously into it. They did all of that so they could drug me.

"Coconut oil," she explains. "It'll help with the hangover."

"I need some boudin."

"Fresh out," she says with a pleasant smile. "Now you stay in here as long as you like. We'll be in the living room chatting when you feel like joining us."

Dreading how she's tainted my Community, I taste the coffee. It doesn't have sugar but doesn't seem like it needs it. Another sip confirms it's not terrible. I've never tasted poison, except in the form of my family's hostility, and it definitely doesn't taste like this. This tastes like someone caring, for once. Beginning to feel human again, I notice more of the bathroom, other than how clean it is. There is a picture of a man in the little hutch over the toilet. It looks like it's from the eighties. He's shirtless… and he should be. They don't make men like that anymore, I don't think. Tan, muscles, and hair in the right places, Jackie has taste in more than good coffee.

Barely outside of the opening of the living room, I listen to their soothing voices. There is a freedom in the way they talk I don't understand. They say things which make no sense to me, but the other always gets it. They don't seem to ever misunderstand each other. While I enter as silently as my drunkenness will allow, I watch their movements. They seem choreographed and synchronized, more things they seemed to have agreed on and practiced for years. They sit as they did before, sprawled on their covered couches. It's still cluttered. But having seen the bathroom I know now it's not dirty. Their goblets of wine swirl as they gesture and laugh.

"Feeling better yet?" Julie asks.

"Yes. Much. Thank you. I'm so sorry about the bathroom. That y'all came in and saw—"

"Your breasts?"

My downward facing eyes cruise up to meet their eyes. The honesty in them diffuses the crass talk.

"Yeah."

"Happens to the best of us."

Sitting in the same chair I did the first time I came here, I relax all the way into it. It is a nice chair.

"Rough night?" Jackie asks.

"Mmm," I mumble, staring into my cup. A replay of Hidalgo, and the stall, and the looks of those two old crows is replaying there.

"Where was John?" Julie asks from the other side.

"Working." I can feel their eyes on me as I stare into my coffee. Catching them communicating to each other with a look, I try to explain. "His job is unpredictable. He never knows if he's fixing to get on the road to go check on one of his tools at any moment."

"And what's that like for you?"

What kind of question is that? What is it like? It's like a lie. But I can't tell them that. "It is what it is."

"And what is it?" Jackie continues.

"Who's the man in the picture in the bathroom?" I hope she'll be nice enough not to make me answer the last question.

"Thomas? He's my ex-husband."

"Oh, I'm sorry," I say, wondering immediately why I said that. She must not be in a bad place if she keeps a picture of him in her bathroom for everyone to see.

"I'm not. It was something amazing. And then it wasn't. He wanted kids. I couldn't have them."

"Oh, I'm really sorry." And I mean it this time.

"Are you always this sorry for things that aren't your fault, Bee?"

What is it with all these questions? Who talks like this? Apologizing is good for everything. When things are uncomfortable for someone, I apologize. If they misunderstand me, I apologize. If I tell them the truth… my truth… I apologize. Because it's always easier when it's my fault.

"I guess I think about what that must be like to not be able to bear children."

"A mixed bag, like most things. It sucks not to have that big piece of womanhood. A piece that seems to define us more often than not. But on the other side of it, I got to have pieces of me, experiences of being a woman, I probably would not have had otherwise. You know? What are some things you always wanted to do but couldn't because you were too busy being a mom?"

"Oh, I don't know."

"Oh come on. Think about it. When did you have your first baby? How old were you?"

"Twenty-two."

"Ok, well then think back to your twenty-two-year-old self. When she looked into the future, what did she see?"

"Just babies. Babies and maybe owning a store. Which I have now."

"That's it?" Jackie asks, surprised. Now I'm getting irritated. This is what I was afraid of. They think I'm not liberated enough or something.

"She would have wanted to be running her own Krewe, I bet." Julie laughs in her betrayal. At first I'm angry because she dragged me into this free woman crap again. When my face stops flushing, and I entertain the thought of my own krewe, I get a little excited.

"Let's stop," Jackie interrupts, watching my face closely. "Bee's night has been hard enough. You don't need to be sorry for anything said or not said tonight. And I've made my peace with what was. Now, you look like you're feeling better. We could either bring you home or you could stay here." I stare into my coffee cup. A new picture swirls into focus. A house, empty, with me crying out my loneliness floats there. I take a sip and look again. The image remains. If I sit here long enough, between saying I want to go home, and not saying anything, I can stretch out this moment where I don't have to choose. "Or there's a compromise. We could talk until you feel like going home. And you can pick what we talk about." Jackie smiles. Julie does too.

"I don't want to impose. And I got to get to the parade early tomorrow. I have to be on the float by seven."

"We can get you there," Julie offered.

Their couch must have been more comfortable than my bed. I can't even remember closing my eyes and then Jackie was shaking me gently to tell me it was five. Julie hasn't complained about a single thing this morning; not waking up at five after staying up until one, not driving me home for clothes and a shower, not during the forty-five minutes it took me to pick something to wear under my costume—in fact she even cheerfully gave me opinions and options. Not even now, as she walks a half mile from where she parked, with an armful of bagged beads that aren't even hers, does she do anything but smile.

"*Bien merci*, Julie. I can't thank you enough."

"My pleasure, Bee," Julie replies with genuineness. I climb onto the float quickly before Betsy and Alice see. But it's too late.

"Beatrice Mouton? Good morning! I didn't know if you would make it, seeing how much fun you were having last night."

"Good morning, Alice. Yeah. It was rough there in the beginning, but I'm here and ready to throw."

"Who's your friend?" Alice's face has all the practiced pleasantness of a Southern woman who doesn't like what she sees and wouldn't dare show it. I hope my version of that face isn't this obvious.

"Alice this is Julie Denburg. Julie is my partner in my store."

"You never told me you had a partner?" Alice adds extra surprise to the statement to make sure I feel framed. I look up at Julie, feeling horrible. It's true I don't talk about her much. Look at how much she's done for me since last night, or even since the moment she walked in my life. There are a million things to choose from which could explain this away or change the subject. Trying to decide on which one could show Julie it was not intentional—though it was— and get Alice to focus on something else, I'm cut off.

"Oh Bee doesn't need to talk about me," Julie says back, matching Alice's contrived pleasantness. "She does so much it's easy to be a silent partner. It's a pleasure to meet you."

"Denburg, you said, Beatrice? Where are you from Julie?"

"Here," Julie says with continued and unwavering pleasantness. "Born and raised in Lafayette."

"Oh. Well it's nice to meet you."

"Yes, Julie is home grown. And a really hard worker," I finally say. I'm not sure if that helped anything.

"Ok," Alice says as if she's had enough of the conversation.

"Bee, I need to let you go. I bet there's a lot of things y'all need to do to get going. Jackie and I will be at the corner of Oakview Boulevard and Johnston, right in front of Fatima church. We'll be looking for you!"

"That's a popular spot. You might have a hard time finding a place to stand," Alice critiques.

"Oh, I know. But that's been our spot since my Momma was a little girl. And I'm sure at least two of my seven cousins are drinking there already, wondering why I didn't join them. So I better get going, too." She leans in and gives me a kiss on the cheek. "Have fun Bee. We'll be looking for you."

The crowds are big, big this year. They seem to get bigger every year. I wonder if people are coming here instead of New Orleans. The thought makes me throw a little less often. But anyone with a Ragin Cajuns shirt gets at least two beads. And of course the kids and babies get some throws. Around Jefferson I take a big sip of my beer and take stock of how much I've thrown. I'm doing ok. I look up in time to see some of my cousins screaming my name. From the looks of it they've been partying all night. I remember it was Vilain's going away party.

Without even opening a bag of beads I toss it to them, and they drunkenly fight over them. I'm glad I didn't go.

We're getting close to Kathy's spot. Looking for hips bigger than mine, and her dirty blond hair that always needs some touching up, I catch sight of T-Guste. Somehow Kathy managed to wrangle her son into coming down to the parade with her. Down in my gut I feel the guilt only a mother can feel at having not gone home to my son last night. But it doesn't matter. He seems happier when I'm not around. My thoughts return to having fun on this float.

"Hey boy! T-Guste!" I yell. He looks up as I catch him in the chest with a cup. He's too surprised and too clumsy, and someone grabs it away from him. Surveying the crowd around him I find Kathy a few feet away. Opening a bag of candy to the ground, I get all the little Black kids distracted, and pitch her the big beads I ordered especially for her. Only in this moment, at this time of year, do I get this smile from her. Despite all of her damnation, she likes how I connect her to the good Mardi Gras. Her hands immediately go back up, waiting for the next throw. She doesn't look at me again. I take another big sip of beer.

We're pulling through USL and I start looking for Addison. Finally, I hear her voice. The only good beads I have left are the ones I bought for myself. I pitch those down to her and follow it up with my last moon pie. She, too, smiles back up at me like I'm the momma she still wants. Pulling past her I feel naked with only trash adornment left around my neck. Sipping my beer, I remember Julie. I didn't keep any good beads for her. Sifting through the bags at my feet, none magically manifest themselves. We're getting close to Julie. The float stops a few lights away from Fatima because Alice wants to offload to some of the clients at her husband's law firm. While she's distracted, I take the chance to steal a box of moon pies from Alice's stash. Passing the Ground Pati, we arrive in front of Julie's street. Quickly spotting her, I begin unloading everything I got, quantity and quality alike. Alice, too, unloads double, triple the haul I'm dropping onto them. Julie, and what looks like her nephews and nieces, love it. As I wave like a *coullion*, I spot Jackie. I wave harder. When we're finally out of eyesight, I chug the rest of my beer and look at Alice.

"She seems nice," she yells over the sound of Wayne Toups singing "Please Explain." I ignore her and keep waving.

Chapter 28

"That's what Tiffany told me," Kathy says with a little too much relish. The smile she'd given me at the parade is gone, replaced by a smug one. Instead of reacting to rumors circulating about my William being gay, I flip bacon.

"You're not going to say anything?" she asks. If I say something, she gets to tell me what a bad mother I am. If I say nothing, I'm complicit in my son fooling around with other boys. There's no room for me to even be *honte* about who my son is becoming. A sister is supposed to support me through the tough times instead of rubbing my nose in them.

"What should I say Kathy? You know my son's a little weird. But I would consider my source if I were you."

"You calling your niece, my daughter, a liar?"

"No, Kathy. I'm calling my niece a drama queen in college. I don't know how—"

"Stop right there, Bee. I don't think you've come down off that float yet. My daughter is telling it like it is. If anything, she's trying to protect your son and your family's reputation."

"Oh, both of you are so selfless."

"You see, this is your problem. You blame everybody else for your problems. I see more and more why no one wants to be around you."

"Where's YOUR husband, Kathy?"

"Here you go again. You're going to try and turn your problems with your kids, and your husband, back around on me. You need to look in the mirror, Beatrice Mouton. That's the only person you need to be talking to like that."

"*Arrête ce combattre. Mais* why y'all ain't done cooking yet? Y'all stop all dat nonsense and finish what y'all are cooking. I doan want to be driving home in da middle of da night," Daddy says with a growl.

"We weren't fighting, Daddy. Just discussing." Kathy says, kissing him on the cheek, that little Judas.

"Y'all can visit while we eat or when we drink coffee." He's in a mood. He's always like this when he comes back from visiting Momma's grave. She was always so mean to him. Going there must hurt.

"I got to chop bacon to put in the green beans. You'll have to come kiss me," I tell him. He does, gruffly. "How was Momma?"

He opens the lid to the chicken fricassee and stirs. "You need more water. It's gonna burn, dat," he grumbles over my shoulder. He always makes his fricassee so thin. And he always tells me how he likes mine.

"I got it, Daddy. Go pour you some coffee and sit down. You been to mass yet?"

"I will. What y'all was talking about when I walked in?"

"Oh nothing, Daddy. Sister stuff." I offer, hoping to cut Kathy off.

"Yeah," she starts. Here it comes. "We were talking about some problems Will's been having."

"What kind of problems?"

"It's nothing big daddy. Let's drop it."

"Bee, *tais toi*! You doan speak to you Daddy like dat. I can go right back home if you gonna be so hateful. You been breaking dat fifth commandment."

Covering the green beans to steam with the bacon, I look up to see Addie wearing the same pleased face as my sister. I can tell it's my roasting she relishes. Pulling the bread from the counter I break it up. It wasn't in my shopping cart. Who bought this? If I can't keep track of my own kitchen, what else am I missing? Everything needs to slow down. All these people working each other, to tell me I'm doing everything wrong, need to sit down and eat. Kathy calls Will to the table.

"Kathy, how was Vilain's party?"

"It was a Breaux party for sure. They damn near tore the place down."

"Daddy, did you go?"

"Me? No. Dat's too late to be driving around. I cain't see at night no mo."

"I would have drove you, Daddy," Kathy says eagerly. "Everyone wanted to see you."

"Dey know where I live."

"You should have seen Vilain, though. He was so drunk he couldn't figure out if he should cry or laugh."

The mood is lightening a little. They are not as concerned with what I did, or did not, do for them. The food and the conversation fixes everything, like usual. But also, like usual, this is not the case for Will. He mopes and picks at his food. His little mouth used to flap away when he'd come home, telling me about his day, the good parts and the bad. His little world is filling up with all the false promises of MTV and video games. Now he has a friend he won't talk about. No one here can appreciate how hard I've tried to protect him. They don't understand what's happening. I can't let Will slip away.

"Daddy did I tell you Will has a little friend now?"

"No. He tole me. Dat's good."

"When did he tell you?"

"When we went fishin'."

"What's he like?" Kathy asks to spite me. If she wasn't my sister, I'd swear she is smiling at the thought of my boy turning out like John. She has never liked how Daddy spent more time with Will than her little angel, T-Guste. It's time to reign Will in. When I tell him I don't like how he's been acting, and who he's been with, I make sure they all see it so they know this family is not falling apart because of me. But Daddy cuts me off, taking sides.

"*Mon Dieu,* Bee. It's not like dat's his boyfriend." This is the conspiracy Will was cooking up. He's trying to turn his Paw Paw against me. Whatever he told my Daddy, Will likely left out how this boy is from a godless part of the country. Daddy doesn't know what's happening.

"Daddy this is not like when we were growing up. We either knew everyone in town or we were related to them. Nowadays—"

"He's gonna be able to go to war in two years, Bee. You got all dese opinions about tings you don't know nuttin' about and you tink we want to hear what you tink."

If someone would open a window, letting the wind rush through so I could scream into it, maybe I could get their attention. I think about sitting on Jackie's bathroom floor. At least they would tell me how I'm a good mother. The scene plays out so vividly in my head, similar to ones from when I was a little girl, that I almost forget I'm in my kitchen with my unhappy children, *mon bouledou* of a sister, and my grumpy father. Looking up, everyone stares at their fricassee, except for Daddy. He chugs his coffee and glares at me. I still need to make this right, make this family right. They need to see how what I do is made out of love.

"How was your visit with the doctor, Daddy?"

"Fine," he says gruffly.

"What'd he say?" Kathy asks, mid-bite.

"He said I'm helty."

"Did he run any tests?" I continue.

"Yeah, he ran tests."

"Well what did those say?" Kathy continues. For all her faults, Kathy at least worries about Daddy as much as I do.

"That's for the doctor to know."

"But Daddy, you—"

"Dammit you two!" He may be angry because we're getting in his business now, but at least he knows why. He understands this fretting is love. He understood it for over fifty years from our Momma.

All of the other men in my life lost themselves in drink, at least for a little while, but I'm not letting my son do it. Will knows that. So I'm floored when he comes home drunk with John. Especially after he'd had such a good day fishing with the one good man in his life, his Paw Paw. I wasn't going to say anything at first, but he is being turned against me by his father. I'm done playing nice with John. Back in the kitchen, I open the cupboards and start a landslide of pots and pans. Seeing Will wince at the noise, seeing how hungover he is, I pull more down.

"What the *FUCK* Beatrice?!" There's the monster now, his shriveled penis hanging out of his underwear like a caveman. "Why in the hell you got to make so much goddamn *noise?*"

"I thought that's what you do when people are sleeping. At least I'm not drunk while I'm doing it. And at least I'm not getting our underage son drunk while I do it. The worst that can happen when I'm making noise is that he learns how to cook."

"Holy shit Beatrice! You're going off about bringing our son home safe?"

Will makes his exit. I really wish he'd stay. He should see this.

"Well?" John asks. "You going to say anything now that Will is gone and you don't have to act like you're in charge?"

"You're being a bully, John."

"And you're being a bitch." Having heard that insult before, from different people, it doesn't hurt. Except this person doesn't have a whole lot of room to call people names.

"Be careful, John," I say grabbing my Magnalite pot and heading for my cutting board.

"You threatening me?" His voice is low. I know what he's thinking. My eyes find the window over the sink. Branches shake as the wind blows through them.

"No," says my voice, though not really sounding like my own. His eyes venture down to my hands and lock on to something there. When he looks back up at my face his fury has turned to fear. The scar on his neck turns purple against the rest of his flushed skin. He continues to look, to watch me, as he backs out of the kitchen. The front door slams, followed by the door of his truck. I wait until the screaming from his tires is distant before I look down to see what he saw. I'm holding my grandma's old chef's knife. The white in my knuckles fade back to pink as I drop it on the cutting board. My shaking hands hurt from holding it so hard. John saw something hidden, something maybe only the wind knew was there. Shaking my head, I call for Will and reorganize pots in the cupboard until he arrives.

"Can you wash the bell peppers and celery, *mon 'tit garçon*?"

"Sure."

I can feel his apprehension. Now is an important moment to try and rebuild our love after so many people tried to pull us apart. Grandma's knife in my hand, I slice through celery. I worry I made a cut too deep, sending a split through the core of this family. This knife is supposed to be a tool for love. It was Grandma's tool, then my Momma's tool, to share love with our family. Now I've used it to sever love. Its purpose tainted, it seems useless now, like the crucifix Jackie gave me. Except I have to wonder who in this scenario sits on the crucifix, the piece broken off from the whole and the holy.

As the days pass, I feel worse and worse for how I acted with John. I wasn't really going to cut him. It was just the way my hand was positioned. I have to keep telling myself that so I believe it. But it's not enough. Extra rosaries don't help. Daddy is the only one who knows what to do with this, to put all of this back together so it makes sense.

Thankfully he agrees to come to Dean-o's tonight and try pizza for the first time.

"I'm so glad you decided to let me take you out tonight. We haven't done this in so long. I miss my time with my Daddy. I get so lonesome. Our family isn't the same. I guess this is how it's going to be now."

"Whatchu talking about, Bee?" he screams over the Dean-o's din. He's trying not to be annoyed.

"Well I see Addie less and less since she started college. And Will is going out with his friends he won't talk to me about. And John—"

"Kids are supposed to grow up, Bee."

"I know Daddy," I respond before a big gulp of wine. I don't know how to get to it. I'm not sure what I'm even getting to. How do people have conversations like this?

"Bee, why can't you let tings just happen? Why you have to try and make it fit da purdy little picture in you head?"

"Because they're pictures of how we used to be... how we should be. They—"

I'm interrupted by the large Tee Rex placed in front of us. Placing a slice on a plate, I hand it to daddy. He inspects it.

"What's dat?"

"Pizza." Not explanation enough, I continue with, "It's got six different meats on it." He still doesn't take it and I drop the plate in front of him. Dishing my own slice, I try to finish my thought. "We don't love each other. I mean I love my kids. They seem to love their father. They seem to love each other. But we don't seem to be able to all love each other at the same time."

He pulls off a big piece of Canadian bacon and chews on it for a while. He looks up at me and says, "*Tu crois que tu es au supplice. Tu tracasses. Tu pleures. Mais toute ta famille s'adonne. À ce moment, personne n'a partie. N'oublie pas, ça.*"

“Daddy don’t talk that much French in public. They’ll think we have webbed feet. And I don’t see how you think my family gets along.”

“Bee, nah listen. I’ma talk like I talk. If dey couldn’t beat French out of me at school den some looks from people in a restaurant ain’t gonna change dat. Dere parents spoke French, too.” He exhales, picking off a few pieces of meat and stuffing them in his mouth. “You always hear just what you wanna hear. I said no one left. Even if y'all are fighting, y'all are still togedder. *Tu comprends?* Y'all still have a chance to fix dat. *Lâche pas la patate.*”

"How, Daddy? How am I supposed to fix them?”

His grey eyes level on me and he scratches at his steely stubble. The sound it makes is a whisper, as if what he wants to say won’t be able to make it to words, and just his gestures have to tell me.

“It’s not da same anymore,” he finally says. “It’s like wit French. People move on. Dey figure ott deir own way. Mix some French wit deir English. Keep some of da past, do something new.”

“I know. That’s the problem, Daddy.” The way he turns his head to look around the restaurant makes it feel like he can’t look at me right now. I don’t know what I did wrong.

“It’s a problem for us, not dem. Your way isn’t my way. You work in a sto instead of keep house. You go out witchou girlfriends instead of family. Nah, deir Cajun gonna look different dan your Cajun.”

“They’re just work friends,” I say. If that’s what this is about I can set him straight. “They just—"

“It’s good you got friends. Dey’ll be family when da kids leave.”

His eyes meet mine again and my face gets hot. I can’t tell if it’s from anger, sadness, or embarrassment. “It’s not the same,” is all I say. I wish I could scream. What does he want me to do? Fix my family, or live alone? He scratches the steel wool on his chin again. He pulls at another piece of Canadian bacon and chews it slowly.

"When cars stopped using carburetors, I hated dat. Dey weren't simple no more. Everybody wanted someting din't burn so much gas. Engines change so fast nah I don't understand them. But dey work. Dey last a long time and dey cheaper. Dey make sense to da young mechanics, da ones who have to work on dem. Dat's what matters"

"Daddy, you know I don't get engines. That's a man's work."

His face turns to pity. It's better than having him expect to move in two different directions at once. Pity is tender. It's better than the anger he had for us when we were little. I wonder if I'll ever be enough to him. His eyes go back to the pizza and he grabs a whole slice and takes a bite. He smiles. "*Mais,* I like dat, me." He puts it down and looks at the condiments. He adds a little of each to the pizza and keeps going. He swallows hard. He's getting tired of talking about this. Whatever he's trying to tell me, this is my last shot to understand it. "Bee, hurricanes always gonna come. You can try and tie ever'ting down, fix da tings the wind breaks. But a tree never worries about dat. The top may bend, and a few pieces may break. Da tree just finds a way to do wit'out dat limb or grow in a new spot. Hurricanes don't bodder trees. When dat wind starts blowin', plant dem roots *ma fille.* You a Chenevert, a green oak. Dem roots are long, and strong."

I shove another piece of pizza in my mouth to keep from shouting. He acts like this is so easy. He gets to say what he wants because he's the Paw Paw, he's the big man. I'm over here trying to hold my grip on being a mom. Even being a wife is ending. He should be able to understand two people growing apart in a marriage.

"You remember how you were with John when we first met at college. You were so upset when I enrolled at USL. You thought it was a waste of money to send a girl to college. But then you were so proud when you met John. At our wedding you never stopped smiling. You loved that I found a husband and I was settling down to make a family. That's doesn't look the sa—"

"I wasn't upset you went to school, *cher.*"

"Yes you were, Daddy. Remember? You'd— "

"I know what I remember. I remember you being sad you din't have no boyfriend. I was upset because you looked so *bouder.* You'd come home and cry. It broke you poor Daddy's heart. When you got married to John, and you was finally happy, you Daddy was happy. I was proud you figured dat out."

"Except John is not like he used to be."

"All dese 'used to be's.' You not da same eida, *cher.* You used to go for what you want and not be afraid to try. Like you school. Like you sto. Like you marriage."

"Daddy, you don't understand."

"I understand enough. I understand you so spoilt you gotta make problems for youself," he says before going to the bar to get a whiskey. Since it's getting so late, he probably wants to go home. I pushed this too hard. He comes back as the check arrives.

"You know the waitress could've brought that to you."

"She take too long. And you would have been talking da whole time."

Chapter 29

"Are you going out?" I ask from the sink, knowing he isn't going anywhere. A mother knows. The excitement isn't there. Just his usual slouch. I'm so happy to see it back. He agrees to watch a movie with me. We settle in and he's already closing his eyes. In this half-conscious state he might give me more answers about his life than he normally does. Daddy always says if you get someone drunk, angry, or half dreaming, they'll tell you the truth every time.

"Will, who is the boy you've been going out with lately?"

Even half asleep he says little, like he always does. The person who sleeps across the hall from me won't let me in on his life. We've always left things unsaid to protect the sanctity of our home. And the grief over what I'm losing, and will continue to lose, pushes the tears out. I hide them at first. But this is what's in my heart. Julie and Jackie didn't make me apologize for what I feel. I shouldn't have to do it in my own home with my own son.

"Will... I'm so alone."

"Why do you say that?" he asks, finally opening his eyes.

I tell him what it's like to struggle keeping this family together. Did Virgin Mary feel this way trying to keep her son alive? But when I look up at my son's warm, brown doe eyes, I don't see love and acceptance. Only pity is there. I've made a fool of myself, throwing my sanity at my own son's feet. It could all be worth it if I get to keep someone who needs me in my life. What would Mary do?

"I'm leaving, Mom. I'm going away to college after next year."

It's almost as if I can hear the devil himself laughing at me. Will's cold eyes look at me with almost no recognition. In trying to be a good mom, who loves her son unconditionally, I've overlooked how he's changed, and turned out like everyone else.

"Where are you going?"

"Does it matter? I'm going away, mom. I can't be this little Cajun boy anymore. This place isn't me. This food isn't me. These people aren't me."

"How long were you going to wait to tell me?"

"I don't know."

Looking at him hurts. I get up to look out of the window at something, anything else. All I see is my reflection in the darkened glass.

I give him one last chance. "I thought you were different. I thought you cared about me."

"This isn't about you."

"It isn't? I'm your mother! I'm who brought you into this uncaring world! The one who wiped your ass and fed you. I was your friend when you had none! And now the minute you make a friend it's ok for you to leave. Tell me which part isn't about me."

"This isn't normal, Mom."

"What? What isn't normal?"

"It's not normal to spend your whole life down the road from your parents. It isn't normal to look at the rest of the world as strange and amoral and cultureless. It isn't normal to judge how good a person is by the color of their roux and who their cousins are."

"You are too young to understand. You're trying to decide who you are by who you don't want to be. You will see how much family matters when you go out in the world and no one loves you like we do."

What he can't see, what I must show him, is that he's chasing a mirage. He's only seeing the rest of the world on MTV. He thinks people will be there for you, take care of you. The world doesn't care about people like us. The British wanted us to swear allegiance to their king in *Acadie,* but Cajuns serve only God. They told us we could keep our religion and our land at first. Daddy told me the real story told to him by his great grandfather, who was told by his father, a survivor of the *Grand Dérangement*, of how we were cast out of Eden by our "caretakers." My great-great-great-grandfather was only seven when they put him on a boat never to see his home and much of his family again. Later, here in Louisiana, they say they love us, promote our food and our music all over the world, but then treat us like we're ignorant, barely better than Blacks. He can't see yet how only the tie of blood can make sure people will stand by you, love you, and never leave you. Will goes on about how much he hates our way of life, right before stabbing me in the heart.

"Paw Paw told me I should leave."

The devil laughs again. The only solid thing I have left beneath me is where my Daddy stands. But he's been filling Will's head with another story since the Sunday before Mardi Gras. I get it now, Jesus. I've had it all wrong. I've been fighting a lost battle. I need to accept it. The last two people I thought would love me have figured something else out. If he's telling Will this, no telling what else Daddy is saying about me when I'm not there. No more point in lowering myself for their pity.

"You're right. You need to find your path. But you don't have to use my father to try and hurt me."

The house will eat me, I'm sure of it. I leave because I don't want to have it take anything else from me tonight. Behind the steering wheel the tears slow, and then stop. Numb is what I want. I want a drink, but I don't want to go to a bar. I go to the next best place. Neither of them ask me why I want to spend the night. They don't ask why I don't talk about Will, or my Daddy, or anyone. They let me talk. They let me be silent. My wine glass never empties. At some point I fall asleep on their couch.

In the morning, Julie takes me to Louisiana Treasures. She handles most of the customers and I drink wine. At closing she drives me to Charlie G's. It's strange being this close to home but not seeing anyone. Jackie meets us at the bar. Her blond hair is tied up in a neat bun above her gray suit. She still doesn't wear makeup, but she looks much older somehow.

"I know. The suit, right?" She catches me staring. "Being an accountant doesn't really fit with the rest of me."

"No, it's just—"

"It's ok. There are days I look in the mirror and wonder if this is me, too."

Moving to a table, the girls talk openly and freely like they always do, not seeming to care who overhears them. At first I enjoy the company of people who seem to like each other. But then I see the looks coming from other tables.

"I'm sorry, Bee. We're going on and on and not including you in the conversation."

"No y'all go ahead. I want to listen," I reassure before scanning the room again. They both follow my gaze.

"They think we're a bunch of lesbians." My eyes whip back around to them. "Let them," Jackie continues. "It isn't the first time, and won't be the last. This way I have the license to act like I damn well please and they'll just think my weird is normal." With a confirmation they are not one of the particularly sinful things I thought they were, I am consoled.

"Were you worried?" Julie asks. I can see she's been watching my face with some amusement.

"Well, I just didn't know. You know?" I exhale.

Jackie smiles. "What else do you worry about in regards to us?" Their eyes peer at me. Why can't they just let some things lie? I remind myself they're not my family. They act like these questions are supposed to make me feel better, instead of put me on edge.

"I worry when y'all talk like you don't believe in God."

They look at each other and giggle again. "You think I grew up that close to Fatima church and never went in?" Julie asks. I shrug.

"Good point," Jackie says, looking at Julie to accept the challenge.

"Jackie and I have kind of come to understand God a little differently than what the church teaches." Wishing I had put my holy water and rosary back in this purse after the ball, I brace myself to hear about their secret identity as witches. "We… um... the way we see God is a lot… well… nicer… than what we were taught."

It must be so easy for them, getting to pick and choose what they believe. "Y'all must think I'm pretty pathetic. I'm a cranky housewife worrying over her little magic beads."

"Quite the contrary," Julie says through a satisfied smile after a long gulp of wine, and a wave to the waiter. "We think you're a pious, loving, amazing daughter, mother, wife, and woman. You take care of your whole family and try to make a home for them. You hold together the language and culture for them. Even when they don't recognize you for doing it." The blood reverses and my face gets hot. They put a name to everything I've ever tried to be. Why can't I get this from my family?

"Are you going to hang out at our place again tonight?" Jackie asks.

"I shouldn't. I need to get back to Will. It's shameful I stayed away again last night. He's probably starving."

"Or in heaven." Jackie laughs heartily, watching the astonishment on my face. "Bee, you have to stop assuming the worst. I said that because of him, not because of you. He's a sixteen-year-old introvert from the sounds of it. He's probably loving the solitude. Or he's probably going out with the new friend you mentioned."

"That's what I'm afraid of. That little *macaque* sounds like *tracas*." A look passes between them. "What?" I bite.

"You didn't go out much as a teenager, did you?"

"Well, shit. What else y'all gonna tell me I been doing wrong all these years?" They smile warmly, but don't offer anything in return. There's no judgement there, despite how much they know about me. I'm ashamed I know so little about them.

"Julie, I know about where you grew up, where you went to church, and that you run my business better than I do. What else can I know about you?"

"Oh Bee, there's not a whole lot to tell. I went to college at LSU, then worked for a while in New Orleans. Went to grad school in Virginia. Came home when my Daddy got sick. I've been here since."

"Virginia? All the way up there with those Yankees?"

She laughs. "You make it sound like it was New York."

"Everything above Marksville is Yankee to me, *chere.*" They both laugh.

"What about you Jackie?"

"My story is not too different. My family wasn't as nice as Julie's, though. And I stayed a while longer up north at college than she did. Northwestern. Chicago."

"Family wasn't nice?"

"Yeah," is all she gives back. Sitting back in my seat Julie's eyes meet mine in unspoken understanding. Jackie's in pain, but she doesn't even want us to console her. Without having to do anything both of these ladies accept themselves, and me, as we are. The ease with which they talk to me makes me uncomfortable. They know so much about me but they're not letting me into their lives. Now this is like my family. How quickly I've gotten used to both their silences and their chatter. My family's problems, something never meant for public consumption, have been too easily divulged. It's messy and wrong. Even if this is what adult friends do with one another, it doesn't make it right.

"I think I made a mistake. Can y'all take me back to my car?"

"What? Why?" Julie asks, nearly spitting out her wine. Jackie puts a hand on her friend. The way Julie immediately understands is both lovely and intimidating. "Before we do, can you tell me for sure that you want to go home because you would rather see what's waiting for you there than stay and share our company?"

"That's not fair. That's not my life. And this isn't my life either. I'm not being the kind of mother I should be." Julie looks at Jackie after I say this. Their faces show pity. I've had enough pity today. I've only needed one thing since the beginning: the love of my family. "What would either of you know? Neither of you are mothers. You sit there, passing condescending looks back and forth. Mothers sacrifice! They put their children first. You would know that if y'all had kids and made hard choices like I had to make."

Chapter 30

Hotels are so sad. All them oil-workers coming and going. I'm sure they'd rather be at home with their families. But here we are, away from our families. They're earning for them. I'm here because my family doesn't want me. Three days through the weekend is the maximum my conscience can take before I go home to cook Will's favorite meal. As much as I want to tell him how hurtful he's been, as much as I want to put him back in the place he belongs, it won't help anything. He's sorry. I know because he's overly nice, using extra "ma'ams" and "thank yous." He goes to school and I go to work. There's a message from Julie. She says she's not feeling well, but swears it has nothing to do with the quiet ride back to my car. I know better. I was so ugly to them. They were just trying to show me a good time. I should cook them something. Thinking of a menu is interrupted by the bell on the door.

"Hi ladies. Thank you so much for coming by."

"Betsy's always told me about your store," Alice Hoffpauir says too nicely. "You have a lot of cute stuff in here." Betsy Fontenot doesn't attempt to mask her disgust.

"Betsy, I still have the stuff I ordered with you in mind. Now it's on post-Mardi Gras sale."

"Hmph," grunts Betsy.

Letting them look around in peace, I go back behind my counter and pretend to look at the computer. There is less room in my life than usual for their judgments today.

"Bee, come tell me about this!" Alice is looking at the jeweled bodice Julie bought this season.

"Oh, that. Well if you really want to step up your Mardi Gras costume..."

"It's scandalous, huh Bee?" Betsy leaves little room in her tone for this to be a question.

"Yes it is," I reply resolutely. "Mardi Gras is supposed to have a little scandal, isn't it?"

"Well you've done your part." Betsy retorts. I don't know why the old bat is buzzing me with her fangs out.

"What do you mean, Betsy?"

"Old Hidalgo sure seemed happy dancing with you." It was ridiculous of me to think they'd had enough of my humiliation in the bathroom stall that night.

"Betsy!" Alice scolds. "What Mrs. Mouton does is her own business."

"No, Alice, it's ok. Hidalgo was hitting on me. And I was enjoying it." The surprise pleasure of the words leaving my mouth is matched by the sight of their jaws dropping. "Every once in a while it's nice to have a gentleman remind you you're sexy. Even when it's not your husband. And that's what this bodice can do for you, too. Are you interested? We can talk about a friends and family discount." Their polite smiles assure me my confession is going back to the Krewe. Did old Bee Mouton finally lose her mind from all that drinking? It's kind of liberating, like Jackie says. I'm free to act crazy if I want to.

"Oh I don't think it would fit me," Alice says.

"Probably not," I respond, warmly. They say their goodbyes, starting their gossip before they even get back to the car.

There's no traffic in the store the rest of the afternoon. Even pouring a glass of wine doesn't help the boredom. I almost regret chasing those two vultures off. The empty time is filled with thoughts of my family, my unkind words to the girls, and my father who doesn't seem to want to help me anymore. When we ate pizza together, he kept trying to get me to do something that isn't possible. He didn't get it.

But today I have all afternoon, time enough to make him get it. Closing shop early I make the drive to Poche Bridge.

"Hey Daddy."

"Bee why you comin' the middle of the day like dat," he huffs from his shed, wiping oil and sweat from his face.

"What are you doing?"

"*Je travaille.* Whatchou want, Bee?"

"It's slow at work and I thought I'd check up on you."

"I'm fine *'tite fille.* If you need some work you can come help me."

"That's man's work."

"Work is work. *Tu connais, ça.*"

"There is something I been meaning to talk to you about."

"*Quoi*?"

"Will."

"What's wrong wit *mon 'tit garçon*?" The way he says it is similar to the tone he used when I was little and I was his *'tite fille.* Life keeps moving, leaving me behind. But my Daddy is a man of principle and values. He won't stand by and let my family crumble. He knows how the Cajun ways work. Even if he doesn't want to, he'll fix this, same way he can bring any motor from his era back to life.

"Will's just been different lately."

"Bee, he's growing up. You got to let go, *cher*. I done tole you."

"I know, Daddy. But he's still in my house for another year. And I'm not talking a little different, no. I'm talking he's mean. He's cold. He's disrespectful."

"Willy?"

"Yes Will."

"Bee, you talked to him? You got a bad habit of calling me before you try to work tings out. You done dat with you sister, you husband—"

"No, Daddy. I've tried. You've seen me. But he doesn't want to talk. He sasses and says things to hurt me. I don't know what I'm supposed to do."

"I'ma see if I can *parler avec lui.* But dis is the last time, Bee. Dis family is yours. God gave you dis family because you need to figure dat out you own way. Time gonna come dey not gonna listen to deir old Paw Paw if I keep telling dem how to live deir lives. Nah, go inside and make some coffee. I'll be dere in a bit. I gotta fix dis motor for ma neighbor before it starts raining."

"No. Daddy. I'll go. You work. *Bien Merci.*"

Now it feels like something got accomplished at work today. But there are other things that need doing. It's hateful what I said to Jackie and Julie. I've already been to confession for it, but now I need their forgiveness. Good thing I know the best tasting penance.

"If it tastes half as good as it smells, it'll be better than anything we've eaten in our house in a long time," Jackie says with a large, joyful, grin.

"It's just a gumbo."

"It's a feast!" Julie sings, refilling my wine.

The praise continues all the way through the meal. Difficult to believe they like it as much as they say they do. They say almost nothing else to me, or each other, focusing on their bowls. When the bowls are empty, they lean back in their chairs, glassy-eyed, rubbing their *ponces.* That's the best compliment a cook can get.

"Y'all are so nice to invite me back like y'all have. I was so horrible the last time we were together."

Now they look at each other. They've talked about this, about me. I can tell. Yet it doesn't bother me. It's comforting in fact. "You were right, Bee. We don't know about motherhood, personally. We're feminist, fornicating heathens. Childless aging women who work and look at art and go to concerts." Jesus help me and prevent my face from showing them how much I agree with them. "People here don't see much use for us. Since we don't have kids, and we're not married, everything else we do doesn't count. There are days I wish my life were more like yours," Jackie says through a sad smile.

The comfort I felt moments before is eroded. Is she being sarcastic? She said it like a fact. The way her flat eyes stay on me, glassy though they may be, tells me she's waiting for a response.

"I don't think you want my life."

"Your life certainly isn't easy. And still with what I know about it, we might trade you. Not because I wouldn't have to deal with judgment. Or because we wouldn't have as many financial issues—"

"But you're an accountant, and Julie—"

"I work for you," Julie chimes in. "You didn't call references, so you didn't talk to my last boss from whom I had to refuse sex daily. He's been getting me back by telling employers how I'd stolen from him and never made a deadline. Jackie's ex saddled her with this house and two other properties. It's a deal that went sour after the divorce. She split it with him because she knew he was no good at money. Now he gets all his income from the properties, so he won't sell and he won't buy her half." Jackie's sad smile begins to hook further downward, her broken heart bleeds through her face.

"I'm so sorry. I had no idea. I'll… I'll give you whatever I can afford. I bet I can get some money from—"

"We don't want money, Bee. We don't want anything from you. But that hasn't stopped you from giving me a job or from treating Jackie with respect. You have things in your life that hurt as well. But you let it go when love is at stake. Somehow, you keep recovering from the hurt. That's why Jackie and I would trade places with you."

We sit, exchanging damaged glances over our empty bowls. Silent cries grow into sobs as we watch each other's pain bubble to the surface like orange grease on the gumbo. In the middle of it all, the weeping turns to giggles. Laughter bursts out in full force. Making my way to each of them in turn, I hug them, the sisters I didn't get to have. Jackie reaches down for the wine bottle.

"Well if wine got us this far, we might as well follow it to the end."

As it turns out, the end must be in Kinder, Louisiana. Tailgating at the casino, we finish our fourth bottle of Zinfandel. Inside I'm met with enough noise and blinking lights to overpower any doubts about this place. The lack of windows disorients time and direction. Quickly thrown into panic when the girls disappear, I begin looking down aisles of slot machines. They return with cards they say act like chips or quarters. They want to play craps. I stick to the nickel machines. This isn't like the antique one my great aunt had. There's no arm, just a bunch of buttons. After three presses, it says I'm a winner – seven hundred dollars' worth. Surprise hits me so hard I don't even make a sound. I look up to see if anyone is watching. The girls remain focused on their craps table.

"That's a pretty good one, honey. Me, I got a fifteen hundred dollar one this past Sunday," a raspy voice says from behind me. A hunched old woman begins to limp down the aisle, pushing her oxygen tank. "You play like Gladys over there does, and you'll be hitting them once a week," she hoarsely calls over her shoulder while motioning to a morbidly obese woman, spilling out of her electric chair. Two oxygen tanks hang from the back. My casino mentor moves on before I can thank her for… well I don't know. Two more times at this machine and I lose several dollars. Another glance at Gladys, and I decide to hold onto my winnings and join Jackie and Julie. They are already walking toward me.

"What's wrong?" I ask, too worried about their faces to tell them about my win.

“The box guy kept staring at my tits, even when I asked him to stop.” Julie says with little blood in her face.

“Well they are out there,” I respond, a little annoyed. Julie gives me a scornful look. “Julie, I’m sorry. But you wear a shirt open like that and men are going to stare.”

More color drains from Julie's face. "I'm going to play some slots."

"Me, too" Jackie agrees.

"I think I'm done. I got jackpot!" I share.

"Well, it's a big casino," Jackie retorts flatly as she walks away. I wish I'd driven myself. This money is a big weekend’s worth of sales in my store. Feeling high class, I wonder what people with money do in casinos when they don't want to gamble. In Vegas they go to shows. No shows are happening for several hours. They eat, too. But, I'm not hungry. There's also those roof top swimming pools. Didn't the girls say they'd packed me a suit?

A full-length mirror in our hotel room shows me something I don't know what to do with. This suit displays more of my body than I'm used to looking at. The way it's cut, though, makes me look nice. The little half skirt hides my hips. The halter pulls my boobs up, making them, and the rest of me, at least ten years younger. Even the red in the suit matches my hair. To my surprise I look longer, turning this way and that, instead of looking away. Somehow my pieces got fitted together. I'd never be caught dead with this somewhere around home. But I'm not home.

None of the people surrounding the pool or in the hot tub seem to care about my presence. Dipping my toes in the water I notice it's been warmed nicely. How long has it been since I swam? The kids were in middle school. I wade in. When my toes can't touch any longer, I begin to float effortlessly, bobbing like an old buoy on my chunky thighs. And I don't care. It's so nice not to care.

"I thought that was you, Beatrice Mouton," a man's voice says from behind me. I turn to find Mr. Hidalgo. His eyes meet my face, but quickly move down to my chest. He must not have seen enough of it at the ball.

"Hi, Mr. Hidalgo. I didn't know you like to come to the casino."

"I come all the time since Sue died." His eyes leave my chest only to survey what floats beneath. No man's eyes have done this in a long time. John never looks at me like this anymore. Writing this off as how men are, another part of me feels guilty for letting him look at me like this. Yet another part wonders why I don't like it, since I never get it. But if I'm honest, like the girls ask me to be, most of me wants his eyes off of all of my pieces.

"Well I'm sure it helps with missing your poor wife."

His eyes meet mine. "She's been gone two years." His eyes go back to roaming. There's nothing to hide behind in this pool. Getting out would only make things worse.

"That's such a short time ago."

"It's longer than you would think. Bee, I never got that last dance with you. Let's you and me talk. I'll go change into my suit and I'll get you a drink. What do you like?"

"Surprise me," I answer. Trying to keep my eyes off the stairs at the opposite end of the pool, he gives me one more look over, and then makes his exit. As soon as the big doors close, I'm out of the pool and heading back to the room. So desperate to get away from those eyes, I take a different way, making sure he can't follow me. I almost get lost. Finally, back inside our room, I crumble to the cold tile of the entryway. Julie and Jackie leave the mirrors where they are reapplying makeup, and rush to my side.

"He wouldn't stop looking at me!" I rasp as they sit next to me, propping me up between their shoulders. It only serves to make me shiver. Julie hugs me tightly, again never asking a question. When I look up to recognition in her eyes, I realize why she doesn't.

"Let's go," she says.

Chapter 31

"Daddy you need to clean up in here," I tell him as I pour coffee into his stained and cracked mugs. There is grime in the corners of the kitchen. The linoleum looks more brown than yellow. His old eyes can't see how bad things have gotten in his home. Seems true for my home, too.

"It's fine, Bee. Why you coming over here early like dat?"

"Sometimes I just need my Daddy, you know?"

"Bee, you can't keep running to me when tings get hard, *cher.*"

"Sure I can."

He takes a long sip of his coffee and his hand shakes a little. That's new. It is cold and early, though. And he does look like I've made him in a bad mood.

"Today is going to be the last time. God gave you dat family because you da one supposed to know how to take care of what you have. You have to go figure out a way."

"Your way always works."

He eyes the pictures on his walls, his brows pumping up and down, like he wishes he could find words to make me understand. I wish the same thing.

"I'm da best mechanic in da next tree parishes. Even I cain't fix a car whose parts is out of production. Nothing works forever."

"Daddy, I didn't come here this morning to argue with you. I'm not trying to make you grumpy. I just wanted to spend time with you."

Getting up from his old leather recliner, the duct tape straining to keep the ragged pieces connected, he sits next to me on his brown plaid couch. Without looking at me, he wraps his arm around my shoulders and pulls me close. My head on his shoulder, I start to cry. My kids reject me. My husband cheats on me. And last night a man tried to take advantage of me. Here is the only place I feel safe and loved. Whatever he's been cooking up with Will washes away with my tears and a big inhale of his smell. Motor oil and my daddy's musk will always smell like home to me.

"Aw, Bee. What I'm going to do witchou? Since you was little you always took it all to heart. It's because your heart is big, big. I always loved dat for you. It's time you start using all dat heart, make room for everybody in it, even you." When I look up at him, he is still staring at the wall. I follow his gaze and see him looking at an old picture of me and Kathy when we were little girls. "You stay home today, Bee. I'ma go to *Moutchon's* game and drive Will. Stay home and take care of you."

If I'd told myself I need a day just to get my heart full and head straight I couldn't do it. Because Daddy told me to, I can stay home, even if it is to clean the house. With the dishes finished I start on the pots, whistling some Bill Withers. This could be what's it's like to stop worrying like Jackie and Julie are able to do. I've made it all the way to the evening without checking on somebody and my family hasn't fallen apart. The quiet in the house is warm. So warm in fact I don't worry about refreshing my dishwater and scrub with the cold, secondhand suds. I know it's the permission Daddy gave me to take care of myself. He's never said something like that, never acknowledged how hard I try, how much work goes into making a family, and the toll that takes on me. My whistle gets loud enough I almost miss the phone ringing in the background. The ID says Lafayette General. It must be some sort of marketing call because I don't know anyone at the hospital. I brace myself for an insurance pitch or something.

"Auguste Chenevert has been in an accident. Your information was found on the back of a picture in his truck. You need to come to the hospital."

Those three sentences make everything else said in the course of a day, or a lifetime, mean nothing. I'd give up all the other spoken sentences of my life to have those three unsaid. To be a loving, happy, respectful daughter was easy. Just keep my mouth shut. I can do that. My hurt feelings, all the times I talked back, the unkind things; I'd keep them down deep, laugh them away, never speak of them again. The world where these three sentences don't exist is easy to imagine because it's only a few seconds in the past.

"Ma'am?" the voice that said the three sentences asks. Her voice is horribly severe and hoarse, likely having been on the butt end of a cigarette for too many years. I hate this voice. "Ma'am?"

When I try to tell her his medical history, it's interrupted by an image of my spry young Daddy, his legs kicking from underneath a car. Again, I try to speak, to say I will be there shortly, but a picture of what my life might be like without him fishing every weekend, cuts off my words. So, I try a third time, but manage only a scream.

Numb finds me. I don't feel a thing after the phone call until I see him in his bed. It's a crime how they didn't finish washing the blood from his face. There's still glass in his hair, too. I'll be talking to someone in charge before he leaves this place. But now my daddy needs to feel my love. My hand finds his, but it's so cold. I wash his face. I pick the glass from his hair. I tell him I'm here, over and over. When I kiss his forehead and breathe in deep, past the medicine smells, I detect motor and musk. All of my energy holds onto that, to the Daddy I know is about to wake up. When Will leaves the room I don't bother trying to stop him. When Kathy calls, I answer with one hand while the other still holds Daddy's.

"What was he doing on the Atchafalaya Bridge?" she sobs.

"I don't know," I hear my voice answer back flatly.

"He didn't want to talk when I called late this morning. What did you say to upset him this afternoon? You couldn't tell he was ill?"

"He's going to wake up," I tell her. "He's going to wake up, goddamn it. So you can hush. He's stronger than both of us. Nothing has ever been able to destroy him. Stronger than whatever that doctor, with his little degree, might have told you."

"There you go, Bee. Not taking responsibility for anything. Why'd they call you, anyway?"

"They said my info was on a picture of me he had in his truck. I didn't know he had that." It's the first time I think about it. We both try to understand the meaning of it from two different directions. He knew something could happen to him, and he had the info ready to go if someone found him in the truck. From her silence on the phone, I imagine she's wondering why there was a picture of me and not her.

"I'll be there in half an hour to take care of him," she says, sounding defeated. I don't have it in me to take pleasure in this. No matter what happens after today, Kathy will always think it's my fault. She'll always think I've had it easier than her despite always being the screw-up in her eyes. Looking at our father in the bed I can finally say her opinion doesn't matter anymore. Only his does. And I've treated his like he'd always be here, like Auguste Chenevert was invincible.

"How are you doing Daddy? You ready to wake up yet?"

At first it looks like his heartrate is going up when we talk. Now, as I hum some *Jolie Blonde*, the lines on the paper don't change. The air is motionless with only the whirring of machines and faint murmurs coming from the hallway. The quiet is almost like my house. His time with me has never been quiet, should never be quiet.

"Come on, Daddy. *Ouvre tes yeux*!"

Never has my father been in a room with me and not responded. He always has something to say. Oh, he'd pretend it was me who couldn't quit talking. His words, his life, all seemed untouchable. Nothing ever tested Auguste Chenevert's will and won. But now he can't wake up. It leaves me wondering if this silence is his will, too. What was he doing on that interstate at night? He hates driving past sunset. He always said he couldn't see good after dark. So, was this on purpose? No, Beatrice. That's a sin. Daddy would never. Still, Daddy never did nothing for no reason.

A long beep is the only noise I get to tell me it's time to tell my father goodbye. He dies with his hand in mine, my hands smoothing his hair. He wasn't invincible. It was all in my head. The world he made for us, wrapped in strength and love, explained to us in both English and French, said on the backs of rosaries and novenas, and served up with hot rice, is gone with him. I'm alone, just like I always felt, but this time for real. I never thought I'd have to worry about how to make my way in the world without him. When the kids come back in the room, I tell them their Paw Paw is gone. The looks on their faces reflect what I feel in my soul. For the first time in a long time, we feel like a family.

Chapter 32

Between metal and wood, he wanted wood. He told me he wanted to be buried in the pine box he made ten years ago, still leaning in his shed. But that's ridiculous. I try to compromise, get him a proper wood coffin, but Kathy, the old *ouaouaron*, insists on metal. It's easier to let her be bossy. His headstone is easy, too. His name is already next to Momma's. All he needs is a death date. One less thing to do. In the back of my head is the picture of Daddy driving on that bridge, and then falling. Wondering what he was doing there seems more important, or at least easier, than this.

Days pass like years until the day of the funeral. My lips are chapped from kissing cheeks and lips, and from talking since eight this morning. My voice is hoarse from the high-pitched hellos to see people who don't have the time to come by for any other reason than a funeral. Smiling, being strong, letting loose only enough tears to ensure people know I care, without letting out a scream, is what's hardest. I want to scream at the sometimes cousins, at my sister who has every reason to be happy but likes making me miserable, at my ungrateful children, and at my cheating husband. Most of all I want to scream at Daddy. I'd scream I love him. I'd scream don't leave me. I'd scream you left me a giant mess to fix and nothing to fix it with.

Daddy's young priest begins the rosary in French. The hand in my purse pushes past Jackie's lonely crucifix to find his rosary. Squeezing it tight I feel him more. The words aren't important today. Maybe they never were. What I need is the rhythm, familiar and predictable. It's the sound of Daddy in the morning while it's still dark in the house and everything is just beginning. The clacking of beads, the tinkling of chains, are windchimes signaling a change in the spirit. This brings him back in the room, making me smile.

What it also brings back is the question: Why was he was on that road at night? When we spoke earlier in the day, he didn't say anything about a trip, though he seemed a little hurried to get me out of the house. If it was a stroke like the doctor said, did Daddy know he was sick? Nobody is supposed to know when a stroke is coming, but this is Auguste Chenevert we're talking about. Why didn't I know? A daughter is supposed to know her father. Unless there was something else preventing me from knowing. Could he have been getting senile? I hear people with Alzheimer's get irritable, and he sure had been grumpy lately. He'd always fuss at us for getting in his business when we asked about his health. I should have pushed. I always assumed Auguste Chenevert had everything well at hand. But I was right to worry about his health. How many other times have I known what was right and backed down? There is one thing for sure—Daddy's way was not invincible or immortal.

Thinking all of this makes a buffer between me and the funeral. I don't remember the rosary. Kissing his face as they close the casket is a blur. The service is all but a blank. Aside from Will getting sick, the graveside service doesn't really make it to my memory either. What is memorable is I don't have to take care of Will because John seems to have an interest in him for once in his life. He even drives Will home from the funeral, even if he just sulks in a corner at the funeral. Nobody wants to talk to him anyway. Funny how God works. Daddy and me tried to get my family to act right for years. Now that we don't try, they're being decent. Except for Addie. She's sulking next to her daddy, apparently thinking the rules of how to be a good woman don't apply to her. On the day my own Daddy is buried I don't have to be nice. Besides, she still has her father, sorry though he may be.

"Addie go talk to your family. You haven't seen most of them in years."

“I haven’t seen them in years because I’ve been in school and most of them have been in trouble,” she sasses, right here at her grandfather’s funeral reception. I’m not taking this today.

“Why you got to talk like that today? Your Paw Paw would be ashamed of you, *Moutchon.*” She slinks away, a little wiser about how to act. It feels like progress.

Time was never my friend. Heartbreak took so much of it. And my happiness in the good times made it move too fast. The good moments slipped through my fingers faster than I could enjoy them. Time is only good at disappearing or standing still. Today, in Julie’s car, time sneaks back up on me as we ride to her house. I'm too embarrassed to ask her how I got here. For once I wish she would refrain from being so respectful and give me some hints about what the hell happened. Sipping tea in their living room I feel the puffiness in my eyes, a brain too oversized for my skull, and the slack in my shoulders—all telltale signs I've been crying again.

“Better?” inquires Julie from her spot on the couch opposite me.

“I think so.”

She smiles, taking a sip of her own tea before giving a worried glance to Jackie. "Has that been happening a lot?"

A sad laugh leaves my lips. "Hard to say."

"You need a break, Bee. Take some time off work. Go to church. Do whatever it is that will help you get through this."

"Thank you, Jackie. But life has to go on." One of their concerned looks passes between them. "Y'all, I'm fine."

"How about you stay here tonight? Your house is so quiet anyway.

“I don’t think that’s a good idea. I need to deal with work and my family.”

“You don't have to do it alone, Bee.”

“Yes I do because they are my responsibilities.”

"And you don't have to shoulder them and your father's death all by yourself."

I exhale. They won't get it. They can't. A Cajun woman makes her family survive. We have been doing it since they deported us from *Acadie*. When the men farmed or left to go offshore, we created a place for love and rest. And we do all that alone. We feel our love best when it's given away. Jackie and Julie only love each other, a complete little circle. That's not the way I was taught. "Here," I say to Jackie, handing her the crucifix. She doesn't look at my hand. I lay the crucifix down on the end table. As I reach the door, my attempt to storm out is foiled.

"Julie, would you please drive me home."

She's kind enough to let me stew the whole way home. The anger starts to dissipate and right when I'm about to apologize I see John's truck in the driveway. Of all the days for him to be home he picks the one when I want to be alone. I slam Julie's door and find him in his La-Z-Boy. He gets up the minute I walk in, as if he were waiting for someone.

"Bee, hey. Why are you home so early?"

"Need the rest of the day off."

Bracing myself, I get ready to hear how spoiled I am. But instead I hear, "Yeah." I head to the kitchen, to do what, I don't know. I turn around to see he's followed me.

"Hungry?"

"Not really."

"You want to go to Judice Inn for a burger?"

If my memory is right, my husband has not asked me on a date for about five years now. Despite having told him I'm not hungry, I agree to go to get a burger. There's no energy left in me to decipher what plot I'm stepping into. Even if this is revenge for what happened in the kitchen with the knife, I don't have it in me to fight. There's nothing left worth having that he could take from me. Besides, this is what I'm supposed to do. Maybe things will start to make sense if I give some love away, especially if it's to the person who's hurt me the most.

The inside of his truck looks like it was recently cleaned. It even smells better. We don't talk on our drive. He opens the door for me when we walk in. He orders for both of us. With food in hand I wait for him to tell me what this is about. He says nothing until he finishes the burger.

"Thought you'd like to come to our old stomping grounds."

"It's very nice John." He's giving me no air of danger. We say little else, and I just try to follow his lead. He drives home too fast. Is he angry? His attitude is pleasant. I make my way to the bedroom, thinking he'll lord over the couch and the TV. But when I turn around from putting my purse down by the vanity, he's in the doorway. The look on his face is similar to the one he had when he saw the knife in the kitchen. I soften, trying to muster the kind of compassion for him Christ would have. I have to forgive. Quickly his face shifts. It's one that last surfaced when we were young. A strained looseness, something like tenderness, grows across his face. The look is out of place on him, and even more out of place right now.

"You know you're still a pretty woman, Beatrice." I smile, trying to accept this comment as proof he might still love me. "I haven't told you that enough."

I face him. "Thanks, John." He winces at the skepticism in my voice. He seems to falter in the doorway. The scar on his neck, the one his daddy put there, glows purple. He lunges at me. But instead of a fist I am met with hard lips on mine. I know it's been so long since I've felt them, but this is wrong. The tenderness in his face isn't in his lips. He pushes me towards the bed and starts to unbutton my shirt, his hands using the same shamelessness Hidalgo's eyes did when I was in the pool. But this is how it's supposed to be. A good wife is supposed to be with her husband. This is what I wanted, the family to get back together. I force myself to kiss back. This is part of the bargain. I can focus on being a good wife and a good mother. Just the wind has to know.

He stops. He pulls away to the edge of the bed, naked. To my surprise, so am I. Time skipped, again. Looking back at him he looks so small. His shoulders hang loose over his big belly. He's not as sturdy as he was moments ago standing in the door. I pity him. He starts to cry and gets dressed. Dressing myself, I sit on the toilet, waiting for God to give me my next step. I uphold my end of the bargain even when He doesn't. Sort of like when I'm at the girls' house, I notice the skin I inhabit. My white thighs disgust me. Except it's not because of the way they look. His hands were on these thighs. Everything... down below... feels jumbled and contaminated. Right now, he's even more unpredictable than when he was ready to hit me in the kitchen. "Auguste Chenevert has been in an accident. You need to come to the hospital," rings through my head. There is no Auguste Chenevert to call to stop him. There is no Daddy to go to. My eyes venture up to the closet across the bathroom, to the open bag of Daddy's belongings I'd taken home from the hospital. It looks rifled through and his red hat is missing. Addie did this, I know. She's so ungrateful. Taking pieces of my Daddy away. With even less of my Daddy in this room with me to prop up the walls, it seems the house is caving in on me. I can't breathe.

There's no need to look at John. I grab my keys and head for the door. "Where are you going?" he calls after me, sounding more like a little boy than a forty-six-year-old man. My car goes straight to Jackie and Julie's house. They open the door and usher me inside without a word.

"My husband tried to have sex with me." Their raised eyebrows await more explanation, but I have none. Not knowing how to explain what happened, I plop down on my chair in the living room. It's a few minutes before I realize I haven't said anything else. My arms wrap around my body. Meeting their eyes, I see the same recognition I saw at the casino. They understand this better than I do. With no more need for details, I can skip to the questions which won't leave my mind alone.

"I mean. I'm supposed to like it right? What woman doesn't want to be wanted by her husband? This is what I wanted. It's been so long since he wanted me, I don't know what to do with it."

"Were you liking it?"

"Huh? "It's... I'm... we're out of practice.""

"Did you want to have sex?"

"That's... personal. I mean..." My lack of answer unlocks something. The silence hangs in front of me, replacing air I'm trying to breathe. The room swirls. I run, ending up in their bathroom, beginning to hyperventilate again. The silence. Everything turns black. The floor rushes up to meet me.

They have never been mothers. Waking up in their arms, beautiful faces staring down, gently running their fingers through my hair, holding my hand, I am reminded of a mother's love. The look on their faces is what I would have wanted my daddy to see before he died. The coolness in Jackie's blue eyes, and the warmth in Julie's brown ones alternate in some sort of rhythm, soothing places in my soul usually only a rosary can find. They see me as I am, not as they wish I would be. What they see, they love. This is God's love. It makes me think I could love what they see too.

"I told y'all I don't need y'all right now. But here I am. What's that say about me?"

"We don't need to go into that right now."

"Why not?"

"Because this is more important."

"Y'all seem so sure about what's important." Julie strokes my hair while Jackie sits quietly. "I wish y'all could tell me."

"I wish we could, too. We hate to see you go through this. You tell us what you need. We could get you help. We can give you a place to stay. We could just sit here. Whatever you need. The way forward is in your control."

"*Je suis cassé.* I'm broken. Now I know what my Daddy felt like when my momma died." Their faces remain gentle and patient, just like the winds. Julie's blue eyes are cool fall breeze. Jackie's are the warm breath of early summer. They hear me, all of me. "I can see how scary it must have been for him, how lost he was." Their eyes watch and see. "He always seemed to have everything figured out, once he got past being broken." There is new recognition in their eyes. This time it is not about the pain the men of our lives have brought us. It's an understanding of what it takes to move forward. I feel like I finally see them. Jackie and Julie do things their way because it's the best they can do with what they were given. Just like my Acadian ancestors did. Just like Daddy did. Just like I must do.

John's truck is still in the driveway at home as I arrive the following morning. The resolve I had when I left the girls' house almost washes away instantly. My legs shake when I open my car door. I reach in my purse to feel Daddy's rosary there. I feel two crucifixes. I pull them out to see the girls have replaced the crucifix they gave me in my purse. Pushing it back in, making sure it is back next to Daddy's rosary, I go through the back door. My knees shake again when I see I won't make it past the recliner, where he is watching TV.

"Where'd you go? I've been waiting up all night."

"I went out."

"Since when do you go out?"

"Life keeps moving while you're gone," I say with perfect confidence. Mary and Jesus, or Jackie and Julie, made me say that. More likely it's all four of them.

"I'm sorry about yesterday. I think your dad's death is hitting me harder than I thought."

I make the coffee, something that will always make the world right. John follows me into the kitchen.

"I waited up all night for you."

I quietly fill the filter with the patience the girls would use. Everything is prepared with the same amount of care Jesus and Mary take with me. As I finish with the water, John is still waiting on me to respond. I sit at the table in the spot Daddy always sat at. I finally get why he liked this spot so much. You can see the whole house.

"You not gonna say something?" John says, standing above me.

"What do you want me to say, John?"

"I was hoping you'd say you understand. That you're sad, too."

"You don't think I'm sad, John?"

"You're not acting like it."

"Because I don't have that luxury. I'm in pain everyday knowing I can't go back, that I have to go forward trying to make sense of the world he left us and build something out of it."

"Bee, please don't be a martyr right now."

His brow and tone lower. Jesus, knowing truly what a martyr is, pulls me to the coffee as John leaves the kitchen. Time threatens to leave me again. Warm coffee to my lips I turn to look out my window, to gauge the wind outside. Nothing is moving. Something new hits me. The wind is nothing. It doesn't make a sound, doesn't become something noticeable, until it hits something. All this time I called into the wind thinking it was catching my voice. Turns out it was blowing through like a hurricane, like the people in this house, making the most racket when it hit this green oak rooted deep. I've bent, lost a branch here and there. With my roots deep in the soil my daddy made for me, I'll show him how strong this oak is.

John is back in his recliner. I stand over him, blocking the TV. "So now you expect me to talk when you want to?" he barks.

"Yes I do. Because I'm not going to do things the old way anymore just because that's what we've done. Everything is going to change. If you want to leave me, if you're that unhappy, you can go with my blessing. I'm done being hurt by you. But I'm not leaving. Because this is my family and I'm going to do it my way, the right way. I'm not letting what you've done change that." He stands up out of his recliner and looks down on me. His jaw sets and the purple scar on his neck glows hot. "Do what you got to do, John. And I'll do what I got to do. Just know it's never going to be like it was."

His shoulders slump. As he gets his things and leaves, I remain in the center of my house, still feeling as if the wind is whipping around me.

Chapter 33

Daddy's place at the table still feels odd. Seeing the whole house is overwhelming. I see places I haven't cleaned enough. There's a cabinet that needs fixing. Or I could just leave it and accept it the way it is. Accepting is what Daddy kept telling me to do. But I wonder if he still thinks so from where he's at. Instead of pressuring him more about his health, I just accepted he knew what he was doing. He'd always been strong, always survived, and I just didn't appreciate how my daddy could get sick. This family is sick. If I just accept it, could it end up the same way? Battered and broken until it dies? I can't afford to make that mistake again.

What's still hard to figure out is why Daddy was on the road. The question still sits in the back of my mind. It lives alongside how scared he must have been going headfirst through the cypress and hyacinth into that swamp. The thought is hard enough to take my breath. The worst part is we'll never know. He took that secret with him. There were many things he seemed to keep to himself, no matter how hard we pressed him for it. After what happened with John the last couple of days I'm starting to understand. There are some things that are just for me to decide. How I want to live, or not live, with them. The next person might not do it this way. Auguste Chenevert would not have handled my husband's cheating this way. But I'm not him. My way will have to do.

Lost in memories and the wide-open feelings they bring, I almost don't notice Will come in. It's not until I see the blood over his eye that I'm drawn away from the comforting expanse of the past back to the problems right here and now.

"I know what I must look like to you with the way I've been acting lately. Going out all the time. Drinking. Getting weird friends. I'm not much like the Will you're used to." Will says. Could the hurricane I've been living in finally be over? Did this oak survive? This sounds like new life trying to come back.

"Hmm," is what I offer back, giving him space to be hurt and scared even though I want to tell him how hurt and scared I am.

"I'm tired of being angry all the time. When the time is right, let's talk about what happens next." The future might not be so messy after all. What I need to do here is just love him, like Jesus, Mary, Jackie, and Julie have loved me.

"*Mon 'tit garçon*. You look like *mon 'tit garçon*."

After the conversation I sleep better than I have in years. It's not just Will who seems to have shaken loose the *misère*. Addie even visits me at Louisiana Treasures, asking for advice, like a daughter would. She wants to know how it was done before her, like I used to ask my daddy. Even though I want to call her out for stealing Daddy's hat from my closet I decide not to. This is all on me now. She deserves to keep a piece of her Paw Paw. I have enough of him inside me I can let her have that. Julie arrives while we visit and I finally get to introduce Addie to her. When she leaves, I can tell Julie wants to assess all that happened during the storm in my house.

"Where did you go when you left last night?" Julie asks.

"Home." She doesn't even try to hide her disapproval. "It's ok. It's ok. I actually straightened some things out." Taking in a long breath, I breathe out, "I'm staying with John."

"Bee, no—"

"Listen. I made a decision. I let him know I'm not tolerating anymore foolishness. But I need to stay because it's the right thing to do. They need me. Even John needs me." Tears rim Julie's eyes. "That means I can't come by your house for a while."

"Why?"

"It's not because I don't like y'all. In fact, it's the opposite. Y'all are so good to me I don't do as much as I should for myself."

"Well you have to come by to tell Jackie."

"I need you to tell her."

"That's not fair."

"I know. And I'm sorry. But I got to stick to this. It was hard enough last night to stand up to him like that. I'm afraid if I come to your house, I'll start hiding out again." She looks angry now. She stares out the window long enough to leave me sure she's about to quit. I wouldn't blame her.

"You're not gone for good, you know that?" she finally says.

"I know, *cher*. Y'all aren't getting rid of this old Cajun momma that easy. I need to get some stuff straight, you know?" She doesn't stop looking out of the window. "You two have been like sisters. The sisters I always needed. I love y'all. Y'all are family."

Chapter 34

Will hangs his head out the window like an old hunting dog. The hugs, and the extra time he's been spending in the living room, makes me think Paw Paw managed to teach him to be a man of his word before he passed. Will hugs his aunt tightly. I'm glad he loves her so much. Without Daddy, we're two ladies dealing with our kids leaving home. Kathy catches me spying things of Daddy's along the wall. She's been to his house, without me, recently.

"I can start on the fish. Where are they?" I say to cover my gaze.

"Still in the ice chest."

"You didn't filet them?"

"I had some things I had to do this morning," she explains. Tolerating her is not in my cards anymore.

"Kathy, *j't'ai écouté quand tu me dis tu attendrais.*"

"*Je suis désolé. Je croyais tu voudrais un peu du temps avant d'y aller.*"

"*C'est ma décision. Ce n'est pas pour tu le faire.*"

Somewhere in between when I was telling my sister to let me make my own decisions, and insisting she call next time she goes to our father's house, Will begins fileting the catfish. Just like his grandfather, he got impatient with our fussing, and did it himself. He's not doing too bad a job either. I catch a glimpse of his mouth turned up on each end.

"*Il sourit,*" Kathy says. He looks up to see us smiling.

Behind us the door opens. Addie walks in and holds a six pack of beer in the air. "I brought Schlitz!" We all yelp. But Addie is sad. It's about a boy, and her Paw Paw. A mother knows.

John

Chapter 35

It's the same damn nightmare. My daddy has the iron skillet in his hand, looking at me like a stray dog underfoot, one that needs kicking out of the way. There's no point in staying in bed here any longer. All the pleasure the place could offer I had last night.

"Make sure you lock the door this time."

"Ok."

"You're not even going to say bye?"

The blood runs through my neck heating it up. My scar there is turning purple, I know. I can feel it. She swore she wouldn't get clingy. "Bye, Linda."

My head swims. I want boudin, but my stomach can't do it. Linda, that crazy bitch, had me doing shots when she knew I had to come into the shop this morning. The shower behind the shop helps. I get my boots on as the first few guys trickle in.

"You smell pretty, John!"

"I just got out the shower."

"That's not Old Spice pretty. That's more like stripper perfume pretty."

"You'd know."

"Hey man, you don't have to hit all four walls. You just gotta give one hell." I nearly piss myself laughing. Yank's got no room to judge. With those glassy eyes, his bulbous chin, and that crooked nose, he's done way worse than me.

"Y'all get started. Gulf Star called and they want all this tomorrow. Which means the old man wants it done by this afternoon."

"Where's he right now? He wants this so bad but he don't even bother coming by the shop."

"You know how it is." Even though this is a perfect moment, today is not the day to put ideas in their heads. They need a little more time before deciding to work for me instead of him. And I need more time to make completely sure my customers would follow me if I were to start my own shop. Then all I'd need to do is lay it out and the old man will sell on the cheap. Fuck his son and whatever claim he has on this shop. I built this place, not him. Over the past three or four years I pretty much lived here. I go home for clothes. There's nothing else there for me, anyway.

The phone rings. It's Oilcon. They don't want tools. One of their baskets busted and they need a quick fix. The Company man sent all his welders to New Orleans. Only ones left on the dock are from Halliburton and he'll be damned if he uses one of those. All those bugs I put in people's ears finally turned into a big company calling. Here's a place for good customer service, the kind that makes loyal customers who would want to follow a guy, whatever he does.

"Yank, I need you to come with me down to Fourchon."

"Why all the way down there?"

"Oilcon needs some padeyes welded and back in the hold, fast."

"Can't they get one of their people on the dock to do it? Or can't the old man get it driven here?"

I lean in close, lowering my voice so only he hears it. "Because someone else will get in good with this guy. And Old Leonard will want you to work on it all night. We can get it done real fast and you can spend your night in Grand Isle. I'll call one of the other boys in to help Swedge here in the shop."

He smiles. He's always ready for a good time. "You're so sweet to think of me."

"I always take care of my people."

We finish the twelve pack right after we pull off Highway 1. The docks look sparse. They're not here yet. We walk around a little, looking for my guy, asking some of the other gulf-hardened boys if they've seen him. Yank moves in his normal, twitchy way, like a bird that's been caught and spat out too many times. Seems a health hazard for a welder. The guys on the dock stare back at us with beady little eyes, set back in cracked eye sockets. Yank goes back to the truck, while I keep looking for our guy for another half hour.

"We could go wait at the bar," Yank says from the truck window while I walk up.

"You better stick to beer. I don't need you so fucked up you can't work."

"It's just alcohol, Dad." He looks past me. "Could that be your man?"

Idling through the service canal is a modified fishing boat, the red, balding head of my guy can be seen leaning off the top rail. I back my truck right up onto the dock and scream up to him. "Don't get too comfortable. My boy is gonna have you rolling back out in a little over an hour."

"That's enough time to catch a little buzz!" He screams back.

Yank's eyes go everywhere but on the Company Man. Why the hell does he do this when the big customers are around? It reminds me too much of Will. "Yank. Yank!" He looks up at me like I caught him stealing something. "Get to work!" He starts to unload the acetylene and arc welders, and my customers load into my truck for the bar. I pull Yank aside.

"What the fuck is wrong with you? You're being disrespectful."

"You know I don't like blowhards like him."

"I know you like employment. Yank, I didn't bring you because you're the best welder, but because there's some opportunities here. You could be getting some big bucks doing underwater welding. Maybe even move up to some management."

"Fuck that, John."

"You'd like underwater. You're the right amount of crazy to want to work with a shark poking his nose up your ass the whole time."

"No. Fuck management."

He won't look at me while he says it. "Well you better pull your shit together while we tie one on. Act like half an asshole, instead of a whole one, when we get back. Here," I say grabbing the ice chest and dropping it onto the deck. "Make sure your lines are straight, though."

"I told you. It's just alcohol."

My Company Guy does Hot Damn Shots, six of them, before I finish my first beer. I'd be impressed, if he wasn't drinking girl shit. I calculate how many more shots it will take for my guy to think the bartender with stringy, bottle-blond hair, and two missing bottom teeth, is a good piece of strange. Like magic, the place gets full in under fifteen minutes. The wood floor creaks on the fifteen-foot-tall pillars from the weight. Crowd like this usually means a boat came in, but none of these guys act like they know each other. Our only female companion behind the bar reads the question on my face.

"Lingerie night."

As if they'd been waiting on the words, three girls stroll in wearing only their frilly *caleçons*. My guy perks up. This is exactly what I need to start the right conversation. The girls make their rounds, visiting the little groups of men, one by one. Company Man's eyes follow them. The shots make his eyes hungry.

"You ever hear the one about Boudreaux going to college?" I ask.

"Nah," Company Man says, not breaking his stare.

"Boudreaux decides to enroll at LSU. When he's at the registrar they ask what his major will be. '*Mais I don't know what dat is.*' 'Well Mr. Boudreaux we'll just put you in Logic since that's kind of part of everything.' So in his first day of class the professor starts going on and on about deductive reasoning. Old Boudreaux raises his hand and asks '*What's deductitive reasoning?*' 'Well Mr. Boudreaux I'll show you. Do you own a lawnmower?' '*Mais yeah, I do.*' 'Well if you have a lawnmower then you have a lawn. And if you have a lawn you probably have a house.' '*Close. I live in a trailer, me.*' 'Ok, well if you live in a trailer, I deduce you live with someone. And I'll take that a step further and say it's probably your wife you live with.' '*Mais yeah, Clotile lives wit me.*' 'Well then if you have a wife you are most likely heterosexual. So you see from learning you have a lawnmower I deduced you are heterosexual.' '*Mais I tink I got it Dr. Professor Sir.*' So Old Boudreaux heads home feeling smart and passes by Thibodeaux's trailer, where he's rocking away on his porch. Thib calls to him, 'Hey Boudreaux. How was you first day of school?' '*It was good, dat. I learned about deductitive reasoning.*' 'Mais what's dat?' '*I show you. Thib, do you own a lawnmower.*' '*Mais* no Boudreaux. I always borrow yours.' '*Well, den you gay.*"

For a moment I think my attempt to tide him over, until the girl can make it our way, is lost. His eyes continue undressing them. The bastard has been on that rig for a while. A moment or two after my punch line lands, he breaks his gaze, looking instead at me in surprise. His laugh is so big it catches the attention of a tall blonde girl making the rounds. Just like me, she can smell the potential of a big ego. She walks directly to him with a knowing smile.

"You want to pet my possum?" she asks. His eyebrows almost go through the roof. "It's only five dollars."

"What do I get for ten?" he asks in all seriousness.

"You can hold it for a while."

He pulls out a fifty and she quickly stuffs it into her bra. She pulls out a box she'd been hiding behind her back. She opens the cover to reveal a hissing possum pup. Company Man nearly falls out of his chair trying to get away from it. I can see now he's citified, probably from Atlanta, or worse, somewhere in Florida. This is all good info to have. He's lost interest in the blonde, who laughs hysterically. I like her style and give her a wink. The dirty little girl winks back before shaking her cute little lingerie butt to the next group. After he finishes another girly shot, Company Man says, “I did not see that coming.”

“Yeah, you never know what can wash into Fourchon. There’s a lot better pickings in New Orleans.”

“I know there is.”

“Listen, you should call me when you get back on shore. I’ll show you some good spots.”

“I got my spots.”

“I bet you do. But a real Cajun can show you the best spots. You might want to try and trust the guy who can do a weld while you take shots.”

He looks away from another lingerie-clad girl, a brunette. “Alright,” he declares with some seriousness, “I’ll call you when we’re done with this job.”

He gets up from his barstool and moves in the direction of the brunette. He works his way around her. Maybe he’s checking out her ass. But then I realize he’s making sure she doesn’t have a box behind her back. As she moves away from a group of boys, he pulls up behind her and grabs her left butt cheek. She’s pissed and lets him know it. One last trip to the pisser and it's time to head back to the boat.

Yank is sitting in the captain’s chair with his feet up. He doesn’t take them down when we pull up. I know he can see us. It’s not until we’re all on the deck, looking at his work on the padeyes, that he decides to walk out. There’s no doubt, that boy has a gift. A little yellow paint and you couldn’t tell it had cracked at all.

“To your liking, sir?” Yank calls down. Dangling from his fingers is a bottle of whiskey. There is no telling where he was hiding that.

“It is. Thank you kindly.” Company Man turns toward me and almost topples over. He looks over the side as if to accuse a rogue wave for upending his balance, except the port is a mill pond. “My girls will get your bill,” he slurs.

"It's on the house. And when you call me after the job, we'll find something better in New Orleans than what was at that shithole."

"You're on!" he says waving his finger in the air, letting everyone know it's time to roll out. After loading up the truck and waving to them, I turn to Yank in the passenger seat.

"That was a little more like it. Not so hard, huh?"

"I did that shit because you asked. He was trying to get laid in Fourchon?"

"Trying, yes. Succeeding, no. He tried to close the deal on that brunette lingerie girl."

"Shit, you and I closed the deal on her on the same night, if I remember correctly."

We adjourn the day for afternoon drinking. All that Rome's in Grand Isle has to offer is bikers. The waitress is more focused on Yank and his mohawk than she is on getting me another Bud Light. Finally, my stomach settles and food is sounding good.

"John! Where are we staying tonight?" His northeastern accent is stronger. He must be doing it for the girl.

"Dunno. Wherever looks nice."

He turns back to the girl. "Does your place look nice?"

"Oh sweetie you were doing so well with the accent and the haircut. Why'd you go and mess it up?"

"I have no problem rightin' my wrongs," he tells her with an even stronger accent.

"Hmm," is all she says before walking over to check on the bikers. He slides back down the bar toward me.

"Where the hell did you get that accent?"

"You don't remember where I'm from?"

"Yank is short for Yankee. Anything else is lost, because every time I hang out with you, I wake up in strange places, with no idea of what happened."

"Just got to remember to check your pockets. Remember two times ago in New Orleans? You woke up in a hotel on the other side of the quarter. You, the girls you were with, and the bed you guys were in, were all naked. And when I told you to check your pockets…"

"Chicken and Vodka from a corner store at 3:13AM."

"It all came back after that."

"I wouldn't say all." We both chuckle while the bartender wordlessly gives me another beer. "Seriously, where are you from," I continue.

"Connecticut."

"Sheeeyut. You know I'll forget that again. All those places are the same to me."

In the silence that follows, my mind turns to po-boys. I really don't want to move. I call the waitress over and ask her to go get me a po-boy from down the street. She can keep the change. Her head cocked back, she lets out a laugh designed to mock me. When I pull the wad of cash from my pocket, and thumb two Grants on the table, her eyes widen. That'll be more than her tips for tonight.

"You serious?"

"As a heart attack. Barbecue. No pickles." She looks at the bikers, who I know were watching this. "We'll be right here when you get back," I reassure her. She quickly grabs her purse from under the bar and heads for the door.

"That was an expensive po-boy, John. A lot more expensive if the guys at the pool table decide they'd like a taste, too."

"You think it's the po-boy I just paid for?" Biker eyes are still on me as I get up and move around the bar. Popping the bar towel, I sling it over my shoulder. "Drinks for the next ten minutes are on the house."

The bikers don't hesitate and move quickly to the bar. I sling out some beers and double Jacks. The last biker up puts both of his hands on the bar and leans in. He smells like gasoline and old sweat. He must be the badass of the bunch.

"I think I'd like the pocketcash," he tells me from behind his tangled hair.

"Fresh out," I say while leaning toward him, wiping down the bar.

"See how you fucked up? You got the only person who'd be able to say something to leave."

Sideways glances pass between the guys behind him, but they don't move. They are content with free drinks. Before I can start talking this guy out of his bad idea, Yank clears his throat. He's laid a .357 and his Ka-Bar on the bar. They back away, even the big badass. I suppress the urge to join them, though I'm glad they didn't see my hand stutter mid-wipe. Yank smiles at all of us. He wants a fight. The big one takes a step toward him, but one of his guys downs a drink, and grabs his arm. Pulling him toward the door they start up their bikes and are gone. For now.

"What the fuck is wrong with you?"

"Me? You're the one flashing wads of cash with felons watching!"

"I had it under control."

"John, you had the other guys under control. That big guy didn't care. I can smell my own. We're going to need to be gone before too long. He'll be back."

"Why'd you have to go and fuck up my night?" I ask, cocking back the Jack in hopes that it slows my heart. I fill another glass before refilling the nearly empty Jack bottle with tea. As I retake my seat at the bar, the waitress walks in and drops a barbecue sauce soaked sandwich in front of me.

"You have me running errands for you, and now you chase off my other customers?" She looks thankful if anything.

"Turns out we need to go, too."

"That's too bad. You were my only company."

"We still can be. Page this when you get off," I say.

"I know what most people think of girls who are bartenders, but you're wrong."

"You wish you knew what I think."

Yank's eyes aren't leaving her, but her eyes aren't leaving me. She likes the old guys, I see it now. Maybe she's got some daddy issues or something. She takes the folded napkin with the number and we head for the door.

"You're a dick, John. I was working on that."

"No, you were fucking it up. But you'll get another chance when it's your pager she calls later. Let's go find another spot. Wait, let me call my cousin and find out if he got his boat out of the shop. He'll let me take it tomorrow and we can find some speckled trout."

Chapter 36

Sunday afternoons at the shop are busy. Guys are getting tools ready for the week. Some guys are finishing jobs near a deadline the boss gave them. The old man might be there. Yank is still asleep in the passenger seat. The coke he snorted before we got on the boat didn't fix what he did the night before. All that dancing on the bar, carrying on, and then beating that big biker in front of his friends, not to mention expensively convincing the cops he didn't need to be in jail, did a number on him. If that didn't, that bartender certainly did. Asshole probably didn't think I'd really make him go fishing with me. One day he'll learn to stick to beer and older women the night before a fishing trip.

Yank sees the old man's truck before I do and sneaks out the passenger door before I come to a stop. The old man looks like he's been at church. He's pissed, so I smile even bigger.

"John, where the fuck have you been?"

"Spreading the good word, Pops."

"You take my best guy out the shop when I got three tools that need to get out. I got half a mind to take you off manager."

"It was Oilcon."

I watch his face change as I step out of the truck. "John, I've told you I want big ones going through me."

"Yes you did. I remember it clearly. I also remember you saying how you need a manager who doesn't need hand holding, and to take care of your shop so you can finally spend time with your grandkids." Leonard's face screws up tighter. I have him right where I want him. "I got a basket all fixed up and back to the rig without them even having to take it off the boat."

He wants to stay mad. This is his baby. Truth be told he's smart to be mad. All he knows is he doesn't trust me. If only he knew all the practice I have dealing with pissed-off, controlling pricks like him. My dad was more than enough education.

"Well. Okay. I guess that's different. Just… you know… okay."

He walks back to his truck, his shoulders hunched, feeling defeated by his success. It's his own fault, being suckered like this. If he'd only treated me like I was somebody instead of another sales guy. Maybe one day I'll have it like Auguste does. He doesn't worry about pleasing anyone. Everyone works to please him.

Swedge accuses me as I walk toward the shower in the back. "I been working for eight straight days. I was supposed to get off early to start my time off. He's gonna keep us on these tools all night tonight."

"You're acting like one of your ex-wives. He's leaving, isn't he?"

"He left his numb-nut of a son here."

"Swedge, you let me handle him. You and I both know he's going to be leaving almost as fast. When had you planned on knocking off before the old man showed up?"

"Five. I was supposed to start my time off today."

"Leave at four thirty. I'm telling you. I got this." I say it loud enough for everyone to hear. A quick glance back and I see them smiling and poking at each other.

Out of the shower, I walk over to Matthew Leonard. The old man's son is sitting behind the desk staring at an order like he's a gynecologist who accidentally walked into an NFL locker room instead of a hospital. The little bastard wanted to go to college. I don't know how he would have survived.

"Hey," I say, sitting on the desk. He gives me only a glance as acknowledgement. Little spoiled shit. "You on top of this order?"

"Not really. This system is so inefficiently designed. I don't understand why there is not an item description next to this stock number."

I squint at the number on the screen. "That's a rotary table." This guy should be delivering pizzas instead of being positioned to take over a machine shop. "Why are you looking at tickets?"

"Dad says I need to learn this system. Since I'm good at computers he thought I should start looking at orders. I think we need to upgrade this system."

"You might be right. How much would all that cost?"

"I'm not sure. But it would probably be pretty pricey."

If there is a person who trusts computers less than me it's Old Man Leonard. He also likes spending money less than me. "Well if he told you to figure out this system, and you think it needs an upgrade, then I think he needs to hear that."

"Dad? He'd never listen."

"Tell you what. You go figure out how much it will be and I'll try and help you come up with a way to break it to him. Sometimes dads need to understand what you're worth." His face portrays someone rescued from an island. "But I bet this is isn't the best place to get… you know… creative. How about you go somewhere better. I can hold this down."

"You sure?"

"I'm sure."

"But it's Sunday and you have a family at home."

My jaw sets. "Yeah. They're there. But I'd bet they'd prefer not to smell my rotten farts."

He smiles and heads for the door. If only this is how it worked at home. At least, this is how it used to work. If it still worked this way, I'd be home right now.

As promised, Swedge is done at four thirty. The other guys I let go at five with the promise they'd be ready to work in the morning to catch up on what they'll miss tonight. The quiet in the shop is deafening. I want to jump out of my skin with nothing to do the Sunday before

Mardi Gras. Maybe it's time to go check in at home. As much as I don't want to, I do need some fresh clothes. Pointing my truck north, I don't get to Highway 90 before my car phone rings.

"Hey, John." The woman has radar.

"What's up Bee? Everything ok?"

"Oh yes, sweetheart. Fine. I'm just calling about tomorrow night."

"What about tomorrow night?"

"The ball, John? I'm going to pick up your tux tomorrow afternoon. We need to leave the house by five-thirty to be at the Hilton." As if I needed any more reasons to not want to come home. All those old hags gossiping to each other, expensive alcohol, and a wife nagging me to dance: it's the absolute worst way to spend Mardi Gras.

"Aw, Bee. Crap. I'm sorry. I can't make it. I'm on my way to Houston for a sales call."

The line gets real quiet. I can hear her breath, heavy, on the other side of the line. Here comes a fight.

"It's ok. I'll... It's ok. Will you be home for lunch tomorrow? I'll be cooking something." I'm pleasantly surprised.

"What are you cooking?"

"What do you want?"

"I don't know. Just wondering." I hesitate. I haven't eaten something homecooked in a while. If I must put up with all her clinginess, might as well be on a full stomach. "I'll be there sometime in the morning."

Immediately I call my cousin. Since I'm not going home into the lion's den tonight and holing up in the shop with nothing but the fans for company sounds like torture, might as well catch up with some of my boys. Under the auspices of thanking him for his boat in Grand Isle, I inquire about his plans for the evening.

"Unlike you I have a wife who puts up a fuss when I don't come home every once in a while."

"That's what you get for marrying a rich Baton Rouge girl," I jab.

"It's a penance, for sure. But I got no plans tonight. What's on your agenda?"

"Turns out I'm in the market for some trouble."

"You want to come froggin'?"

"That's some teenage shit, ain't it?"

"The adult stuff will come afterwards."

"Well then count me in. Where we going?"

"Forked Island."

"In whose boat?"

"Mine. My new one."

"Damn it, Dud! How many boats you got?"

"Every penance has its perks."

A final walk around the shop to make sure all the doors are locked, I notice Swedge left all his tools on the floor near the pipe he was working on. That boy treats his works space like a living room. I pick up his two most expensive wrenches, the ones he bought himself, and throw them in the trash.

Heading south, Creedence blasts through my radio. I'm transported back to high school, seventeen years old, and feeling free since I would not have to go to war. I'd also managed to get out of the warzone in my home. Because I did what I had to do, no one was killed there. The only thing getting killed tonight are some frogs and time at the bar while I wait for Dud. After having checked into my favorite haunts in Abbeville, drank beers with the people who can be counted on to be on the same stools any day of the week, I arrive at the Curve Lounge to wait for Dud. He doesn't keep me waiting long. Solid buzz secured, we head out to the landing.

"How'd you get away with getting another boat?"

"Because he was practically giving it away. And this is the first time I'm putting it in the water. Help me out check it out. I was pretty drunk when I bought it yesterday."

Scoffing, I run my hand around the hull checking for cracks. He flashes his light at the engine. After following a few wires, and touching a few gaskets, he seems satisfied. We load the ice chests. As he puts one down near the back he cusses.

"That son of a bitch! The drain's all rusted out. It doesn't even have a plug in it."

I laugh.

"It ain't funny you asshole." I laugh harder. For a man who likes to throw around his money he sure gets his feelings hurt when he's been swindled. He gets angrier. I laugh even harder. "Do you think one of your guys can weld that? Maybe your father-in-law?"

I stop laughing. Walking to his cab, I rummage through the sediment on the floorboard. A trash bag or some a plastic tarp would be good. A leather glove will do. At the back of the boat I stuff it into the rusted gap.

"Cut your shit, John. Let's head back to the Curve Lounge."

"No, you cut your shit. You drag my ass out here. Now we're going froggin'."

"Do you know how many gators are in that water?"

"Too many to count. And you know as well as I do they'll leave us the hell alone."

Dud grabs the ice chest and makes for the bed of the truck.

"Launch me," I dare. "If the boat starts to sink after ten minutes we'll head back to the Lounge. I'll buy your drinks." His lemon boat bobs in a symphony of frogs and crickets. Something large splashes in the dark behind me. Not a word passes between us. We don't break our stare. Occasionally he glances at his watch. When and why he stopped trusting me with his life escapes me. We've run from cops in Texas and shot back when we were in the wrong neighborhood in New Orleans. A wife softened him, which means our team softened. Another glance at his watch and he shines his pistol gripped spotlight down to the back of the boat. The glove is wet, but it's holding. "It's ok if you want to go, Dud. I understand if this is too difficult for you."

He hands—no, throws—his ice chest down to me. Thankfully, the engine starts. Head lamps on, I shine his spotlight down the bayou. A conservative estimate puts the number of blood red alligator eyes staring back at me around thirty. Damn, I hope this glove holds.

We putt around, looking for frogs on the banks, but the water is high. Dud pulls up to a pair of diamond white eyes on the bank. I end up catching some shit from him because I hesitate. I'm buzzing hard enough to not be able to differentiate between a snake and frog on first glance. The moon is full, casting an eerie glow on everything not touched by our spotlights. He trolls me from canal to bayou. Boredom is setting in. I can tell by the number of cans at my feet. Downing my current beer, I hang it off the side of boat, letting it fill with water and sink. In the light of the moon it glints as it goes down. Something nasty down there will go after something so shiny. Reminds me of bars.

"How are your kids, John?"

"Your guess would be as good as mine."

"Working too much?"

"Yeah."

"Man, I've been wondering more lately what it would be like to have kids."

"I can save you the trouble. Take whatever money you have and put it in the trash. Have someone yell at you when you didn't put it in the right trash can. When you try to get the right trash can, they tell you are the reason for all the unhappiness they've ever felt."

"You're on some dark shit."

"There's one."

It's a good-sized bullfrog. The slippery son of a bitch almost manages to push out of my hand. His blinded eyes meet mine. They're empty. I toss him in the ice chest for a slow freezing death.

"Well at least there's always a *chouchoun* on the side to keep you company."

"Let's head back to the Curve," I suggest.

"Come on! You just got a big one."

"I think the glove might be giving way."

Chapter 37

Rolling through the spotty pictures in my mind of the night before, I remember Dud rubbing up on this lady with white rubber boots, going on and on about how it meant she was his Cinderella. The pictures come back between images from the nightmare again, except this time it was me holding the iron skillet, ready to throw it at my dad. Watching the ceiling fan slowly turn above us, I try to get gumption to leave Linda's trailer. How did I even get here? Did she call me? Groaning as I sit up, she stirs and wakes.

"Do you remember what you said to convince me to come get you in the middle of fucking nowhere?" Holy shit. What the hell have I done? "You said you'd leave her."

"Linda—"

"Do you remember what I said back to you?" I stay silent. It hurts to think. "I said I don't need any more pot-bellied oil men stinking up my house and then leaving right when I get used to their stinking pot-bellies. Yet here you are, in my bed, after I drove from a perfectly good bar to come pick you up, as if I really did want you to leave your wife."

"Linda—"

She opens her blood shot blue eyes to look at me. "Don't talk, John. You're horrible in the mornings. Especially when you're leaving here to go to her. I just wanted all of that on the record. Lock the door on the way out."

Auguste's old Ford is in my driveway at home. Bee did not tell me her father would be here. She does this shit. She'll leave out information so I'll get all clammy and my scar will show purple. I explained it all to her when we first got married. She said she understood. Now I need to get my head right to be able to talk to him and not panic. I need to remind myself this is my house and I'm a grown ass man.

"Mr. Chenevert! I didn't know you'd be here today. It's good to see you!" I put on the biggest smile that will fit on my face.

"John. *Ça va?*"

"Oh I'm doin' alright."

Almost forgetting I should kiss Bee, I hurry and put one on her cheek.

"Hi, John."

"Hey, Bee. Let me go put all this up and I'll be right back."

Dumping out my dirty, sex-saturated swamp clothes in the hamper, I shove fresh ones back into my bag. Since the door to the closet is so squeaky, I open it slowly. The last task is to get this bag back down the hall and somewhere out on the back porch where she won't see it. But I can't even get close to the outside because she is coming down the hall. She must have cameras in here.

"You're not even going to stay and eat with your father-in-law?"

"Yes I am. I was just putting this in the truck so I don't forget it."

"As if you'd forget you were leaving."

"Bee, I just walked through the door. Don't start."

There's not a spot on my plate not filled with food. If I can keep my mouth full, I won't be made to answer a bunch of questions. Bee is already pissed with me, though. She won't run interference for me with Auguste like she used to.

"John, has work been busy?" I shovel more food in. "John?" Bee insists.

"Hmm?"

"How's work been?"

"Good. Busy. Ole Leonard got me runnin' all over the place selling these tools. I can't wait to get this damn liberal out of the White House so the business is good and they come to us." Sometimes he likes to talk politics. Really, he likes to talk work. But if I can get him on those godless young voters, I can get off the hook.

"You ever get out to da rigs?"Auguste asks.

"Me? God, no. That's mechanic work." Oh shit. Now I did it. Just because he's got that old coonass ambition, the kind where you make just enough to feed your family and everything else is *lagniappe*, doesn't mean I should have to feel ashamed for advancing my career.

"You too good for mechanic work, John?"

"Aw come now Mr. Chenevert. I meant no disrespect. I got guys especially for that is all I'm sayin'."

"Dat's what dem big bellied Texas men tought, too. Dem rich Texas boys din't want to be out on dem rigs so dey got us to do it for dem. At least we weren't Black. Dey din't even tink about lettin' Blacks work deir rigs. Beside, you can do some good fishin' at da rigs. We used to pull up all kinds of stuff. *Les tambours, les plies, les sheepheads*; and we'd cook dat right on da rig. And we din't have all dem safety rules, no. Dem company men would've shot us if dey'd known we was using open flames near all dat oil."

Fishing is what I should start with. I forget he distrusts any politician. "Only thing missing was some beer!"

"Oh we'd get our beer. We'd catch so much fish we'd trade some to da fisherman who would come to our rig. We'd lower down a bucket and dey'd send some Schlitz up. Nah da Company Man definitely din't want to know about his coonasses drunk on da job."

This isn't so bad. It's almost like when he was drinking after Mrs. Chenevert died. We could talk and drink for hours. We move to the living room and I get in my recliner. As he sits across the end table next to me, I see the deep purple bruises on his arm in the lamp light. It's been a while since I took a good look at him. He's aged.

"How long you Daddy been dead, John?"

"Shoo—must be twelve years now?"

"Dat long?" He whistles through his teeth. "I tole you I met you daddy when he was going fight in da war? Dat he was da reason I decided to go fight in Korea?"

"Many times."

"Dat temper of his got him in trouble. You and you brother and sister came along and he seemed to become a family man. Always at church, *lui*."

In a perfect universe I could see my father the way Mr. Chenevert does. There are a lot of things I could do like Auguste Chenevert in a perfect universe. I wouldn't flinch anytime I see brown belts. My words could be kind. My anger would show up only when it was about people getting hurt or screwed. I'd eat gumbo. It'd be nice if I could tell old Auguste my universe is closer to perfect since my daddy died.

"Yeah. His kind is dying off."

"*Mais* you right. You daddy worked a lot, but it was always for his family."

"Yeah." I wish he'd leave this alone.

He chugs at his beer. "John, you work in dat shop for long hours. But you fat like a man who don't got enough work to do. Why you not comin' home to *ta famille*?"

"I'm one of the bosses now, Mr. Chenevert. My job is to look after my guys. Make sure they're doing what they're supposed to." The corner of his mouth cocks up and I can see where this is going. This is going to turn back around on me, telling me I don't look after my family. Except he doesn't live in this family. And he acts like he wasn't happy to get my wife and her fat ass sister out of his house. He's just a good ole boy thinking he knows better than everyone else. He never got beyond being a roughneck and he thinks that's where real work is. "I worked hard to get where I am, to get what I deserve."

"Deserve. *I'dit* deserve. Only God knows what you deserve. *Tu comprends*?"

I do understand. I understand that despite how good he's been to me he still doesn't appreciate everything I've accomplished. That God he always goes on about, the One he suddenly got close to after he nearly drank himself to death after Mrs. Chenevert died, wasn't taking care of my family when I was growing up. He cocks his beer way back to drain it.

"John you take care, nah."

While I watch *Men in Black* my head swirls to a young me. I looked a lot like my son does now. I was nearly as scrawny, except I liked being outside. I liked hunting and fishing with my dad, getting my cheeks smeared with blood on our first deer kill. It was one of the only times I knew he was proud of me. I smile.

"It was good to see you and Daddy laugh," Bee interrupts, killing the memory. My smile is gone now.

"Yeah."

"Y'all used to visit like that a lot."

"Yeah."

"John where are you going to be tonight?" First Auguste, now her. They're tag-teaming me.

"Told you, Bee. Gotta work."

"On Lundi Gras?"

"Don't start."

"John, I don't ask you for much—" She's been doing this more lately, pressing me for answers on things she doesn't want to know the truth about. She must be reading some Oprah shit if she thinks she wants those answers. She can't tell me what I owe her, not under the roof I put over her head.

"Damn it, Bee! Don't you act like some sort of victim here. You knew what this life was like when you married me. Your daddy did this work. You like your house? You like this ball you're going to? Because you're not going to have these things selling junk to housewives. Until you're responsible for the roofs over thirty other people's heads, I don't want to hear it. Have fun at your ball. Because I'll be working."

"John—"

"Shut the hell up, Bee!" Turning the volume up makes her shrink. She'll think twice before starting crap like this again. Her neediness hovers behind me and she finally goes outside. I'm finishing my damn movie.

"Hi, Daddy."

Half expecting Bee again, I see Addie. All that softball has thickened her legs and slimmed her face. She's growing up into a woman, which means I have only days or months left before she starts hating me like every other woman. When she asks to join me, I have to wonder if Bee put her up to this. Women like to gang up.

"You gonna fight with me?" I ask. She hands me a beer. Maybe she can still be salvaged. "How's the season starting?"

"Not bad."

"Good."

"You got any good stories for me?"

"Shiiiitttt, you know I do. Have I told you the latest one about Yank?"

"Oh lawd. What did that freak do now?"

While telling her the story I get to look at her round face with those dark eyes. This is the one I taught how to pitch and catch and shoot. The one who made me cry when she got queen at Prom. God damn I was proud. She still wants to know her Daddy. This feels like it always did. When she leaves, I feel a little better knowing someone here still thinks I'm the man who hung the moon.

All this reminiscing makes me hungry. Heading back to the kitchen, I find Bee lingering again.

"Is there any sac-a-lait left? Or potato salad?" I'm regretting it already. She's got a look.

"John, I don't want you to go back to work tonight."

"Tough," I declare. If she's smart she'll pick up from my tone I'm in no mood.

"Fine. Then I'll tell it like it is. I don't want you going to another woman's house tonight."

The little boy, a young me, hears her words. He's been caught. He's caught cutting the grass the wrong direction. He's caught asking a question when his daddy is drunk. He's caught playing earlier than when his daddy said it was ok to. But the grown man, who owns this house, and made this family, decided to never feel caught again in his own home. I get angry. Fire burns through my chest and up my neck. My scar there gets especially hot. My blood is fire that will burn her if she doesn't stop.

"I'm going to believe you're drunk right now. Drunk and not crazy. And I don't care where this bullshit is coming from, but it's going to stop right now. I'm heading to work tonight. That's all there is to it."

"What about this home? What about me? You always have a priority that doesn't involve us. You always—"

She doesn't seem to see this fire. Or maybe she does and she doesn't respect it. I'll make her respect it. "I'm going to give you one last chance."

"If you beat me, what do you think my Daddy will do?"

The flames blow out and the little boy is back and center. "Huh," is all I can say with a laugh. The words that caged the rage, finding that scared boy again, are nothing more than "I'm gonna tell my Daddy." But it's Auguste.

Staying drunk is the only way to make it through the next week. The last time I did that was when my dad died. The guys at the shop can't tell the difference. I'm not sure I can either. As I inventory what I drank the night before, and how many Bloody Marys got my eyes open this morning, the sound of shouting captures my attention. Looking around the shop I see the guys staring at Old Man Leonard's office.

"Forget it Matthew. I've been in this business for thirty-five years. That's before you were alive, in case you're no good at math either. We spend money on tools and on labor. That is this business."

"Why are you so afraid of technology?"

"What the fuck are you talking about? My whole industry is technology!"

"And it sucks. You're bleeding money."

"You don't know what the hell you're talking about!"

"Half of your inventory isn't even coded in the system. Your payroll might as well be in another language. I don't know how your accountant figures anything out. Or, he's where you're bleeding some money."

"Shut your fucking mouth you little cum stain! I like Doug more than I like you. He's been with me since the beginning."

"Then maybe he should be buried in the same coffin with you and this company. Mom was right. I shouldn't bother. You're running this company into the ground."

From the vantage point he's taken to watch the fight up close, Swedge grabs Old Leonard's arm before he can finish his swing. His fist never makes it to his son's jaw. "Get out of my shop," is the blow he deals instead. Matthew grimaces and stomps out of his dad's shop, grabbing his flannel leftover from Nirvana's heyday. Leonard thanks Swedge. Everyone is back to work within a few minutes, except for Swedge. His face belongs to a nine-year-old who got his bike stolen.

"I can't find my two good wrenches."

"Where'd you leave them?" I ask.

"Probably by the pipe I was working on before I left. The boys usually pick them up."

"You check with them?"

"Yeah. They ain't seen 'em."

"Maybe Matthew? Leonard's kid. He's been trying to run the shop you know."

It takes work not to smile while the vein pops out of Swedge's neck. With the boss mad at his son, and the boys about to be mad at him too, thinking he's the one who took Swedge's tools, I make my way into Leonard's office at the back of the shop for the kill.

"I can honestly say I know how that feels," I convey with fatherly sympathy.

"Do you? Your kids already old enough to think they know better than you? Are they planning your funeral too?"

"They know better than to tell me what they'll spend my funeral fund on."

"This business is changing. I think I chose a good time to look for the door."

"Important parts are still the same."

"Maybe," he glances over at this computer. "John you got lunch plans?"

"Now I do."

We pass up several perfectly good restaurants and bars, but he has his heart set on T-Coon's. The Lent menu looks good, reminding me I haven't eaten since that loveless lunch at home Monday. It takes a moment to decide whether I want a beer, but it would be rude to make him drink alone. His son did just tell him to go fuck himself and opened the door to me getting this company without a fight. A beer is in order either way.

"You want my company, John." I stare at him. His voice went down at the end. This is not a question. He makes me wait. "I thought about selling to you, but I know you don't have the money. You piss it away all the time. And you're still married. So I know for sure you're not hanging on to money." We laugh together. I continue to wait. But he doesn't say a word, or even look at me, until the food comes. One bite into the special, he breaks the silence. "Why'd you really pull my best welder off a job on a fast deadline to go weld a piece of shit padeye on a dock?"

Wiping fried catfish crumbs from my mouth, I don't skip a beat. "Because Oilcon is a big fish. You taught me to cull the little ones when a big fish shows up."

He takes two more bites of his special. "That company man is connected to an old friend. You jeopardized our relationship when you did that."

"Then it's a good thing we finished on time."

"You always have an answer, don't you?"

"Only when there is one."

He chuckles then takes another big bite before stretching in his chair. "You are one untrustworthy son of a bitch. And you're good at this."

He dragged me here to make me beg him for his company. But I'm the son of a bitch. He'd save his breath if he understood the likelihood of me ever asking a man for some sort of kindness again.

"Time to upgrade to a real drink." He grabs the inner thigh of the waitress walking by and pulls her to the table. "Gimme a crown and seven, baby. John?"

"Jack and Coke"

He stares at her ass as she walks away. "I love T-Coon's."

Chapter 38

Five more minutes is all I'm giving that turd before I leave. What kind of dumb shit has me waiting in front of a college architecture building, with my flashers on, when we are supposed to be heading to a strip club? I shouldn't have to work this hard to clear my head. A campus cop idles down the street as Yank walks out of the building.

"Thanks for coming to pick me up. We ended up working longer than either of us thought."

"Either of who thought?"

"Me and this professor dude. He saw some of my art and wants to incorporate it in this new building idea he's working on."

"Art? What kind of fairy shit are you talking about?"

"The kind of fairy shit that got me welding. I started out doing metal art. Took metallurgy for two semesters. Stayed until I learned what I wanted to. They had these ridiculous no drug policies in their workshops." Half the time he talks I'm left trying to figure out if he's telling the truth.

"Alright. So why did you decide we're heading to the butt hut tonight?"

"I have a date."

"You need to be joking," I command.

"Wouldn't joke about love."

"Love?"

"Yeah. Met this girl at City Bar in Maurice last Sunday. When I told her I'd pay her tab if she could outdrink me, she left me with a two hundred twenty dollar bill and the first hangover I've had since I was fifteen."

"And you're meeting her at a strip club."

"No, I'm meeting her at work."

"Yank, what have I told you about those strippers?"

"Something too hard to remember. I do a lot of drugs."

Lipstick's always feels desperate. Not radioactive, like the club sharing a road with a chemical plant out in Ascension Parish. Not shiny and contagious like clubs on Bourbon in New Orleans. It's full of people trying to mimic those things and falling sleepily short. It's dim lights and smoky atmosphere, but it always feels like some horny uncle's living room.

"Tell me we're not gonna sit around and wait for her shift!" I yell the thumping music. He points to the main stage. A beautiful blonde weaves her perfect body around the pole. I can't take my eyes off her.

"Pretty amazing, right? And she's even smarter than she is pretty. She's like me. Transplant. California."

In the middle of being mesmerized, I felt of tingle of confusion. Or it's curiosity. I've never met someone from California. Much less something like her. We sit at the stage. Her body shimmers and shifts like water beneath a rig until she's in front of us. No fruit smelling perfume wafts. She smells like sweat and woman.

"I didn't think you'd show. You were so drunk you couldn't remember your name, much less mine," she tells him.

The song changes. She stands, moving into the new rhythm. Her tops comes off, undone by invisible fingers. Those are California tits: no stretch marks, implant scars hidden, and not a tan line to be seen. For Yank's sake I try not to stare too hard. But she grabs the pole and makes gravity disappear. Making her rounds on the stage, she gets fives and tens in her G-string. In this place they might as well be hundreds. Honestly, she deserves more. She finishes her dance in front of us. Yank smiles, a smile I haven't seen on him before. When she makes her exit, he turns to me with the same goofy smile. "Nice huh?"

"Yeah. Nice."

"I think I'm in love."

"You keep talking about that."

She comes out of the back room wearing little more than she did when she went in. She thanks all her customers before sitting in Yank's lap.

"Michelle this is John."

"Tonight it's Amber."

"Sorry. Amber. This is John Mouton."

"You're Cajun, John?"

"*Mais* yeah, *cher?* Who's ya daddy and what color is his roux?"

"Oh I love Cajuns!"

"Mais, you in da right place!"

Yank glowers from behind her blonde mane. "John's my boss."

"Oh. Well. This is weird. I'm not part of a deal for getting you a raise, am I?" She set him up so well. I wait for him to start closing his deal.

"Absolutely not. John's also a good friend. He's here to make sure I don't screw this up."

This little monkey is actually in love. And from the way she's settling more in his lap, it seems she's on it too. It's weird. The setting makes it weirder. These fellas are here for very specific reasons. Two people having real feeling, real love, is screwing with the illusion, pulling the reality of desperation back into the room.

"Yank tells me you're from California. How the hell did you end up in Lafayette, Louisiana?"

"Nursing school. You guys have a good one here. And it's so cheap."

"You can get it done on this salary?" I chuckle.

"And then some," she responds seriously, looking me in the eye. "It's how I got through undergrad too."

"Shoo, you got some skills, you!"

She smiles her work smile. The kiss she puts on Yank's cheek is not work-related, though. Leaving his lap, she goes back to work her room. Even though her dance ended four songs ago, it's still her room.

"John, you don't talk like that," Yank barks into my ear.

"What?" After my eyes get off her ass, I meet Yank's very serious face. "Oh. I was just playing up the Cajun thing. You do it with your Yankee accent all the time."

"But why her? I'm trying to get with her."

She's by the bar, running her fingers along the collar of a sports coat on an elderly man. "I'm buying a dance," he declares, starting to get up.

"Yank, why don't you ask her out on a regular date so we can just enjoy our evening?"

"See you later, John."

The whipped little son of a bitch leaves me at the foot of the stage. He taps her on the shoulder like some goofy kid. She doesn't even tell the old fart she was working on bye when they head to a dark, velvety corner. My attention gets re-occupied by the backwoods stripper who now takes the stage in front of me. Her smile counts less than fifty-two. Looking back at the pair, at what little I can see through their crack in the curtain, I can tell it's not strictly business happening in there. They've officially made this place worse than it already was.

Sick of love in the wrong places, sick of men who don't act like men, I peel out onto Johnston. I can't even figure out why I'm so pissed, or whatever this is. Grabbing my car phone, I dial Linda's number without needing to look at the keypad. No surprise when she doesn't answer. Then I dial her favorite watering hole. No answer there. And why should there be at ten o'clock at night on a weekend? Something weird is happening in my head. My five-day drunk must be wearing off and it could not have picked a worse time. I need to get out of my element for a little bit. Back to Back on Pine St. always has good blues. Even if it is on the other side of town.

Turning down Simcoe I remember why I don't take the back way at night anymore. It's like I took a wrong turn into Africa. They are everywhere. All of them move so damn slow to cross the street. The girls are the worst because they can't walk in the damn six-inch heels they stole. I scream and honk at one group because they decide to hold a fucking family reunion in the middle of the road. They glare at me like I'll get scared of them. Let them touch my truck, and they'll see how fast I can turn them into a streak on the road. The worst is when I see these big Black boys with their white trophy girls. Like these two about to cross at the next light. She looks like she came straight out of a trailer, wearing baggy jeans and everything. With the hangover headache approaching, and being done with all this foolishness, I decide to let this white piece of trash know where she belongs. My words get stuck in my throat when I realize it's Addie.

Chapter 39

This morning I don't have to open my eyes to know where I am. Linda's voice is behind my throbbing eyelids. "Get up, John. Go to work." Despite the tenderness in her voice, it acts like a knife through my skull. She's running her finger over the bump of the scar on my neck. Her hand might as well be sandpaper. How drunk did I get last night? "What do you do when I'm not here to make sure you don't fuck up your job? Or your life?"

"Well, I do sleep a lot later."

She laughs. "One of these mornings you're going to stop pretending you don't remember what you tell me when you're drunk." That's been true other mornings, but not this one. When I try to remember the night before, it all stops as I was leaving the strip club.

"Shut up, Linda."

"Whoa, there. Be hungover. Be pissy. But be disrespectful, and we stop this thing we have."

Why did I get so drunk last night? Did Beatrice call?

"Have a good day, sweetie," I whisper as I lean over and kiss her.

"You always did strike me as someone who learns the hard way."

Inside my truck I hear my phone ringing before I open the door. Old Leonard must have been calling all morning. "Get out of whatever hooker's bed you're in and get your ass to work. If you really think you can land Oilcon for more than some dock welds you better be here in the next fifteen minutes."

He's waiting for me in his gravel lot when I arrive nine minutes later. The look on his face is disgust. I smile through the headache.

"Look at you." He coughs. "No. Smell you. I should have done this myself."

"I got this Leonard."

"You stink, John! I'm not letting you talk to Oilcon looking and smelling like that."

"Three minutes for a shower."

"He'll be here in two."

"Two minutes, then!" I yell while grabbing my bag out of the back of my truck. Exiting the shower, I almost run into the Company Man I'd taken to the bar in Fourchon. Totally different in presentation with a collared shirt and shiny shoes, he cuts a wide alligator grin upon seeing me. I really hope the old man is watching.

"Just the man I wanted to see!" Company Man blurts.

"Because you need someone you can trust when you got your guys on the rig and you're going kelly down?"

"We'll see how that sounds after we get back from New Orleans. I'm here to collect on your offer. And I warn you. I've been out for thirty days."

My stomach drops to my feet. I can't entertain these boys in New Orleans solo. My salvation comes in the form of Yank ducking behind some pipes in the back of the shop. "Let me collect my associate and we'll be ready to get on the road in about an hour. Can I send you to a good place for lunch?"

"I am feeling a mite peckish."

"Talk to our secretary and let her know what you're in the mood for." Turning to go find Yank behind the pipes, I catch a glimpse of Leonard staring from his office. He's got a half smile on his face. It'll be hard to convince him I can run this place if I fuck this up. Walking into the piping in the back, I find Yank putting his welder's helmet on.

"I need your help."

"I knew you were gonna ask again as soon as I saw those guys in the shop."

"They want to go party in New Orleans. We need to show them a good time."

"Can't help you."

"Come on Yank! Your new girlfriend can come along and bring some of her stripper friends."

"Definitely can't help you."

"What the fuck, dude? I go to bat for you all the time. I can work on getting you a big welding gig, at a better place, this way! They have to get to know you."

"I don't want to get to know *them.*"

"What the hell is your problem? Grab your balls, man!"

"My problem is fake-ass motherfuckers like that Company Man who think they own people. Worst part is you're starting to sound and act like them."

"You're not making sense, Yank."

"John you turned on the Cajun act last night when a stripper thought it was cute. You didn't even care that she's a girl I like. Now you want me to bring her as a party favor."

"She's a stripper! You've dated three at a time before. Listen. None of last night matters right now. Let's get you a big boy job."

"Stop talking to me like you know what I need!" It's a good thing the fans are running. Otherwise people like Swedge would be taking a little too much notice.

"Come on, man. We're pals."

"Yeah, we're pals. When we want the same things or we're ready to party. But I'm not fucking up this thing with Michelle just because you want to feel big. I don't have anything to prove to anybody. You go do what you gotta do. I'm gonna melt some metal."

He lights up the acetylene torch, chasing me away with the brightness. Screw him. It's like they don't make real men anymore. If he'll bite the hand that feeds him, I can find someone else to party with. There's got to be a thousand welders in this town. Still in the market for a party pal, I know the next best guy to call.

Dudley packs them into his brand-new suburban. I'll be damned if my cousin doesn't own anything more than a year old. Heading toward I-10 East with a full ice chest, we make one stop at the daiquiri shop before hitting the road. The two guys with Company Man are only along for the ride. One of them doesn't even seem to work for him. We stop in Baton Rouge to pee and listen to Company Man making disparaging remarks about LSU. Now I know he's from Georgia. Good thing I went to USL and I don't care much what he says about this damn place.

The secretary put us up at the Inn on Bourbon. It smells like the rest of this city: piss, vomit, liquor, and sin. The Company Man likes it because it's right on Bourbon and feels authentic. He's hungry again. No wonder his belly is bigger than mine. Sweat perpetually beads on his red, fat face. It's worse in this sunken paradise, New Orleans being a below sea level pressure-cooker and all. His sparse strawberry blond hair sticks to his scalp. I watch for his head to explode the way that collar clinches his neck. Tonight will be a slow moving train wreck while he comes unhinged.

At Brennan's I order the biggest ribeye they got. They try and sell me on sides. Why is it so weird that I only want the damn meat? He orders something with shrimp and extra sides. All of it has tons of butter. And he's still drinking some damn girly drinks, cocktails with tons of sugar. Now I'll need to worry about him getting sick. I know his two friends won't babysit him. Dudley is holding his own, entertaining the other two without creeping them out. He was a better choice than Yank.

"All right. Is it time to cut loose?" I offer.

"Y'all got some clubs you can take me to? You said you know this town," Company Man challenges, eyes gleaming.

"Yes sir. You want a bar? A place to meet women—"

"Strip club, John. It's got everything you just mentioned, and then some."

"Well here we go. Got a place tucked away that should suit you."

While signing the check I leave extra tip on the company credit card, because fuck Old Leonard. Heading out the door, Dud walks close to me and starts to whisper.

"I can't go to a strip club."

"You allergic?"

"My wife doesn't like when I go to strip clubs."

"Well it's a good thing it's tucked back, kind of like your balls are right now. Only people who know about it are the people who know about it."

"She'll be so pissed at me."

"How will she know? You got a private eye following you?"

"I think I do." I stop, but make sure to keep my trio in sight.

"You're fucking joking."

"I didn't see his car on the way here, but there's been an old Pontiac around every time I leave work lately. She knew about the boat, John. I never brought it home and I paid cash. Tried to make me believe she gets it through gossip."

"Goddamn it, Dudley!" I storm off after the trio. I'm solo now, keeping these three boys happy all by myself. If his wife hears about this, she'll tell Bee, or worse, Auguste. I'll be explaining this shit for years. They don't understand this business. They don't understand what it takes nowadays. "Go back to the hotel."

"If he's here, he's gonna suspect something is up when I break off from you."

"Yeah. He'll know how big of a pussy you are and how you can't stand up to your wife. Why'd you come here in the first place?"

"I thought we were just going drinking!"

"You know better, Dud. You've been in this business before."

"Never went to a strip club on company funds while being a roustabout, John."

"Go back to the hotel. Or go find a bar to prop up. Or whatever. Just go."

Catching back up to the trio I lead them away from Bourbon Street to my spot. We pass two iron gates, walk through a dark courtyard, past a giant jigaboo bouncer, into the belly of the most scandalous place I've ever been able to talk my way into. A few conciliatory words to ensure them we would be gentlemen in the gentlemen's club, along with a heavy cover, and we are granted entry. In the compromised state I was in during my last visit, it escaped my attention how this is a converted residence. With windows blacked out, light gets sucked out of the bulbs. Only the spotlights on the small circular platforms dotted throughout the room provide light. A sparkling, sweating, completely nude body populates each of the raised floors.

"So fellas, this is the place. Anything you want—and I do mean anything—is within your reach. Pick all of your poisons," we're told by the greasy, skinny white guy checking ID's at the door. My crew all go to the first platform before realizing there is no point sharing. Each find something to scratch an itch they didn't know they had. This is where I close the deal.

My own flavor is twisting herself around the pole in the right corner platform. I'll share her with only one other guy. She looks like that California girl, Yank's girl. I put a fifty down as goodwill. She looks me in the eye when she smiles. These girls are professionals. Blond hair, long, thin limbs, she's the opposite of every girl in south Louisiana. She's exotic. The song finishes and she steps down from her stage still nude. I watch her perfectly formed ass saunter away from me, wishing I wasn't so gentlemanly before she left. Another song starts. Thankfully this place doesn't play any thumping booty music, only jazz and rock. I hear heels clicking from my right and look to see who my new flavor is. I almost fall out of my chair. The girl in front of me has sweet, dark brown curls, dark eyes, a round face, and big ass. She could be Addie's twin sister. My heart seizes like an unoiled engine. I stare at her face to confirm my daughter is not nude in front of me. I have no choice but to keep my eyes on hers, otherwise I risk getting a hard on for a replica of my daughter. She smiles when she notices I'm watching her face. Frozen, I can't smile back. She dances more, thrusting her hips in rhythm, looking over her shoulder as she shows me everything. Eventually she leans in front of me, cupping her small breasts together as a billfold. When I don't move she puts her hands on my shoulders, and brings her tits to my face, before sliding her lips down next to my ear.

"I know you like what you see. You want something more private?"

The first bill I can find in my pocket is a hundred. As she backs up to the stage to wait for my reply, I stuff the money in her hand, and head to the bar.

"Bud Light."

"No beer. Cocktails and Wine only."

"Bourbon."

"What kind?"

"Just… whatever."

Something about her, something more than the way she looked, reminds me of Addie. Fist filled with bourbon, I turn back toward the scene. It's changed. What's in front of me is not the crazy night I came here to find again, the one where every sexual fantasy plays out. From this vantage point the girls, probing their customers eyes for cues on how to get paid, while the customer's imaginations probe their bodies, are working this room the way I work the shop. Despite the place being classier than Lipsticks in Lafayette, men gawk with the same empty, desperate faces. As the red-faced Company Man goes to the back room, closing his deal and mine, I don't feel satisfied. It's Yank's fault, him and his little blonde from last night. The spell of this place is broken.

All I can see is a bunch of people who wish they had what those two seemed to have but are settling for much less. But that doesn't explain it all.

"That was a big tip. You seem a little shy. How about you let me take the lead." I'm frozen again. It's the girl from the stage. Her eyes are lighter than Addie's.

"I'm ok. Thanks sweetie."

"You sure? I'd like to thank you for being so generous. I can be generous, too."

"No. Thank you. Another time." I despise the words as soon as they're out of my mouth. I rarely ever see my daughter anymore, and here is the last place I want to be reminded of her. She takes my averted eyes as an invitation. Usually I have all the words in the world to talk my way into or out of anything. As I wish I could wash my eyes with holy water, divine intervention finds me. With the sound of a shriek, the bouncers and the two other guys with the Company Man rush to the back rooms. By the time I join them, the big jigaboo bouncer looks like he's trying to pull a red balloon off a collared shirt. I push through the throng to where the Company Man is gasping for air.

"Hey brother!"

"Fuck you!" gets spat back in my face. This bouncer must be six foot four.

"I'm pressing charges!" cries the stripper the Company Man was sharing the room with. She's got a purple mark forming under her eye. The Oilcon deal is about to be choked.

"For a thousand dollars you could save yourself the paperwork," I force my mouth to say to the aggrieved stripper.

"Fuck you," spits into my face again from the Black mountain.

"Twelve hundred! And your friend could get three hundred for the trouble of having to manhandle this fella." The Company Man's head is turning from red to purple in the big Black hands.

"Let me see the money." Pulling the wad from my pocket, I hand it to her. She counts it. "This is eighteen hundred. I'll take it. Let him go, Derrick."

"Fuck this dude!"

"Here." She counts out eight hundred and sticks it in the big dude's pocket. Then she reaches into the Company Man's pocket. She pulls out his wad and counts it. She gives another four hundred to the bouncer and keeps the rest for herself. "He's not worth it. He's oilfield trash. They don't learn anything unless you make them pay. From the sounds of it, this one is from Lafayette. He's so ignorant he doesn't know how he's getting fucked worse than me."

The big Black man lets go and the Company Man falls to the floor. It's the first time I notice his pants and boxers around his ankles.

"Y'all bitches better make yourself scarce before I stop listening to my associate."

From behind the big Black man the Addie lookalike walks up to find out what is happening. The two of them next to each other pulls a memory from my brain like a bill from a G-string. I've seen this before. It was last night, right before I tied one on tight. My daughter was on the wrong side of town with the wrong kind of man. A hot fire burns from my chest to my neck. I can't deal with this right now. The need to get out of here just got even more serious. The sweaty, red Company Man struggles to his feet, and then struggles to get his pants on. His two tagalongs, who watched the whole incident behind me, don't offer to help. Grabbing his shoulders from behind, I shove Company Man to the door. We quickly make our way back into a more populated part of the quarter. The streetlights seem like sunrise after the hole we crawled out of.

"Alright. I guess we'll call it a night."

"The hell we are." The sweaty crawfish starts back for the gate we exited. I've lost all ability to tolerate this. My eyes ask his friends to intervene, but they smile. They've seen this all before. I walk around and stand in front of Company Man.

"Get out of my way asshole! I'm teaching that bitch a lesson."

"She's been taught. I promise."

"You pussy! You pussified little coonass! Y'all never stand up for yourselves! Ignorant swamp rats!"

The fire burns hotter and licks my neck, setting my scar ablaze. Old Leonard can piss me off, but he never talks to me like this. No one gets to talk to me like my father did. I don't ever have time for this. Right now, I need to find my daughter and tear her a new asshole before she throws her life away on some trash. This needs to wrap up, now.

"That's enough. Nothing good is coming out of you going back in there."

"That's right nothing good. And that bitch is about to find out."

A clip from the nightmare plays in front of my waking eyes. Those were his words when I stood in front of him, me only thirteen years old and one hundred and ten pounds, while he spoiled for a fight with my mom, reeking of whiskey. Since the first cold front of the fall had come through, he wanted a gumbo. All she did was cook the roux dark like he liked it, only to end up burning it. Instead of throwing that hot, skin-peeling roux on her, I stepped in front, and it ended up on me. Most of it landed on my shirt. Only a little ended up above my collar, searing a red scar into my neck that turns bright purple when hate hits my veins. The Company Man's face overtakes my father's in the vision.

"You're useless. You know that? How'd I ever think you were going to be worth a damn to me?" I ball my fist. When I was fifteen, I swore I'd never listen to this again. Not without making the person who said it to me regret it. I should have cracked my father's skull open to watch all his hate spill out onto the kitchen linoleum. Knowing I'd be no better than my father, I swallowed my own hate. I didn't want a future burnt and blackened beyond recognition by my daddy's roux. I knew I had to be better than this, better than this man, this trash. The bones of that day are buried in my stomach, under pressure. My business is all about making something useful out of the death of the past. It must be why I'm thinking more about Addie than teaching this Company Man a lesson. She could make it out. She didn't have to start out being a dumb coonass. My whole life I've tried to get away from trash and she wants to be closer to it. I can't believe this. My blood moves at a rolling boil through my veins. Staring at the Company Man's oversized, red, sweating head I could finally put all this fire to use, spilling his brains on the greasy New Orleans street.

"You're not even gonna fight me you pussy? Well… if you want my business you should get your ass back over here now." I could do it; rub this sanctimonious asshole into the ground. It's what he deserves. But I deserve to be where he is. The reward for a whole life of beating the dealer is at stake. This fire inside me can burn anything it touches, but it also powers my success. I'll need to break my own rule, be beaten again, if I want to win.

"Well if we're going back in there, we're gonna need a few more shots. I'm buying," I say, pushing the pressure of the night back into my belly.

"You better buy, you pussy."

Back on Bourbon he's attracted to the shiny strip clubs and flashy bars. It doesn't take much to finish him off. His friends decide to stay in the club while I lug his sweaty carcass back to the hotel room. Dud is long gone.

Chapter 40

This time the nightmare is about what happened after the roux. My mom, with a bloody nose, dabbed aloe vera at my neck. My siblings were still hiding in their rooms. She cried. The dream stays stuck there, us sitting on the floor defeated, believing that's all we'd ever be.

Today I'm going to save Addie from a life like that. Trash is all the same. My first thought is to take her truck away. But I have a big problem. If I tell her I saw them, that it was me that honked, she'd ask what I was doing on Simcoe and where I was coming from. I don't have to tell her. But if I don't, she'll know I'm hiding something. I could lie. I'm a good liar. But Addie always knows when I'm lying. Even as a little girl, she'd look at me with her huge brown eyes and see through my smile. Already she doesn't see Superman when she looks at me anymore. Convincing her I'm better than anybody, even that porch monkey she was with, will be impossible if I do it with a lie. I'll do the thing I hear other dads do with daughters. I invite her out to lunch.

"You remember when I used to bring you here when you were a kid?"

"I thought that's why you wanted to come here."

"Yeah, maybe so."

We bury our faces in our po-boys. The Jack Miller barbecue sauce continually smears across my face and I'm thankful for it. All the wiping gives me time to figure out what the hell to say next. Man, I wish I'd thought past grabbing Old Tyme and taking it to Girard Park.

"You alright, Addie?"

"Me. Yeah. Doing fine. You?"

"Oh, I'm good, babe." I take another bite and work on my strategy. "I've been worried, no, thinking about you more lately. We don't get to do this enough anymore."

"We have busy lives now, Daddy,"

"I know. Just… wish we could talk more. You know?"

"We can talk now." Damn it. How do I say this without incriminating myself?

"You remember that time we went fishing with Paw Paw and he shot some nutria. I think it was the first time you saw nutria. Those ugly little bastards grossed you out. You even screamed when you first saw them!"

"They still gross me out. I don't even like staying in this park at sunset."

"Yeah. I remember you said you were glad Paw Paw shot them."

"Yeah. I think they should all be shot."

"Hmmm."

She's got the idea. So now how do I connect that to her choice in men?

"You want to go fishing soon?" she asks sweetly. Looking over to her slowly swinging, mayonnaise at the corner of her pouty mouth, her big brown eyes on me, expecting me to give her the world, I chase her stripper version from my head. She still sees the real me, the man I've tried to give her since my own father was so awful. She still looks to me for answers. Maybe I don't need to teach her something today. It could have been a one-time thing, testing things out. I've done my own testing. For now, I can let it go and just keep a closer eye on it. She talks about fishing and her Paw Paw. I almost lose interest until she asks how work is going.

"Work? Work's good, I guess. Always like a derrick. Up and down. As long as it never tanks like it did the eighties, we'll be alright."

"You still like what you're doing?"

"Yeah. Gets the bills paid."

I forget how beautiful she is. How nice she is. Being with her purges all the weird feelings I had with her stripper twin in New Orleans. She's all the best parts of me and her momma. When I look at her again, she has a weird smile on her face.

"What?"

"What?" she echoes

"You're smiling."

"Oh. Just thinking about something one of my friends did recently."

"Like what. I could use a good story."

"Oh, it's stupid. "

"Those are my favorite."

While we laugh, I see this is part of what I've been avoiding. It can't last, especially not with the other two living in that house. Bee can't be made happy. Will is too far gone. But that thinking turns south when I get a call from Will after dark. Immediately I suspect Bee is up to something. "What are you doing calling me?" Worse than Bee's plotting, he's interrupting a deal I'm about to close with this pretty young thing.

"Figure I'd make your dreams come true. I'm at a lame party and don't have a ride home."

"A party huh?" I'll be damned. I'm proud of the little *cawain.* "T-boy I'm a little busy right now."

"Too busy for a free beer? I'll buy if you order."

Back where memories don't hurt, I see a young man, a young me, having his first beer with his Daddy. It was a rare time I ever got to see Daddy smile at something I did. I'd always hoped I'd get to do it with my son. Funny how after you give up on people, they can still surprise you. Fifteen minutes later my son is crawling into my truck to come have a beer with his Pop.

"Put those goggles where I can see them. I've been looking for them. So where we going T-boy? We could go find something in Broussard or we can stick closer to the house."

"I'll let you choose."

"Let's go to Parrain's. There will be some people I could introduce you to."

Both of my kids are acting like they like me in the same week. Maybe I've gotten them all wrong. Or maybe they're growing up and coming into their own. Will's shoulders are starting to square a little. His girl arms dangle from wider spots. If he can start thinking for himself he won't believe half the shit my wife says about me behind my back.

"So, what were you doing there? I thought you only liked playing video games."

"I met some new friends."

"Girls or guys?" Need to make sure.

"Guys mostly. But some girls."

"Just wear a condom. I'm not paying for grandbabies this early. You need some condoms?"

"No, Dad. Thanks, though. What's this bar?"

"Place I go after work. They have 'Bikini Fridays.' Too bad it's Saturday. Most of the same old boys will be there."

Trudy gets a Bud Light ready for me as I approach the bar. Cocking my head toward my son I let her know I need one more. He doesn't wince when he takes a sip like he did when he was ten. We start making the rounds, getting him to shake firm, working man's hands. The little brat is awkward, but I think that's because he's fifteen. No, wait. He's sixteen now. He doesn't laugh when they pick at him but doesn't try and hide behind me or anything. The younger guys, some of whom I got jobs, come and tell Will how good of a guy I am. The old bar maids tell Will how much he looks like me. Stick a bigger belly on him, and we might be twins, they say. Linda slides her hands under my arms and over my chest. She whispers in my ear, telling me I'm mixing family with pleasure. She needs to stop touching me like that for now.

"You're Will?" she asks. Her voice is a tease like the rest of her.

"Yes ma'am."

She smiles at me. "So polite, *cher 'tit bebe*! And you're handsome like your daddy, too! My name is Linda."

"Nice to meet you."

She gives me a sarcastic thumbs-up before walking away. She'll throw this in my face later. Will is giving me a look. Last thing I need is for this little marsh hen to run back to his mother about this. Nobody taught him how this works. He doesn't know how to be a real man in his world. A new beer coming across the bar without me having to order it. I'll have to explain this to him.

"How does Paw Paw say that? *Quoi tu peut faire avec une femme comme ça?* What you gonna do with a woman like that? I don't think your mom should know. She'll probably think the wrong thing. That lady has had a thing for me for a while, but I know better than to stick my dick in that alligator's mouth." He doesn't seem to care one way or another. With enough work maybe he'll even turn out like one of these guys, or maybe even like me. "How about a shot with your old Pops! Trudy! Get us a couple of red snappers! And maybe shots too!"

Even without painful morning light, the fan above me is unfamiliar. Linda doesn't have a ceiling fan in her room. And she doesn't get out of bed before me. She certainly doesn't cook. But the smell of trinity mixes with the end of the nightmare. This time the nightmare had my daddy with the pan ready to go, but was frozen. Auguste stood over his shoulder. I kept waiting for Auguste to do something. Splitting dream nightmares from real ones, an angry clang comes from the behind the closed door. I know exactly where I am.

"What the *FUCK* Beatrice?!" Stumbling down the hall I find my son walking away from a head-splitting racket in the kitchen. She is punishing us both. "Why in the hell you got to make so much goddamn *noise?*"

"I thought that's what you do when people are sleeping. At least I'm not drunk while I'm doing it. And at least I'm not getting our underage son drunk while I do it. The worst that can happen when I'm making noise is that he learns how to cook."

"Holy shit Beatrice! You're going off about me bringing *our* son home safe." Behind me I hear him slink off toward his room. Fine. I don't care if he sees me put his mother in her place again. "Well? You going to say anything now that Will is gone and you don't have to act like you're in charge?"

"You're being a bully, John."

"And you're being a bitch."

"Be careful, John."

She knows better. After all these years, she should have learned. I don't get talked to like that. It was enough for that blow-hard Company Man to treat me like that. She picked the wrong day to do this. I'm not swallowing it this time. "You threatening me?"

"No."

Her soap opera soaked brain makes her think shit like this is normal. I've had enough of this. Any time I enter this house, I pay for it. Moving toward her, contemplating the ways to break her, once and for all, I glimpse something shiny. Over her shoulder, I see her clutch the chef's knife. Her grip on it is not one she uses to chop onions. She intends to hurt me. She's lost it. The fire that had been relit when she started banging pots is now an inferno. Readying myself to teach her, I catch her eyes peering over her shoulder. They are terrified. A glimpse from the past, and those eyes, cuts into the moment. The eyes from my past belong to my mother. Bloody and bruised, she looked at me from under the covers of her bed. We were sure she would die. She stayed there for two weeks before she could walk without help. It was me who held the knife back then. My knuckles were white just like Bee's as I told my father to leave and never come back. Her eyes show me who I am in this picture from my past. The fire instantly gets extinguished. I'm the scared little boy, again; scared of the person the knife is meant for.

Walking back to my room, I put on pants and grab my bag. Without thinking, I open Will's door on my way to my truck.

"You coming my boy?"

"Paw Paw is coming. It's Sunday," Will says

Auguste is the last person I need to see right now. The man who should have been my father will see the look on his daughter's face and know I put it there. "I'm tired of being a piece of shit," fumbles out of my mouth before I make it out of Will's doorway. My tires squeal as I struggle to put road between me and this place. Passing Mr. Chenevert's truck aiming for my house, I desperately hope he doesn't recognize me.

Chapter 41

Yank is quiet at Edie's. He munches on his biscuits without saying much. I get the impression he's mad at me. But I can't tell for what. It's like I'm taking my wife to lunch.

"You gonna say something? Or should I have come here alone."

"What do you want me to say?"

"I don't know. You've been acting weird. You haven't come out in forever."

"I got a girl now."

"You're still with stripper girl?"

"Michelle. Yes. And she doesn't strip anymore. She moved in. I've been paying her bills so she doesn't have to dance."

"She moved in? That's a little fast, huh?"

"Yep."

"Where the hell is Yank and how do I get him back?"

"See. This is why we don't hang out anymore. You think you know me, John. Just because we used to run around and get in trouble together don't make us best friends."

"Ok. That's true. But you are acting all different all of a sudden."

He stares straight forward, chewing slowly on his biscuit. "I come from money. So much goddamned money. I hate it. All of them fake pieces of shit. I'd get into trouble just so the name would get tarnished. I got into welding because I needed something blue-collar, you know. I knew it would piss them off. Usually blue-collar people are more down to earth. Plus, it worked well with my art thing. I did it enough, shit, until they got tired of me. They give me keep-away money now. Like an allowance as long as I stay away." He sops up the last of his gravy and smacks his lips. He looks me in the eye. "You were one of those down to earth people when I met you. I had no intention of staying in the shop because I was having fun drifting. But you were nice to me. You looked out for me. Then you started getting a hard on for running the place. You want to run people. And you're starting to do it like my dad does." Looking down at his blackened hands, he continues, quieter, "But now I can't quit. I got someone who's real. Who's messed up in some of the same ways as me. And who wants me to be who I am, without changing me into something else. And the two sets of bills I got to pay for, plus her school, is enough for you to keep seeing my ugly Yankee face." He smiles at me with the last statement.

"Yank. Man, I'm sorry. I was never trying to be— "

"I don't want your apology, John. Because you don't mean it."

Little bastard thinks he's better than me. It's time he learned what real life is like. "You're right, I'm not sorry. Because there was no silver spoon in my ass when I was born. Some of us fight to get through this world. While you're busy throwing away someone else's money, I've earned all of mine with blood, sweat, and tears."

He crosses his legs in turn, checking the bottom of his boots. Silently he picks at the dirt caked on the bottom of them. I can't tell if he is purposely ignoring me or he's that messed up from all the drugs. Maybe he's even more fried now that he lives with a stripper.

"I guess I didn't realize how much you and my dad are alike. You and I were roughly in the same place when we met. I assumed you still thought of people as people. But really, I was on my way down to earth and you were on your way up, to whatever the hell this is."

"You sound like a fucking liberal, Yank. Come on man. This woman has you talking like a pussy. I do what I do because this is how you get ahead in business. You can't get mad at me or your dad for that."

He looks up with a big smile. He turns his welders cap forward over his slightly crooked nose. "The fuck I can't, John. There you go, assuming you know me. You never knew me. I'm gonna go. Here." He drops thirty dollars on the table. “This is my dad’s money. I’d like him to buy your lunch.”

So many pussy-whipped friends and cousins are in and out of my life. Proves my point: no real men anymore. Yank has gone crazy. This girl seriously messed up his mind, made all his priorities get out of whack. He should be happy I’m so loyal. I’ll still be here when she leaves him, taking all his money, and saddling him with regular doctor visits to have his dick looked at. The brat doesn’t show back in the shop when I get back from lunch. He’s completely crazy if he thinks he can pull that shit for much longer. Before I can get to my desk to check for sales call backs, I hear old Leonard scream my name over the din. It’s the first I notice his son in the office with him. They must have kissed and made up.

“John, have you heard back from your guy at Oilcon.”

“Not yet, I—"

“It’s been a week, John. That sale is going cold. Give him a call. You can show Matthew how this is done.”

What’s this son of a bitch doing here? Is he trying to scare me? Finding the Company Man’s number in my rolodex I call him up. Either by miracle or by curse he picks up in his office.

“Hey, John. You caught me right as I was about to head back out.”

“You recovered from that large time I showed you.”

“Heh. Yeah. Sort of.”

“Well now that you’re about to head out you might remember us when you need some tools.”

Old Leonard and his offspring stare at me while I grip the handset. I give them a big smile.

“Yeah. Maybe. We’ll see. Look, I need to head out, John. We’ll reconnect later.”

“Oh yeah. Sure will. We’ll be ready when you need something.” When I put the handset down Leonard waits for me to say something.

"He's heading out. Said he'd get back with us when he's on the rig and has a chance to figure out what's going on."

"Don't hose me, John. You spent over a grand in bars and at restaurants. You've been running around behind my back with this guy for a while. You need to shit or get off the pot. You have a week to close or you'll have to run all future spending through Lilly in the front."

Matthew, the little butt spelunker, giggles as his father scolds me. I'm getting screwed by a Company Man who has a few loose bolts, and a computer geek who probably gives his daddy handjobs. Add to this Yank's little hissy fit and I'm done with this shop for the day. Given my standing with Oilcon I try to think about some other customers I could round up, but nothing is popping off the boards lately. This must mean I'm supposed to call it a day. Maybe I can go see how Dud is doing with his private eye.

Dud's paranoia must have rubbed off on me. After his secretary tells me he went home for the day, I start checking my rearview mirror. It takes a few miles to convince myself no one is behind me. But paranoia comes right back when I pull off East Broussard onto Dud's street. In front of his obnoxiously rich house is my father-in-law's old clunker. I nearly get cold feet. Then the paranoia strengthens, and I worry it would look worse for me to leave right after I pull up. When I get out of my truck, I can see two silhouettes under the boat cover.

"Dud I told you I could get one of my guys to fix your boat! Why'd you drag poor Mr. Chenevert all the way out here?"

"He offered. We met up at a traffic light after I'd gone to pick up my boat from the time we took it froggin'."

"*Bonjour* Mr. Chenevert."

"John."

Using a MIG welder for aluminum is crazy. He's lucky he doesn't burn his arm off or cut right through the bottom of the boat. Upon looking at his patch I can see it was stupid to doubt him.

"You thirsty? I'll go get some beer. What do you drink Mr. Chenevert?" Dud offers.

"Schlitz."

"Is Coors ok?"

Auguste pushes the shield up on his helmet and looks at Dud seriously.

"I'll take Dud and get you some Schlitz, Mr. Chenevert," I declare. We don't even make it out of the driveway before I start in on Dudley. "What the hell are you doing bringing my father-in-law to your house to weld your stupid ass boat?"

"I told you! He offered! My wife has been up and down my ass for everything. When I came back from New Orleans, she told me she would start selling my shit. To calm her down I said I'd do it myself. I needed to get the boat fixed before I could sell it, though."

"Lemme get this straight. You are helping your wife sell your shit?"

"Not helping her. I'm selling my shit."

"Damn Dudley. You are a bigger pussy than I thought."

As my wheels reach the Circle K parking lot he starts yelling.

"Fuck you, John. You act like you got your wife on a leash. You're never around. Which means she has lots of time on her hands to think about a life without you. Oh yeah. My wife sees your wife in her store or around town, buying groceries. They talk. She sees how your wife is getting more and more unhappy. How long you think that will simmer but not boil over?"

Slamming the door behind him, he gets down and heads inside the Circle K. He thinks he knows how to handle women. His wife handles him. Besides. I'd say things with Bee already done boiled over. I contemplate leaving him here. With Auguste waiting, it's not an option. I'm stuck between all these gossiping women, spineless men, and Auguste Chenevert. The truck door opens, and he gets back in without a word.

"So you're an expert on relationships now. Mr. I-had-a-private-eye-on-my-ass."

"That private eye got on my ass because of the stupid shit I've been doing with you."

"You're going to blame me for your marriage problems?"

"No. Not all of them. Only the ones where things were fine until you showed up. It's never enough for you. You see beer and you have to have whiskey. You see a bar and you have to have a strip club."

"You didn't complain at the time."

We pull back up to his house and Auguste is loading the MIG gear back into his truck.

"Don't come around anymore, John. At least not for a while. Not until I tell you it's ok." What is happening to all the people in my life? It's like a damn conspiracy. Why can't it just be easy like it used to, before all this 90's "family man" bullshit started? I stick by my kids and my wife. Why do I get punished for being successful and not trash? The last thing I need is Auguste getting into me about something. I don't want to get out of the truck but disrespecting the old man like that is not an option. At least not for me. Dud gets out and hands Auguste a six pack.

"*Mais, non.* I only need one."

"Go ahead Mr. Chenevert. I don't drink that brand."

"What's wrong witchou? You too good for what made Milwaukee famous?"

"I stick to what makes Dudley drunk. How much do I owe you for the weld?"

"*Rien.*"

"Oh come on Mr. Chenevert. That was at least a seventy-five-dollar weld."

"I keep da beer and we call it even."

"Well, *bien merci.* You want to come inside and drink it? Or come sit on the swing?"

"No. I need to go. Tell you wife I said hello."

"Thank you so much Mr. Chenevert. John…"

"Yeah, I better go, too. Was just passin' by to say hello. You know?"

"Yeah. Probably just as good." Dud can't look at me when he talks to me, now. "I got some dishes to save. Y'all take care, now."

Dud makes his exit, leaving me and Auguste Chenevert under his big oak trees. Auguste takes a long swig of his Schlitz, and then offers me one. We drink in silence leaning against our respective trucks, him against the old Ford, me against my two-year-old Chevy. I'd like an old truck like his, but I don't want to put in all that work to keep it running. We finish our beers without saying a word.

"You want to go have a beer in a bar somewhere? We can get some ice from Dud to keep those cold."

"Doan worry about ice. Schiltz is still good when dey get hot."

At City Bar in Maurice there are more beer selections for me. The bar is peppered with the typical amount of people you'd expect in a bar in Maurice on a weekday afternoon. Auguste's brow furrows when they tell him they don't have Schiltz. The double Jack I order him seems to put him in a better mood.

"That's a nice hat," I say, eyeing the new red hat with a pig stitched onto it. He doesn't acknowledge my attempt to start conversation with him.

"Auguste Chenevert!" an aging man calls before hobbling over.

"*Monsieur* Gremillion! *Comment ça va?*"

"*Je ne peux pas l'appeler, ça.*"

"*Moi non plus.*"

"*Monsieur* Gremillion, dis my son-in-law, John Mouton."

The old man hobbles forward and locks my hand in an iron grip. His cloudy eyes come closer to my face than I'm comfortable with. It seems like any second his big, hooked nose will brush against mine.

"I knew you Daddy, John. You look like him. But wit a big 'ole belly."

"It's from all that good food my wife cooks," I say while patting it and looking at Auguste.

"You daddy helped me out of *malchance*… er… you call dat bad luck."

"Oh, yeah?"

"You work for Philip Leonard?"

"Yes sir." My eyes dart back to my father-in-law who is paying perfect attention.

"Philip worked for me when he was a young man. He's a hard, hard worker, him. You stick wit dat good company."

"Yessir. Nice to meet you Mr. Gremillion."

"Auguste, *cet un vieux chapon.*"

"*Je connais.*"

Settling back in his stool he takes a long sip of his whiskey and smiles to himself. These are the moments I always live in dread of. His smiles always say he knows something, but he never lets me in on what it is. If I had to choose between his cryptic silences and my father's tendency to purge every nasty little thing he thought while whipping us, I might choose two whippings.

"What?" I ask.

"Hmm? Oh, I'm smiling about Gremillion and you Daddy."

"What happened with them?" Feeling my jaw clench, I wait for a story about my father inconsistent with my memory.

"You daddy jus talked his way alongside Gremillion into a bad deal. Den he talked bote of dem out of it with an extra five hundred dollars.

You and you daddy have dat in common. Y'all can talk people in circles."

Not since my wedding day, when Auguste smiled at me unendingly, have I felt this good. These people I'm around all of the time never seem to see what I'm capable of. My own boss doesn't appreciate how my gift of gab made him successful. Yet here is a man, whom I barely talk to, who gets it. He takes a big gulp of the whiskey and sets it down on the counter with a bang. He stares at the empty glass until the bartender silently refills it. He takes another sip. "You daddy told me one time you more American than Cajun."

Here we go. I'll have to listen to laments about how our way of life changed after the wars and the oil companies. Nobody talks about how connecting to the rest of America, to commerce and industry, made us strong again. Everybody forgets how our forefathers in rebel grey fought to make sure we have the same rights and opportunities as other men. We're not stuck in fields and swamps anymore. The food, the music, the good times, we can keep. Get rid of all that other nostalgic crap. "I don't think Cajun means much anymore," I say to my beer, hoping he'll stop talking about the past.

"Dat company got you tinkin' you sometin you not...*comme tu n'est pas Cadjin.* You don't tink you still Cajun or sometin'. *Écoute.* You daddy was rough on y'all. Probly too rough. He drank like you and it brought out his bad side. But he din't lie like you. And he din't stay gone all the time. Dat's not Cajun. Just today, I raised you boy, I *taa-taa'd* you daughter, and I gave a shoulder to you wife, all before I helped you cousin and den came drinking witchou. Dat's being a man. Dat's Cajun."

It's not like Auguste to stick his nose in other people's business. If he knew how rough my father really was, he'd know I would have preferred him gone. I would have preferred a soft lie to any one of my daddy's hard truths. I am a refined product of my father. I do well despite what he did to me, not because of it. Maybe I've put too much stock into Auguste Chenevert's take on things. He can't call me out and then try to make me apologize for doing what my job makes me do, what he himself just said I was good at. He, of all people, should know there's more to being a man than just hanging around your family.

"Mr. Chenevert—"

"Before you wife was born, I had a neighbor, a Broussard, who lived down da road. I'd help wit his crawfish. His brother died one day. I learned one day da dead brother's wife, Broussard's sister-in-law, pulled Broussard aside and tole him her son had been messin' around with her daughter. Da wife never tole her husband because she tought he'd kill his son. She din't know what was right now her husband was gone. A couple of weeks after da funeral my neighbor got sick wit pneumonia. I tole him I'd work his ponds. *Il dit,* '*Non, non,* dat's too much *tracas.*' But I went ahead and took his pirogue and started working. It was warmer dat day. I worked my way to da back corner to da shade of a water oak. The traps under dere were full of crawfish. Dat's when I saw Broussard's nephew, da one dat messed wit his sister. He must have been dere for two or tree days. I never tole Broussard what I saw, or nobody else."

I take a sip of my beer. My son finally acts like a man, and then backs down when his mommy gets a little pissed. My daughter is screwing some Black man. At work my best friend goes from the good kind of crazy to the bad kind. Dudley turns out to be no better than my son. And now this. What is this? What the hell is that story supposed to mean? Is he trying to teach me something?

"Good story, Mr. Chenevert."

"Come to ma truck. I want to show you something."

Out of the last bit of respect I have for him, I follow him to the old Ford. The sky got dark fast tonight. I drain my beer to help tolerate whatever coonass wisdom he's going to try and impart. At the door of his truck, he stops. He spins toward me, faster than I can follow, with his fist raised. My fists go up, too.

“Hit me, John.”

“What?”

“*Poquer*!” he yells, before trying to land a left hook. I block it as he takes a jab at my chin. I duck it. “You been wantin’ to fight someone you whole life, boy. *Allons!”* He says before faking another left hook before landing a solid fist to my gut. I back off from strike range and look at him. The fire in me is lit, burning where his fist was. But it won’t get to my arms or my feet. When I finally get my feet to move, they spin me toward my truck. As I try to slide into the cab I hear, “*Si tu veux d’arrêter ton misère, trouver Notre Dame. Trouver ta famille.* Huh? You understand? Go pray, John. Take care of dat family. *Lâche pas la patate.*”

Chapter 42

What I need is my bar with my people. The bartenders at Parrain's on the edge of Lafayette can tell I've had a bad day because they bring out my Bud Lights two at a time. Talking to the mayor of Gueydan I find out what's happening with crawfish season. It helps to calm me down from the fight I never wanted to happen. The mayor complains the two brothers, who no one seems to know the names of, still got their hands wrapped around all the crawfish in that little town. They forbid anyone to let them distribute unless it's through them. If anyone does, they make sure no one is buying. The mayor sure seems worried. All I can think about is how genius this is. Once I'm on the other side of business like them I won't have bad days like today. I'll call the shots. And I could not have called a better shot than Linda walking through the door. Ending up in her bed tonight will be some salve on this shit day. Her face drops after her eyes adjust to the dark and she sees me. She's done up even nicer than usual. She walks over to me and orders a drink.

"You're here early," she grumbles.

"Shitty day. Figured I'd get busy making it better. You walked in and helped that out." She doesn't even smile. She sips her cranberry vodka and chats with the bartender. Stroking her upper arm softly, I try to get her attention. She turns and pulls her arm away.

"What's wrong with you?"

"John I'm meeting someone else here in a little bit."

"That's fine."

"It's another guy, John."

Red fire burns through my scalp and in my chest, but I don't bother pulling my collar over my purple scar. My hand dents my can a little, but I stop short of crushing it.

"Don't act pissed. I've been a good side girl for you. Time's up."

“You weren’t even going to talk to me about it?”

“Not much to say about it. You can’t end something that never was. I had fun, John. You should know that.” She thinks she can do that. She thinks she can make that decision. The fire rages. No point in trying to contain it anymore.

“Let’s go outside and talk more about it.”

She peers into my eyes like she’s studying them. Then a look spreads across her face. It’s a look like Bee’s when she had that knife in her hand.

“No. I’m good. I’ll go drink at the end of the bar.”

“We need to finish this conversation,” I say firmly, letting her know it’s not a negotiation. Linda looks at Trudy, who’s been watching while stocking beer in the back cooler. Trudy wipes her hands on her ass as she walks up to us.

“You look like you’re still thirsty, John.”

“Not now.”

“John you leave this woman alone, you hear?”

“So you been telling people about this behind my back? Wait… has he been here before?”

“John, you best calm down or you’re gonna have to leave,” Trudy barks.

“How many times has he been here?”

“John, I’m warning you.”

“Calm down, Trudy. It’s a little domestic dispute. She’s a big girl. She gets to pick who she spends her time with. In fact, let me buy you a drink, Linda.”

“No, thank you,” Linda responds coldly.

“Linda, go ‘head on to the back. John, you either sit still in that chair or leave.”

“How did she turn you against me, Trudy?”

"Ain't nobody turned against you, John. You act like an ass at my bar and your ass gets kicked. Same rule as always."

A few quick chugs and I finish my beer. When I pay, I grab Trudy's hand and slip her a hundred dollar bill. She looks at it and her eyes narrow.

"You can't pay me to let you hurt her." She stuffs the bill in what must have been my open fly. "Get your ass out of here, right now."

At the Hole in the Wall in Scott they don't kick people out when they get too drunk. They can't afford to when I'm one third of the business. I feed the jukebox and listen to Hank Williams, Junior and Senior, on repeat. A hankering to dance appears, but there are no women in the place. Stumbling to my truck I go to call Linda on my car phone. But I must pass out. I'm roused out of a dream by my car phone. The dream was the same. There was me and a frying pan of burning roux. This time, it was me with the frying pan, throwing the roux not on my Daddy, but on Auguste Chenevert. As his skin burned he opened his mouth to scream. The scream ended up being the car phone. Hoping it's Linda, I reach down and see a number I don't recognize. My wife tells me my father-in-law was in wreck and it's not looking too good. Without letting her finish her explanation I start up the truck, promising to be there in a little bit.

It's a miracle I make it there in one piece. Grabbing the mouthwash I keep under my seat, I take a big swig, swish, and swallow. It's hard to get my feet to move straight but I find a rhythm. I've done this enough before. Inside his room I can hear my wife bitching at someone, so I decide to knock. I find my sister-in-law and my wife hovering over Auguste Chenevert.

Looking at Auguste, pale and still, a little bloody, lifeless, makes the world come into focus. I'm suddenly sober, completely clear-headed. His arms, which I always took for sturdy rods, are limp on top of the sheets. There are so many tubes and bandages; they cover up the strength I'd come to trust. From the looks on the women's faces, and the lack of machine noise, I know he's dead. A terrible thought arrives. I was the last person to see him alive. Oh, shit. I got him all drunk and pissed before I took off. Oh… shit. My whole body feels blistered and raw, like my skin after the roux. Except this is much worse.

Chapter 43

They said it was a stroke, but I know I killed him. On the day of his funeral I decide I shouldn't drink. I'm a mess. The funeral director closes the lid. The noise it makes sounds exactly like when my daddy landed the first punch after I stood up to him. To the outside world these noises are brief and not very loud. But these echo throughout my life. The difference between the noises, and the way I react to them, can be seen only in the men who created them. One noise started the explosion which left fire to burn anyone who gets close. The other noise shuts off the possibility of learning how to put out that fire. As if answering my fear of never getting to extinguish what's inside of me, liquid begins to pour from my face again. I nearly drop the casket. It gets worse when I go into a church for the first time in almost a decade. It smells the same as the day I married Beatrice in here, the day Auguste was so proud of me, maybe for the last time.

Bee believes the stroke made him miss the exit. I think the stroke sent him over. But being drunk on the whiskey I was feeding him likely made him blow past his exit. The drinking, the fighting, and being out at night were all things that killed him. Those are the things from my world. It's my world that killed him. If it could kill the strongest man I've ever known, why doesn't it kill me? Am I stronger than even Auguste Chenevert? Likely not. Nuclear fallout doesn't kill cockroaches, but it doesn't turn them into unicorns either. He did everything for them, I've done everything for me. All this money, this work, this good timing doesn't make anyone respect me more than they did him. Since I'm the one who took him from them, I'm not sure I respect me much either.

During the mass people come up and say some of the nicest things. They tell stories about how Auguste changed them, made them into better people. He fixed their motor. After a storm he helped them clear a fallen tree. I should stand up and say what he did for me, how he showed me what a good man is. He cared about what I do more than I do. It always felt like he was getting in my business. He wanted the best for me. He cared what happened to me, more than my own blood, more than his daughter, more than my kids. They can screw themselves. Crap. If I said that up there Auguste would rise from his coffin to crucify me right next to Jesus. He would tell me to do right by my family as he drove nails in my wrist. Shit. That's what his goddamned story at the bar was about. Doing right is bigger than family, more important than your money or your job. It's what makes a man. Without it, evil will eat everything, your family, your job, you, from the inside.

"I'm sorry about your father-in-law, John," Old Leonard says from the doorway of my office. "Listen, take the time you need for that Oilcon guy. If you get him, great. If not, whatever."

"Thanks," I say. I can't find anything to follow it up with. He smiles and goes back to his office. I'm taking that as a sign. I walk out into the shop to where Yank has the MIG torch burning away. He turns after I shout his name.

"Hey man, I'm sorry I acted like that around your girl. I was… it—"

"It's alright, John. I appreciate it."

"You want to go grab lunch?"

"Not today. Maybe another time."

"Oh, yeah. Good."

Back at my desk I start looking for what sounds good for lunch. I'm usually counting minutes before I can go to a bar-and-grill. Today I'm wondering where it would be quiet. It'd even be nice to have some church-type quiet. It reminds me of how Auguste told me I should invest more time there. My memory is getting better since I quit drinking. I leave the shop before I start crying.

Voices mumble sins in the little confessionals at the back of St. John's Cathedral. I can't do it. The priest couldn't handle it anyway. If I told him about all the women I've had affairs with, all the times I chose drinking over spending time with my kids, all the ways I've tried to steal Leonard's shop from underneath him, and finished it with how I killed Auguste Chenevert (whom the priest would likely know since everyone knew him), that poor bastard would collapse right there in the confessional and then I'd have to say I killed a priest. He'd tell me I made my son a wimpy excuse for a man, I drove my daughter to Black men, and I might as well have put that knife in my wife's hand. As I listen to the muted mumbles, it's comforting knowing someone, even if it can't be me, will walk out of that little room cleaner than they came in. I try to absorb their peace.

During mass I go through the motions. We get to the part where we get to confess our sins in silence. This will have to do. That man in the sky is just like my real father. He doesn't give guidance, doesn't give forgiveness, and never says he's sorry. Even Auguste Chenevert was better than that. No one seems to mind when I elect to stay on my kneeler during communion. When it's over I stay in the pew, even as the lights go out. When the last person leaves, when it's been silent for more than fifteen minutes, the tears come back. I won't be somebody he can be proud of for a long time. There might not be enough masses to attend, good deeds to do, or confessions to make. I've heard undoing takes longer than doing. If so, I'll be spending the rest of my life undoing. I killed him, after all.

"Take care of dat family," he said. His thick accent rings in my head. That is where I could start undoing. It would be easier to start with the kids. There seems to be a little bit there to work with, unlike with Bee. But if I'm going to do things the way Auguste Chenevert would do them, I have to start with the hardest part first. My wife and I need to start acting like a married couple. Old Leonard will understand if I need to take the afternoon off. He's understood a lot. I'll wait in my recliner until she comes home and we can fix our marriage. Luckily, I don't have to wait long.

"Bee, hey. Why are you home so early?"

"Need the rest of the day off."

"Hungry?"

"Not really."

"You want to go to Judice Inn for a burger?"

To my surprise she agrees. On the ride I feel like crying. Every time I swallow, I'm stifling the urge to say how much I miss her father. There's plenty of room in this truck for me to say I'm sorry for whatever would've made her want to come at me with a knife. There's probably lots, going back for years, I need to apologize for. I could even tell her things are over between me and Linda. Instead, I say nothing. At Judice Inn I go ahead and order. I thought she'd be impressed at my ability to remember she liked the double burger with grilled onions every Thursday night before we had kids. I even order fries, knowing they don't serve them, just to try and make her laugh. She doesn't bat an eye. And when she doesn't say anything while we eat, I realize this is not going like I had it in my head. I was about to lay it all out there. She looks like she couldn't care less.

"Why'd you bring me here?" She finally speaks.

"Thought you'd like to come to our old stomping grounds."

"It's very nice John." Maybe this could go right. But then she asks, "Can we go home?"

"Why?"

"I think I need to be alone."

"Oh, ok. Ok."

Here I am, doing what I'm supposed to do, what her father would want me to do, and she's playing tough guy. You can't ever make this woman happy. My foot presses down on the gas. But before the fire makes it up to my face or through my hands, I remember. Auguste Chenevert never did this. He never let a bad feeling stand in the way of doing what he thought was right. That was part of his last story, too. Some secrets you hold in and manage yourself, like a man. No one can take care of it for me. So when we arrive home I decide to try again. Bee tries to retreat and gets all the way to the bedroom. She looks surprised to see I've followed her. Looking at her face, past jowls and crow's feet, is the face of a dark-eyed beauty.

"You know you're still a pretty woman, Beatrice. I haven't told you that enough."

"Thanks, John."

She's so damned cold. I don't know why she's acting this way. Seems to me a normal person might want to connect with their long-lost husband, prodigal son style. Fat lot of good church did her. Standing at the door, Auguste's charge nags at me. His face from our wedding day looms. I want to be worthy of pride again. Mustering what left I have of my dignity, I walk toward Bee and kiss her like husbands are supposed to kiss their wives when they love them. I get her to the bed and start undressing her. She finally starts kissing me back. She doesn't seem all that into it, but she's not stopping either. I've gotten too used to the way Linda is in bed. Bee is wearing worn out cotton panties instead of red or black thongs like I'm used to. The sex is even more awkward than the panties. It's like she's forgotten what to do. Damn, it can't have been that long. Her face is the worse part. She stares up at me with this flat look. She could be watching one of her chick flicks on the ceiling for all I can tell. This is not how it's supposed to be. I stop. Even when I try to do the right thing it comes out all wrong. I was never good enough for my dad, and I won't be good enough for Bee, so there's not much hope I'd be good enough for August Chenevert's memory. I wait for the fire to arrive in my chest, setting the scar on my neck ablaze. Something moves from deep down in my gut. When it reaches my head it turns into tears, more goddamned tears.

They make me sick to my stomach. I grab my clothes and start getting dressed. She heads to bathroom like she always does. I swallow hard a few times, praying I will eventually get to live Mr. Chenevert's life.

The thought is interrupted by Bee rushing out of the bathroom her shirt barely on, grabbing her keys, and then heading out of the doorway. "Where are you going?" I call. She doesn't answer.

What feels right, no, what feels normal, is to head to a bar. Slipping into a cold can would be a homecoming. This was stupid. This has been broken for years. Auguste couldn't even get this to work. Whatever he was trying to get me to do, it won't happen. Maybe I'm more like what my father said I was than I'm willing to admit.

Fine. Fuck him. That drunk son of bitch gave me nothing that ended up being worth anything. My life didn't get better until I went to college and met Bee and became Auguste's son-in-law. I'll never get to tell Auguste he saved my life. All I can do now is figure out the right thing and keep doing it, hoping he sees it all. I go to my recliner in the living room and wait for Bee to come home.

Chapter 44

Morning touches the recliner, but Beatrice does not. The action movies ran out on cable. I stare at the local news. The guy who gives the fishing report is entertaining. The door finally opens behind me.

"Where'd you go? I've been waiting up all night."

"I went out."

"Since when do you go out?"

"Life keeps moving while you're gone."

"I'm sorry about yesterday. I think your dad's death is hitting me harder than I thought." Her eyes lock on mine. Before I think she will say something, she turns and heads for the coffee pot in the kitchen. He said I have to keep trying. *Lâche pas la patate.*

"I waited up all night for you."

She acts like she doesn't hear me and makes coffee. Sitting down at the table, she remains silent. I've been doing the right thing all night. She has to meet me half way.

"You not gonna say something?"

"What do you want me to say, John?"

"I was hoping you'd say you understand. That you're sad, too."

"You don't think I'm sad, John?

"You're not acting like it."

"Because I don't have that luxury. I'm in pain everyday knowing I can't go back, that I have to go forward trying to make sense of the world he left us, and build something out of it."

This shit again. If she could just see how hard I'm trying. "Bee, please don't be a martyr right now."

Leaving the kitchen so she can pout, it starts to feel like progress. At least she's talking. She'll come back in, say she's sorry, and we can start doing this thing right. My recliner feels comfortable again. I watch the news a few more minutes and she's back in the house. But when she stands in front of the TV, blocking my view, I know this is not normal. She thinks she can railroad me like she tried before. But there's no knife in her hand today.

"So now you expect me to talk when you want to?" I ask.

"Yes I do. Because I'm not going to do things the old way anymore just because that's what we've done. Everything is going to change. If you want to leave me, if you're that unhappy, you can go with my blessing. I'm done being hurt by you. But I'm not leaving. Because this is my family and I'm going to do it my way, the right way. I'm not letting what you've done change that."

That was it. That was any chance we had at being good again. She's screwed any chance at forgiveness. I should hit her. I want to show her she can't stand over me, telling me I've done everything wrong again. But I can't do it. Because she's right. She's doing what Auguste Chenevert would do, something I can't seem to do. Hitting her would be what Daddy would have done. When he threw that roux on me, he burned something into me I can't seem to get rid of, something that's just in me. The best I can do from here is give her what I think she wants, and maybe deserves. I get dressed like I always do, pack the bag I always pack, and leave out the back door where I always make my exit.

I'm only a mile from home when the phone in my truck rings. It's the Company Man. "Well ain't it a coincidence you're calling me this early," I chide with all of my practiced warmth.

"Had no idea I'd catch you. Why's it a coincidence?"

"I was just about to head to New Orleans."

"Oh no, I'm done with that place."

"It beat you?"

"Hell naw. I feel like I beat it."

"Care to give it another shot at the title?"

"Maybe. Let's talk business first," he says.

"You in town? Let's do it over Bloody Mary's. You ever been to Fred's in Mamou?"

He seems to understand my directions on how to find Tante Sue dancing with her Hot Damn in her holster. Heading north, I stop to grab coffee. There are cheap baseball caps hanging from the plastic case of cigarettes. I buy a red one to commemorate Auguste's last hat. A thought occurs to me. What if Mr. Chenevert wasn't too drunk to miss the exit? What if there was some *chou-choun*, some side piece, he was crossing the basin to go find? He never made mention of it, but then again why would he? That would make Auguste Chenevert a lot easier to understand and even easier to be like.

Linda loves Fred's. I bet I could convince her to join us.

Acknowledgments

So much of Cajun culture has shifted in the last fifty to seventy years. There are lots of people to thank for helping me remember and appreciate. First there are my grandparents, may they rest in peace and happiness. Their stories, their French, and their attitudes gave me a base to work from. The *Dictionary of Louisiana French* (edited by Albert Valdman and Kevin J. Rottet) and *Cajun Self-Taught* (by Rev. Mgsr. Jules O. Daigle) helped to take our mostly unwritten dialect of French and get it on paper and into Auguste Chenevert's mouth. For the gaps even these extensive language books could not cover, I thank my parents for answers to my strange texts and phone calls asking, "How do you say ____?"

Several people helped me look at my culture and these characters from the outside. Dr. Joey Hannah and Karl Spencer both shared their wisdom and experience to help these characters be more accurate and real. David Cartwright understood this story better than I did and made sure I understood the deeper messages. Dr. Maria Timm breathed new life into this book, believing in it when I had all but lost hope. Emily, my sweet, strong wife, never let me settle.

About the Author

Toby LeBlanc is a mental health therapist in Austin, TX. Writing is a way his own tales can have life alongside the countless stories of courage and strength of his clients. While he and his family sleep under the Texas stars, he will always say he's from Louisiana. He enjoys wearing period-specific pirate costumes and fishing. His dream is to one day do both at the same time.

CPSIA information can be obtained
at www.ICGtesting.com
Printed in the USA
LVHW110725120822
725756LV00004B/106

9 781956 692266